RACHEL CANWELL is
the Fens, has lived and work
Her short fiction has a
Her collection of flash fictio...
in 2022 and her novella-in-flash *Magpie Moon* in 2023.
Paper Sisters is her first novel.

CW01460712

PAPER SISTERS

RACHEL CANWELL

NORTHODOX

PRESS

Northodox Press Ltd
Maiden Greve, Malton,
North Yorkshire, YO17 7BE

This edition 2026

1

First published in Great Britain by
Northodox Press Ltd 2026

ISBN: 978-1-91-700509-8

This book is set in Caslon Pro Std

Cover and Interior Design by T J Keane

This book is a work of fiction. References to real people, events,
establishments, organizations, or locales are intended only to provide a
sense of authenticity, and are used fictitiously. All other characters, and
all incidents and dialogue, are drawn from the author's imagination and
are not to be construed as real.

Printed and bound by CMP (UK) Limited,
G3 The Fulcrum, Vantage Way, Poole, Dorset, BH12 4NU

To Matthew, Joshua, Zachary, Samuel and Lucy,
who believed I could.

'I'm tired of being enclosed here. I'm wearying to escape into that glorious world, and to be always there: not seeing it dimly through tears, and yearning for it through the walls of an aching heart: but really with it, and in it.'

Emily Brontë, Wuthering Heights

'A ministering angel shall my sister be.'

Hamlet, act 5, sc. 1, Shakespeare

PROLOGUE

THE WASH, 1894

The sound, dragging, and unfamiliar, pulls the family from their beds. Forcing them out into the yard.

Where they stand, Father to sleeping babe, each wrapped in the warmth of the summer's evening; the hospital at their backs, bedecked in new paint and hope. Waiting, peering into the velvet darkness; each straining to hear as they push past the blunt edges of sleep and try to understand.

To place this noise, travelling across the river, cutting through the languid June air. Circling the moon just once, before reaching the Hospital, where, winding its way around the red brick walls, it skims the newly tiled roof and open kitchen window, looking for places to settle. To infiltrate.

They move as one, shuffling in the twilight, edging towards the river. Silent, breathless, seeking the comforting shadow of the infant Port nestled in the darkness of the opposite bank; their minds continue to scrabble around this sliding sound. Slow, dreadful, yet strangely gentle.

Until it isn't.

For now, it changes. Becoming louder, faster; unstoppable, until the intermittent splashes that pepper the night air are impossible to ignore.

At its source, across the river, the sound stills the watchmen, pulling them away from their chatter and cards. Rousing those left after months of planning, dreaming, and toiling, peeling them from building materials and the first load of cargo, calling them to the water's edge. Where, stupid with shock, they peer into the ink of the hungry river, their hastily gathered lamps held high in shaking hands.

This sound, having raised the alarm, is impossible to silence. Drowning out protests and stealing away hopes, it continues, day after day. The truth dawns gradually, and finally acceptance settles.

The new port has fallen.

Has crashed, piece by piece into the muddy waters below. Concrete, wood, engines. Dreams.

All bob, then sink, pulled under by the swell of the Nene.

And the Port Hospital?

Inexplicably, nobody looks their way.

CHAPTER ONE

ELEANOR - MAY DAY 1914

Eleanor stands at the window. Her left hand grips the head of the tap, as the right strokes her sister's hair. With long deliberate movements, she tries, yet again, to push someone else's fear away; her fingers catching on unwashed curls and years of pain. Her hands moving in their familiar, persistent rhythms; her tongue clicking in automatic response.

'Shh, Lily.'

Lily, hunched on the kitchen chair, shoulder blades proud through the cotton of her dress, presses her forehead against her sister's thigh. The feverish heat that leeches through Eleanor's clothes brands her with duty and yet another reason to stay. The only sound is dry sobbing and an occasional moan.

Against her ankle, Eleanor feels the knock of a tail. Alfred's dog: a reminder she can do without. She fights the urge to kick it away.

'Not now, Piper.'

The dog whines, slinking off to the door. Briefly, Lily lifts her head, then weeps harder.

'Even Piper wants to be away from me today.'

Irritation, ancient and unchecked, rises. Eleanor's gaze drifts back to the window, out to the never-ending sky; vast, buttressing every leaf, reed, and clump of grass. Today its cornflower blue is marked by just a wisp of early summer cloud. As always, the sky dominates, claiming her eye and this place as its very own.

For this is the land of sky. A place so vast, so open and stark, in which Eleanor remains entirely trapped.

Beneath her hands, Lily's tears become vibrations, tracking up to Eleanor's wrists, through her shoulders, coursing to the top of her skull. Where they settle like tiny brown birds, that flap and fight at the centre of her brain. Their song, a lulling hum of sorrow, filled with the power to hold her at this window. To abandon the day's plans and keep herself at home.

Then something catches Eleanor's eye. From behind the empty hospital, staring faceless and useless at the marsh and fields beyond, darts a hare, dancing one way and then the other, limbs long, fur sleek and eyes bright. Spinning in seconds of beautiful indecision, before, finally, it breaks its cover and is away, over the narrow dyke and out onto the golden, slowly warming fen. Making no backward glance, the hare now fully committed to this one, glorious burst for freedom.

Eleanor gasps, suddenly pulled from this dangerous reverie. The hare's dash restarts her heart and reminds her where she wants to be.

It is May Day. Her day. Their day.

She has wasted enough time on delays, caught by the snares thrown out so expertly by Lily. Today she refuses to be kept here. For once, she has other plans.

Snatching her hand from her sister's shaking head, Eleanor open the single rusting tap, sending water crashing into the sink below. Lily yelps, falling back as the icy spray hits them, and Piper, milling at their feet, gives one sharp bark, before retreating once again. The rush of water, coupled with the scraping of the chair on stone, are enough to end the moment. To break the spell.

Lily shrieks and shrinks. 'Oh Eleanor, how could you?'

Eleanor tries not to take pleasure in her sister's shock. Lily whimpers, shaking out her long, white fingers, so delicate and unlike Eleanor's own. But she feels it; that small swell of victory, warm enough to invigorate her and reignite the fire that has been smouldering in her stomach since she agreed to this day all those weeks ago.

'Sorry. Here,' she takes a cloth from the back of the chair. 'Dry yourself off.'

Taking the cloth, Lily releases her sister, and instantly Eleanor is lighter; emboldened and free.

'I need to be off.'

Unfastening her sopping apron, she decides that her carefully chosen dress, although damp, will do. She ignoring the pleas that follow, she steps away and crosses the room.

'Eleanor, please don't. Don't leave me here alone.'

'Lily, it's one day. I'll be back before you know it.'

At the mirror, Eleanor straightens her faded straw hat, wishing again she had bought a new one, despite knowing there had been neither the opportunity nor the time.

'A whole day, Eleanor; anything could happen. You know that.'

Dodging the barb, Eleanor sweeps Piper from the floor and dumps the wriggling dog into her sister's open, imploring arms.

'You aren't alone. Piper's here. But I have to go.'

Lily glares, her sunken cheeks glistening with tracks of disbelief; the one final sting of guilt and bitterness that chases Eleanor out into the yard. Closing the kitchen door, she pauses just slightly. Then turns the key.

Ignoring Alfred's voice, and her mother's. Both asking what kind of monster locks her sister in the house, alone and on the wrong side of the river.

A monster who is tired.

A monster who has someone waiting for her.

And besides, the river is too close for it to be any other way.

Half walking, half running, Eleanor makes her way up the steep cinder path that leads out of the garden and on to the embankment. The morning is mild and full of promise, but she is hopelessly late and in danger of missing the train.

Out of habit, she holds her frustration under her breath, cursing silently, even though apart from the circling gulls, there is no one to upset or send off in the wrong direction. She grabs the bicycle she and Lily share.

Once shared.

At her back sits the house. And beyond it, the hospital. Dark, squat against the earth, an abandoned sentry to the fen beyond. She looks away, determined that today all its ghosts will stay at home.

From the right comes the whisper of a salt-tinged breeze; a reminder of the marsh and the past; as always, pressing too close. To her left, spanning the wide churning river, soars the great arch of the swing bridge, the gateway to the village; where she must get to if she hopes to rescue the day. Silently, she gives thanks that the river is quiet, meaning that the bridge is not standing open.

Mounting the bicycle, skirts tucked, she fights to lose her anxiety in the rhythm of the pedals and the clacking of the chain. Leaning into the slight headwind, she relishes the immediate resistance and the comforting cushion of a warm breeze.

There is no shelter here, for Fenland air is never still. Always something lurks; some force, seen or unseen, ready to send her spiralling out on a different course, to tug her thoughts in the opposite direction.

Enveloped by this vastness, Eleanor senses a growing, glorious sense of danger, of both joyful abandon and encroaching doom. She knows, given half a chance, her mind will split and her thoughts, normally so neatly parcelled, will spread from her core like the blackness of the river, ready to seep into places unseen. All of them insipid and murky.

The places she can't leave. But doesn't want to be.

Today she won't let that happen. She won't become tangled in those dark and complex hollows, where the voices of yesterday wait to remind her of how it all went wrong. Even now, she can hear it. The ruin of the port, singing quietly to her, its notes reaching out across the expanse of churning water.

But Eleanor refuses to listen determined to be held in place by what belongs only and entirely to her.

On she pedals. Grasping at her thoughts as she goes, pulling them into one tight spot and letting only a rationed amount of simple and sustaining goodness in. Her cheeks flame and her mind races, but Eleanor knows she hasn't locked her terrified sister in the house on a whim.

Travelling along the embankment, with the marsh at her back and the river, rushing beside her, Eleanor employs an old trick, self-taught and never far away. Fraying the edges of her vision, she shrinks the world into its softest focus. Lifting her shoulders, staring straight ahead, she picks out one unyielding landmark, reducing and taming the horizon that taunts her with its openness: so unreachable and impossibly far away.

Pushing on the pedals with determination, Eleanor keeps her gaze on the bridge, and the steam rising beyond its frets, marking the place she needs to be. Pushing against the expectation still surging within her, she reminds herself to see this day for what it is. What it can only ever be.

A one off. Nothing more.

A single chance to step away.

By the time she arrives, Eleanor is breathless, dizzy with the effort of fighting against the wind and enormity of the day. Leaving the bicycle half hidden in bushes at the gate, she makes her way into the station, pushing through the crowds.

Most of the village is here, pressed within these whitewashed walls; young, old, they spill out in every direction. Everyone making the same journey, all heading for the coast; allowing themselves a break from the plough or boat.

Eleanor picks her way through the crowd, desperate to both find John and avoid all other eyes. She recoils from the gazes, the unspoken questions she feels upon her back, resting there longer than she can bear. Most faces blur, but some, suddenly and without permission or warning, jump out at her in sharp relief. And the harder she tries to close her ears to the whispers, the louder the voices of surprise and shock seem to become.

'Have you seen?'

'Where's the sister? She can't have left her at home, surely? Not for the whole day!'

Eleanor's face burns, but still she pushes on, shrinking from every arm that brushes against hers, every pity-filled look that comes her way.

It is nearly three months since that night in the dark, when she stood in the shallows of the river, holding Lily and screaming into the blackness. Three months of pretending everything is improving and making the small world she and Lily inhabit smaller still.

John is the only thing that could bring her here today, and with each face that swims before her, the need to find him grows.

But it is Clara that Eleanor sees. Standing on the edge of the platform, in a hat ribboned with a band of blood red, a warning stripe against the fading brim. One defiant splash, for which Eleanor is sure her sister-in-law will later pay. But still her heart lifts, the sight of her friend steadying her nerves.

Instinctively, she looks for her brother, finding him seconds later, not too far behind, joined to Clara by a raggle-taggle of children; a living, seething rope.

Already, there is a bottle in his hand. And already, Frank's fist is curled.

Lurching unsteadily from his family, he jokes loudly with lads who are years younger, years freer than him, and Eleanor's stomach clenches with the knowledge that tomorrow is taken care of by a visit to Clara. After they have dealt with whatever Lily and Frank throw out as punishments for today.

But tomorrow and all its evils are pushed back, erased completely by the sight of John.

Leaning against a post, John's face is fixed, shadowed by the iron canopy of the platform. At least one head taller than most milling around him, even in this fevered May Day excitement, he stands totally still. So still, in fact, he could be taken as a bystander, a mere casual observer, set apart and unaffected by the carnival of the day.

Yet even from this distance Eleanor senses his tension, can smell his brewing disappointment. The slope of his broad shoulders and the downward cast of his eyes give him away; he thinks she isn't coming. That after weeks of stolen moments, short evening walks, with the house and the river always in sight, after the hidden notes and quiet understanding, she has failed to achieve what she promised. That she has been unable to pull herself away from Lily. Even for one day.

She pauses, indulging herself in the time to watch him, calming herself with the glorious realisation that she is not too late. She marvels at the sight of him, her heart plunging as all the small dark things that continually scuttle and bore about her mind lift and fly away.

Seizing upon this lightness, she starts to push through the crowd, just as John darts forward, and with grim determination, heads towards the train. Standing, one foot on the carriage step and one hand on the door, he turns his head towards the throng of chaotic bodies and joyful voices already inside.

For one black moment, Eleanor is sure he will simply step up and away: giving up on their day. On her.

Panic fills her, propelling her forward, through a group of men, ignoring the comments that follow her as she goes. She starts to call out, desperate to catch John's attention and stop him in his tracks.

But even before the words leave her lips he looks back, his head high, straining once again above the crowd. And he sees her.

His face lifts and his hands, flying from the edge of the carriage, pat nervously at the pockets of his coat. A coat too heavy for the warmth of the day. Jumping down from the train, he runs towards her.

CHAPTER TWO

CLARA

Already she regrets the ribbon. Crammed in the carriage, a squirming child against each hip, Clara holds her hat, staring at the uneven stitches added late last night with thread begged from Eleanor.

For Clara owns no red cotton of her own.

She had lied about mending something for Molly, avoiding her sister-in-law's sharp, wary eyes. Unable to give voice to the fact that just this once she had wanted to create something good for herself, to simply attach a second-hand ribbon to her old hat with a colour that matched.

To be respectable and have just one occasion where she is seen.

But now, here in the heat of the train, with Frank sitting opposite, his eyes like flint and face constantly changing from intense scrutiny to faraway, Clara can't imagine what she was thinking, drawing attention to herself with this wide scarlet band. Her fingers itch with the urge to unpick each stitch and crush the ragged satin deep within her palm.

Why hadn't she been satisfied with persuading Frank to make this journey to the coast? With the chance to enjoy this one, rare day with her children, a day away from the dark terrace house, and its press of obligations. Why had she pushed for more?

Beyond the window, the platform empties, as family after family, couple after couple, moving up the steps and into the already packed train.

Clara leans forward slightly, hoping to spot Eleanor. But the press of bodies is dense, and her growing anxiety makes discerning faces too hard. Instead, she sends out into the crowd a quiet, drifting hope that Eleanor is amongst their number; that she has escaped Lily and is out there, on the capable arm of the blacksmith, who, only two years in the village, is unencumbered by the weight of expectation, family, or a past of any kind.

The carriage is almost full. Her own small family and their expectations pressed together on one side, while across the aisle two women gossip, quick and loud, under the shade of large straw hats, dressed with ribbons that are new and suitably pale. Their eyes range over and assess their fellow passengers, before landing on the bottle clutched in Frank's hand; lips curled in disapproval, they shift their bulk nearer to the window and away from Clara's shame.

Opposite them sit three farmhands, marked out by their weather-beaten cheeks and hands, rough and barely touching clean. Laughing together, their tone is light, respectful. The right kind of young men, Clara thinks, gazing at Frank and then looking away.

The air, hot with excitement and breathless laughter, is undercut by the sharp call of the guards, impatient to get the train under way.

Stealing one quick glance at his father, Billy tugs on Clara's sleeve and whispers, 'How long? Before the sea, Ma?'

She smiles. His excitement is the reason she has pushed so hard for today.

'A while yet.' She murmurs, ducking her dry, hesitant lips to his cropped hair. 'We've to move first.'

Her son's round cheeks are flushed, eager and impatient. His voice, untethered and unchecked, lifts too quickly through a whine to a moan. 'When Ma? But when will we move?'

Frank's shoulders rise, his gaze locking onto them both. Clearing her throat, Clara bobs her head lower, creating a barrier between her husband's eyes and her squirming son.

'Soon. It won't be long now.'

The words are a plea, pulling at her throat. Clara hates how they drag like sandpaper over her tongue. Bringing her hand to her mouth, she attempts to cough her cowardice out, resolving for the hundredth time that she won't allow Frank to spoil their day. She pulls Billy closer and through the press of her body, wills him to patience.

If they can just get to the sea, then she and the children can slip away. She eyes the bottle, already half empty, cradled between Frank's thighs, before checking the others tucked under his seat. These are his true companions for the day.

In her mind, she counts the coins in her purse. Two saved, two borrowed from Eleanor. All hidden from Frank. So many things she's gone without in the past weeks to give them this one day.

'Is everyone on yet, Ma?' Peeling away from her, Billy pushes his body up from the seat.

'The guard's got his whistle.' Tommy calls. Her older son kneels, pressed against the window, his hand and face already grimy with soot; his wriggling body blocking out the sun. Clara tenses. Frank grunts, swigs, and stares.

Upright and too close to her father, Molly tugs anxiously at her brother's shirt, trying to persuade him, wordlessly, back into his seat. Ignoring her, Tommy pushes his broad nose to the glass; his hair, damp with sweat, sticking out around his pink tipped ears.

'He's waving the flag!'

'Let me see!'

Overcome, Billy leans forward, pushing his brother's bulk aside. At the same moment, the train lurches, pitching him headfirst into Tommy's back. Knocked off balance, Billy's hands sprawl, grasping at the seat, his left leg swinging wildly, catching Frank hard and square on the shin.

'Christ!'

His roar is sudden and short. All three children freeze, then fold themselves back into their seats, instantly diminished; thoughts of guards, flags and whistles forgotten and put away.

Frank, on the other hand, grows.

He leaps to his feet, his anger filling the carriage as beer spills, first across his lap then Molly's. She flinches, just once, before falling unnaturally still.

Drawing in a quick, silent breath, Clara straightens her back and lifts her chin. Every inch of her longs to scream.

Looking down at his trousers, Franks face is scarlet with disgust, his fist primed and curled.

'Stupid little bleeders. Look what you've done!'

Clara swallows, holds his gaze, but nobody speaks. Against the dusty red leather of the seat, Molly's face is a smudge of chalk, as gingerly she lifts the sodden fabric of her dress, peeling it from her thighs. Quietly, Billy begins to cry, and the carriage, so recently alive with clamour, is now unnaturally still.

'Look, look at the state of my bloody trousers!'

Throwing himself back into the seat, Frank pushes his legs out, his dusty boots striking Clara's worn leather shoes. He lifts the now empty bottle high, its wild arc barely missing Molly's pale cheek. Again, Clara sees her flinch.

Again, she bites back her rage.

From bitter experience, she knows stillness is the best option, but the train, it seems, does not agree and, with a final lurch, they are on their way. Neither of her sons rushes to the window to see.

'Look!' Frank thrusts the damp stain of his groin towards her, as the women opposite, retreating behind gloved hands, turn away in disgust.

Clara wishes that she could do the same.

'See? Told you your damn kids couldn't bloody behave.' Frank staggers to his feet, unsteady from anger and the jarring movement of the train. Looming over her, he slaps one hand flat against the seat behind her shoulder; the dark hairs of his wrist grazing the shelf of her jaw. Clara's stomach contracts.

His other hand, curled tight against his chest, still grips the neck of the bottle. From the corner of her eye, Clara sees the dark shapes of the women, now pushed beyond their limits, gathering their bags, before moving off, further down the train.

The farmhands, no longer joking, suddenly seem younger than their years.

Over her father's shoulder, Molly starts to slide, slipping from her seat. Her eyes still locked on Frank's, Clara gives a slight shake of her head and, to her relief, her daughter, practised at such silent signals, stills. Creeping her fingers out on either side, Clara's hands find two pairs of bony knees. Billy's shift a little closer, Tommy's inch further away.

Without taking her eyes from her husband's, Clara absorbs that very particular jolt of pain.

'What?' Frank stoops, his face is level with hers, his breath, hot and sour against her own; his lips twist furiously, knotting themselves into wide shapes and tight red lines. Working themselves up to his next spittle-soaked tirade. Clara pushes back against the worn seat, hairpins shifting and digging into her scalp. Still, her eyes, now smarting with the effort, meet his. Her head remains steady, but her mind is racing, as if trying to keep up with the clack of the train.

Frank snarls. 'What the hell am I supposed to do now?'

From nowhere, Clara is seized by a violent urge to laugh. Or maybe shrug or sing. Even spit.

She does none of these things.

Instead, in her softest voice, she replies.

'Sit down, Frank.'

Frank draws back. His face, strangely blank and passive, seems caught between anger and disbelief; the rapid flickering of his lips is now coupled with wide staring eyes. His hand peels from the leather, slicing the silence with a slow ripping sound. Clara's neck burns with tension; her children are shadows at the edges of her view.

Frank stands upright, his stocky legs wide apart, his arms tight into his sides. On the opposite seat, Molly curls, tearful and tight.

'Sit down?'

Clara answers with a barely perceptible nod.

He looks down at his trousers, before raising his empty hand, pumping it high into the air, muscles primed and taut exaggerate the curve of his waist. His movements are practised, deliberate; familiar. Instinct drags Clara's breath inwards, as her elbow push the boys away, but her eyes never Frank's hand, as it continues to rise.

Only to be stayed by another, whose strong roughened fingers, are suddenly tight at Frank's thick wrist.

'The lady asked you to sit down.'

Behind Frank, stands one of the farmhands, holding his arm high, keeping it above his head. With a grunt, Frank tries to twist his body, his face contorted by the effort, hot and enraged. But the boy, tightening his grip pitches Frank backwards. Towards Molly, who pushes harder into her corner, whimpering.

'Let go of me, you bastard.'

Frank squirms. Held like a puppet his feet knock hard against the carriage floor, and behind their friend appear the two remaining farmhands, nervous looks flitting between them.

'I don't think I will. Not in this carriage anyway.' The lad, looks towards Clara, waiting for her to contradict him. She glances at him, once at her husband, before turning quickly and deliberately away.

Refusing to look back until she hears the bang and click of the carriage door.

No matter the price, she and her children have their day.

When they arrive, she waits until the train is empty; holding the children, still subdued, back in their seats while everyone else disembarks, refusing the help of the farmhands whose sympathetic eyes she has struggled to avoid. Making the children stand behind her, gingerly she puts her head out of the carriage and scans the platform. Unbelievably, Frank is nowhere in sight.

Neither is he lying in wait by the ticket office or the waiting room, nor hiding in the lav when Billy insists, he needs to go. Only when they leave the station and find themselves moving amongst the lightness and laughter of the crowds, does Clara start to believe they might be allowed it. This one stolen day.

It is then that she catches sight of Eleanor, walking with John, arm in arm. Passing through the crowds like water. Their heads close together, their shoulders rubbing gently as they move along. She watches them turn to each other, their faces breaking into shy and fleeting smiles.

Torn between envy and delight, Clara watches them drift away.

She takes this as a sign, and with every step further from the station, nearer to the sea, Clara's heart lifts; the sun, high in a blanket of blue satin, is warm on her back. Together they push on, becoming part of this whirling crowd, and until finally she relaxes enough to let the children move further from her, releasing her grip on their eager hands. Touching the ribbon on her hat, she draws a little more strength into her belly.

They reach the beach, the boys out in front, darting off, then wheeling back along the prom. They beg her to hurry, and she finds herself laughing at their desperation, her mood buoyed by their uncomplicated and unbridled joy; only to be tethered by Molly still resolute and silent at her side.

Clara finds a spot, tucked in by the breakwater, where the sand, damp and unbroken, is speckled by just enough shade and just enough sun. Away from the gaze of other families and not immediately visible from the height of the prom. And where Clara can see most of the beach.

Just in case.

As the boys divest themselves of layers, Clara unpacks her basket, spreading out a thin sheet and keeping another back for drying off wet skin. Then, gripping the boys' shoulders, she lays out her rules.

'Stay where I can see you. No fighting. Paddling is allowed, but don't go in above your knees.'

'Ma.'Tommy whines, hopping from foot to foot.'We can swim.'

'Paddle or stay here. It's up to you.' Tommy's eyes flash, briefly defiant. Clara remembers how he pulled away from her in the train.

Pausing, he weighs up his options before a grin breaks out and his features lift. Throwing back his head Tommy yells at Billy, 'Race you to the sea.'

Billy looks to her, and she nods. And with one final whoop they are gone, limbs white and long, streaking like greyhounds across the strips of shingle and sand.

'They'll swim, Ma.' Molly, gazing at the horizon, pushes her white toes into the wet sand.

At the sight of her daughter's tight, anxious face, Clara's heart lurches.

On a whim, she unbuckles her shoes and rolls down her stockings. Standing up, she pulls Molly to her feet.

'Then we'd best make sure they don't.'

Running across the sand, hand in hand with her daughter, Clara whoops, calling out with unexpected, forgotten voice, alive with the salty taste of abandonment and joy.

A voice that finally feels like her own.

The boys are, when they reach them, surprisingly, only wet to the thighs; the rules stretched but not quite broken. At the sight of Clara, their eyes widen.

'Ma?' Billy whispers. 'What are *you* doing here?'

Gathering up her skirts, Clara wades into the water, shrieking at the cold, laughing at Billy's stricken face.

'Paddling, like you.'

She looks back at Molly, still standing uncertainly at the edge of the sea, her eyes sending nervous glances up and down the beach. Clara stops, calling back with all the gentle conviction she can find.

'He's not here, Mol.' She crosses her fingers, twining them beneath her petticoats. 'I promise.'

And with one last look, Molly smiles and steps into the waves.

CHAPTER THREE

LILY

Lily retreats to her bed.

Drawing the curtains against the brightness of the day, she slips between sheets still tangled from last night's fight with sleep and rage. Somewhere below, Piper barks.

Picking up her shoe, Lily slams it hard, once against the bare boards of the floor. The barking stops. Lying back on the pillows, she sinks, first into the silence. And then rage.

Lily has known about Eleanor's plans for over a week. Heard them whispered beneath her window following one of those evening walks, taken when the tide and the bridge have allowed; but whose regularity and duration has steadily increased over the past months. Despite John having never entered the cottage, never setting foot beyond the kitchen door.

But knowing about the plan was one thing. Lily never dreamt her sister would dare to see it through. Never believed Eleanor would find the strength to fight through the days of turmoil, she, Lily had so carefully created and curated; foiling all the traps, each one laid with the bait of guilt and fear, designed to keep her sister close by. To keep her at home.

With each passing day, as Eleanor showed no sign of yielding, Lily had felt the walls pushing in on her. Until compressed by the emptiness and space of the Fen, her world was overtaken entirely by disbelief and rage.

And her anger was red and hot, continually knotting itself in her chest, before unfurling to wind itself around her limbs and invade every waking hour.

Anger that chattered, taunting until Lily became its puppet, unable to make any movement or utter any words that it hadn't sanctioned. Anger that drove her to stay in bed for days, closing her throat against food and speech, that drove her to scream in the dead of night until she was sick and hoarse; and Eleanor came running, begging for calm.

Anger that ran its red and black ribbons throughout the house, laying a trail for her to follow, hiding Eleanor's carefully pressed dress, smashing plates and basins, spoiling food. That spoke to her in the early hours, whispering the ways she could keep Eleanor alert and close. The ways to keep herself safe. But still, this anger has been beaten. All its ministrations, however terrible, wild and dark, have been unable to keep Eleanor at home.

Because Eleanor has gone. And locked the door. Leaving Lily alone with only this terrible rage for company.

Balling her hands into two sharp white fists, Lily thumps the mattress beneath her, drumming her rage into the straw and sending it bouncing up into the air. As if this wild tattoo will summon her sister and bring her back home.

How dare Eleanor leave her here alone? Not just for the usual hour or so, but alone for a whole day.

Lily's displays have never failed her before.

In the two years since Alfred's death, rage, harboured and carefully cultivated, has always shown Lily the way. From its quiet but insistent beginnings found in grief and genuine fear, through to its unexpected power and control, anger has extended its hand and taken her to places she would never have dared tread alone.

It has been her warrior and protector; a manipulator of the strangest and most magical kind. Able to shift its shape and to appear often as something it is not.

Anger in all its enchanted forms is what keeps her safe. There is no use arguing with anger.

Lily knows that, and Eleanor knew it too.

Until now.

Pushing her head back into the pillow, Lily screams into the silence, feeling the tide of rage surge, breaking over her, again and again. Grinding her teeth, clutching at the sheets beneath her, she fights to stop herself being swept entirely away.

She can't, won't let it overwhelm her.

It takes almost an hour. An hour in which Lily shifts uneasily in her bed, searching for a cool space in which to breathe, to whisper, trying to trick her anger into giving her the answers. To find something that will make Eleanor pay.

And when she finds herself at the door of Eleanor's room, it is a quieter, colder rage that sits in her gut and guides the way.

She knows exactly where to find the letters.

Knows that there are ten, safe in the second drawer of the dresser, slipped between her sister's clean linens; a tight bundle tied with string. Knows each is thin, the paper cheap and brittle, in danger of being torn, so she takes extra care as she unfolds and reads each one.

Dearest Eleanor...

Lily has read them before, picking through the spelling mistakes and faltering handwriting. Through words and phrases that betray the writer's inexperience; composed by a man of deeds not words. The earliest, dated over a year ago, is wholly practical, no more than a scrawled invitation.

I know it is hard to get away. But maybe a short walk by the river?

Over time they change, becoming peppered with flakes of gentle, growing adoration and the smallest declarations, each more animated than the one before. Alive.

Seeing you in the village today was a welcome change...

I have been thinking of you; wondering when we might meet again...

These little slips of paper are rare and precious things. Lily knows her sister prizes above all else. And believes them to be hidden; entirely safe.

That is why Lily doesn't hesitate.

She reads them twice, reminding herself of their simple beauty, before drawing them back into their tidy bundle, envelopes and all. Then, stroking the careful folds, she crosses the room.

As she opens the small window, she feels calmer than she has in days. Laying each letter on the narrow sill, she orders them, carefully, chronologically, one after the other and with the placement of each envelope her spirits start to rise.

A breeze lifts from the river, curling the furthest paper. Quickly, Lily reaches out, holding all the letters flat, spreading her palms to keep them still. Waiting for the air and anger to yield once again to her control.

Only then, with deliberate, methodical care, does she begin.

Withdrawing the first letter from its envelope, Lily touches it lightly it to her dry hot lips. Kisses it.

And then lifting it to the light, she begins to tear.

She takes her time. Making sure the pieces she creates are regular, the fragments small. But recognisable. Otherwise, there is no point.

Ripping slowly until nine precious letters and their envelopes are destroyed.

Holding the final letter up to the light, she pauses; remembering how Eleanor had read it, hungrily in the weeds behind the hospital, her face flushed and smiling, thinking herself unseen. How she had pushed the loose strands of hair from her cheeks and let her hand idly stroke her throat; in a gesture so unconscious and tender, that her strong fingers had looked quite unlike her own.

Lily reads it now. The few short lines.

'Sending love from the right side of the river. Wishing you were here tonight.'

Lily spits on the paper. Only she decides on which side of the river her sister belongs.

Gritting then grinding her teeth, she tears again. Page after page.

And opening the window wider, she scatters what remains of each letter onto the path beneath.

Laying a trail to guide Eleanor home.

CHAPTER FOUR

ELEANOR

By the time they arrive at the coast, the taste of the last few days has nearly left Eleanor's throat. Stepping into the heaving mass of the station, she has almost laid down her guilt.

Almost.

John stumbles after her onto the platform, landing directly in the path of barrelling children and scolding parents, impossible to work out who belongs to whom. Eleanor's laugh is high and infectious, and smiling John reaches for her hand. Pulling her towards him, the rise of his hip nudging at the soft curve of her waist, Eleanor feels her body respond, as the past, both recent and distant, retreats a little more.

'Flaming bun fight, this is,' John mutters. Instinctively, she tenses, but his breath in her hair is the counterbalance. His is an idle, good-natured grumble, containing no hidden barbs; just a throwaway comment, briefly caught, then immediately lost in the heat of the day.

Not like at home

With John's lips on her crown, Eleanor inhales his familiar musk of heat and soap, soaking him in, before the momentum of excited bodies propels them on; along the platform, through the station, finally spitting them out into the blinking bright sea air.

'Where to?' John asks, relinquishing, as he always does on these stolen times, complete control to her.

She replies with a greedy simplicity, 'The sea.'

Arm in arm, another faceless, nameless couple, they move with the crowd; becoming a blank slate, upon which anything could be written.

Here, on John's arm, sandwiched between the reek of the whelk stalls and laughs of children, wrapped in brine and sunshine Eleanor feels she is no one. And yet finally someone.

It is she who is first down the steps and on the beach. Reaching behind her, pulling John down, towards the water that rolls and breaks, whispering beyond the shimmering sands. Filled with anticipation and longing to walking across the pooling, mirroring light to reach the waves, she briefly relinquishes her hold on John, turning back, impatient, to see him paused at the bottom of the steps. His brow, drawn in a line of taunt concentration, he is patting furiously at the sides of the coat, now hooked over his arm. The sight of him provokes in Eleanor a sudden, overwhelming rush of love. He looks up; catching her eye; his face clears as he steps towards her on the sand. She kisses him full on his wide warm mouth, delighting in his blushes.

'Come on.'

Tugging him onwards, they walk together, hand in hand, shoulder to shoulder, over the sand, beautifully ridged by the tide. Without speaking, they stoop to remove their shoes. Eleanor, stockingless in preparation, waits with ill-concealed impatience, as John removes his socks and rolls up his trousers. Barefoot they continue, hands entwined, shoes swinging loosely by their side. With each step Eleanor's shoulders drop, the gentle sink and pull of the wet sand tugging all tension downwards and away.

At the shoreline, they stop, standing stock-still beneath a high, intense, marvellous sun. Just, Eleanor thinks, as it should be. As she always wishes it could be.

She gazes out, lost to the offing, where the sea gives way graciously and gratefully to a dappled mackerel sky, in which gulls' wheel, cry and swoop. It's as if they are standing on the very edges of the earth. At a bright sunlit gateway: where she can escape everything, shake off all that is cloying and rotten about her life. Perhaps even touch what it was that once made her whole.

For since Alfred's death and all that has come after it, Eleanor has fractured. Her being, her life splintered piece by minute piece. Each month and each small trial or tragedy has resulted in her giving up a little more of herself. The more detached Lily becomes from the reality of life, the more life tightens its grip on Eleanor.

But here, at the edge of the sea, where the lace fringed waves lap rhythmically and comfortingly at her feet, she glimpses the shadow of the person she was, echo of the person she might have been.

The sand shifts, pushing beneath and between her toes, the water cool about her ankles. Barking dogs, squealing children, cricket bats, laughing men and calling mothers, all circle around and above her. Ebbing, flowing, at the edges of her consciousness, but they can't break the spell.

Eleanor won't let them; not yet.

She turns to John, smiling as she meets his eye. But his features, although familiar, are somehow not his own. His usually passive face shines, beads of sweat standing at his temples. His mouth is ringed, white with tension, as he turns his cap over and over in his work-ridden hands.

Something is wrong. Terribly wrong.

And with a terrible, practised ease Eleanor slides from joy to the black despair.

Her eyes dart back to the shoreline, combing the sea and the sand, searching for whatever the trouble might be. But all seems calm; she can spot no obvious danger.

Confused, Eleanor steps towards John, bringing her hand to his head, as if she is nursing Lily through one of her debilitating and convenient fevers.

'John?' Her voice rasps, little more than a whisper. 'John? Are you ill? You look ever so strange.'

He stops twisting his cap and drops his eyes to his feet, a low strangled laugh escaping his lips.

'Strange, eh?' Lifting his head, he blurts out, 'Oh Lord, this isn't how I had it planned.'

'What isn't?'

All Eleanor's carefully cultivated contentment is leeching from her like water. John is her stability, the one constant, solid part of her life. She has never seen him like this. Wings of panic begin to beat, pattering deep within her throat.

'The thing is…' He starts, then stops, as grasping at his hand, Eleanor pulls him towards her. Clinging to him, stuck somewhere between the desire to know what is wrong and an overwhelming urge to scream.

But more than anything, she wants to still him. To delay the unspoken words that she is convinced will ruin everything.

She tries to speak but John stops her. Laying his hands on her shoulders, he spins her round. Once, twice; turning them both in the shallows, the beach becoming a glorious, terrifying blur. When he stops, the sun is behind him, gilding his dark hair with a bright edge of red gold. His features are blurred, only his eyes visible, shining black and intense, their usual gentleness stolen by the light.

John pauses, bringing his breath into line with the swell of the water still lapping about their feet.

'Eleanor, I am tired. Of us having to hide. Of snatching moments here and there.'

She opens her mouth, ready to justify, excuse and promise. But again, John stops her, snatching her own hand up in his.

They are moving towards forbidden ground, treading unspoken terrain; rough and uncertain.

'I want… want things, us, to change. I love you, Eleanor. And I think you feel the same.'

As John swallows his way to clarity, Eleanor, overcome by a rolling wave of emotion, knows exactly what he is about to say. And what it he is now searching for in the folds of that stupid winter coat.

Yet still, it is a shock to see it. The small blue box, sat in his palm. A shock to see his rough fingers fumble with the clasp.

She is transfixed. By the glinting, winking ring, snug in its velvet nest, whose tiny chip of stone catches the sun's rays. Reflecting and refracting the essence of this perfect day. Keeping her eyes on the light, captured and condensed, playing out its magic, Eleanor nods; answering a question that hasn't yet been asked.

John, speechless with relief and love, lifts her from the sand, spinning her around. And in the blur of gold and blue, beach and sky, Eleanor allows herself to believe that this moment, and all that will follow, is possible. Setting her down, John kisses her face, his lips moving slowly from her brow and before seeking out her own.

And beneath their gentle pressure Eleanor sets about convincing herself that this can work.

CHAPTER FIVE

LILY

The spare key is in its usual place.

On the top shelf of the larder, wedged behind their mother's preserving jars; now rendered useless by the fact they are far too big for two people's needs. Taking care to remember their exact placement, Lily is careful not to disturb the dust.

It won't do to let on to Eleanor that she knows about this key.

Piper, now released from the kitchen, sniffs hopefully at her feet, but Lily has no intention of letting him betray her with muddy paws. Ignoring his whining, she crosses the kitchen, unlocks the door and steps outside.

The garden before her is littered with the evidence of her destruction; scraps of paper caught in the grass, bushes and flower bed, white and stark against the green. Lily smiles in satisfaction and moves on.

Immediately she notices that the bicycle is gone. Even though Lily never uses it, its absence irritates her. Another liberty Eleanor has seen fit to take.

She walks the path that curves to the top of the bank, crossing the dyke marking the edge of their land. Pausing just briefly, she takes in the river and the village beyond. To her right stands the lighthouse, the sentry of the sprawling marsh; to her left, the bridge, one great web of rusting steel.

And there, on the opposite bank, low and ruined, squats the remains of the port, its timbers dark with time and water, as skeletal as the hopes and dreams it had so fleetingly bred; now sinking, each year a little further, into the river mud, where its rotten footings, splintered, to be carried off unseen on the tide.

Soon Lily, Eleanor, and the hospital, will be the only tangible things that remain. Even more reason to cling on, to fight. To keep everything the same.

Reacquainting herself with the caress of air on her skin, Lily absorbs the sense of open space and the possibilities of this high, vaulted sky. She takes it in, in measured sips, this familiar haunting view. For since that night, almost three months ago, out in the darkness, Lily has rarely stood here alone. The night she came dangerously close to overplaying her hand.

Mostly Eleanor's terror suits her, but it limits her too.

It helps that today the wind is in the right direction, carrying only the scent of newly cut pine stacked on the wharf, and the occasional cry of an unfortunate child. Another poor soul left behind. Maybe one of her brother's brood; it would be just like Frank to keep his family at home today.

Because for all her growing confidence, so carefully concealed, Lily can't stand here when the wind blows in from the right, allowing the marsh, too close and insistent, to overwhelm every sense. When the tang of salt coats her throat with the taste of the past.

Decisive and defiant, Lily throws back her head and turns to the comforting surety of the sky. With slow, deliberate steps, she tests her position, shifting beneath this sky, which is everything. Lowering herself to the warm grass, she keeps her eyes fixed above, even as her tangled hair mingles with the earth. Arms outstretched, she comes across a molehill. She starts, then relaxes, as her fingers sink beyond its warm ,crumbling surface, seeking out the cooler and damper, earth. The contrast grabs and calms her; anchors her to this place. As her fingers probe, pushing and poking at the hidden and unseen, the last of her rage finally lifts.

Her hands move slowly, continually through the dirt, her gaze still on the world high above her.

The sky is still there. Huge, waiting for her. Even after all these months of being inside, the sky hasn't gone away. This sky that will always dominate. Whether soaring over the garden or marsh, or fragmented and captured in a grubby windowpane. Fierce with the orange and violet of a winter sunrise, or leaden with rain blown from the west, the fen and all within it will always belong to the sky.

Today it arches over Lily, painted the kind of blue of nowhere elsewhere. A colour unmatched in any of the threads she sews with, or the flowers that Eleanor tends in the small square patch she calls a garden.

Sky blue. Laced here and there with wisps of trailing white; almost clouds that slowly break apart, torn by breezes too high, too slight to perceive. Now and then a bird appears; some darting, there and then gone before Lily has time to register them. Others, birds of the sea, climb higher and linger, circling and wheeling far above her head. Once, Lily would have strained to hear their cries. To pick out the calls and put a name to each one. Just as Alfred would have done.

Another thing her brother taught her. Something else they shared; that had died with him.

Now Lily finds it is easier not to listen.

Removing her hand from the earth, she reaches out, her fingers closing about a clump of grass. She tugs, filling her fist with long blades. Bringing them to her face, slowly, rhythmically, she draws them, one blade, then another over her skin, pausing as she reaches her lips and chin. Lifting her neck, she immerses herself in the sensation and pushes the call of the birds beyond her reach. Eyes closed, Lily tips her face towards the sun, inviting the light, absorbing its warmth as it dances across her skin. Behind her eyelids the colours change. It is pleasant, disorientating.

And only then does Lily invite Alfred's memory in, allowing

it to rise, slowly, gently. Until her brother stand on the very edges of her mind.

There are only certain ways and in certain places that Lily will conjure these thoughts. When she is calm and her skin is warm. When the sky is clear and open. Only then can she think of the brother whose death turned the world on its head. Outside and in these conditions, her grief doesn't always feel too big. Or mixed up with and spoilt by the anger and spite that now dominates her days.

Only here is there sufficient space for her to unleash her loss; examine it and let it breathe. And when it threatens to engulf her, here Lily can find the space and strength to push it all away, sending it back to the marsh, where it came from and where it still belongs.

The summer colours dancing behind her eyelids begin to still, and suddenly Alfred is before her.

Her brother. Her other half. She had always believed they were equally matched in spirit and temperament. Only when he was gone did Lily realise that she had stolen all her bravery and joy from him. Or maybe he had stolen hers?

Because when he was here, appearing at mealtimes, there when she went to bed and entered the kitchen in the morning, Lily wasn't the person she is now.

When Alfred died, that Lily, the fearless, joyful, laughing Lily, died too.

They had belonged to the marsh, disappearing for hours; together, lost in their shared existence. Alfred shouldering his gun, Lily, striding out with Piper at her heels. Anything had seemed possible.

Until possibility died with him. Until Alfred taking it out onto the frozen marsh, had squandered it, trapping it with him in the creek. Allowing it to leach like poison into the mud that had held him fast, swollen by the tide that pulled and buffeted his body. So, by the time they brought him back, shrouded, disfigured, with filth caked in his hair, possibility and the future was long gone.

And with it, all hope and light. All lost and left to drift aimlessly in the Wash, where it fractured and slowly sunk, before coming to rest, ragged and abandoned on the rocks and sand beneath.

Lily knows it all. Knows it with a certainty that grips her by the throat; that all she loved, and all she was, is drowned. And though she might catch occasional glimpses of it in the flow of the river, or taste it briefly in the swirl of a sea fret, she will never ever be allowed to possess the whole of it again.

Lily freezes, her body suddenly rigid, hard and cold against the earth.

She has opened the door too wide. Has allowed these unchecked thoughts, to grow, to spiral into feelings. Into emotions that she can't hope to contain.

Filled with panic, she opens her eyes, to find the sky is no longer arcing, not wide or high. Instead, it is heading towards her, falling rapidly and without mercy. A dark and shattered sky.

Snatching at the air, Lily turns her face. And, pressing it to the earth, she screams.

CHAPTER SIX

ELEANOR

'You'll tell her?'

Eleanor nods. Her bicycle, retrieved from the station bushes, stands between them, as passengers stream past on either side. John's hand moves from her waist to rest lightly on her shoulder, one finger twisting itself amongst the fine and escaping strands of her hair. Her own hand flies to meet his and her eyes catch yet again on the shine of the ring she still can't believe is there.

'I'll tell her. I'll just need to find the right time.'

John's hand strays to her cheek, lifting her face. Dipping his head, he meets her eye.

'It won't come. The right time. And it will only get harder the longer you leave it. If we are to marry, Lily has to know.'

Eleanor looks away. She doesn't want to talk about Lily now.

'Come to the smithy tomorrow, in the morning. Let me know how it goes.'

'I'll try, I promise. And John…'

With a sudden stab of panic, Eleanor catches at his arm.

'Don't tell anyone. Please, promise me. Not 'til Lily knows.'

His kiss is soft and hot, and she takes it as an agreement; then with a final, gentle whisper he is gone.

John had wanted to walk her home, to see her safely back along the river, through the rapidly falling violet dusk. But Eleanor is not ready to risk bringing Lily and her fiancé face to face.

Looking down at her ring, she mouths the word.

Fiancé.

She looks around to see if anyone has noticed, letting the thrill and fear of implication pass through her and slowly drift away.

She grips the handlebars but doesn't move until John has disappeared, becoming another shadow amongst the many that weave unsteadily over the cobbles, another part of the village making his way back home.

Only then does Eleanor head in the opposite direction, moving against the tide as always, over the bridge and away.

She pedals slowly, her thoughts tangled in the remaining warmth of the day, now cut through with the enormity of the promise she has made.

Along the road out of the village, past the last of the day-trippers and the overtired children carried by weary parents, past the laughing couples and groups of young men. Along the narrow track that runs the length of the bridge, she lingers. Dallying and dabbling in memories and moments, slipping back to the sounds of the beach, the feel of John's hand in hers and the persistent rhythm of the sea.

Yet, by the time she has crossed the river, turning left onto the uneven, deserted road that tops the furthest bank, the feelings of dread she has tried to suppress begin to rise, accumulating and sitting like stone beneath her ribs.

As she moves closer towards the sinking sun whose wide orange and crimson bands spilt the evening sky, her legs become stubborn, sluggish with reality, and her mind teems, alive with thoughts of how to break her news to Lily. Trying and failing to picture a moment when this might be possible.

And, as always, thoughts of Lily are followed, quick and hard, by those of Alfred.

Without permission, her eyes slip to the marsh, its horizon dark against the garish clouds; a permanent reminder of what it is that they have lost. And, assailed by the familiar wash of love, grief and burning resentment, Eleanor is temporarily halted. Pulling hard on the brakes, she dismounts, walking a few yards before being overcome anew; this time with a sudden cold terror of guilt. It is hours now since she locked the door and cycled away from Lily.

Anything could have happened.

So, the last half mile is covered at speed, until Eleanor tumbles, sweating and hopelessly conflicted, off her bicycle, to pull hard at the rusting bolt on the gate. She pauses only to remove the ring from her finger, stuffing it hurriedly into the pocket of her dress. Silently, she asks the evening and John for forgiveness.

From inside the house, the high, excited barks of Piper, are accompanied by a rapid scratching at the kitchen door.

Eleanor rushes through the gate, before something stops her in her tracks.

Out of the falling gloom jumps a fragment, an unexpected flash that catches her eye. White, irregular, it lies at the edge of the path. As Eleanor stoops to collect it, her gaze falls upon another, slightly smaller, then immediately several more. She is surrounded. By a misplaced and disparate trail of what she realises now is paper, inexplicably and carelessly tossed around the garden, quite impossible to fathom or follow. But Eleanor knows that whatever they might be, these scraps were not there before.

Confused, she hastily sweeps three pieces into her palm, then steps towards the house, the gathering shades of evening preventing her from identifying what it is she holds. Retrieving the key from her pocket, she unlocks the door. Immediately Piper is upon her, jumping up, his claws catching at the folds of her skirt, before darting into the garden beyond, where he turns tight and desperate circles in the twilight, relieving himself in the centre of the grass. He is surrounded by more of those strange fragments, like bone against the earth. Eleanor calls out, turning the rags of paper over in her hand.

'Lily? Lily? Where are…'

She stops, horror and recognition damning the words in her throat. Quickly, she grabs and lights the oil lamp, then arranges the scraps of paper in the light's puddle of gold, her heart pounding as she runs her finger over the broken yet familiar ink.

With a cry of pain and rage, she pulls back. Knocking against the nearest chair, she flies out into the garden. As she runs down the stone steps, a floorboard somewhere above her squeaks.

To and fro Eleanor dashes, scrabbling in the short grass, dirtying her hands and skirts, as she pulls piece after ruined piece towards her, desperate hoping that all is not lost. Piper, restless and intent upon the game, scampers beneath her arms, occasionally trying to tug the fragments that fall from her shaking fingers with his sharp, insistent teeth.

'Away!' she shrieks, stamping her feet towards him and sending him yelping in the direction of the house.

Behind her, a curtain twitches. And through the thickening darkness, the lighthouse lantern begins to sweep.

Finally, defeated by the failing light, tears and fists overflowing with paper, Eleanor admits defeat. Kicking the kitchen door shut, she calls again into the stillness of the house, making her way towards the narrow hallway. Her feet are thunderous on the stairs.

'Lily. Damn you, Lily, I know you're here!'

Clasping her bulging fists against her chest, Eleanor stares at her sister's closed door. The only sound is Piper, claws scrabbling on the kitchen flags.

In blinding desperation and with a final flash of hope, Eleanor turns and darts towards the open door of her own room.

Flinging the paper down on the counterpane, she heads to the oak dresser, where she begins wrenching out the second drawer, before casting the contents upon the floor. On her knees, she tears wildly at fabric, lifting garment after garment, shaking each one before thrusting it from her.

All the letters, all his letters, every single one, is gone.

Throwing back her head, Eleanor roars into the silence. An extended cry of pain and betrayal echoing off the walls and scraping the bare boards.

Getting to her feet, she forces her way through the sea of discarded cloth and paper, to stand, shaking, outside her sister's door. Thrusting her hand into her pocket, Eleanor retrieves the discarded ring and pushes it on her finger, before thumping hard and fast on the door.

'Lily!'

She rattles the handle before banging again. Her fist smarts and her throat burns.

'Open the door, Lily. I know you're in there. And I know what you've done.'

The house creaks in the dusk. But from beyond the door there is no response.

Infuriated, Eleanor pushes her ear to the wood, straining through the grain and silence. And just when she feels the familiar gnawing of dread start to erode her fury, she catches the thread of a distant whimper, which spools slowly to a moan. Her anger catches, reignites, then flares again.

'Lily?' She pounds, her knuckles raw and her breath ragged. 'Lily, open this door.'

Silence, stretching on and outwards, followed by the faintest slip-slide of stocking feet and the slow drag of a rug. Eleanor can feel Lily now. Can see her standing there, waiting, deciding, on the other side of the door. Swallowing, she fights for an inch of control.

'Why, Lily? Why did you do it? Rip them up like that? They were my letters, Lily. Mine! Nothing to do with you.'

In a quiet, broken voice, that sounds like it weaves through tears, Lily whispers.

'I was scared. That I'd be left here alone. That you wouldn't come back, like…'

Her voice descends into a succession of quick dry sobs. And the almost-reference to Alfred both stills and enrages Eleanor, bringing her back to the place they have been a hundred times before.

But she will not be talked out of her anger today.

'Of course I was coming back. I always come back.' She bangs again, harder. 'Open up this door.'

'Please, Eleanor…'

'*Please, Eleanor*, nothing. How could you, Lily? Those letters. *My* letters. Just one thing of my own.'

'I told you; I was scared.' Lily's voice, higher now, comes closer, then wheels away from the door. Eleanor pictures her pacing, her fingers working at and around each other; rapid and imagined movements that infuriate her even more.

'Being scared is no reason to do what you have done.'

'You locked me in, Eleanor. Alone. What was I supposed to think?'

There it is. The first stirring of guilt, sharp. An ebony knife, slicing through the anger, and reminding Eleanor of her carelessness. Carving out the suggestion that maybe this is really her fault. Enraged, she fights it, slamming her foot down on the floor.

'Think? You didn't think at all!'

Lily's weeping begins again, settling to a constant, pressed hard and tight against the door. Eleanor lands one final thump against the wood, closing her eyes as she does so, hoping that Lily recoils in shock. Trembling, she stares at her hand and the ring, now twisted, its small stone biting into her flesh.

Tell her.

Her head swimming, she snatches her breath and falls hard against the door. She is ready to tell her.

Opening her mouth, starting to press her news into the grain, she is halted by Lily's throaty whisper.

'I was scared, Eleanor. So scared, here on my own. It was…'

Lily pauses. Eleanor hears her gulping at the air. She feels herself becoming entrapped once more.

Tell her. Now.

She presses her palms and face flat against the door.

But it is Lily who speaks first.

'It was like the day Alfred left. You left, and the whole world went dark, and I knew it… it was going to happen again.'

Drawing her fingernails down the grain, Eleanor sinks and sags, hating herself as the anger in her belly starts to dissolve.

'I was sure you would never come home and…'

A fresh round of weeping begins into which Lily's words disappear.

And that softening, the weakening that always starts at her very centre, seeps outwards, overtaking Eleanor's brain. She steps away from the door.

'Come out, Lily.' Her words are wrapped in their usual worn velvet. Her legs, suddenly deprived of adrenaline, buckle and shake.

And somewhere in the distance, she hears Lily draw in a long, triumphant breath before turning the lock and slowly opening the door.

They face each other. Lily in her long cotton nightdress, crooked at the neck, one thin shoulder half exposed. Her toes curl, clenching in nervous folds against the floor; her dark hair hangs limp and loose about her face and down her narrow back. Her lips are cracked and bitten, her eyes shadowed and sunken in her tear-stained cheeks. After a day of such lightness, such love, Lily, framed in the doorway, appears lost and haunted. Wild and unkempt.

Before Eleanor has time to speak, Lily throws herself forwards, forcing her sister to catch her in her arms.

'Oh Eleanor. You don't know what it's been like, trapped here all alone.'

Pushing her hot face against Eleanor's chest, Lily's arms creep up to cling about her sister's neck, tears soaking the collar of her dress.

Lifting her head from the urgent heat of her sister, Eleanor fights the urge to scream.

Habit pulls her hand down to the crown of Lily's head, where it falls into the familiar stroking. That gentle rhythm halted as John's ring catches fast in the knots of Lily's hair.

Crying out, Lily tries to pull away as Eleanor desperately tugs the ring free. Filled with panic, she steps back, attempting to tuck her hand away.

But Lily, now strangely dry-eyed, is too quick, too sharp. With no sign of fear, she twists Eleanor's hand towards her, dragging her to the narrow landing window.

In the lighthouse's revolving glare, the ring glints then fades. Revealed, then hidden, caught in the endless circle of night and day.

Lily grips Eleanor's fingers.

'Did he give you this?' Her voice thick with accusation, hisses just above a whisper.

Eleanor stares at the wall, tracking the dizzy combination of shadow and light.

Lily squeezes tighter, rocking her sister's hand in one small but spite filled shake.

'This ring… John… did he ask you to…'

'Marry him.'

Eleanor finds her voice. Lily's face, shadowed but insistent, emerges from the gloom, only to retreat again; her eyes burn with something Eleanor is afraid to read. Into the soft lines of her palms, she feels the press of Lily's nails, sinking deeper as their gazes and hands remain locked. Together.

'And?' Lily spits.

Eleanor trembles, desperate to look away from Lily's insistence that she should put into words what is already known. Her answer, when it comes, barely breaks the darkness or the silence. Is just a bubble of air. The blackest of sighs.

'I've accepted.'

Lily's eyes widen in shock. Her fingers previously so rigid, suddenly slacken and release. Seizing the moment, Eleanor snatches away her hand and hides it deep in the pleats of her dress.

'You've done what?' Lily consumes the inches between them, until her breath, rancid and wet, bursts hot against her sister's cheek.

Every inch of Eleanor aches, to sink, to drop to the floor. Stepping back, she gropes, hands outstretched, desperately seeking the support of the wall. Forcing out her reply, she wills her words to fill the space and create some kind of shield.

'I've said I will marry John.'

'And what about me?' Lily screams, her shoulders back, neck outstretched; the darkness surrounding them, writhing with her rage. 'What am I supposed to do?'

'Lily, stop. There is no need…'

'There's every need. After everything we've been through… I am telling you, Eleanor, I will not be left alone here.' Lily's voice splinters, scattering like ice and merging with shadows on the floor.

'Lily…'

Eleanor moves nearer to the window, to the light. Lily follows. Closer, too close. On tiptoes, she pushes her face into her sister's, words rattling against her teeth.

'Never. Do you hear me? I'm never going to be left here alone.'

'Lily, nothing is settled yet. We haven't talked about…'

'Oh, talk away. You and *him*. You can talk and plan… fool yourself that this is going to happen. But…'

Lily's fingers creep, snaking their way into the nape of Eleanor's hair. Her scalp burns as the roots twist. She gasps once.

'… no matter what it takes. This will always be your home.'

Lily stands for a few seconds longer. Eye to eye, her fingers knotted in Eleanor's hair.

Then, releasing her fist, she stalks back across the landing, slamming the bedroom door.

CHAPTER SEVEN

CLARA - MAY 1914

At the sound of the gate, Clara starts, then seeing it is Eleanor, instantly settles. As much as she dares. All day she has been wound like a spring, assailed by memories of yesterday; the scene on the train and all the simplicity and pleasure of the hours that followed giving way to the anticipation of what she knows is coming.

Frank had arrived home in the early hours, collapsing in the kitchen chair, then left before breakfast without uttering a word. Lying in their room above listening to his snores, Clara had been trapped between relief and the knowledge that the inevitable was only delayed.

Now, smiling at Eleanor, she walks into the small kitchen without a word, only raising her eyebrows to the thumps shaking the ceiling above them.

'The boys,' she explains. 'In disgrace. Fighting, with each other and them next door. Molly's trying to get them into bed.'

She lifts the kettle onto the stuttering range. The evening light, yellow and low, is retreating little by little from the narrow confines of the kitchen and the yard beyond. Picking her way, through the shadows, Eleanor sits at the table, just as another crash is followed by a wail.

Clara throws her hands up, jabbing wildly at the air.

'Those boys. They'll be the death of me. Don't know where they get it from; do you?'

Eleanor smiles weakly. The house is possessed by the usual air of barely contained chaos, the worn table still covered with the remains of the evening meal. As the kettle begins to sing, Eleanor gathers plates and cups, brushing breadcrumbs into the palm of her hand.

'Come all the way over here to clean up, have you?' Clara says.

'Might have.'

Clara makes the tea, and the crashing continues, until finally she walks into the narrow hall and shouts up the stairs.

'Do as you're told, you two, or there'll be hell to pay.'

An uneasy silence settles, and Clara eyes the front door. Still no sign of Frank. Again, the relief followed immediately by fear. On an impulse, she steps forward and draws the bolt. Then, thinking better of it, draws it back it again.

In the kitchen, Eleanor, two cups of tea poured in front of her, sits at the table, toying with her cuff, shifting her spoon. Eyeing her, Clara sits down and lifts her cup.

'Well?'

'Well, what?'

'How was yesterday?'

Eleanor smiles shyly.

'Was going to ask you the same thing.'

Remembering each part, Clara is assailed by a complex string of emotions, joy, delight, fear. And the certainty that the debt remains unpaid.

Forcing brightness, she nods towards the ceiling. 'They loved it. Especially the boys.'

'And Frank?'

'He seemed to enjoy it.'

'Seemed to?'

Despite the tea, Clara's mouth is suddenly dry. She doesn't want to go into all that now.

'We lost him. In the crowds… like I say, he seemed to enjoy it.'

Eleanor says nothing, just watches as Clara spoons sugar

into her cup. Sugar she doesn't usually take.

'Anyway, I asked you first. How was *your* day?'

Flushing, Eleanor looks down at the washed-out table, at her fingers, idly following breadcrumbs and butter.

'It was lovely.'

She lifts her eyes to Clara's.

'Really lovely.'

Clara takes Eleanor's hand in hers.

'Good. Because you both deserve a lovely day. I saw you, in the station, way ahead of us. You looked happy.'

'You could have caught us up. Come and said hello.'

Clara laughs.

'Not likely! As if you'd have wanted us cramping your style! I'm just saying it was nice, to see you smiling. Nice to see both of you smile.'

'Did Frank see us?' That note of uneasiness, something sour creeping in.

'No, he wasn't with us then.'

Avoiding any more awkward questions, Clara tries again.

'Enough about your brother. I want to know about you. What d'you do?'

'Walked on the beach. Talked and...'

Eleanor stops, her gaze and fingers pausing where the wood is nicked and swollen.

'And?'

Reaching beneath the table, Eleanor fumbles, then brings up her hand and holds out her palm. The sounds of children have fallen silent; the air is still; the kitchen a web of dusky shadows. Reaching out, Clara lifts her sister-in-law's hand into what remains of the light. She draws in her breath.

'Oh Eleanor. Is that...'

'A ring, the last time I looked. John proposed.'

Clapping her hands, Clara laughs. Dancing around the table, she pulls Eleanor to her.

'Oh El, what wonderful, wonderful news.'

Within her embrace, she feels Eleanor stiffens. Clara pulls away, regarding her at arm's length. She looks back at her hand, now closed tight around the ring.

Wordless, Clara turns, lighting the oil lamp on the sideboard; Eleanor flinches, then pales in its buttery light.

'You said yes I hope?'

Eleanor nods.

'So why is that ring still in your pocket?'

'Lily...'

Clara's gut recoils. Biting back everything she longs to say, she sinks in her chair and waits for more. Here they are, just where they always end up. For Eleanor, all things, good, bad, even indifferent, always return somehow to Lily. Just as for her, they return to Frank.

Clara reaches for her sister-in–law's hands, but shaking her head Eleanor moves away.

'You've told her?'

'More she found out.' Eleanor is crying softly now, tears sliding down her cheeks. She makes no effort to wipe them, letting them fall onto the dirty pine.

'When I got back yesterday, she had ripped up John's letters. Every single one, torn to pieces. Left them all over the garden where she knew I would see.'

'The cow!'

Eleanor shoots her a quick look.

'Sorry Eleanor, but...'

'I was furious...'

'I'd have bloody killed her...'

'So, I put the ring on and banged on her door. I was all ready to tell her. I was so angry, I shouted at her, kept hammering on the door. But...'

'But what?'

'When she opened it, the door, I could see in her face how

scared she was. How awful it must have been for her yesterday, locked up all alone over there. I should never have done it; locked her in, left her like that.'

Clara snorts.

'Don't be so ridiculous. What choice did you have? After last time…' Clara's voice trails away, as she watches Eleanor's thoughts fly back to the water. Pulling at wet clothes, alone in the shallows of the river, pleading and praying. Grasping at Lily and the riverbank with desperate searching hands. And not for the first time, Clara wonders what would have happened if Eleanor hadn't found her sister that night, if that single gust hadn't caught the open back door and sent her hurling into the darkness. For when Eleanor ends up here, in this kitchen, hurt, lost, and wholly defeated, Clara thinks quietly of the blessing it might have been had there been no wind at all. Then, filled with shame she pushes the thought down as quickly as it rises.

But it is there all the same.

'I shouldn't have gone.'

Knowing it is pointless to argue, Clara tries to move the conversation on.

'How'd she find out?'

'She was upset, so I held her and the ring… it caught in her hair.'

'And what did she say?'

'That the wedding would never happen, that the hospital was my only home. Then locked herself in her room. Went off and slammed the door.'

'Didn't mind being locked in then, did she?' It is out before Clara can stop it, spat over the teacups.

Eleanor recoils.

'All night I heard her crying, Clara. All night! And she's barely spoken since. Hasn't eaten a thing all day.'

Clara stares back, harder. Eleanor continues.

'It's impossible…' She slumps forwards, folding in on herself, limb after limb; so obviously defeated that Clara's anger is swallowed by sadness. And the desire that Eleanor should have the thing that she herself has never found. The sure simplicity of a love that sustains, given by someone who is completely on your side. Even when your side is the worst place to be.

'Nothing's impossible, Eleanor.'

'It feels it.' Eleanor's voice is muffled, woolly with tears and frustration 'You know better than anyone what happens over there. What it's like. How it all changes in the blink of an eye. You know!'

'But John knows too. And he's still asked you.'

'Not all of it. He'd never have asked me if he did. I can't bring all of this down on him. It's not fair.'

'He's a grown man, Eleanor. One who can make his own choices. And he's chosen you.' Clutching at Eleanor's hand, Clara whispers. 'You have to let him in.'

'And then what? If I open the door, everyone will see what I see. Lily'll never be able to stand that. It'll make her worse.'

Clara shifts in her seat, wondering what could possibly be worse than this, this half-life. A life constrained and defined by someone else's pain and fear, determined to keep them all imprisoned by the past. Embolden by the unfairness of it all she pushes on, into a place from which she knows she can't return.

'Lily isn't a child, Eleanor. No matter how she behaves. And the way I see it, right now, all three of you are miserable. Lily might get better. She might not. It's been two since Alfred died, and two years' too long live like this. But a lifetime? That's even longer.'

'But if it makes *her* worse again Clara. What if…'

'I'm not sure that it can be any worse, Eleanor.'

Silence falls, sitting thick between them, a mantle attempting to deaden their unspoken words. Clara pushes it aside. 'Well, if you're going to marry John, then something's got to change.'

Eleanor nods slowly. Her face is white; a ghost against the smudges of the window and the dancing shadows beyond.

'I know, but…'

'But what...?'

'On the beach, with the waves and sunshine, I didn't think... it all seemed so easy. That just saying yes and really wanting it was enough.'

'And why isn't it? El, people get married all the time. For better or worse, they're all ready to tie themselves to some poor fool.' Clara grabs at her own bitterness, refusing to let it unspool.

'Other people don't have Lily, don't have the hospital...'

'You can't look after her forever Eleanor. No matter what's happened, Lily's a grown woman.'

'I'm all she's got.'

'She's young and healthy despite what she'd have you believe. Others worse off than her have made their own way.'

Eleanor tugs at the neck of her blouse. Clara reaches over, once more, taking her hand.

'And she has another brother. One that's not dead.'

'Frank?' Eleanor's laugh is hollow. 'When was the last time she saw him? Or the last time he came to the hospital? He hates the place. He won't even let you come.'

'Maybe it's time that changed. Time I changed, too.'

Eleanor stares in disbelief.

'Frank'll never stand for it.'

'Let me worry about Frank. But for a start I can come over, a couple of times a week, while the little ones are at school. Sit with Lily, or whatever else you need me to do.'

In the evening light, Clara sees Eleanor's eyes glow briefly as her expression flits between hopeful and hopeless and then back again.

'Clara...'

'Clara nothing.' She squeezes Eleanor's hand, the ring insistent at the centre of her palm. 'I won't let you give up on this. Together we'll make this work.'

CHAPTER EIGHT

LILY – MAY 1914

She wakes to a flood of light, Eleanor having been in and pulled back the thin curtains; allowing the sun to play in bright patches on the dusty floor.

Instantly irritated by the implication, Lily pulls the blankets high over her head and turns her face to the wall.

But the smell, sour and keening, of her own body and breath, forces her head back out. Lily hasn't washed in days.

Submitting to the sounds of the house and the world beyond, she tries to establish where her sister might be. She longs to stretch out her body, but she won't give herself away by footsteps on the boards if Eleanor is in the kitchen below.

So, she waits, encased in moments of almost silence, until from the yard, comes the clack of metal on stone, followed by the bang of a door. Confirmation that Eleanor is in the hospital; that, for now at least, she has given up on Lily and made a start on her day.

Smirking, Lily slips from the bed, narrowly missing the tray left on the floor, complete with cold toast and a grey, milky scum that might once have been tea. With the side of her foot, she slides the tray away, ignoring the roll of her stomach and the fact that she hasn't eaten properly in days.

Keeping to the edges of the room, careful to stay out of sight, Lily approaches the window, where, screened by shadow and curtain, she peeps out. Piper lies on the path, head on his paws, looking towards the gate. The hospital door, visible through the budding trees, is propped open by a bucket and mop. Eleanor, no more than an occasional shadow or sound, moves within, going through the daily, practised, and pointless routine. Folding towels, washing floors, chasing spiders from the beds in which no one ever sleeps.

Then, without warning, she appears in the doorway, her arms filled with a mountain of sheets. Lily ducks back behind the curtain, heart thumping, afraid she has been seen, but when she looks back the linen is heaped in a basket on the steps, and Eleanor is gone.

Since the night of the letters, Lily has held the upper hand. Eleanor has never been able to argue. The fight in her is quiet and constant, like their mother. It is not the fire that jumps and flares through Lily and Frank's veins, the heat of their father, that is only ever a moment away. It had taken Alfred's death to quench her father's rage, grief knocking all the fight out of him, before slowly carrying him away. Lily feels it now, briefly leaning into it; that cold, familiar hand of loss, squeezing at the base of her spine. She rolls her shoulders, shrugs it off. She can't lose her focus, not yet, not today.

Since that night, after the ring and the torn paper, Lily has felt Eleanor pushing against their familiar pattern, putting up a gentle but constant resistance, but so far, on balance, things have gone Lily's way.

Just a few more days. A few more days of this and Lily is sure that the idea of John and marriage will be given up, cast away completely. As long as Lily keeps to her room, not eating, barely speaking.

But this hunger! She has never had to go this long before, surviving on snatched and illicit meals, while all the time her stomach gnaws and aches. Even now, leaning on the windowsill, she feels the black dizziness catching at her edges. She longs to eat; even the cold tea and toast on the floor looks inviting. But eating that would betray her, and this might only be the beginning of the game.

Besides, if Eleanor is only at the stage of stripping beds, then she'll be out in the hospital for a while longer. Long enough for Lily to risk sneaking down to the kitchen without being seen; maybe she can even collect something for later and stash it under her bed.

Stealing one final glance, she dips down beneath the window and, crouching low to the floor, crosses the room. Edging open her bedroom door, she pauses in the stillness before making her way slowly down the stairs.

Her bare feet are chilled on the stone floor; the narrow window, high in the wall opposite, is open, pulling in the sounds of the river. The familiar beat of the water, overlaid by shouts of carters and fisherman, the wind rattling through the thick beds of reeds. Pushing down the longing to be out there, Lily steps carefully, silently into the kitchen beyond.

The room, running the length of the cottage, is flanked by a small window at each end, one looking out onto the fen and the hospital, the other the road and water beyond. Two armchairs sag in front of the range, a book lying open and face down on the nearest arm. Piper's basket resting, on Ma's ancient rag rug, sits snug against the hearth. In the centre of the room, the pine table, washed and worn by hands and years, is covered in the remains of Eleanor's breakfast; a cold teapot, jug of milk, an upended loaf of bread surrounded by crumbs. It is unlike Eleanor to leave things in such a state, but then, Lily thinks, she has been distracted these past few days.

Since May Day, Eleanor has stayed close to home. Just one short trip to the village and Clara. And one late evening when, from her bed, Lily heard John's voice at the kitchen door.

Despite pressing her ear to the floorboards, Lily had not been able to make out their conversation, only the rise and fall of whispers all uttered from the doorstep; John, as usual, did not step inside. A brief conversation followed by footsteps on the path. The sound of retreat.

Smiling at the memory, Lily tucks the victory neatly away.

In all these months, Lily has only allowed herself glimpses of John, stolen from behind a frame or a curtain. She has never spoken to him and rarely of him, never even looked him in the face.

And she wants to keep it that way.

Approaching the mess of the table, Lily strains to investigate the garden. Reassured she is safe she reaches for the bone-handled breadknife, resolving not to take too much, to make the cut as neat as Eleanor's. She will do nothing to give herself away. Not risking jam or butter, she takes the bread quick and dry, and with her eyes still on the window, she lifts an enamel mug from the low shelf, filling it from the single tap. She drinks deeply, the sound of gulping loud in her ears.

Then, without warning, Piper dashes past the window, a blur of brown and white, tail up and barking, intent upon the gate. The mug falls from Lily's hand, crashing against the stone of the sink, filling the kitchen with a metallic ring. Panic, hot and instant, seizes her and dropping to the floor, she pulls her nightgown to her chest, wedging herself between the wall and sink.

'What a row! Piper, get down.'

A woman's voice cuts through the barking. Lily curls up her toes. It's Clara. Clara who never comes here.

Suddenly Lily's sense of safety and quiet triumph leeches away.

'El? Eleanor?'

The gate clicks. Clara's footsteps move down the path, her voice louder as she approaches the kitchen door. Lily looks up; the key sits in this side of the lock, meaning the door is open. Clara will be able to let herself in.

Cursing softly, Lily wonders if she has time to fly across the kitchen and lock the door. But both Piper's barks and Clara's shoes are now almost at the door. Lily inches closer to the wall. The steady tap of feet on the steps, and then the handle dips.

'*Clara!*'

Eleanor's voice, high and surprised.

The handle stills. Then rights itself.

'Well, don't sound so bloody pleased! Where on earth are you?'

Lily rises from the floor. Crouching, she waits, one hand on the wall.

'In the hospital. Clara, what on earth are you doing here?'

Eleanor's voice is clearer now, closer, and Lily lifts herself a little higher. Ready to move, ready to run.

'Stay there. I'll come to you.' Clara's feet, now back on the path, move away, her shadow

crossing the table as she passes the window. Lily waits, her limbs tense and joints locked, just the briefest pause; then she leaps, sprinting the length of the kitchen and flying back through the hall and up the stairs. Where she takes to her bed, breathing hard into the pillows, cursing herself for almost giving the game away.

CHAPTER NINE

CLARA

'If she's that ill, then she needs a doctor.'

Clara, standing in the middle of the hospital, her coat open, grips the corners of the sheet stretched between herself and her sister-in-law. Eleanor steps forward, matching corner to corner, intent on both folding the sheet and avoiding Clara's eye.

'She's not ill. Not really…'

'Not eating, lying in bed, and refusing to wash. Refusing to speak? Sounds ill to me.'

'It was a shock, her finding out about John and the engagement. She needs time.'

'Time? It's been over a week Eleanor. Nearly two.'

Eleanor takes the sheet, adding it to the pile stacked at the foot of the nearest bed. Fiddling with the seams of the linen, she keeps her back to Clara.

'I saw John yesterday.'

Clara waits for a reaction. Eleanor's shoulders tense and her hands still.

'Where?' Eleanor's voice is odd, controlled.

'In the village. Billy went barrelling into him outside the smithy. Nearly took the poor man off his feet.'

Eleanor half turns, a quick, painful smile on her lips.

'Sounds like Billy.'

Then, turning her attention back to the sheets, she starts counting, softly beneath her breath.

'Don't you want to know what we talked about? What he had to say?'

Eleanor shrugs, and Clara steps closer.

'He was asking if I'd seen you. Said he came over a few days ago, and you kept him on the doorstep. Then sent him away.'

Eleanor flushes but makes no reply. Reaching for her shoulders, Clara turns, pushing her gently but firmly onto the edge of the bed. She sits with a thump next to her. As she lands, she winces. But Eleanor, distracted, seems not to notice.

'Clara. It's no…'

Clara shoots her a look, and Eleanor stills, before beginning a feeble protest about them sitting on clean sheets.

'And who's going to care about that? No bugger ever sleeps in them. Anyway, stop changing the subject; we aren't talking about sheets.'

'I wasn't talking about anything. It's you doing all the talking.'

'Someone needs to. And not to me either. It's John that you need to speak to, instead of holing yourself up over here.'

Clara sweeps her hand around the room, over the neatly made up but empty beds, the high windows, and whitewashed walls, surveying this room, built up of relics; fragments of the past. Clara can't remember the last time she came here, to this shell of dreams, devoid of life and purpose. The hospital is one of the few things she and Frank agree on. That all of this belongs to another time.

Eleanor's face is alive now, with indignation and frustration, as she jabs her finger in the direction of the house.

'And who's going to keep an eye on her, while I slip off for this little chat? Who is going to make sure Lily doesn't end up in the river again?'

Clara snorts.

'Lily isn't going to end up in the river. Not if she hasn't been out of bed for days.'

They stare at each other, eyes locked through sunshine and

falling dust.

'Have you changed your mind, Eleanor? About marrying John? Is that what this is all about?'

'No.' The word flies out, with a force, a passion that makes Clara smile. Grabbing Eleanor's hand, she squeezes it, tight.

'Pleased to hear it. So, in that case, where's your ring?'

She tugs once at Eleanor's bare fingers.

'In my pocket. I don't like to wear it when I'm working…'

Clara imagines the effect the ring has on Lily and the hours it stays hidden away.

'Well, put it on. You're not working now, and there's nothing in this God forsaken place that won't wait for another day.'

'I can't. There's the rest of those beds to strip, and then the floors.'

Clara laughs; shaking her head, she rolls her eyes to the rafters, then waves at the open door.

'What, for all those ghost sailors you are expecting, the ones arriving at the imaginary port? Get that ring on and get over that bridge. Go and tell that man that he still has a reason to hope. Don't let him slip away.'

She nudges her hip against Eleanor's. Pain, hot and immediate, flares through her back, stabbing fire in her stomach. Unable to stop herself, she flinches, her breath sharp and sudden, teeth sinking into her lower lip.

This time, Eleanor sees. Reaching across the sheets, her eyes fill with quick and familiar concern.

'Clara?'

Moving away, Clara throws up her hands.

'I'm fine.'

Eleanor regards her in quiet disbelief. Clara meets her gaze.

'Don't fuss. I said I'm fine.'

Eleanor raises her eyebrows but says no more.

'Go. Get that ring on and go. And take a coat. There's a fierce breeze along that bank today.'

'Lily…' Still Eleanor protests.

'Lily isn't going anywhere.' Clara sets her face. 'And besides, she's me for company today.'

Finally, Eleanor leaves. Clara lets herself into the house, Piper following hard on her heels.

After locking the back door and, listening briefly for Lily at the foot of the stairs, she sinks into one of the worn armchairs, her body screaming in silent protest as she bends. The house remains quiet.

Clara hasn't been in this room since the early days of her marriage. Back when Frank's parents were both alive, before Alfred died and her husband still occasionally tried to win his father's approval, and love. Yet it all looks the same.

Letting her head fall back, she tries to quell the faint throbbing behind her eyes and concentrates on the window and the square garden, beyond which she knows the river snakes slow and wide. She is grateful for the barrier the water provides between today and last night, between the quiet shadows of this kitchen and her untidy cottage left hurriedly behind. She feels it, this line, gouged through the landscape, laying between her and Frank, her children, and the yards full of women, whose gossip and laughter stop when she passes. Women who take care to avoid her eye, but whose judgement follows her, carried by their whispers and stares.

Clara shifts slightly, ignoring the pull of her ribs, and closes her eyes, only to find herself back in the early hours of that morning. There on the cobbles of the yard, watching the blood from the collar of her nightdress bloom out into the pail. Watching, with strange, detached wonder, this drifting, flower form and then disperse, as over the row of cottages the morning light grew, and the village came to life.

Finally, it happened. Last night, the debt incurred by that stolen day at the beach was settled. Swiftly and without warning, fuelled and emboldened by a night of drinking, Frank had claimed his dues with feet and fists.

And in the afterwards, familiar, dark and raw, Clara had lain, motionless and beaten, the smell of old pine and dust, filling her throbbing nose, coating the metallic tang of blood; lulling her back to being as she fought to hold herself still. As, trying not to breathe on the bare bedroom boards, she waited for the seething mass of her husband to fall into sleep.

As she listened for the regular ragged breaths that meant release, Clara had lain there; angry, beaten and her body and mind both screaming for change.

Now, holding her hip from the frame of the chair, she thinks that maybe she is getting slower. That she should have anticipated the way the evening was going and found a way to avoid the inevitable. But the pauses she has come to rely on, those between Frank's outbursts, are becoming shorter, less predictable; harder to read. Any semblance of the pattern that had established itself earlier in her marriage is dissolving, disappearing. Clara can't seem to keep track anymore.

Hers is a marriage that, since Alfred's death, has been stamped and sewn with violence, punctuated with knuckles, teeth and sometimes worse. But in the past, there was always respite. Glimmers of gold, small tantalising patches of light when the man she danced with, laughed, and loved, the man she married, came back into focus. And she was able to reconcile, no matter how briefly, the choices she has made with the life she lives now.

The life her children have now.

The life her daughter sees.

For day after day, Clara watches Molly tallying up the bruises, and the broken plates they can't afford to replace. Feels her daughter's eyes fixed on her during the silences that are somehow worse than all the noise. During this past year, it is as if Molly has woken up, shaken off her innocence and started to assemble the pieces of the jigsaw, to see the picture of their lives as a whole.

And every time Clara sees another piece drop into place her heart breaks. Eleven years old is too young, she thinks. To face the truth of the family she is born to. Clara doesn't want to have to make excuses for Frank anymore, doesn't want to talk about what has been and what they all know will come again.

A wave of nausea rises, and Clara, pressing her hand to her mouth, pushes back the urge to scream or vomit. Twisting her aching spine into the seat of the chair, she fights the misery that knots in the pit of her stomach. She is light-headed and overwhelmed by her pain. By her life.

Then, from above comes a noise, small and mewling. Faint at first, something weak and newborn. Piper, curled in his basket, pricks his ears, lifting his head slightly from his paws.

A voice. Coming again, louder, now with a promise of tears and maybe anger.

'Eleanor? Eleanor?'

Clara levers herself to her feet with a grim determination.

Her life is not the only thing that has to change.

CHAPTER TEN

LILY

Lily calls for Eleanor, despite knowing that her sister is not there.

Not an hour before, she had watched as her sister slipped out of the gate and Clara let herself in at the kitchen door. She had also seen Clara's grimace as she twisted towards the house. Had noted the way Clara paused, steadying herself on the wall before climbing the two steps to the back of the house.

Lily had quietly taken it all in.

Using Piper's scurrying and barking to mask the sounds of her own footsteps, light and practised, she had crossed the bedroom floor, where, sinking onto her mattress, she curled herself into a convincing pretence of sleep.

And there she waited. For the door to open, for Clara to come in and check on her, maybe to softly call her name; indeed, it wasn't long before she heard feet crossing the hallway, approaching the bottom of the stairs.

Then nothing.

Just silence, filled only by the sound of Lily's own shallow breathing and the scratch of her toenails cycling slowly beneath the sheets.

Clara did not come. Instead, she headed back to the kitchen, her feet echoing on the stone floor.

Now Lily lies, unmoving, wrapped in perfect uncertainty.

The truth is, Clara has always been a mystery. Frank's wife and Eleanor's friend; kept at a distance and seen occasionally but to Lily, barely known at all.

Rolling tentatively onto her back, wincing at the creaking of the springs, Lily watches the dance of sunlight on the ceiling and wonders which way to play her hand.

She would prefer Clara to come to her, but as impatience finally gets the better of her, she draws in breath, before calling out into the quiet of her room.

'Eleanor. Eleanor?'

A question, plaintive. A plea. A call.

Clara does not come immediately, and when finally, Lily hears her climbing the stairs, it is with a slow, deliberate tread. Each step a concession, a compromise, for which Lily should be grateful, thankful Clara is coming up at all; movements entirely at odds with Eleanor's quick, light, and obliging steps.

Repositioning herself within the folds of blankets, Lily calls again, weakly, then falls back against her pillows to wait. Scrabbling at the conviction that she remains in control.

The footsteps pause, before the door is opened, pushed wide on its hinges, and Clara appears in the doorway, her body straight and square within its frame.

'Eleanor?' Slowly, Lily raises her head. Hands at her brow, she shields her eyes from the non-existent light.

'Eleanor's gone. Out.' Clara's voice, steady with fact and authority, invites no comment or objection.

From her bed, Lily seethes.

Feigning confusion, she pushes herself half upright. 'Out?'

'Yes. Out. She needed some air. I've sent her to see John.'

Lily stares at Clara, knowing she is waiting for a reaction. Beneath the covers, she locks her knees.

Conjuring tears, she looks down at her hands and grips tighter at the sheets.

Clara says nothing. Just remains solid, unmoving, with one hand on the doorframe, giving nothing away.

Lily sniffs loudly, wiping her nose on the back of her hand, then glances at the open door.

'When...' She makes a show of swallowing, as if choking back some great misery. 'When will she be back?'

'I don't know.' Clara shrugs, stepping forward. 'I didn't ask, and she didn't say. But it's a beautiful day out there, so if I was her, I wouldn't hurry.'

The room seems instantly smaller with Clara in it. Lily, pulling at the blankets, sets her jaw as she considers her options, fighting to keep her irritation at bay. Clara moving closer, peers at Lily, meeting her eye. A small smile passes about her lips. Lily catches the challenge, sensing her sister-in-law laughing at her in her own quiet way.

'I don't like to be without Eleanor.' She stutters the words down into the bedclothes. 'I don't like to be alone.'

Raising her eyes to the ceiling, Clara folds her arms slowly across her chest. And Lily catches it, the immediate roll and tension of her shoulders and a fleeting flash of pain. She pictures her brother, and smelling weakness, something within her sparks, then glows.

'You aren't alone though Lily, are you? I'm here.' More threat than comfort, Clara's words are forced through a thin smile.

The glow dims.

'I know, but...' Lily toys with a thread at the neck of her nightdress. At the foot of her bed Clara waits.

'But what, Lily?'

'Oh, nothing. It's... well, Eleanor always knows just what I need.'

Moving from the foot of the bed, Clara makes her way to the chair at the side, where lie the clothes that Lily wore on May Day. Removed and abandoned after the letters, their fight and the sight of that ring. Normally, Eleanor would have tidied them away. Instead, it is Clara who rolls the petticoat and underclothes into the crook of her arm, before dropping them to the floor with a look of amusement and disgust. Lily flushes. Her belly burns as Clara slowly peels away her layers.

Lowering herself to the now empty chair, Clara turns her face to the ceiling, and Lily connects with her slight gasp of pain.

'So, Lily. Why don't you tell *me* what it is you need?'

'Oh, no. Really…' Lily shakes her head against the pillows, one hand half covering her face. 'I wouldn't want to trouble you.'

'No trouble, Lily.' Clara leans over, pulling at the counterpane, twitching it tight across Lily's knees. 'No trouble at all.'

Recoiling, Lily lies a little straighter. Eleanor does not behave like this. She thinks of weeping again but somehow knows that it will have no effect.

'Oh, come on, Lily. Please. Tell me what I can get for you. Don't make me guess.'

Sitting back in the chair, Clara laughs softly. 'I'm terrible at guessing games. Better to just be honest. Say what you think. That's what I always find.'

'Oh yes. I agree.' Lily whispers, before adding. 'How's Frank? Does he know that you're here?' Just for a split-second Clara's face freezes, and something within her eyes dulls and falls.

She regards Lily with coldness, before quickly recapturing her smile. Slowly, she pats the mattress as if settling an argument and then rises from the chair. Triumph followed by relief tugs at Lily. But Clara does not leave.

Instead, she walks slowly across the room, stopping to peer at the two faded paper prints hanging high on the furthest wall, examining them on tiptoes with a slight dip of her head.

'Pretty.' Clara murmurs, not turning around. 'Did you choose them?'

'They were my mothers. This room was hers.' Lily runs cold with confusion; she can't seem to keep hold of the edges of these moments. Suddenly, she can't find her place.

Clara nods, stepping on. Running her hands lightly along the dresser, she lifts Lily's mirror and brush, unstoppers and sniffs a small bottle of scent. Grimacing, she coughs once. As she puts it back, the glass strikes the wood with a bang.

Suddenly all confusion evaporates, and in her bed Lily seethes.

Clara pauses, then swooping, she grabs something from the top of the dresser, thrusting it towards the window and tilting it in the afternoon light. Lily's heart lurches as she realises Clara holds the photograph. The only one they possess. Taken by the Port Authority on the day they moved into this house, all six of them, huddled in optimism in front of the hospital. Her family, frozen in time. It is an image she knows only in sepia, can only paint in shades of white and brown. Just a baby when it was taken, Lily is forever wrapped in her mother's arms.

And yet every detail is burned into her brain, every line, every angle scorched on the inside of her eyes.

It is the only image she has of Alfred, even if he is a toddler, pressed hard and unsmiling against her father's leg, half hidden by the skirts of Eleanor and the shadow of Frank.

Without thinking Lily pushes back the covers, then forces herself to still, fighting the urge to rise and rip the frame from Clara's filthy hands.

'Would you look at that! I've never seen this before!' Clara holds the image high by the window, sunlight glinting off the dusty glass.

'It's very special. It belongs to the family, belongs here.' Lily struggles to speak.

'Oh, I can see it's special. And I am family after all.'

Clara smiles. Lily shrinks.

'Do you know I think Eleanor might've mentioned it, this photograph. Look, all of you are in it! Honestly, it's quite a thing.'

Bile rises in Lily's throat. Her face feels numb, and her limbs distant, as if they belong to someone else. She can't bear it, the way Clara is stroking the glass, the cold amusement sparkling in her eyes. Sitting up in the bed, she draws her knees tight to her chest.

'So strange to see your mother and father again. Look how young they are! And Frank! He looks just like Tommy, don't you think?'

Clara wheels around. The frame, loose and careless, swings

wildly in her hand.

'Please, be careful!' Lily reaches out before she can stop herself, her voice loud, her body unmistakably strong, as she flings one foot out of bed and plants it on the floor.

Clara smirks and brings the picture in close.

'Oh, I will be. Because,' Clara's voice is slow and thick with meaning, 'this is such a precious thing.'

She stares down at the photograph again, tilting it this way and that, the glass flaring bright in the sun.

'But now, does Frank look like Tommy? Or maybe Billy. What d'you think?' Clara holds the frame out, her hand tight on its edges, her eyes daring Lily out of bed.

Lily, withdrawing her foot from the floor, sits back, determined to appear disinterested and resolute, while every nerve vibrates and fibre screams. She shrugs.

'I haven't seen Tommy or Billy in months. I have no idea.'

'It's the glass.' Clara licks her finger, rubbing it across the surface of the frame. 'The glass is so dirty; makes it hard to see. Oh wait, I think the dust has got inside, between the frame and the picture.'

To Lily's horror Clara turns the photograph, and pushes back the clasps, ready to slip the thin picture from the old wooden frame. Without thinking Lily throws back the blankets and jumps from the bed. Her hands clamp around Clara's wrists.

'Please don't; it is so fragile. So old. What…'

Clara stops, the photograph half in and half out of its frame. She stares at Lily, her eyes hard and cold.

'What, Lily?' Clara tugs her hands and the photograph away, her fingers flicking at the edges sending its age and brittleness crackling through the air.

'No!'

Lily lunges, but Clara steps back, holding the photograph higher; high and away.

Clara laughs. 'What Lily? Are you worried that I might tear

it? Is that it?'

Lily stops, both hands raised; a scream expanding in her chest.

Clara's eyes narrow. 'Because it would be terrible if something so precious, so irreplaceable somehow got ripped. Wouldn't it, Lily?'

Clara makes a grab for the window catch. Lily yells, then leaps.

'Give it to me. That belongs to me. You have no right.'

Wrenching the frame and photograph from Clara's fingers, she pulls them both in tight. Clara glares. All trace of smiles and teasing erased, all insincere warmth completely gone. Stepping forward, with one hand on Lily's shoulder, she whispers in her ear.

'I know you, Lily. I know your brother, and I know you. I'll be watching. And I can see through everything.'

Lily closes her eyes.

And when she opens them, Clara is gone.

CHAPTER ELEVEN

ELEANOR

The smithy is filled with heat and dust. Despite the sunshine, John has pulled the old oak doors closed, and Eleanor watches him, returning his occasional smile as he works.

Silently, she thanks Clara. And tries to ignore the doubts that peck like sparrows at her heart.

John, reaching for a file lying on the bench behind her, drops a kiss on her hair, its imprint remaining long after he moves away. She smiles. Lifting her fingers to its warmth, she allows herself to contemplate what it would mean to take such gentle familiarity for granted and experience this every day.

To separate her life from Lily's and move beyond impossibility; to breathe air, clean and untainted by the past, by duty and her sister's clinging needs.

Gazing at John, his broad back, bent over the anvil, his muscles shifting beneath his collar, she observes his complete concentration on the metal as he turns and shapes it beneath his hands.

Sensing her scrutiny, he looks up and laughs.

'You trying to put a hex on me?'

Blushing, she shakes her head.

'Just watching. Thinking.'

'Think away.'

So, she settles against the narrow back of the chair and gives herself permission to dream of a future, with John at its centre, coming home to her each evening, sharing her bed. She imagines him lying, curled against her, legs pressed together; waking with his fingers in her hair, his breath soft on her neck. The thought makes her shift in the seat.

Never has she allowed herself to stray this far, and now, here in the heat and semidarkness, she feels hemmed in by possibilities, realities and everything in between. Bringing her hands to her face, Eleanor lets out a sigh.

'As bad as that, eh?' John straightens, lowering his tools.

'What?'

'Your thoughts? As bad as that? I reckon you'd hear that huffing out on the river. You want to tell me what's on your mind?'

'Do you need to ask?'

'Might help if we talked about it. About her. If we stopped pretending and came up with a plan.'

'You say that like it's easy. Like I haven't been trying to think up a plan every single day.' Eleanor is surprised by her own sudden anger; the bitterness she feels at John's oversimplification of the tangled web that is her life. There is no plan. Just inescapable, impossible facts. She can't even begin to explain the knot that is Lily, let alone unpick it. There is so much John doesn't know, can't begin to understand, and Eleanor is afraid that if she tells him all this will vanish. That the reality of Lily will scare him away.

So, she stares, hard eyed and desperate, burning with the unfairness of it all, waiting for him to recoil under the intensity of her gaze.

Instead, he steps forward. Slipping his hands into hers, he pulls her to her feet.

'Not easy. Nothing about this is easy, El. But necessary. And you can't work this out alone. It's not your problem. It's ours, and it won't go away.'

Sagging against him, she rests her head on his damp shirt, inhaling the sweat and smoke, whilst biting down one dry and brittle sob, her anger and fear replaced by frustration and familiar despair.

'Come on.' John squeezes her to him. 'Best thinking's done in the open. Reckon I'm due a break.'

He locks the worn oak doors, then hand in hand, they move through the streets. Past the women who stand in their open doorways, arms folded, laughing, and gossiping; too busy, Eleanor hopes, to look her way.

Occasionally, Eleanor steals a glance, trying to imagine what it would be to live here, like this. To be one of those women; with neighbours and a yard at the back window rather than the sweep of the glowering fen. To have someone within a wall's reach who wasn't her sister or Clara, to be in touching distance of people outside of her family; people with whom she might share the simple pleasures and fears of her day.

If she leaves the hospital and fulfils the promise she has made, then this life would be hers. Other women and full days; filled end to end with chatter and bustle, rather than empty beds and never-ending hours.

It makes her breathless, overcome with the urge to stand on the corner of the street and take everything in, to see if the answers she seeks are to be found in the faces of these women. But she doesn't dare pause; instead, she walks faster holding tight to John and keeping her head down. Willing her feet to move silently over the cobbles, rather than clack and rattle, drawing attention to the two of them together and agitating her brain.

Beside her, John - head up, unashamed, and undeterred - strides out. Past the wharf and the drifting sounds of men and heavy horses, stamping in their harnesses. Past the wood stacked in precarious piles and rats scurrying between sacks and along the walls.

Finally, reaching the riverbank, they settle themselves without speaking at the edge of the ruined port. Where they sit, and kiss, holding each other amongst the brick footings and tufted grass, legs intertwined, hands knotted, their eyes drifting from each other to the river and the fragmented light that moves there. Running her fingers along John's forearms, through the mat of dark and dusty hair, Eleanor lingers over ridges of small nicks and scars, wondering idly how each came to be. Face to face, skin to skin, with so much she doesn't know. And how much John doesn't know and can't begin to understand.

John who appeared in the village, soon after Alfred's death, having inherited the smithy upon the death of his uncle. Who, after an initial flurry of speculation, had slipped quietly into the practical seams of village life, accepted and assimilated by both the virtue and necessity of his role; helped along by his unassuming air and willingness to please. A man untainted by the past failures of people, the port and its lingering grief, he appeared to accept everyone at face value. Embracing the honesty of the present, he was wholly unconcerned with what had come before.

But here, today, amongst these splintered footings, broken chains and weeds, the past is undeniable and close at hand. Eleanor can feel it, creeping from the water, a miasma that swirls about her knees. She shifts away, breaking the spell of their closeness and lifting her foot, drops it down to the cracked concrete, clouds of dust rising as her heel strikes the ground, vindictive and sharp.

'It's time all this fell into the river. Sank into the mud with the rest.'

John looks at her, amused.

'Looks like it's going, slowly. Don't seem like it needs any help from you.'

'It's not going quick enough. Not for my liking. Does no one any good having this sitting here. Staring at us every day.'

She kicks her heel at the dirt again, harder, wincing slightly as she does so.

John reaches forward, picking idly at seeds tangled in the ends of her hair. 'I don't know much about it. The port and all that. But surely it's all in the past, all such a long time ago.'

Eleanor stiffens, inching further away. She shakes off his touch, opening up a space. The breeze picks up and slides between them.

'Well, think yourself lucky because some of us have no choice. Some of us think about it, stare at it, every single day.'

John nods, acknowledging her anger. But he doesn't apologise, neither does he look away. In the face of such calm acceptance, Eleanor is instantly unsure of herself, her anger beginning to leech away. Moving into him again, she tucks her back against John's chest and lifts her face towards the sky, acknowledging the thrill of his breath as it moves through the roots of her hair.

Her voice, when she continues, is tempered and reserved.

'I saw it, you know. Or heard it at least. The port, the night it fell.'

'You remember it? You were a child!'

'Not much. Maybe not at all. But Da used to talk about it, especially later, when he'd had a drink. Maybe he convinced us all that we remembered it.'

She trails off.

'But I do have a sense... a feeling of... something. Of us all, together, standing over there.' Gesturing to the other side of the river, she screws up her face at the memory. 'Lily, only a baby, crying in Ma's arms. Standing, listening to these strange splashes coming out from the dark. And knowing that somehow, in one night, we had jumped from a beginning to an end.'

'But it wasn't an end, was it? You stayed. You're still there.'

'I was a child; what choice did I have?' Her words leap, instantly hurt and defensive.

Bringing his hand to hers, John strokes her palm with firmly with his thumb. As if he is trying to tame her. To hold her in place.

'No choice. Not then anyway.'

Choosing to ignore the implication, she fixes her eyes on the ground, watching as a trail of ants making their way through the dust and grass.

'Your parents? Didn't they want to move on?'

'Everyone kept saying the port would be rebuilt. Bigger, better than before, and Da believed that. And no one told us different. The supplies, they kept coming, and their wages too. Still does. So, we stayed. It was Da's pride and joy, the hospital. Keeping it clean, keeping it ready. Waiting for the day we would be needed.'

'And it has really never had a patient?'

She shakes her head, her hair brushing softly against the faded cotton of his shirt.

'Not one. The only person who has ever laid on those beds is Alfred. And it was too late for us to help him.'

She shuts her eyes, pushing away the memory of her brother's bloated and muddied body. Of his hands, shredded at the knuckles, his face, swollen by submersion and bruised by the pull of the tide. Closes her throat against the ghost of the stench, that even as she hovered by the door, had made her swallow and heave.

Tugging at John's arm, she wraps it about her, anchoring it across her chest. In response, he tightens his embrace; lowering her lips to his forearm, Eleanor tastes iron and smoke. She breathes him in.

But still, Alfred refuses to leave.

'Three days.' She whispers. 'Three days we waited for them to find him. Three days of Ma silent, weeping. Of Da hobbling up and down the bank, screaming at Frank every time he came back, empty-handed and alone. Three days of trying to keep Lily from going out onto the marsh after him; trying to keep her from drowning as well.'

Silently, John shifts closer, folding the creases of his body until they align with hers. Now she has started on the story, she can't stop. But still, she won't tell it all.

'He'd got himself trapped in a creek, yards from where he should have been. At the inquest, they said he misjudged the light of the buoys and lost his bearings. It was Frank who found him in the end. He carried him in.'

She closes her eyes, choking back the next part. She isn't ready to tell John how Da screamed at Frank, telling him it was his fault. How he fell across the corpse of his younger son, while his eldest ran out the door. And how she can count on the fingers of one hand all the times her brother has been back since.

She pauses, gently raking her nails along his arms. John doesn't move.

'It killed Da when they brought him back. Alfred was Da's future, the one who was supposed to take the hospital on. Might have taken months, but it killed Da. And that killed Ma. And as for Lily...'

She trails off, her gaze once again on the far side of the river, where the chimney of the cottage rises, just visible above the furthest bank.

'Sounds like it is time for you to move on.'

Unable to find the words, Eleanor sits in wonder, simultaneously captivated, and bemused by the simplicity of his reply.

'Do you want to? Leave, I mean.'

'Of course I do, but it's not that easy.'

'I never said it was easy. But if we are going to be married, we need to find a way. Work out what's stopping us and find a way around it.'

'Lily. She's the only thing stopping me, stopping us. If it wasn't for Lily, then I'd lock the door and never look back.'

'Then bring her with you. Or if you can't do that, then I'll come to you.'

'Live over there?'

She nods across the river, her eyes wide in disbelief.

'Why not?'

'But the smithy, your work...'

'Christ, El, it is only over the bridge. I've got legs and I reckon I can manage a bit more of a walk every day.'

'You'd do that? Come and live over there? Live with Lily.'

'If that's what it takes. I'm a patient man, Eleanor, but we can't wait forever. We have to find a way. Otherwise, what's the point?'

He doesn't know what he is saying, can't imagine what living with Lily would be. What it would mean. But still Eleanor wants this; to be with him, despite being terrified of all that it means. She longs for it, to believe that this other life is possible. That marriage to John could bring the end to this all-consuming tiredness, to the days that stretch out in front of her.

John is here, offering her this chance.

Through her dress, the heat of him draws her closer. Kneeling in front him, she pushes her body between his thighs. Leaning forward, cupping his face in her hands, she lets her breath dance across his lips and play upon his cheek.

'No point at all. I think it is time you got to know Lily. Time you came to tea.'

CHAPTER TWELVE

ELEANOR

Arriving back at the hospital, Eleanor is filled with dread, but also quiet resolve; determined that no matter how hard it maybe, she is going to fulfil her promise.

She is going to marry John, marry him and take his name.

Lily and the hospital, they are secondary to what she wants. What they both want. Emboldened by his kisses and the memories of his hands upon her skin, Eleanor tells herself that with John by her side she can do anything.

She enters the gate, her heart flipping in her throat. Immediately her eye falls on the back door, standing open, and she is seized by a familiar wave of dread. Breaking into a run, she half-trips up the kitchen steps, ready to meet whatever unnamed disaster lies within.

In the doorway, she stops, frozen by disbelief.

At the kitchen table sits Lily, her hair wet, streaming in a dark sheet down her back, her face pale but clean. She clutches a cup, her knuckles white as she lifts it slowly to her lips. Looking up at Eleanor, she greets her with a silence and a scowl.

Behind her stands Clara, working with determination and a brush at the tangles of Lily's hair. In contrast to Lily, Clara's face is purposeful and serene, as she ignores the hunch of her sister-in-law's shoulders, her rhythmic intakes of breath and obvious discomfort. A jug and basin are upturned and draining by the sink; the smell of lavender water and soap hangs lightly in the air. Piper lifts his head from his basket before curling back into a comma of sleep.

Eleanor stares.

'Oh, you're back.' Clara meets her eye, smiling in the face of her bemusement. 'There's tea in the pot.'

Mesmerised by Clara's quick hands, Eleanor pulls out a chair and sits opposite Lily, drawing a cup towards her. Seeing the ring still on her finger, her heart gives its usual lurch of dread. She looks quickly to Lily but does not take it off. Instead, she rubs the pad of her thumb over the small stone, absorbing its permanence through her skin.

'Pour one for me, while you're at it.' Setting down the brush Clara picks up a comb, applying it sharply to Lily's temple, oblivious to her wincing and the slow closing of her eyes. 'I've nearly finished here.'

As Clara combs, then twists and pins Lily's damp, gleaming hair, Eleanor drinks her tea. It tastes of wonder and unease.

'There, all done.' Clara steps back, admiring her work. 'Much better. Don't you think?'

Looking across at Eleanor, she shakes her head. 'It was a right state. Tangled, matted, and the dirt! I've told Lily she needs to make sure it doesn't get like that again. But if she is struggling, I can always come over and help her wash it.'

Lily visibly blanches at the thought. A smile appears on Clara's lips, her fingers curling into the shelf of Lily's collarbone with a decisive squeeze.

'I don't need help.' Lily's voice is no more than a whisper, pressed down in her throat with a blade of humiliation. Her eyes remain closed. Eleanor shifts uneasily in her seat and tries not to think about what'll happen when Clara leaves.

'Good girl.' Clara pats Lily's hand. Sitting down next to her, she reaches for the newly poured tea. Blowing across its surface, she asks cheerfully, 'How was John?'

Eleanor says nothing. Instead, she looks from Clara to Lily, then back again; a thousand questions jostling in her head.

Lily hasn't been downstairs for days, hasn't let Eleanor touch her, has refused to eat and drink. How on earth has Clara managed to get her out of bed and upright? Where has this strange and strangled compliance come from?

'John?' Clara asks again, rattling her saucer with a spoon. 'You did see him, didn't you?'

Across the table, Lily's eyes open, revealing sudden black windows of spite and hope. Determined to keep hold of her newfound resolve, Eleanor looks away.

'Yes. We went for a walk, enjoyed the sunshine.'

Clara beams. 'Perfect.' Raising her cup, she pats at Lily's hand again. 'Isn't that lovely, Lily?'

Lily pulls her hand away. Eleanor's stomach clenches, and Clara smirks. 'Well, Lily and I've had quite the afternoon. Washed her hair, stripped the bed, opened a window or two. I think we both feel better for it. Don't we, love?'

Lily turns her face to the window, and amusement flashes across Clara's face. She lifts her eyebrows.

'Had a chat, me and Lily; decided it's time we got to know each other better. I've told Lily that now all the children are at school we should make this more regular. Me coming here, helping out. Giving you a break.'

Lily stands abruptly, her knees jolting the table, her chair scraping on the stone floor. Without a word, she leaves, heading for the hall and the narrow stairs beyond. Unfazed, Clara calls out, 'Until next week, Lily. And mind you don't get back in that bed. I don't want to have to get you up again before I go.'

Her smile never wavers, but Clara's voice rings with an edge of steel.

Caught up in her sister-in-law's casual cheerfulness, Eleanor grasps at the last of the bravery she felt out on the riverbank, and half rising, calls out,

'Before you go, Lily, just so you know I've invited John over...

to come here one night for his tea.'

Lily stops, one hand on the doorframe, one foot across the threshold of the hall.

'Here?' A whisper of shock and spite.

Still, Eleanor refuses to shrink. With Clara's eyes are upon her, she braces herself against the table, and longs for the steadying frame of John's arms. Forcing herself straighter, she meets Lily's backward gaze.

'Yes. I thought it was time you got to know him. Time we all started to make some proper plans.'

'When?' The word hits the floor. Bounces off the walls. Like a marble. Or a bullet.

Eleanor swallows once, forcing the air into the depths of her lungs. She replies with a brightness she doesn't feel.

'Soon. Next week.'

Wordless, Lily turns and walks away, her tread heavy and deliberate as she makes her way up the stairs.

Legs shaking, Eleanor sinks back into her seat.

'Well done.' Clara lifts her cup, toasting her with tea.

'How on earth…?' Now Lily has gone, all the questions she has suddenly refuse to assemble.

'Did I get her up?'

Eleanor nods. 'How did you do any of it? Eating, drinking… she hasn't done that for days.'

Clara laughs. 'Let's say I encouraged her. Might have told her a few home truths. Nothing for you to worry about, anyway.' She reaches for the pot, topping up their cups.

'And you're wrong. At least about the eating and drinking. Judging by the crumbs in those sheets and the plates under her bed.'

'What?'

'She's been taking you for a fool, El.'

'How…' Eleanor's voice is fractured by shock. 'Clara, are you sure? Honestly, that can't be…'

Holding up her hands, Clara shakes her head.

'I'm only telling you what I've seen with my own two eyes. I haven't lived all these years with your brother not to be wise to a lie or two. But we know now. And she knows it, too. So, let's just concentrate on what happens next.'

Eleanor feels the first stirrings of anger, buffeted by waves of shock and disbelief.

'John coming here is a good place to start.' Clara stands, lifting her coat from the back of the door. 'It's getting late. I need to get back before they all get home from school. And before Frank rolls home from wherever it is he has been pretending to work today.'

'Does he know you're here?'

Clara busies herself with her buttons. Her reply, less confident, is directed at the floor.

'Oh, you know what he's like. About the hospital and all.'

Eleanor knows all too well. She can't remember the last time Frank willingly brought himself here, the last time he stood in this kitchen or even knocked at the door. Too many memories, too much both said and unspoken. Even in Lily's darkest moments, even after her parents' died Frank has stayed away, and made sure his family have too.

'You shouldn't have come, Clara.'

'Oh, I should. And long before this. What Frank doesn't know won't hurt him.' Her smile is brave, but Eleanor hears the vulnerability in her voice.

'I'm not worried about Frank.' Eleanor catches hold of Clara's coat, holding tight to its fraying seam. 'It's you I'm worried about.'

'I can look after me. Now I'm going. But I meant what I said. I'll be back next week. Before, if you need me; just let me know.'

As she follows Clara out into the afternoon sunshine Eleanor notes that the stiffness she saw earlier is still there. Without comment, she steps forward, folding her friend in her arms and ignoring the short intake of breath.

'Thank you, for everything.'

Clara steps back and winks. 'My pleasure.' She looks up. Lily's window stands open, curtains swelling outwards in the breeze. Tipping back her head, Clara raises her voice.

'And if Lily gives you any trouble, you remind her how much I liked that photograph.'

CHAPTER THIRTEEN

LILY – EARLY JUNE 1914

All week Lily carries the humiliation left by Clara; the image of her stripping back the bedclothes and discovering the grease-stained cloths and stolen food hidden beneath.

Nothing had been said. And somehow that was worse, generating enough shame for her to submit to the washing of her hair, undertaken by Clara in accusing silence.

In just one afternoon, Clara had rewritten the rule book, taking the power Lily has so carefully cultivated and ripping it to shreds.

As soon as Clara left, Lily had hidden the photograph. First, she slid it beneath the mattress, but every day since she has moved it, from piles of clothing to rumpled sheets, but still nowhere feels safe.

Because after months of pretending to be filled with fear, now Lily is alive with it; that and the knowledge that Clara is playing her at her own game.

And, worse, Eleanor too is changed.

No longer does she bring Lily's her breakfast, padding into her room with soft, apologetic feet. Instead, clattering below in the kitchen, she talks pointedly to Piper, before leaving bread and jam on the table and going about her day. Waiting for Lily to decide if, and when, she eats.

Since Clara's visit, Lily made sure she is up every day. Keeping her movements deliberately slow and sulky, she eats only small amounts in Eleanor's presence, careful to keep up a token protest. But the thought of Clara keeps her clean and upright at least.

She will do anything to keep that woman away.

Each day, staring out at the wide expanse of land and sky, Lily watches the wind ripple the virgin wheat carpeting the fields. Seeking within the view she has known all her life, some kind of inspiration, a loose thread from which she can weave a plan; a way to shut down the world that is expanding, opening up without her permission and at an alarming rate.

At night, lying now truly sleepless, as the slow sweep of the lighthouse lamp creeps beneath her door, Clara's threats echo in her head.

The truth is Lily knows little about her sister-in-law. Even before Alfred's death, Frank had stayed away from the hospital, from Da. Clara and Frank might only live across the river, but their lives are and always have been strange and remote. Eleanor alone befriended Clara, visiting the children, and helping out where she could, but even she avoids Frank.

In the nights that stretch out from her humiliation, Lily becomes convinced that Frank is Clara's weakness; that somehow the restoration of order lies with her brother and his hatred of the hospital.

Eleanor's conversation too has changed. Every day growing steadily bolder, increasingly, peppered with John's name and opinions. As Eleanor builds him, limb by limb, Lily's resentment of him grows. She listens in silence, making no comment beyond the occasional clearing of her throat, fighting the urge to thunder upstairs, throw herself hard on her mattress and scream. Eleanor takes her silence as permission to continue, a sign that Lily has accepted her engagement and is now willing to fall in with their plans. Unaware that Lily has plans of her own.

And today, John has come to tea.

Here they sit, the three of them, each balanced on the edge of their chairs. Eleanor, at the head of the table, fusses with knives and plates, her face flushed, her mouth drawn tight, flitting rapidly between a grimace and a smile. Lily and John face each other, separated only by Ma's cake stand and an expanse of once-white cloth.

'Tea?' Eleanor holds the pot in John's direction, a tremor in her hands and voice.

'Please.' John lifts his cup. As he turns, Lily takes the chance to study him.

Before today, her only impressions have been based on those ill-fated letters, and the occasional low rumble of his voice beneath her window. Now, Lily takes in his skin, glowing with perspiration and the appearance of being violently scrubbed. His dark hair is damp, curling about his ears, and down onto the worn collar of his shirt. As he reaches for the sugar, she observes the grime of his work deep in the bed of his nails and lines of his palms. She imagines those hands, reaching for her sister, resting on her waist or burrowing gently into her soft, thick hair. Her breath catches.

John looks across and smiles. Instantly, Lily looks down at her plate. Something molten and unfamiliar burns, hovering between her stomach and her throat. Into the uneasy stillness drifts the sound of a solitary crow; all three turn towards it, as if hoping it might have something poignant or useful to say.

'Please, help yourself.' Eleanor, half standing, offers a plate of bread and butter, and John, nodding his thanks, helps himself. Lily puts up her hand and shakes her head.

'Not eating, Lily?' John's tone is light, friendly.

'Not hungry, Mr Hobson.' She bridles at his familiarity, the fact that he feels able to comment on what she chooses to do in her own house. Their house.

'You must have a will of steel to resist all this.' Cutting cheese, forking slices of ham John loads his plate. 'It's not often I sit down to a spread like this. And please call me John.'

Lily shrugs, sipping her tea and feigning indifference.

'Enjoy it. A special occasion calls for special food.' Eleanor nudges Lily's elbow. 'Are you sure you won't have something? A slice of cake to go with your tea?'

'No.' A glance passes between Eleanor and John, quick and desperate. With a flicker of satisfaction, Lily begins to hope.

'It's a lovely spot.' John turns to the window. 'Quiet, by the river. Peaceful.'

'Oh, it is!' Eleanor leaps, seizing on his words. 'Wild in winter though, you're seeing it at the best time of the year.'

'I can imagine!' John's voice is bright with forced eagerness; Eleanor grin is wide and foolish in response. Lily burns.

'I like the winter.' She spits. 'Dark days and no unwelcome company. Winter suits me just fine.'

John, fork halfway to his mouth, bursts out laughing. Eleanor reddens and sighs.

'Lily, really…'

'No.' John holds up his hand. 'Best to be honest, to tell it like it is.'

Twisting her mouth into a smile, Lily sits straighter and sets down her cup.

'Then, Mr Hobson, can I ask for some honesty from you?'

'Be my guest.'

Putting down his fork, John lays his hands wide on the table. The room is warm, filled with challenge and the scent of river water and honeysuckle drifting through the open door. Eleanor stiffens.

'How did you meet my sister? And what do your own family think of your plans, Mr Hobson?'

Lily refuses to refer to this engagement by name.

'John.' He corrects her. 'And that's two questions.'

'Then pick one.' Lily pushes her back against her chair, seeking strength in her spine. 'I don't mind.'

'Lily…' Eleanor murmurs, but John shakes his head.

'I met your sister in the village, Lily, not long after I arrived.

Spent months watching her walk past the smithy, and then one day I got brave; decided to introduce myself. Considered myself lucky that she didn't turn on her heels and run away.'

Lily looks slowly at Eleanor, who nods with flaming cheeks. Looking back to John, she flares her nostrils, daring him to go on. Meeting her eye, he barely blinks and for a second Lily wonders if she has underestimated him.

'And your family?'

'No brothers, no sisters. Both my parents are dead. I inherited the smithy from my uncle. So, I thought I'd come here. Try my luck.'

'And by 'luck' you mean finding another family, worming your way in like a cuckoo in a nest?'

'Lily!' Eleanor now on her feet, screeches. 'That's a dreadful thing to say!'

Delighting in her sister's anger, Lily keeps her eyes on John, watching his face struggle to remain passive; claiming a small victory in the tightness that creeps and turns around his lips.

'Some might say life would be easier if I'd carried on alone. After all, I've a trade, a home. Everything a man might need.'

'Not quite everything, it seems. Do you know what I think, Mr Hobson? I think you heard about our *situation* here. Father and brother gone, two women living quite alone. And you thought we might be able to provide *exactly* what you needed.'

'Lily, that is enough! John, I'm so sorry.' Eleanor, furious, moves behind him, planting her hands on his shoulders and glowering at Lily. From beneath the table, sensing agitation, Piper whimpers and breaks for the door. Lifting his hands to Eleanor's, John squeezes at the tips of her fingers, with an ease and affection that Lily simply cannot bear.

'I'm sorry you feel that way.' John's voice is heavy with empathy and weariness. 'And I'm sorry for the past few years, for everything that's happened. Eleanor's told me how close you were to your brother…'

The thought of the photograph, hidden today beneath her

linens, rises and without warning, it splinters the fragility of Lily's control.

'How dare you mention him?' She stabs at the air, suddenly wild and hissing, her spittle coating the cutlery and scones. 'You, you know nothing about him. Nothing!'

Eleanor flinches, but John remains infuriatingly calm.

'I know you loved him. And now I love your sister. Things move on, Lily; nothing stays the same.'

Violently, she pushes herself away. The table jerks, its white cloth dissolving into a puddle of tea. Eleanor, edging further behind John, makes no move to console or comfort Lily. Just watches her sister through a mask of disbelief and anger, disappointment, and pain.

With a final cry of irritation, Lily flees, out into the yard.

CHAPTER FOURTEEN

ELEANOR – LATE SUMMER 1914

Then, from nowhere, nothing is the same.

Coming from a direction no one expects, the change is far larger than Lily's fears and manipulations; than Eleanor's promises; larger even than this place of churning water and open skies.

The first words of war arrive with the scant hospital deliveries, spoken by a man known to take delight in black news and other people's misery. Eleanor, consumed by the heat of summer and her own alternating sense of hope and unease, finds it easy to dismiss his gossip.

But, before long, his predictions are taken up by others, this time in voices louder and more insistent. Suddenly and slowly, like a curious riddle, change is everywhere, and the air, full of harvest dust, rings loud with the chimes of war. In the village, on the river, in the field, wharf and street. It is all anyone can talk of, taste, see or be.

And the weather, as fevered as the speculation, does nothing to ease the tension. In the face of the climbing heat, the usual marsh breezes vanish, trapping the community in a bubble of fear, excitement, and disbelief. Overnight, conversations move from the conviction that nothing is afoot, to a community counting the days to war.

The streets are dotted with strange and inescapable signs of reality, as the number of men working on the wharf shrinks with each passing day. Trains departing the station are draped in flags, leaving weeping mothers, and upright fathers in their wake.

But as August slips like butter to a hot September, John stays. Held fast to the village by the necessity of his trade, he watches others leave, saying nothing as he immerses himself in iron, flame. And Eleanor.

For since Lily failed to bully him into submission, John's visits across the river have settled into a pattern and slowly begun to swell. This evening, they sit together in Eleanor's small garden, beneath the remains of the low hanging lilac, where the last bees drift lazily in the dying sun's haze. Resting on the grass, shoulders touching, in a small pool of togetherness, they capture the remaining warmth of the day.

And Eleanor steers the conversation from war to John, to his family and his past. The truth is Lily's outburst all those weeks ago had shocked her into realising how little she really knows. Being so caught up in her own family's troubles, their ghosts, and entanglements she has rarely stopped to consider John's.

So over recent weeks John has obliged her, painting scenes, fleshing out the unknown characters of his life piece by piece. Now, resting on his shoulder, surrounded by the scent of hay and heat, she asks, 'Tell me more about your father.'

Lowering his head to hers, John runs his thumb slowly across the back of her hand, and in Eleanor's stomach, something flips.

'He was a gardener, on the local estate.' He looks down at her, amused. 'I've told you all this before.'

He has of course; way back in those early months, when they would meet, on the bridge or in the smithy, and exchange snippets of their past. The carefully curated fragments that barely build a life. But now, having made this commitment, Eleanor finds this patchwork of facts is not enough.

'I know,' she lifts her head, catching his breath in her hair. 'But what was he really like? Was he tall, short? Quiet, loud? If I'm to marry you, I ought to know.'

Reaching up, she brushes his dark hair from his forehead, his face flat against the palm of her hand. John kisses her softly, his mouth warm on her lips. She leans in and then away, fighting distraction.

'Tell me.'

'Dad was…' he searches for the words '… strong, relentless. On the go, working in the estate gardens, morning to night, rarely smiled, never complained. He died as he lived, just fell down one day. No warning, no ailing, quick and decisive, like everything else in his life.'

He smiles sadly, leaving Eleanor with the sense that briefly he has stepped somewhere smaller, far away.

'And you didn't want to follow him? Become a gardener I mean? He must have taught you about his work?'

John shakes his head. 'My Dad was a man of few words, not the teaching kind. And besides plants, all that, it never interested me. Horses were always much more my line.'

She knows this is true, having watched him from the corner of the smithy, calming a nervous horse, clicking and murmuring in admiration, speaking a strange, shared language. She has seen the way his shoulders bend to his work, his brow lifting, furrowed in concentration as he shapes and files.

Pushing back on his elbows, John looks to the sky. It is darkening now, light seeping from its edges, the first pinpricks of stars piercing the dusky blue. Breathing out, he folds himself around her and, forgetting her questions, Eleanor softens into his quiet, generous sense of ease. Yet again she envies the simplicity of his life, his ability to hold a day without complications. Without Lily.

Lily, who remains sullen and lazy, doing little around the house and making just the right amount of trouble where she can. Except now, each day she rises, dresses, somewhat carelessly, but always combing her hair, making a special effort if Clara's weekly visit is overdue.

Since their first explosive meeting, Lily has settled into an apparent - if wary - compliancy around John. Now, occasionally when he visits, she will sit with them, just slightly apart, and listen silently to his tales. Last week Eleanor thought she saw Lily half-smile at one of John's jokes and later heard her call him by his Christian name. It should feel like progress, a step closer to what Eleanor wants and needs. Yet it doesn't.

Instead, it increases her feelings of unease.

Tonight, Lily is a shadow, flitting in the violet dusk of the kitchen. The back door stands open, and Eleanor knows that beyond it her sister is waiting; hoarding everything she hears and sees. She shudders slightly, and John pulls her in close.

'Cold?'

She shakes her head, trying to push the thought of Lily away.

'Anyone else gone?'

Each day John brings news of the men who've joined up; many names are familiar, but some not. She pictures the village slowly emptying, leaking its boys and grown men, all of them slipping away.

Immediately she feels tension in John's arms. There and gone, a jolt. A flicker. Looking beyond her, into the garden's lengthening shadows, as Eleanor tries to read his face.

'As a matter of fact, yes, but sort you'd expect.' His words drop into the darkness. She stills, waiting for an explanation.

'Young lad came in from one of the farms, brought a mare. Fine horse, chestnut; polished to a gleam. He was good with her, the lad. Patient, steady like. He couldn't be more than fifteen, but he had the knack. We're strong, too…'

'Fifteen?' Eleanor cuts him off, unable to keep the horror from her voice.

John looks bewildered.

'Fifteen?' She repeats the word, unable to understand why he doesn't share her sense of shock. 'A boy of fifteen off to war?'

'What… oh no. No, he isn't going nowhere… well, not so far as I know…'

Breaking off, John's free hand tugs at the grass, rolling blades into ropes between his fingers. Eleanor waits, confused, but aware of a quiet dread.

'He was upset, though. Kept saying how much he'd miss the beast when she was gone. I thought the farmer was selling her, local like; told him that he shouldn't worry, that horses get sold and likely he'd see her around.'

John drifts to silence as Eleanor scrambles to understand.

'Maybe he will…'

His reply is quick, unusually harsh.

'But he won't, that's the thing. Because she isn't being sold around here. She's being sold to the Army. The horse is the one going to war.'

'What?' She stares in disbelief. 'The farmers won't stand for it, surely? Not when those horses are needed here.'

'Doesn't look like they've much choice. The lad showed me a piece of paper, all screwed up in his pocket, God knows where he got it from. Said it was…' John stammers slightly, tripping on the words. 'A 'Compulsory Purchase Order…'

Eleanor looks blank.

'Means they have to sell them to the Army. Like I said, they've no choice.'

'But the land. How'll they work it without horses?'

John shrugs. 'Don't know, but that mare's not the only one. Saw two more like her this afternoon. Apparently, they're rounding them up next week. The canny farmers are getting 'em ready, sprucing 'em up, to get the best price.'

'You'll be busy then…' She regrets it as soon as she says it, but she can't think of anything else to say. John nods slowly.

'For now, at least.'

She has never seen this before in John, this raw vulnerability. It is a hidden part, that fills her with both fear and a quiet thrill, as though she has discovered a secret path. Reaching for his hand, she squeezes it; a quiet pulse of love and understanding. For the first time, she feels stronger, having the opportunity to offer John reassurance and comfort, some kind of balance and repayment for his patience. She leans into him.

'I think it's time we...'

'Eleanor!'

Lily stands at the edge of the lawn. A wispy silhouette caught in the light spilling from the kitchen door.

'Not now, Lily.' Eleanor turns back to John.

'Eleanor! It's Piper. Eleanor, please.'

Clenching her fists against a body that hums with frustration, Eleanor breathes in hard. Beside her, she feels John freeze.

'What about Piper?' Still, she refuses to move.

'I can't find him anywhere.'

'He can't be far...'

'Eleanor, please.' Lily's voice is ragged with desperation, and Eleanor, letting her hands fall from John, grips the fabric of her skirt.

'For God's sake...' She looks at John, who smiles and levers himself up.

'Best you help her. We'll both help her.'

Eleanor pushes him down, her hand quick and firm at the centre of his chest. She doesn't want him to see Lily like this. Suddenly she is overwhelmed by the certainty that whatever Lily wants, John shouldn't be involved.

'No. It'll only take a minute; Piper does this all the time. He is probably not even missing.'

Before John has time to protest, she stands, brushing grass from her skirt, hands slapping and stinging at her knees. Striding towards Lily, she sets her jaw.

'Oh Eleanor!' Lily sways on the path, eyes darting back and forth, her neck bobbing, rodent-like, one hand working frantically at her blouse. The other is out of sight, tucked behind her back.

'I've looked all over the house. I can't find him anywhere. One minute he was in the kitchen, and then he just disappeared.

The back door… what if he has run off into the fields?'

'Calm down, Lily. So, what if he has? He's been out there a hundred times before?'

'Oh, but last time it took hours for him to come back.'

Eleanor opens her mouth to say that Piper has always found his way home. Even when Alfred was lying upon the marsh. But she thinks better of it.

'He'll be in the garden somewhere, chasing moths, or rats. Have you even looked outside?'

'I was going to, but the dark…'

Shifting from foot to foot, Lily glances back towards the door. Irritated, Eleanor pushes her aside, and steps into the kitchen. Piper's basket lies empty.

Seizing a lamp from the sideboard, she heads back into the garden, where Lily is now openly weeping. Ignoring her, Eleanor lifts the light towards the low tangle of bushes lying beyond the path. John stands, advancing towards the circle of yellow light.

In desperation, she calls into the shadows.

'Piper! Piper, come!'

Behind her, Lily wails.

'For pity's sake, Lily. How will Piper hear with that racket?'

Holding the lamp aloft, Eleanor walks towards the back of the house, calling as she goes. 'Piper… Piper…'

Rounding the corner, she waits, facing the darkening fields. To her right, the hospital looms stark against the navy sky, the sun now no more than a sinking strip of burnished rose.

Then, somewhere to her left, she catches the faintest sound.

'Piper? Piper!' Trying not to stumble Eleanor leaves the regularity of the path.

The noise comes again, now recognisable as a bark.

Lifting her skirts, she steps onto the scrubby patch of grass that lies between the hospital and the half-tended vegetable beds, bald and worn to dust by chickens and heat. Swinging the light, she catches sight of a roosting hen, who opens one eye before burying its head beneath its wing.

'Piper, where are you?' Again, a bark, this time rising to a sharp, peeling volley.

Eleanor follows it to the old tool shed.

'What on earth?'

She yanks at the door, which, to her surprise is closed. Not just closed but latched. So firmly that it could only have been secured by deliberate hands. Eleanor wriggles the rusty catch, until it gives and the door swings open.

From the gloom Piper bursts forth, leaping at her skirts, panting, and pawing at her legs. Within the lamplight, he capers, allowing Eleanor to see that although his coat appears soiled, the dog seems otherwise unharmed. Setting the light down, she bends and hooks two fingers through Piper's collar, before leaning back to shut the door.

The catch takes some force before it clicks. And with Piper straining under her hand, Eleanor stares at the door, bemused.

Now released from the shed, the dog wants to run. His fur is unpleasantly streaked, and the air foul. Recoiling from his filth, Eleanor unhooks her finger from his collar and watches as he disappears around the house. Lifting the light, she runs her hands over the splintered wood, lingering over the impossibly stiff catch and wondering how long Piper had been shut inside. Under night's cloaks her thoughts jangle with unease.

'Oh Piper! There you are!'

Eleanor rounds the corner, just as Lily pulls the dog into her embrace. Licking her tears, he lets out a series of excited yaps.

On the path stepping away from her sister John stumbles slightly, as though he has moved too quickly. A flash of white disappears into his pocket, then, seeing Eleanor, he tugs his hand free.

His face, half in shadow, changes. Something shifting, there and then gone, fleeting and unidentifiable. Surprise, unease or even guilt; from this distance and in this light, it is impossible to say. But immediately within Eleanor springs a familiar dread.

'Oh!' Lily holds the dog from her, dropping him in obvious disgust. 'Piper, you…'

'Stink.' Eleanor spits the word, her gaze still on John. She wills him to meet her eye. Instead, he shifts further away.

She turns to Lily. 'He stinks.'

Pulling at her stained clothes, Lily wrinkles her nose in disgust. From nowhere, Eleanor wants to laugh. Then bite and scream.

'Where was he?' Lily says.

Eleanor pushes her reply out between clenched teeth afraid she might vomit. Or worse.

'In the shed, Lily. He was in the shed. Locked in.'

Stepping closer, she holds the lamp to her sister's face and to her blouse, streaked with the dog's filth.

Lily flinches, and within Eleanor something screams.

'The door was shut tight, Lily.'

'Oh, poor Piper.' Lily looks at John.

'Forgive me, Mr Hob… John…'

His name again.

Bile burns at the back of Eleanor's throat. Swallowing, she fights the urge to spit.

'I'm sorry I made such a fuss. It's just that Piper was my brother's dog, and if we lost him…'

John puts up his hand, but before he can speak, Eleanor snaps out into the darkness.

'The door, Lily, why was it fastened? *How* was it fastened?'

Lily steps back; Piper snuffles at her skirts. 'How should *I* know? Maybe the wind slammed it shut?'

Eleanor snorts, and John starts.

'Wind? There's barely been a breeze in weeks.'

'Well, I don't know how it closed. What does it matter anyway?'

'It matters because…' suddenly Eleanor can't find the words. 'Well, however he got in there, he's filthy. He needs a bath, and since I found him, I think that pleasure is yours.'

Lily glares, then snatching the lamp from Eleanor, calls the dog; retreating, she slams the back door.

Eleanor stares after her, one hand on her stomach, pressing into the whirlpool of anger and disbelief.

'I think I should be going.' John, at her shoulder, kisses her lightly on the cheek. As he turns, Eleanor reaches out, pulling him back. Fighting a sudden urge to curl her nails into his skin.

'What was going on? Between you and Lily, when I came around the corner.'

Waxy in the moonlight, John's expression is rigid with disbelief. Or discomfort. The lack of light suddenly makes everything so hard to read.

'Nothing was *going on*.' The edge to his voice is slight but unmistakable. 'She was fretting about the dog. I was trying to stop her from getting so upset.'

'And did you?'

'What?'

'Stop her… from getting upset?'

'I didn't need to; you came back with the dog. So, everything was alright.'

'Oh yes, everything's *alright*.' Eleanor recoils from the sound of her own voice.

'Eleanor, what… ?'

'Your pocket.' Stepping forward, she points at his trousers. 'Did Lily give you something? There in your pocket?'

Stark against the twilight, John's lips folding themselves into a stubborn white line.

'For God's sake, Eleanor…'

'Just answer me.' She longs to back down, to break into a smile; to tell him this has all been a huge mistake.

But she knows what she saw.

'What did she give you?'

John turns to the gate. 'You're tired, Eleanor, and like I said it's time I went.'

He heads up the path, leaving Eleanor caught in a maelstrom of anger and regret. Again, the urge to deny reality rises, to ignore whatever she saw and step back in time.

But she can't.

At the gate, John stops. He calls back, his words floating through the darkness, gather like gnats around her head.

'Don't assume the worst, Eleanor. You know, Lily might just surprise you one day.'

Eleanor can't speak. Standing there, on the path, she is held fast by the all too familiar feeling of safety spiralling away.

CHAPTER FIFTEEN

CLARA – OCTOBER 1914

Removing her hat and soaking coat, Clara steps out of her boots and shakes herself like a dog. The heat of summer has finally, violently, yielded to autumn; October arriving wrapped in sheets of rain.

'Christ, this weather!'

Eleanor, loading dirty plates into the sink starts to run the tap.

'Leave all that.' Clara moves to push her aside, stockings damp on the flags, skirts pooling water. 'It'll give me something to do while you're out.'

'It's fine. It'll only take a minute.' Eleanor's eyes remain fixed on the running water.

'Don't be daft.' Again, Clara nudges her with her hip. 'It stopped raining as I was coming along the bank, but the sky's black. If you make haste, you might dodge the next shower. Save you from turning up at the smithy soaking wet.'

'I've said it's fine.' Eleanor sweeps cutlery from the draining board, stepping back from its clatter and splash.

Clara looks for a moment, then moving away, sits down at the table, spreading her wet skirts around the legs of the chair.

'Please yourself.'

Eleanor works in silence, and Clara, drawing her finger through a pile of crumbs, waits. Looking around the familiar chaos of the kitchen, she seeks an answer to her friend's hostility. In all the weeks she's been coming, Eleanor has only ever met her with warmth and gratitude, usually at the doorstep, eager to leave.

The truth is that today Clara longs to sink into this stolen time of solitude, for it is not only Eleanor's behaviour that is unsettling; Frank, too, has developed a new and unnerving attitude. For nearly a fortnight now, her husband has been at home in the evenings, smoking silently on the back step, keeping watch as Clara tidies the kitchen or stands ironing by the range. His drinking, now confined to home, means that thick brown bottles are set down amongst the tea things, filling meals with the clatter of glass and the reek of stale yeast.

Without comment or explanation, Frank has invaded the familiar rhythms of her domesticity with his unspoken judgement, and at night, Clara lies sleepless beside him and tries to work out his game.

'Anyway, I'm not going straight to the smithy. I've a few errands to run.'

Eleanor's words break into Clara's thoughts, bringing her back to the present.

'You should've said, I could've brought things over if you…'

'I can manage!' With a sharpness and a thrust of elbows, Eleanor turns away.

'Have you and John had a falling out?'

'No! I've got things I need to get, that's all.' Eleanor stacks the plates, offering no further explanation, and despite Clara's hope for respite, the rain begins again.

Clara catches hold of Eleanor's sleeve and watches her freeze, then flinch.

'Eleanor, what's…'

'Oh, Clara. I wasn't expecting *you* today.'

Clara looks up. Lily, fully dressed, her hair tidy, leans against the doorframe.

'I'm going then.' From nowhere, Eleanor's reluctance morphs into almost indecent haste. She pushes herself away from the sink and Clara's hands.

'Yes, you get off. You don't want to be late for John.' Making her way to the armchair nearest the range, Lily picks up an apple from the table as she passes. Bringing it to her lips, she looks at Eleanor, smiling slowly.

'Remember me to him, won't you?'

She bites into the apple, holding it out in front of her, examining the white flesh, exposed and inexplicably, Clara feels, obscene.

Clara raises her eyebrows at Eleanor, only to be greeted by the slamming of the door. Whatever might be going on, Eleanor is clearly more repelled by her sister than she is reluctant to see John.

Getting up from the table, Clara hurries to the window, Lily eyes following her every move. Moving aside the thin curtain, she peers through the veil of water. Head down, Eleanor strides out; buttoning her coat as she goes, her shoulders and hat already dark from the rain.

Clara fights the urge to follow her. To run away.

'Has she gone?' Lily sits, a book open on her lap, but all her attention squarely on Clara.

Absently Clara rubs at the glass, searching for clarity, somewhere beyond the rain.

'I think so. Going anyway.'

'Good.' Again, Lily bites slowly into the apple.

Letting the curtain fall, Clara turns back to the kitchen, which today has the air of a new and entirely unknown place. Transformed by both sisters' inexplicable behaviour.

'But I didn't think she'd go today.' Lily returns to her book, letting the comment hang, heavy with meaning.

'Why? Has she argued with John?' As soon as the words are out Clara regrets them, cursing her own curiosity as Lily's face, wolfish and eager, looms out from the cushions. Leaning forward, she digs her elbows into the arms of the chair, pushing at Clara's uncertainty and weakness.

'What makes you ask *that*?'

'No reason.' Trying to summon and then exhibit a confidence she doesn't feel, Clara settles herself at the table, where she takes out the pile of mending she has brought today. In all the weeks she has been coming here, Lily hasn't sat in the same room with her for more than few minutes. Usually, it is Clara who climbs the narrow stairs, to make her presence known, offering company and tea. And Lily who scowls and refuses, cowering from Clara's firm gaze and gentle teasing. So used to being on the backfoot in her daily life, Clara has quite grown to relish this strange, hot sensation of being the one in control.

But today everything is different.

Lily is different.

Threading her needle, her hands quivering, Clara holds up the cotton, catching what little there is of this grey afternoon light in its eye. Biting off the thread, she begins working at the frayed collar of Frank's shirt, seeking comfort in the rhythm of her stitches. She glances at Lily, who, legs tucked up beneath her, seems absorbed in her book with Piper, lying at feet chewing on her discarded apple core. To any outsider they paint a picture of contentment, a quiet moment, warm and domestic. But held within the portrait, Clara sits unsettled, even afraid; as if she has stepped into a game where the rules, without warning, have changed. Where the moods, the whining and withdrawing, the sulking and tears have abruptly vanished, to be replaced with a calm confidence, that hangs vapour-like about the room.

'What are you sewing?'

Lily's question is like gunfire, rapid and unexpected. Clara jumps, stabbing herself with the needle. Blood blooms, instantly, marking the collar of Frank's shirt.

'Damn.' She sucks the spot. Lily rises from her chair, reaching out.

'You've pricked yourself? Here, let me see.' Clara pulls her hands close and fights to compose herself. Her face is hot, her back running with sweat. In the face of Lily's concern, her own anxiety flares.

'It's nothing, just a jab. I do it all the time. Should have used my thimble. It must be here, somewhere...' Rambling, desperate to avoid Lily, Clara rummages in her bag, spoiling the rest of her mending with falling petals of scarlet.

Lily shrugs. But does not retreat. Instead, she steps nearer, picking up the shirt from where it has fallen, standing so close that Clara feels herself recoils. Shaking out the fabric, Lily tilts it this way and that, before bringing it close to her face. She breathes it in. Holding it there, against her skin, her eyes dark, glinting above the fading cotton, before folding it carefully and running her fingers along the seams.

'Frank's shirt.' Lily announces, placing it gently in Clara's lap.

Clara swallows and nods.

What is happening? Who is this girl, so upright and sure of herself? What does any of this mean?

With shaking hands, Clara balls up the shirt, pushing it into the depths of her bag. Lowering her eyes from Lily's, she begins to wind up her threads, the skin across her shoulders and chest drawn, uncomfortably tight. Against the window, the rain continues its relentless drumming.

Drawing out a chair, Lily sits, stretching out her slender legs. Forcing herself to look up from her tidying, Clara sees the colour high in Lily's cheeks.

Head on one side, Lily asks carefully, casually, 'And how is Frank?'

'Sorry?' The sewing bag slips from Clara's hands, hitting the floor as her anxiety crystallises into shards of dread.

'Frank. My brother? Your husband? How is he?'

Clara wonders how she should answer. Should she start with the lack of money, or the drinking? The outbursts of violence, the silences that can stretch on for days? Or the Frank whose hot and beer-soaked breath rises and falls on the base of her neck, while Clara lies at the edge of their narrow bed? Or about the morning whistling that screams its daily warning daily in her brain?

But perhaps she should describe the Frank of recent weeks; so close and quiet. The Frank she is unable to grasp and whose watchful silence has sent her anxiety spinning out of control.

Instead, she swallows it all. All thoughts of her husband, all metaphors, memories. All questions. Returning to her tidying, she replies.

'Frank? He's just the same.'

Lily raises an eyebrow.

'I've been thinking; I'd like to see him.'

Dropping her scissors, Clara slides her hands beneath the table, not wanting Lily to see them shake.

'Maybe I should go to visit him, or perhaps,' Lily leans forward, her face eager, twisted into a smile. 'I'll see him at the wedding?'

Clara stares in disbelief. Lily has never spoken of Eleanor's marriage as a tangible thing. As far as she knows, there is no date set, and if Frank is even aware of the wedding, she couldn't say. Clara avoids all mention of Eleanor and the hospital, knowing it is a subject that is guaranteed to provoke his rage.

'I… I don't think…'

'But surely, I will? I mean, as Frank is the only man left in the family; he is the only one who could possibly give Eleanor away.'

Disorientated by the conversation, by the heat of the kitchen and the overwhelming strangeness of the whole afternoon, Clara gets to her feet. Eleanor is unlikely to be back for an hour or more, but Clara is seized by an unbearable need to leave. Eleanor's distance, Lily's strange new confidence and Frank's recent behaviour, all of them colliding, have rendered the room airless and dangerously small. Suddenly everything is too much to bear.

Grabbing her bag from the floor, Clara makes for the door; forcing her body into the wet wool of her coat, then fumbling with the sodden laces of her boots.

'Where are you going?' Lily doesn't leave her chair, but her voice trails, heavy with mock concern.

'I need to get back.' She has no explanation. She has never left Lily alone before, promising Eleanor that she never would, but now the urge to be gone is so strong, so crushing that Clara can barely breathe. Or think.

'But Eleanor…'

'She'll be back before you know it.'

Without looking back, Clara wrenches open the door.

'Lock up if you're worried.'

'Clara!' Lily, still sitting, calls out. Her voice, clear, bell-like, is calm and totally devoid of fear.

Bareheaded and flustered, Clara plunges out, into the rain bouncing high on the path and cutting narrow channels through the flower beds. Behind her, the back door slams, and from the house comes one surprised bark.

Clara does not turn. She heads on, pulling her bag and coat tight against her body. Soaked to the skin, shivering with cold and fear, she bumps straight into Frank, solid and silent, waiting at the end of the path.

CHAPTER SIXTEEN

ELEANOR

Walking to the village, Eleanor is so caught up in her thoughts she barely notices the rain. It is two weeks since that night in the garden, the flash of white in the darkness and John's hand thrust deep in his pocket. This, coupled with his unfathomable reaction when challenged, still haunts her.

Each day, she drifts on this new icy pond of doubt, fearing that beneath her lies something dark and unseen; lurking, lazy in the shallows and preventing her from putting her feet down.

She has waited for John to explain; to allay these wild fears that seem to grow with each passing day. But no explanation has been forthcoming, perhaps because neither Eleanor nor John have raised the incident again.

But she feels it. Sitting there between them, a boulder of doubt and confusion, hardening into a rock face of anger and betrayal; each day she mourns the loss of their softness, convinced that their coming together is spoiled beyond repair.

More than once, in the evenings, when she and Lily have been alone, she has started to ask her sister about what happened that night, but each time she has stopped herself, refusing to let Lily believe she has succeeded in derailing their plans.

Yet there are no plans. On that evening in the garden, she had been on the verge of telling John that it was time, that she was ready to set a date. Then Lily had called from the edge of the lawn, setting in motion the chain of events that had blown

113

all that hard won certainty away.

She dwells on this now, waiting in line at the grocers, standing apart from women as they exchange news of men and war.

'We only got our first letter last week.' A woman, near the counter, rests her hand on the arm of a young girl, who, half hidden beneath her hat, fights back tears. 'How long's he been gone?'

'Three weeks.' The girl sniffs. Eleanor recognises her in the vague, uncertain way she sees most of the villagers. And the way she herself is seen. 'I thought we'd have heard by now.'

'Well, there you go. It was very nearly six weeks before we heard anything. All that moving around, and let's face it, they aren't much of letter writers, are they? Boys?'

Seeking support in her pronouncement the woman swings about, finding herself immediately and unexpectedly faced with Eleanor. She grimaces. Eleanor's voice is not one she wants to hear, her face not one she wants to see.

'But he promised he'd write. Knowing how worried I was...' The girl, trails off, blowing her nose. Her companion bustles closer, blocking Eleanor from view.

'And he will! But he'll be busy, love. Caught up in it all. Having the time of his life no doubt...'

'Sorry to interrupt, ladies, but your order, please.' Looking anything but sorry, the grocer brings the conversation to an abrupt end, the queue and the shop descending into order once again. Eleanor, still ignored, waits her turn, wrapped in the stench of paraffin, potatoes, and wet wool. Lost amongst these shuffling women and her own misery. Whether she will call in at the smithy, she still hasn't decided, but instinctively her thumb seeks out the shape of her ring on her finger through her soaking gloves.

It is then it hits her, as her fingers push against the slim, hidden band. A simple truth, dawning, even as she sweats in this line of distant, unwelcoming women. For all her doubts, whatever she may or may not have seen, John is still here.

He hasn't gone, hasn't joined the ranks of men leaving their homes. His profession and duty to the village, his commitment to the horses, and to her, all are keeping him here, not more than half a mile away. And here Eleanor is, deciding whether she should take the time to walk down the street to see him. Taking for granted the quiet privilege these women would give anything for. Hurriedly, she collects her groceries, quickly tucking suddenly pointless packets into her basket, before heading in the direction of the smithy.

The rain, lighter now, is cool, a welcome mist against her cheeks. The roads and cobbles glisten with the promise of sun. At the entrance to the station, a small group of soldiers smoke, laughing loud and long; trying on bravery like a new coat.

As Eleanor watches them, trying to pick out the faces she knows, the words of the women come back again.

Eleanor is lucky. Whatever Lily has done or is trying to do, John loves her. And she, Eleanor, loves him. He is here, working right at the heart of the village, while so many men have been ripped away. He hasn't left, hasn't followed the horses. Instead, he seems determined to do his duty by keeping the smithy open for the people of the village and the farmers left behind.

With a clarity she hasn't felt in weeks, Eleanor realises that she can't let the first hurdle her sister throws in their path fell her. Fell *them*. She will go to the smithy; will make herself forget what she saw. After all, what did she see? There in the almost dark she had been frustrated and tired; likely it was nothing, just a strange trick of the light. No, the only thing keeping her and John apart is her own stubbornness, and misplaced pride.

She steps on, past the churchyard, where, perched on a gravestone, a blackbird shakes his wet feathers, notes rising through the last of the rain. Beyond the beech trees, turning from green to copper, the sun finally breaks the grey, and Eleanor feels a lightening, right at her core. Touched by that golden light, a glimpse of the summer they have bathed in, whose warmth she longs to feel again.

She is nearly at the corner of the high street when she sees Frank, walking ahead of her, head down, keeping tight to the row of cottages. Eleanor pauses, the usual reluctance to encounter her brother pulling her back, but then, curious at where he could be going at this time of the day, she quickens her step.

She doesn't have to wait long to find out. Halfway along the street, Frank ducks across the road and into The Anchorman, the only pub in the village that remains open all day. No great drama or mystery, just Frank repeating the patterns of so many years. Eleanor weighs up whether she should warn Clara or if this knowledge is best kept to herself. The pub door swings and the autumn sun, glinting off its glass, catches on the road.

Pushing the thought of Frank to the back of her mind, Eleanor turns into the maze of streets that lead to the smithy and the wharf beyond. She moves quickly, stepping higher; a new sense of urgency pushing her on. She hopes that John hasn't got a customer, wanting to step alone into his space of heat and dust, to push her back to the narrow brick walls and shut the world away.

Rounding the final corner, she is in sight of the smithy when she stops in her tracks. Ahead of her, by the rough brick wall, is a woman, hunched so far over that her skirts pool about her; so stooped and low she could be mistaken for a heap of sodden rags. One foot is stretched inside the smithy yard; one arm grips the top brick of the wall.

'Hello?' Eleanor's voice is unsteady, constricted by a dry, hot dread. Immediately she thinks of Lily.

She steps closer. The sounds of the wharf fall away, muffled by the rasp and wheeze of the woman's breath, pumping like bellows from the depths of her coat.

'Hello? Are you..?'

The woman shifts, crying out, her fingers curling tighter around the brickwork.

Not Lily. Clara.

Horrified, Eleanor drops her basket, its contents spilling out across the stones. Rushing forward, she props up her sister-in-law. Wrapping her arms about her chest, she absorbs the weight of Clara's helplessness and winces at her groans.

'Clara! God, Clara, what on earth…' Eleanor positions herself, wedging Clara between her hip and the wall, holding her upright, one arm folded behind her sister-in-law's back. With her free hand, she lifts Clara's face, recoiling at the bruise, already livid on her cheekbone, and the cut above eye; the blood matted in the dark wave of her hair.

Looking behind her, Eleanor gives silent thanks the lane remains empty. No one can see Clara like this. She looks towards the smithy's slightly open door.

'Can you walk?' she whispers.

Clara nods. 'Walked… here.' Her words are almost nothing, just low, breathless whistles, punctuated by pain.

Tightening her grip, Eleanor levers Clara to her feet. Knocked sideways by the sway of her limbs, she pauses, steadying them both, before shuffling forwards.

'Frank?'

Clara bites her lips, nodding towards the smithy.

'Inside…'

They cover the final yards without speaking. Eleanor turns, leaning her back against the half-open door. The wood gives, swinging open so quickly that she struggles to keep them both upright.

John, bent over the anvil, looks up in surprise. There follows the sound of iron striking the stone floor.

'What the hell?'

'Get me a chair, quick.' Now inside Clara loses the last of her strength, and both she and Eleanor sink beneath her weight.

Darting forward, John pushes a stool against the nearest wall and together they guide Clara, setting her against the brickwork. Kneeling before her, Eleanor pushes against Clara's shoulders, holding her sagging body in place.

'Who did this to her?' John squats, his hand hovering by Clara's skirts, uncertain and incredulous, afraid to touch.

Clara finally meets Eleanor's eye.

'Frank?'

Eleanor asks again. Clara nods.

'Frank? Her husband?' John stands, rocking back, high on the balls of his feet. 'Her husband put her in this state?'

Clara looks up, her face pale but defiant, her voice no more than a croak.

'I'm still here you know.'

John flushes. 'Sorry. But… my God.'

He stares for just one moment longer, before turning and heading for the door.

'Where are you going?' Eleanor doesn't want to be left here, in this cavern of a workshop, squatting in the dust and holding her bleeding friend alone.

'To find the bastard…'

'No!' Clara shouts. Her voice, surprising and almost restored, bounces off the walls.

'What do you mean *no*? Look at the state of you!' John snarls, his face half in shadow as he pulls at the door.

'John! That's enough.' Eleanor glares at him, trying to bring the whole situation under some kind of control.

'But he can't get away with…'

'Why not? Got away with it a hundred times before… I don't need you going after him.' Making it worse.'

Clara's voice, fragmented by effort and pain, falters.

'I'll bloody knock him into next week!'

'And then what? Move in and protect us? Sleep on the doorstep and stop him every time he comes in half cut?'

John sags, but his eyes remain alive with fury and disbelief.

'I thought not.' Clara, exhausted by her outburst, leans back against the wall. 'Men. Men and their fists. All the bloody same.'

John reddens, opening his mouth, but from her place at Clara's feet, Eleanor reaches out, touching his leg. 'If you want to help, get me some water to bathe these cuts. And tea, sweet and strong. Yes, Clara?'

Clara nods. Closing her eyes, she murmurs.

'And lock the door while you're at it. Don't need any other bugger seeing me this way.'

Eleanor smiles, pleased to feel something of Clara, *her* Clara, in the room.

John grimaces, then nods. Bolting the door, he steps into the shadows. Eleanor shudders at what she imagines he is thinking. First Lily, now Frank. Each of her siblings laid bare, each one a source of shame. She forces herself back to Clara who is now shrugging Eleanor's hands from her shoulders.

'You can let go now.'

'You sure?'

'It's not as bad as it looks.' Clara's breath is steadier, her words arriving in streams rather than fired out like shots. 'I made it worse, trying to run here. But I wanted to warn you.'

'Warn me?'

'Tea's on. Here, sit down.' John, stepping forward, drags out a low wooden chest. Then hands Eleanor a bowl of water and a semi clean cloth.

Eleanor leans over, starting to work her way gently along Clara's cheekbone, pausing as her friend winces.

'Sorry. What do you mean warn me? Warn me about what?'

Then, before Clara has a chance to reply, another thought strikes Eleanor, a thunderbolt of panic rearing up behind her eyes. The familiar action of bathing a pale face triggering reality in her brain.

'Lily!'

Eleanor leaps to her feet, water spilling across the floor. The cloth in her hand drips, pink and thick, into the dust at her feet.

'Has something happened?'

Clara nods, her face stony.

'You could say that. But don't worry. Lily's more than capable of looking after herself.' Clara's voice is as cold as the fear and panic that is building inside Eleanor. Staring at her friend's swollen face, her mind flips from disbelief, to sympathy, to anger and then quickly back again.

'Something's happened and you've *left* her?'

Flinging the cloth from her, Eleanor buttons up her coat, trying desperately to work out how quickly she can get home. John steps forward, mugs of tea in his hands and eyes cloudy with confusion.

'Eleanor, stop. I don't think Lily's the one we should be worried about now...'

Looking between them, Eleanor stands poker straight, defensive.

'If something has happened to Lily, I need to go. If it's like last time, neither of you understand...'

'Oh, I understand.' From the folds of her skirt, Clara pulls something, thrusting it into Eleanor's trembling hand. Between her fingers sits an envelope, carelessly torn, its corners curled and wet; addressed to Frank. And despite their smudges, the letter's loops and curls belong, unmistakably, to Lily.

'Lily's written to Frank? That makes no sense.'

'Read it.' Clara's breath is even now, her voice square and strong; all its usual force, cutting through the afternoon gloom.

Wrong-footed and defiant, Eleanor shakes her head; trying to shake the pieces of the day into some kind of sense.

She pushes the letter back towards Clara.

'No. You've read it; you tell me what it says.'

'Eleanor...' Standing behind her, John's tone is low, filled with warning. Irritated and terrified, she steps away.

'You're wrong. I haven't read it. Frank read it to me. I say read, he spat the words in my ear, with my arm up my back and my face against the side of the bridge. But still, I think I remember the gist.'

Clara snatches at the letter. Eleanor releases it but doesn't look away.

'Fine. This letter *kindly* tells Frank that his wife has been visiting the hospital. And that *of course* his wife, as one of the family, is always welcome. But Lily felt that Frank had a right to know.'

At Clara's words, all Eleanor's anger drains away.

'Lily sent that? To Frank?' Fighting against confusion and disbelief, she looks at John. He is frozen, his face and lips pale.

'For Christ's sake, Eleanor! It's all here in the letter…'

'But how? She hasn't given me anything to post. Besides, she never writes letters. She never even leaves the house…'

Holding out the envelope, Clara jabs at the fraying corner. 'No stamp. It's been hand delivered.'

'But by whom? Who would do that? Lily doesn't see anyone. Apart from you and me, there…' She stops. Blinded by a sudden flash of white in the twilight.

At her side John groans.

Without looking behind her, Eleanor runs out the door, heading for home.

CHAPTER SEVENTEEN

LILY

Watching from the window, Lily smiles tightly as Clara charges along the path, almost tripping over her own ugly feet. Smiles until she spots her brother waiting, stock still and tucked in at the gate, his shirt rolled up to the elbow, and one arm reaching out through the rain.

She gasps as Clara, head down, barrels straight into her husband's chest. Flinches as Frank grabs the collar of his wife's worn coat, lifting it high and holding it fast in his tight, red fist. Lily ducks behind the curtain, heart thudding, her pulse drumming in time with the rain.

When she'd slipped John the letter, that night in the garden, whispering her carefully planned story to explain the contents, Lily never imagined Frank turning up here. Her only wish was that her brother would keep his wife away.

Clutching the edge of the curtain, she hears the gate bounce once on its hinges, a crack answered by Piper with a bark. Eyes closed, Lily shrinks, terrified against the fabric, waiting for the door to swing open and Frank to burst in from the rain. She thinks of running, but her legs seem locked, right at the knees. So, she stands, tense and powerless, straining to catch whatever it is that's happening on the path outside. But she hears nothing beyond the rush of her own blood, and the steady drone of rain. At her temple, a lone pulse throbs.

Lily can't say how long it is before she opens her eyes and daring to inch back the curtain, peers out into the rain-soaked garden.

The gate swings idly in the wind, but of Clara and Frank there's no sign.

Unable to believe it, Lily longs for reassurance, to be able to send someone else out into the garden; to check that Frank and his anger have really gone.

But apart from Piper, Lily is alone.

Minutes pass, and the tension in her joints creeps from discomfort to actual pain. Tentatively, with one ear still on the garden, Lily makes her way to the table, as the rain sweeps softly over the house. Through the back window, out beyond the fen, she sees the clouds begin to part, sliced by a seam of gold. Cushioned light and silence, Lily finally lets herself breathe; a breath that, without warning, bubbles to a laugh. Pushing her fists to her mouth, her knuckles knocking against her teeth she pushes the sound down. And her belly floods with the warm, liquid of hope. And power.

Unbelievably, against the odds, her plan has worked. All by herself, Lily has managed to send Clara away.

Falling into the nearest chair, she surveys the familiar; the coal in the scuttle, a half-eaten loaf, the mismatched cups stacked upon the dresser. Taking in each detail, each line and crack, she reclaims the house as her own.

Taking her time, for now she has plenty.

For Eleanor unaware that Clara's gone, has no idea that Lily is here all alone; meaning she can revel, undisturbed in the fact that she has succeeded in turning the tide. And can start to plan how to truly bring her sister home.

Stretching herself out, Lily marvels, here, resting in the afterwards, at how simple it really was; giving John the letter and persuading him that what she was asking of him was in Eleanor's best interest. Frank turning up might not have been her plan, but at least now she knows beyond doubt that her message was delivered. Knows for certain that Clara won't be returning here alone.

It was all so much easier than the last time; back in the winter when Lily first felt Eleanor slipping away. She knows now that the late-night dip in the river had been foolish and far too risky. How the bank dropped away so steeply and the river had pulled at her limbs and tugged at her clothes. But that, too, had worked. All the chaos, the doctor's visit and the gossip in the village; all of it had been worth it. Reminding Eleanor that she and Lily together are everything, all the other could ever possibly need.

On the table lies a newspaper folded and half read; beside the sewing scissors that in her haste Clara has left.

Lily has no interest in the paper and no desire to know about the world outside these walls, but recently Eleanor has started to read it, bringing it back from the village and then discussing its contents with John. Another unwelcome development, another way in which their world has expanded, it borders slipping further from her control.

She draws the paper closer. Picking up Clara's scissors, she lifts them to her ear. Slowly she works the blades, listening to metal snap, then slide. Bringing the scissors to the corner of the newspaper, Lily makes short cuts that swiftly progress to meandering lines. Long ago, back in the safety of the past, she remembers her mother's warning, that cutting paper with scissors made for fabric blunted the blades. The thought of ruining something of Clara's gives Lily a sharp stab of pleasure.

Carefully, Lily lays out a fresh sheet of newspaper. A blank canvas into which she folds and then cuts a memory, her fingers nimble, gathering speed as the past fires, sparking in her brain. Snipping curves and lines, she works, recreating the paper dolls Ma taught her and Eleanor to make all those years ago. Steadily she slices, head down, absorbed in her task and her surroundings forgotten. Cutting, turning, shaping. Working until the table is covered; littered with row after row of paper dolls. Faceless girls, each with long skirts and pigtails. Side by side. Hand in hand. Line after line of Lilys and Eleanors; endless and together.

Paper sisters. Standing together, with no one in between.

Again, comes the slam of the gate, this time followed by the immediate, urgent drum of feet on the path. Lily looks up, the scissors open, high in her hand. Whoever is out there is almost at the kitchen door. Her mind flies first to Clara; maybe she has fled from Frank and run back to the house. Perhaps Frank is behind her, and they are both about to come crashing through the door.

Dropping the scissors to the table, Lily pushes the paper dolls away. Some crumple, folding in on each other, while others drift slowly to the floor.

Their togetherness fractured by sudden chaos.

Her mind racing, Lily heads to the door, praying there is time to turn the key before the storm she has created breaks. In her haste to cross the flags she slips, one foot sliding on a line of fallen dolls. Crying out, she grabs at thin air, her body twisting painfully as she falls.

Now on her knees and helpless, she looks up, just as the door springs open. Staring upwards at Eleanor. Within two strides, her sister is upon her, towering and breathless, hair falling about her face.

Eleanor. Neither Clara nor Frank. Just Eleanor home again.

In sweet relief, Lily sinks to the floor. Only to look up into eyes so black and filled with rage that every ounce of comfort melts instantly away. Her gut contracts, with realisation. Eleanor knows.

Hastily weighing up her options, Lily decides to stick to the plan.

Eleanor's anger is raw, tangible, pulsing through the air, her breath ragged and uneven. Lily brings her hands up to her face, letting her shoulders drop she begins to weep.

'Eleanor. Thank goodness. She walked out and left me.

Clara… Clara, she's gone.'

Eleanor makes no response. Her silence is cut through by water dripping from the gutter and the river's occasional growl. Head still lowered, her hands pressed to her face, Lily waits, until Eleanor startles her anew by slamming the door. Lily hunches, curling tighter. Through shaking fingers, she sees Eleanor standing by the kitchen sink, her mud splattered skirts and sodden boots just a fingertip away. But still, she doesn't speak.

Ducking her head still lower, Lily shivers, taking a single convulsing breath, before commencing her sobbing once again.

'She left me, Eleanor.'

'How could you?' Eleanor's voice, flat and unstable, comes from far above her. It fills Lily's stomach with ice. Raising her head just slightly, her eyes sit level with the back of her sister's knees.

'I don't know what…'

Eleanor turns, spinning on the spot, her skirts lifting, flicking up from the floor. With a roar, she grabs the nearest chair, lifting it high, before slamming it down, hard and fast into the flags, its feet landing just inches from Lily's face. With a yelp, Lily retreats beneath the table, pressing her back up hard against the leg.

'I know, Lily! About the letter, about Frank.' Eleanor is voice, wild and unchecked it fills the kitchen. 'I know about it all.'

The ice in Lily's stomach spreads, hardening as it goes. Drawing her knees close, wrapping her hands about her shins, she searches for a scrap of warmth and steadiness.

Eleanor's face, shining and livid, looms beneath the lip of the table. Reaching out, grabbing Lily by the shoulders, she hauls her across the floor.

'Get up!' Eleanor's hands push in beneath Lily's armpits, until her fingers link painfully across her breasts. 'Get up, damn you! I won't have it! Have you hiding down there! No more pretending to be scared.'

Barely is Lily upright before Eleanor pushes her down again.

This time hard and into the nearest chair. Under the force of her sister's anger the chair tips, and Lily, grabbing wildly at the table, fights for balance and breath.

'Eleanor!'

Eleanor stoops, her face so close that Lily's lips burn beneath the touch of her sister's scalding, sour breath. Her words curling and curdled, stalk the sweating angles of Lily's face, each little more than a snarl.

'That letter. The one you had John take; do you have any idea what Frank has done to her? What *you've* done?'

Lily opens her mouth, but the words refuse to come.

'He's beaten her. Frank. Our brother. Held her up against the wall and beaten her. Until the blood...' Deliberately, slowly Eleanor drags her fingers across Lily's cheek. 'Until blood ran down her face.'

Staggering under the weight of her own rage, Eleanor steadies herself against the table.

Lily stares, rigid; recalling Frank out there on the path; his face twisted. Clara shrinking from his hands, back into the rain. Closing her eyes against the memory, she tries to convince herself that what Eleanor has told her isn't true; to ignore the sick feeling in the pit of her stomach that tells her she should have known.

'What on earth?' Eleanor's whisper is heavy with disbelief.

Lily opens her eyes, and slowly Eleanor drifts into focus. In her hands, she holds a chain of crumpled paper dolls. Instantly, guilt is replaced by hope, springing high in Lily's chest.

Eleanor will surely remember them, these dolls, just as Lily did. Two sisters, joined together. United against the world.

'I made them.' Lily tries out the words, her mouth dry. She longs for water.

'When Clara left, I was trying to keep myself busy. So I made them, like we used to, with Ma.'

Eleanor sifts through the scraps of paper, her eyes widening as she takes in the number of dolls, strewn across the table and spilling onto the floor. Emboldened by her sister's silence, Lily pushes on.

'Remember? How Ma showed us? How to fold them and where to cut?' She talks quickly, feeling the weight of each word.

'We used to make rows of them, do you remember? And Ma said they looked just like us. Sisters, sticking together like…'

Eleanor picks up another row of dolls. Laughing, she lays them out along the table, in one long chain. And Lily feels she is getting somewhere.

Slowly, she stands; creeping next to Eleanor, her thighs resting against the table as she props herself up. Reaching for the scissors, she holds them out to her sister, the closed blades, cool against her palm. Lily points at the nearest row of dolls.

'I gave them all plaits, see? Just like us, when Ma used to tidy our hair just the same.'

Nudging the scissors towards Eleanor, she lays the handles carefully in the curve of her sister's hand.

'You could make some too.'

Eleanor stares. First at Lily, then down at the scissors resting in her palm. Lily stands. Watching. Waiting.

Without a word, Eleanor moves, slipping her fingers into the handles of the scissors; easing open the blades.

Then she flies.

In one swift movement, she lurches towards Lily, grabbing at her hair. Pins scatter, as Eleanor pulls hard at the roots. Both sisters fall to the floor.

Hands folded above her head, pressing into her crown, Lily drags up her knees, fighting to curl her body into a ball. She screams.

'Eleanor! No!'

Eleanor grips tighter, pulling harder until the skin at Lily's temple grows taut. Lily tries to speak, to think, but nothing is real. This sister, this woman, made unrecognisable, shrieks above her, with alien fingers coiled about her hair.

Against her scalp, she feels the cold press of metal, as Eleanor slides the scissors between the roots.

'How could you?' Eleanor snarls once. Then closes the blades. One metallic snap, as on to Lily's skirt falls a clump of dark and tangled curls.

Lily shrieks, thrusting her elbows upwards, slamming her feet down. The sound of the scissors comes again.

'Eleanor, stop!'

Another voice. Not Eleanor's.

And not hers.

Louder, deeper. Cutting through the room, carried on a slice of cold air. Lily feels an instant relief as Eleanor releases her grip.

Everything shrinks to silence. From frantic, uncontrolled energy to nothing in the space of seconds.

Staring at each other, both sisters are suspended in the void. In the moment.

And through her tears Lily watches as Eleanor's rage turns to horror.

Standing in the open door is John; too big for the narrow frame, he fills every inch. Still and silent. As if what he has witnessed has turned him to stone. The only movements, the rise and fall of his chest and the steady blink of disbelief. His face, usually so open, so calm is white, his lips invisible and pulled in; his expression impossible to read.

Eleanor, too, remains fixed. Her hands balled, shake at her side; the scissors, open and accusing, lie abandoned on the floor.

Lily moves first. Seizing her moment, she stoops, picking the scissors up, before setting them down purposefully on the table.

Without speaking, she steps away, past her sister, slipping like water from the room.

CHAPTER EIGHTEEN

ELEANOR

They sit in silence, either side of the table, Piper watching from the floor. Sounds of Lily moving above their heads drift down, making Eleanor flinch. Outside, the rain resumes, falling like needles into the dirt.

'Clara?' Eleanor speaks first, whispering into the silence.

John's eyes keep to his hands, before him on the table, as if looking at her face causes him pain.

'I took her home. Not that she wanted me to, but I thought I should. To make sure. That's why I came... to tell you.'

Eleanor nods.

'Frank?'

Scowling, John shakes his head.

'No sign. But she wouldn't let me in, wouldn't let me stay.'

Briefly, she thinks of telling him how Frank will still be in The Anchorman, bragging that he's taught Clara a lesson. But, rather than drawing further attention to her family shortcomings, she lapses back into silence.

'The letter...' John starts, and Eleanor waits.

In all the confusion of paper girls, scissors, and her blinding rage, she has almost forgotten the beginning. That letter, that pale streak luminous in the darkness.

Her disbelief flares again, becoming a bright spot, burning through her own shame. Eleanor snatches at, grateful to push aside her own behaviour and focus on somebody else's mistake.

She might have cut Lily's hair, but John delivered that letter.

'Why? Why did you take it?' Brittle, harsher than intended, Eleanor's words make John sit straighter in his chair, his face instantly defensive.

'I didn't know what was in it. I'd never have taken it if I did.'

'But didn't you wonder? Why she was suddenly writing letters? Lily, who speaks to no one? And to Frank of all people? Frank never comes here...' Her words cascade, one over the other, her head pounding as she fights for control.

'But I don't know *why* he stays away. You never talk about Frank; you don't talk about any of it.' John is sweating, indignant.

'Do you blame me? After what you saw this afternoon?' Eleanor's voice climbs, up to where she knows Lily is listening and waiting, crouched above their heads. She damns it all; John, Lily, her own destructive anger, but still she cannot stop. All consuming, the day, her breath, her body; each has taken on a life of its own.

'All I'm saying is it'd have helped to know...' John tries again, stumbles, '... before...'

Eleanor stands, her palms pressed hot and hard against the table, her fingers aware of every inch of the grain. Stretched and molten, her senses swell, racing far beyond the limits of her control.

'Before what? Before you got too involved? Before you asked me to get wed?'

She doesn't want any of this. To be saying these things, riding high on these waves that keep churning in her stomach. Instantly she wants to take it all back, but the words insist on coming. Rising, splitting her tongue, filling her mouth with something foul and brackish, coating her tongue with the rich taste of the marsh.

'No! Before I took the letter. That's what I was going to say!'

There, shining out of John's hurt and disbelief, Eleanor catches an unexpected flash of steel, the heat of the smithy lodged deep within his pupil. A glimpse of a stranger, quickly hidden as the purple edged thunder cloud passing over his face.

Her heart lurches and her stomach drops away; with trembling legs she lowers herself to the chair and down into the safety of silence.

Minutes pass. John calls to Piper, running his hand along the dog's dusty back. Eleanor sits, summoning all her courage to try again.

This time she drops each word slowly and with care. Like a path of white pebbles laid to guide them both home.

'What did Lily tell you? About the letter?'

John's shoulders drop. Leaning back, he rubs hands slowly over his face. He groans.

'She told me…' his face reddens, 'and it sounds so bloody daft now, saying it out loud, that she wanted to surprise you. That she'd an idea, a treat for you and for Clara. Something to do with the wedding. She wouldn't tell me what, just said that she needed Frank's help.'

'A treat?' The idea is so ridiculous that Eleanor's hard-won composure explodes with a high, bitter laugh. 'Frank and a treat?'

Looking uncomfortable, angry at his own foolishness and her reaction, John pushes himself back from the table. Eleanor clenches her fist at the scrape of wood on stone. Pushing her nails into her palms, she fights for calm.

'I know that now. But like I said, I only had half a story. If you'd…'

From nowhere Eleanor's anger reignites.

'So, it's my fault, is it? That Lily wrote the letter, and you took it. My fault that Frank read it and beat Clara after to death.'

'That's not what I said. You're twisting it. Twisting everything I say.'

'Am I?' Eleanor's voice shakes, spiralling upwards.

'Yes. You are! What's wrong with you?'

There again, deep in the pit of her belly, is the fire, a warning that this has all gone too far. But now she can't stop. Everything has gone so wrong, so quickly. She might as well ruin it all.

'Wrong with *me*? I'm not the one listening to Lily, delivering her letters full of poison…' On her feet again Eleanor leans over the table. Towering above those paper sister abandoned there.

'And I'm not the one keeping secrets about my family. And hacking at my sister's hair!' Their words collide, combust and the room, instantly devoid of light and air, plunges into the worst kind of silence.

John walks to the window, staring out into the rain-washed fields. Leaving Eleanor behind, searching for the words to describe everything that has led up to this day; to explain her family, the grief that consumes and warps them. Instead, she sits, stiff and searching for a way to face what she is sure is coming next.

'How often…' John keeps his back to her. Eleanor longs to reach out, to catch hold of his sleeve and turn his face to hers. But she does not move.

'How often, does *that* happen?'

Her mind scrabbles; she refuses to understand what he could possibly mean.

'*That*?'

'Arguments, scenes like that. How often do you two end up fighting that way?'

'Never!' Now she reaches out, snatching at his jacket. He flinches. Shocked, Eleanor snatches her hand away. 'That's never happened before.'

'Never?' His words are heavy, thick with disbelief.

Eleanor lays one hand on his arm.

'Never, nothing like that. But she…'

She breaks off. John turns, his face pale, and his eyes filled with hope; a want to believe.

Eleanor tightens her grip.

'I was so angry; I couldn't believe she'd written it, that letter. She must've known what Frank would do. And then, to find she'd been sitting there, after putting Clara in danger. Sitting there cutting out those paper dolls…'

'But cutting her *hair*? I know what she did was wrong but…' John's arm tenses beneath her fingers. She feels him pull, just slightly, away.

'I lost my temper. I know I shouldn't have, but I did. It isn't just the letter. It's…'

Eleanor stops, unable to put into words the scale of the betrayal she feels. The time she has lost to this place, the months locked in by fear, grief and lies, struggling with the hospital, and keeping everything going. The overwhelming responsibility. The burden of keeping Lily alive.

Covering her face, her words now no more than a wail.

'It's everything! Lily has lied to me for months. Years, even. All this time I thought she was ill, helpless. And she was nothing of the sort.'

She sobs, chest heaving with the effort. John, stepping forward, brings her into his arms. She rests her head against his chest, grateful for his familiar warmth; yet still his body doesn't yield. Within seconds he eases her body away.

'I should go.'

'Go?'

John lands one quick, dry kiss on her forehead before turning abruptly to the door.

'I need to get back to the smithy. What with Clara and everything going on, I'm not even sure I locked up.'

'But you can't just go. We have to… everything is different now.'

John stops, one hand on the door.

'Different?'

'Yes. Now Lily… now I know what she is been doing… there's no reason for us to wait, to get married I mean…'

She moves towards him, her feet and mind trying to keep pace with her words. John looks down and half away.

'We could set a date. Now. There's nothing to stop us.'

He reaches out, both hands gentle on her arms.

'We'll talk later. When all this has calmed down and we've both had a bit of time to think…'

Eleanor shakes her head.

'I don't need to calm down or time to think. Don't you see? We can get married *now*.'

'Best not to rush, not with everything going on. Lily, Clara, and Frank. This damn war…'

'Rush? War… John!'

Desperate, she grabs at him. And John catches her hand, squeezing it once, before walking out the door.

CHAPTER NINETEEN

ELEANOR – LATE OCTOBER 1914

Despite living her whole life on its fringes, Eleanor's never spent this much time on the marsh. As if the isolation of the hospital isn't punishment enough now she forces herself even further away. For the past week, accompanied by Piper, she navigates the suck of mud and the marsh's ever-changing channels, her mouth brimming with the taste of salt and brackish water. Each day she sets out, her face hard against the wind, her back turned from home. For hours she watches the ebb and flow of The Wash, sliding over the marsh, spreading like molten steel. And when the tides and sky conspire, she lingers as the sunset transforms the water into a sea of burnished gold.

Constantly she thinks of John and Lily. Stopping only to think of Frank. And finally Alfred, balling her fists and screaming up at the high white sky, cursing her brother for daring to leave.

Yet it's all futile. All the walking, the shouting; none of it relieves her pain.

Her mornings are spent in the hospital, obsessively making and remaking the idle beds, cleaning every corner, every groove and windowpane. But no matter how hard she scrubs, the memory of that afternoon, the cold feel of the scissors against her palm refuses to fade.

Trapped in a dark hole of remembrance; its sides so black and steep that Eleanor doubts she'll ever climb out.

The morning after the incident, after a night Eleanor had spent awake and despairing, Lily had appeared, in the kitchen, barefoot, her eyes wide and hurt, one hand pressed against the uneven patch on her scalp.

Feeling her throat close, Eleanor watched Lily's face settle into its familiar mournful expression, sliding into the well-trodden paths of self-pity and dependence. Pushing down hard on the door handle, Eleanor had deliberately flooded the kitchen with ice cold air.

'Eleanor...' Lily whimpered, one hand outstretched, starting across the room.

Recoiling, Eleanor stepped out into the garden, calling back over her shoulder.

'Stay away from me. For Christ's sake, and yours Lily, just stay away.'

Shaking on the path, every part of her had longed for John. Lily's actions, with Clara and the letter, had been utterly exposing, but still Eleanor was lost, left with no idea how to move forwards. Again and again, she was assailed by the image of John, stepping away; his eyes wide, the pain of his rejection rubbing her raw.

And then there was Clara.

For days, visiting her sister-in-law remained out of the question. Eleanor was familiar enough with the pattern of Frank's rage to know that the danger would not have passed. Every night, gazing out over the slow-moving river, she prayed that Clara and the children were safe; resting her forehead against the cool glass of her window and trying to convince herself that things could not be as bad as she imagined. Before the sight of Clara hunched by the smithy wall reoccurred and the sick and certain terror rose again.

At night, she counts the rotations of the lighthouse, a sweep of light and shadow across her wall. Listens to the lonely call of seabirds, broken occasionally by Lily's footsteps in the room across the hall. Just the soft shuffle of her sister's feet is enough to turn her quiet terror back to blinding rage.

But now, unable to bear it any longer, Eleanor finds herself at Clara's back door. She taps twice, her eyes darting behind her as she waits.

Clara opens the door, and immediately Eleanor is overtaken by relief, flooding through her in a warm, glorious burst of colour and hope. Collapsing against each other, they take it in turns to hold the other upright in an unrelenting and desperate embrace.

'Frank?' Eleanor breathes his name into Clara's shoulder blade.

'Working.' Clara whispers back. 'Or so he claims.'

Easing herself away, palms on Clara's shoulders, Eleanor takes in her friend's drawn face, her eyes ringed by violet shadows. And watches Clara appraising her in the same way.

Clutching hands, they move to the table, where they sit in silence, overwhelmed; each wondering how to begin.

'I've ruined everything.'

Eleanor's words burst forth, to be swallowed by an immediate storm of weeping. Clara reaches for her, listening as the story begins to unfold. In jumbled, jagged pieces Eleanor tells of the scissors, paper dolls and then cutting of Lily's hair; John's horror and his subsequent retreat.

'But he can't blame you, surely? He must see that she pushed you too far. For God's sake! The letter, Frank...'

Clara's expression moves from confusion to anger. Removing her hands from Eleanor's, she grips the arms of her chair.

'But how it must've looked, Clara. Me, grabbing at her, chopping at her hair. And how he looked at me...' Eleanor trails off, sinking back into despair.

'Have you seen him since?' Clara's voice is flat, controlled, but Eleanor sees her fingernails pushing, worrying at the wood of the chair.

Eleanor nods. 'I went to the smithy, once. And last week, one afternoon, he came up to the house. But he wouldn't come inside. We went up to the marsh, but Clara, nothing *feels* right. Every time I speak to him it likes he's slipped further away.'

'What about Lily?'

Eleanor's cheeks flame. 'I can't even look at her. Every time she walks into the room I want to get as far away as I can. But I don't care about Lily. Clara, what do I do?'

Thrusting her face into her hands, she begins to weep again.

'Here!' Pulling her chair alongside her Clara wraps both arms around Eleanor's shaking body. 'Come on now, enough of that.'

'But Clara, if it's over; if John's decided he's made a mistake, how will I ever get away? I can't stay there with Lily, not after what she's done.'

Thumbing Eleanor's tears away, Clara pulls her towards her, resting her friend's hot forehead against her own.

'John loves you. You know that. Lily knows that. That's why she sent that letter in the first place. Give him time. He'll see. He wouldn't throw everything away just because you lost your temper.'

'I hope you're right, Clara. God, how could I've been so stupid?'

Clara snorts.

'Lord, you're only human, El. If it was me, I'd have scalped her, never mind giving her a bloody trim.'

Eleanor smiles weakly and then, edging away from Clara, she reaches into her bag. On the table, she sets down a pair of scissors.

'You were there in spirit. I used your scissors.'

Roaring with laughter, Clara lifts them to the light.

'Couldn't think of a better use!'

There, in that snatch of shared laughter, Eleanor feels lighter than she has in days.

But then Clara glances towards the small brass clock on the kitchen mantle and the spell is broken; Eleanor sees her face fall.

'El, sorry, but it's getting late. They'll all be back soon. Molly won't say anything, but the boys... well...'

Understanding is immediate; Frank can't know she's been here.

Getting to her feet, Eleanor pulls her friend into one final tight embrace.

'Thanks for listening, for trying…' Her voice breaks.

Clara whispers into her hair.

'Honestly, John won't give up. Not on you. Not just like that. And neither should you.'

Fighting back tears as Eleanor heads to the door.

'I hope you're right.'

'Why don't you go and see him? Go now!'

She shakes her head. Seeing Clara has left her exhausted. Now out in the yard, her eyes stiff from crying, she blinks in the weak sunlight.

'Go! You'll feel better once you do.'

Except I won't, Eleanor thinks as she lets herself out the gate and starts up the alley. Even though the smithy is less than two minutes' walk away, going to see John this afternoon is beyond her; the remembrance of last week's coldness enough to fill her with dread. If their engagement is over, then she can't bear to know today.

She walks on, out onto the High Street, each step dogged by a terrible loneliness and, worse, the feeling that she has nowhere to go. The thought of heading back across the river to Lily and the hospital makes her heart and feet feel like lead. On impulse, keeping her head down, she crosses the road and makes her way through the narrow gate into the churchyard.

The church, a square, blocky building, glistens as the afternoon sun kisses the flint that adorns its walls. Eyes straight ahead, Eleanor steps through the gravestones and up to the great oak door.

Inside all is cool and still; her footsteps ring out on the aisle, drifting up to the vaulted ceiling. Sliding into the nearest pew, breathing in the silence, she tries to catch and claim this small splinter of calm. But all she tastes is incense and dust.

To the left of the altar, at the base of the pulpit, a line of candles flickers. Each marking their own moment of prayer.

Or despair. Each a quiet, bright reminder that while Eleanor's own life has been falling apart, the war continues, shattering the lives of others in the village.

And for many stealing the luxury of uncertainty or hope.

She looks up, just in time to see the light around her change. A shaft of sunlight, piercing the stained glass, coating the walls into an immediate, shimmering wave of violet, crimson and blue. Transfixed, she steps out into the aisle and the sudden ocean of light; following it, watching as it shifts and pools, drifting across the red and black tiles, coating their ancient geometry with a new, watery brilliance.

Spellbound, she plunges her hands deep into the rainbow beams, letting her fingers dabble in their kaleidoscope. A moment of simple beauty, dancing on her fingertips. Blue fire sparking off the tiny stone and illuminating the gold of John's ring, with its unexpected and sudden brilliance.

A fleeting flash of hope.

CHAPTER TWENTY

CLARA – NOVEMBER 1914

Clara's bruises fade quicker than her rage.

Even now, she can feel it, heavy, and insistent, dragging at her spine as she walks through the village. Tugging at her calves, each step threatening her from the inside out, to split her skin and open up her veins.

It is three weeks since Frank delivered his beating, and still Clara wants to scream whenever she thinks of Lily's face, watching from the window as her brother lingered by the gate.

As she held Eleanor in the kitchen, Clara had found herself whispering reassurances that she tried hard to believe, and long into the following night, Clara had remained troubled. Her anger tied up with a curious sense that somehow, she too was to blame for her friend's misery.

So, on this bitter November morning, heels bouncing nervously on the cobbles, she stands outside the Smithy, her back resting against the icy wall, as she waits in the shadows for John's customer to leave. The wind blowing in from the river, cuts down the street. Clara's eyes smart, and each minute she waits feels like ten.

Finally, the smithy door opens, immediately Clara turns her face to the brick, bracing herself as the sound of hooves and boots move into the yard.

'She'll be good for a couple of months now. If you keep her that long.' John's voice. Followed by the quick, snorting breath of a horse and the creak of a saddle as someone unseen mounts.

'Much obliged. And I'll be keeping her as long as I can.'

The man's reply is clipped, his are not the vowels of a working man.

'And you'll think about it? What we spoke of?'

A pause, then John replies.

'I will, aye.'

Steadying herself, one gloved hand against the brick, Clara waits until horse and rider round the corner. Then, just as John is about to close the door, she steps forward, into the road.

His eyes catch hers, widening in recognition. He straightens, then attempts to smile.

'Clara? Are you... what are you doing here?'

Wordless, she pushes past him. Stepping inside, she sits in one of two low wooden chairs, holding her hands to the glow of the furnace. The warmth stings her palms, and she winces as life returns to her frozen skin.

Taking one quick glance down the street, John follows and closes the door.

'Don't worry. Frank hasn't followed me.'

Clara can't tell if the scarlet of John's cheek belongs to fury, heat, or shame.

'I wasn't worried about that. Well, not about me... I just...'

Clara throws up her hand.

'It's fine. I'd have checked too.'

Seeing John so bemused and uncertain, Clara is instantly irritated. Suddenly alive with the conviction that he should know precisely why she's here.

Fleetingly it occurs to her that he might challenge her presence. Will turn her away; this strange, unwelcome creature, blown into the smithy at the wrong end of a bitter morning.

Straightening beneath his glare, she lengthens her frame against the chair.

'The kettle on?'

John makes a show of shoving coal into the fire before setting the water off to boil. Clara flexes her frozen hands as he searches his workbench, shifting tools, clanging, and muttering until he comes across a second mug.

He hands it to her, and Clara sees the tremor of unspoken questions running through his hands.

She sips slowly. About her feet, the stone floor is littered with straw, dust, and iron filings. From the corner of his eye, John watches, a mug at his lips, blowing across the surface of his tea.

They drink in silence, Clara stealing careful, occasional glances, taking in his face, the rise and fall of the muscles working at his wide, sloping jaw; a strange, stirring combination of strength and gentleness shifting beneath his obvious tension.

It isn't hard to see what Eleanor finds so attractive, and Clara can't help but wonder if anyone looking at Frank would understand what it was she first saw. If she could ever describe what drew her to him; his vulnerability, the overwhelming glimpses of that lost little boy.

As a girl, Clara had always been one for rescuing, never giving up on anything or anyone broken, twisted, wounded; damaged beyond repair. So, perhaps it was inevitable she would tie herself to someone like Frank. The lonely farm boy, who looked at her through black haunted eyes.

Well, she was paying for it now.

Interrupting her thoughts, John speaks.

'You still haven't said why you're here? Is it Frank? I've been meaning to…'

He tails off.

'I'm fine. And Frank…' she shrugs, 'Is still Frank.'

She washes down the familiar knot of fear and revulsion with the hot, faintly metallic tea.

She waits, giving nothing away. Let John work it out, piece together why she's here.

He shifts in his chair.

'Nothing wrong, over there?' John inclines his head, nodding towards the door and the river beyond.

Clara bristles, then glares.

Through the silence comes the click of coal settling, shifting in the furnace and the odd holler from the street outside. A gust of wind blowing under the door brings leaves and winter in from the yard. She shivers in the chair. Finally, she speaks, her voice low and barely controlled.

'I wouldn't know, would I? Not being able to go over. Or have you forgotten about the letter?'

John looks down, squirming; ashamed.

Clara hates herself for enjoying this, even a little bit, but she is sick of it all; of being so powerless, of having to play by rules of which she has no part.

Still, she reins her feelings in, reminding herself that, for all his recent faults, John isn't Frank.

'Eleanor came to see me, though. A few days ago, when Frank was out.'

John drinks deeply from his mug, then knocks out the dregs on the bricks of the furnace. The last drops of tea turning the dusty floor dark.

Clara continues.

'Told me, about Lily. And you, walking in, seeing Eleanor with the scissors... well, she told me everything.'

Still, John says nothing, and Clara's irritation and sense of injustice rises once again. Leaning out of her chair, she pushes her face into the dust and space between them.

'She's worrying herself sick over there you know? Convincing herself that you don't want her. That whatever you saw, or thought you saw, is keeping you away.'

'That's ridiculous. She was here; I saw her, just the other day.'

His indignation, bursts from the silence. Too quick, too sharp. A hot denial whose burn Clara knows all too well.

'Seeing her is not the same.'

'The same as what?'

'As wanting to see her. Wanting to be with her.'

'I don't know what you mean.' But even as he says it, John looks away.

Clara leans closer, finger jabbing wildly at the air.

'Have you asked her? About cutting Lily's hair. And why she did it?'

John bites, snapping back; a terrier at heel.

'I know why she did it. I was there; don't forget.'

Clara spits.

'Do you? Seems to me you're having trouble remembering what really happened that afternoon, or at least the important parts. Me, turning up here, everything Frank did; all because of Lily and her bloody letter. The letter you delivered.'

John's face flames, his eyes bright from the fire and shame.

'Of course I haven't forgotten. But Eleanor; she was so angry, vicious even. I've never seen her like that. Like she wasn't Eleanor at all.'

Clara laughs; high and hollow out into the dry, dusty air. Feeling its force in her still-aching ribs, she clutches at the half full mug, trying to prevent it spilling as she shakes.

'You think you know it all, don't you? Everything about Eleanor and the life she's lived. You've known her for a bit more than a year, and you think that everything's squared away. That might not have been *your* Eleanor there with Lily, but it was her just the same. If living with Frank's taught me anything, it's that all of us have got more than one person knocking around in here.' Clara brings her fist down hard at the centre of her chest.

John picks up a poker. Turning back to the furnace he jabs again at the flames.

But having found her voice, Clara is unable to stop.

'So, you didn't like seeing Eleanor angry? Thought that, maybe, you might be getting more than you bargained for?'

He slaps the furnace door shut.

'You can say that again.' The words spark, metal on flint.

'Go on.' Clara squares herself, facing him head on.

Pale with regret, John shakes his head.

'I shouldn't have…'

Beneath her frustration, Clara feels the stirrings of relief; the hope that finally someone might actually speak the truth. For a the briefest second, she considers reaches out to him; instead she tucks her hands into her sleeves.

'No, go on. Say what it is you mean.'

Turning from the heat, John grips the back of his empty chair.

'I don't want to upset you, Clara. But these past few weeks…' He pauses, and she nods, urging him on.

'Well, it's been a lot to take in. Lily and Frank. Then the letter and what happened to you. How Eleanor reacted…'

He trails off, his knuckles white against the chair.

Clara's heart sinks.

'And you're wondering what sort of family you are about to tie yourself to?'

Making no response, John pulls back hard on the chair; small clouds of dust rise up into the air.

'Do you regret asking Eleanor to marry you?'

It's a risk, this question, so bald and quiet, but Clara asks it anyway.

John shakes his head.

'No, I don't. I don't regret it. I love her but…' He swallows 'It feels like there's a whole side of her, a whole life, that I don't know.'

'So, ask her about it. Get to know.'

John gazes into the cave of the workshop, eyes blank. Silent.

Clara continues, treading a path that feels too narrow. But she owes Eleanor this.

'What you saw was a woman, bent out of shape. Pushed beyond her breaking point. Turns out we've all got them.'

John looks up, and Clara wonders if his own breaking point is all that far away.

'Since Alfred died, Eleanor's been the one keeping things together. Looking after her mother, her miserable bullying father. Managing Lily, the best she could. Not to mention keeping me sane. You might not have seen her at her finest, but if you want my opinion… after what she's put up with, it was too little, too late.'

John starts to speak, but Clara silences him; raising her hand as she steps out into the freezing yard. She pauses in the doorway.

'I've said my bit. Whatever you saw, or think you saw, that's for you to make your peace with. To try and understand. But Eleanor's what she is because of the fire she's been cast in. And you know better than most that with the right hands metal can be reshaped.'

CHAPTER TWENTY-ONE

LILY

Sitting on the stairs, Lily's shoulders stiffen as she anticipates the familiar slamming of the door. The one Eleanor doesn't bother locking anymore; the key, abandoned in the lock, taunting Lily with this new reality.

Lily's hands drift to her head, where they seek out the stubby patch of hair.

Every morning since their argument, Eleanor has shut herself up in the hospital, before collecting Piper from the kitchen and taking herself off towards the marsh. Finally, she arrives home, mud splattered and chilled, framed by the last of the daylight, the tightness of her face forbidding Lily to ask questions or challenge her in any way.

Lily had followed her once. Driven to desperation by Eleanor's silent avoidance, she had yanked on her boots and set off running along the bank. Determined that, if Eleanor refused to acknowledge her presence in the house, Lily would force her to speak outside.

She had been about to call out when Eleanor had turned. Eyes locked, they stood facing each other, just yards apart, the late October wind making tangled streams of their hair. Immediately Piper had lunged towards her, but grabbing at his collar, Eleanor had held him back. Lily remembers the two small haltering steps she took towards him before her sister stopped her with a slight shake of her head. Then, turning away, Eleanor walked on.

Leaving Lily, buffeted by disappointment and weather, to head home alone.

She hasn't tried again.

It is true that Clara never comes. But there is no need for Clara now. Not now Eleanor is no longer afraid of leaving Lily alone. Thinking of Clara is like pressing on a bruise, a dark patch of guilt that refuses to heal. Lily had never wanted Clara hurt, had never imagined that Frank would do what he did. She had only wanted Clara to keep to her side of the river. Just wanted Clara to leave them alone.

At least, that's what she tells herself as she lies in the darkness, unable to sleep. But it doesn't stop the memories of her father and his rages, playing themselves out whenever she closes her eyes. And it doesn't stop Frank stalking her dreams.

Now in the afternoon shadows, Lily reaches into her pocket, seeking the familiar, comforting curl of the photograph, released from its frame. Holding it to what little light penetrates the hallway she traces Alfred's infant face with her finger; hoping that thoughts of one brother might chase the other away. Willing Alfred back to life.

Alfred. The brother who should have kept her safe. Who was going to run the hospital and look after her, making sure she always had a place to stay.

Maybe it is Alfred, or the gentle dream of him, that guides her to the hospital; pressing the key into her hand and helping her to shoulder open its swollen door. Because it is a surprise to Lily to find herself there; standing beneath the rafters, breathing in the damp, frigid air scented by paraffin and late autumn rot.

Since Alfred's death, Lily has rarely entered the hospital and certainly never alone. No matter how hard she clings to the past it represents, but she leaves it to Eleanor to tend day to day.

Now, walking slowly down the centre of the room, she runs

her fingers along the cool steel of the bedframes; only lifting her hand when she reaches the bed by the wall, the one on the left. The one where Alfred lay. Whose mattress she knows has been turned to hide the stains.

Each bed is made up, clean and neat. Evidence of Eleanor's care and attention that renders Lily breathless with a sudden and overwhelming sense of loss.

Dragging a chair from the wall, she sits between the feet of two beds, positioning herself in the middle of the floor. She looks up to the beams that crisscross the ceiling and then slowly down to the worn pine; planting her feet wide, she lets herself remember.

How she and Alfred had played, chasing, in and out of the open door; dodging her mother, made slow by pails of water and piles of sheets. How they rolled marbles along the length of these wide uneven planks, before sitting on the step beside their father, breathing in his tobacco and the smell of new paint, and listening to his assurances; that it was just a matter of time before the Port was rebuilt. Watching as he wove the precious golden threads of their future importance through the stale air, long after the rest of the village had given up hope. As she and Alfred had sat, cocooned by the knowledge, the only thing required of them was to believe.

That had been the problem with Frank and Eleanor. The cause of all the trouble; the questions they insisted on asking and their continued refusal to commit to their father's dream.

If they had only accepted that this was the place for their family. This hospital was their kingdom. The place where everything made sense and where, set apart from the rest of the village, divided by land and water, they could all be free.

All they'd needed was patience and belief.

But her older siblings had insisted on pushing, always looking for more. At school, Eleanor had tried to infiltrate the close-knit circles of girls in the yard. Village girls, to whom she and Lily were at best a curiosity and at worst an irrelevance; relics of the past, whose very existence taunted the community with false hope and broken promises. A reminder of the past that refused to go away.

'They'll never play with you.' Lily told her sister as they crossed the bridge, Eleanor dragging her feet while Lily marched ahead, desperate to be home.

'They aren't like us, El. They don't understand.'

Scowling, Eleanor would push Lily, hard, before running past her, out onto the dusty road. But the next day she would try again. Circling the girls, desperate to find a place in a world to which she didn't belong.

And now Eleanor thinks that marriage is the way out. Another circle that Lily knows her sister can't close.

Lily stands. Walking to the back of the hospital, where, with the bunch of keys she doesn't recall picking up, she unlocks the store. Immediately she is assailed by yet more memories. Of rainy days. Endless games of hide and seek.

Narrow and musty, the storeroom smells faintly medicinal. Its wooden shelves line the walls, barely a shoulder width apart. It is cave-like, barely lit by the grey afternoon light;

Lily's eyes, adjust to the gloom, then begin to wander. At eye level sit piles of linens — sheets and pillowcases, spare blankets — all stacked beneath rough but never used towels. Below are cubby holes, filled with rolls of bandages, each wrapped in yellowing paper, and packed together, neat and tight. Blue and brown glass bottles run in rows that almost touch the low ceiling, lined up by size, gleaming and free of dust. Lily reaches for the nearest one; pulling out the cork, she holds the bottle to her nose, immediately something acrid floods her nostrils and stings her throat. Coughing violently, she bangs the bottle down, her hand rubbing at her neck.

She turns to the other wall, where the shelves are deeper and their brackets spaced further apart. More wooden boxes lined up and filled with paint, tools and carbolic soap, alongside tin pails, ladders, brushes, and mops. Far more than will ever be used.

But all of it brings Lily a strange kind of comfort; to know that despite everything, these supplies are still here, ordered, tidy.

That despite everything that's happened, Eleanor hasn't given up on this space.

Looking back out into the hospital, Lily sees the smear of her footprints, a track of autumn damp spreading across the floor.

She curses. After the events of the past few weeks, there is no real reason to hide her presence in the hospital from Eleanor. But old habits die hard.

Gathering a mop and bucket, she drags them out, smudging the dirt further across the floor. She stops to remove her shoes, setting them down by the heavy rush mat just inside the door, not wanting to add more filth as she works. With the soles of her feet catching on the uneven boards, she lifts the pail down into the deep, lightly crazed sink.

As the water plunges and bubbles, she is caught up once more in memories; she and Eleanor set to clean while Alfred roamed the marsh with his gun. Try as she might Lily can't think where Frank might have been.

On impulse, she thrusts one hand deep into the water. She gasps, and the water.

rocks then slops. Lily steps back sharply, but not before it the pail overspills, soaking her feet. Briefly, she considers setting the small wood stove, heating the water and warming herself by the fire. But it's been years since she watched her mother light it, and even if she could remember how, there would be ash to rake out and dispose of. Cold water will have to do.

In the cupboard, she searches for something to add to the pail; trying and failing to remember what her mother would have used. In desperation, she snatches up a bar of carbolic soap, then, removing the brittle, faded paper, drops the hard cake into the bucket, where it sinks, striking the bottom with a metallic ring and staying stubbornly whole. She wonders if Eleanor counts the soap and whether it will be missed.

She lugs the bucket to the back of the room, her shoulders tightening, her body already protesting at the most work she has done in years. She slaps the mop hard against the floor her strokes broad and careless, interrupted by small twigs and leaves. Wringing the mop makes her hands ache, and her feeble efforts do little more than dilute the dirt, spreading it further across the floor. Within minutes, the hem of her skirt is dark with water, and her lower back aches.

Abandoning the mop, Lily picks her way through the puddles, freezing water nibbling at her feet. Returning to the store, she pulls down an armful of thin towels. She has no idea of the time, but the afternoon light is already fading, and she wants to be back in the house before Eleanor arrives home.

In haste, she tugs at the linens, until they topple, then unravel in a heap at her feet.

Lily yelps and then stops. Unable to believe what it is that she can see.

There, nestled behind the stacks of pillowcases and blankets is something Lily had believed no longer existed.

A long wooden box, that, unlike the rest of the hospital, is coated in a thick layer of dust; its once polished grain and brass catches dull and tarnished. As is the key that sits undisturbed and snug in the lock.

Lily drops to the floor.

Slowly, her heart pumping at her throat, she reaches through the stacks of wool and cotton, hardly daring to believe that this precious thing is here. That the past she has so often longed for is sitting here undisturbed, just within her reach.

'Eleanor?'

John's voice rings out.

Snatching her hand back, Lily quivers on her haunches.

'Eleanor? Are you in there?'

John's voice again. Louder now and coming from the front of the hospital. He is on the path, if not already at the door.

Since the day he walked in on that terrible argument, Lily hasn't spoken to John. His one visit to Eleanor, conducted in the garden, had been unusually brief. The matter of the letter and its contents has never been discussed.

'Eleanor?'

She waits, counting John's footfalls on the narrow concrete steps. With one hand outstretched behind her, slowly she pushes the cupboard door back into place; and gives silent thanks for the fact her muddied shoes are on this side of the hospital door.

John calls out again, and Lily closes her eyes, trembling with dread and anticipation.

Then there is silence.

Still she sits. Rigid, for what seems like hours, before finally she lets herself believe John has really gone.

But the case remains. Still on the shelf, untouched.

With a smile and shaking hands, she collects the fallen towels, folding them carefully, and rebuilding the neat stack. She risks taking one and, on her hands and knees, uses it to dry the floor.

And as she works, the image of the box grows and hums. And Lily hums along with it. Ready to sing the long song.

CHAPTER TWENTY-TWO

ELEANOR – DECEMBER 1914

To dance in the middle of all this seems wrong, but that's what they do.

The villagers left behind; the mothers, the fathers, sisters and lovers, the men still working the land and tending the wharf, the old and infirm, the too young but eager. Together they welcome the coming of winter by throwing open the doors of the village hall and setting out the flags as they dance for their boys.

They tell themselves they aren't doing this for their own sakes, but for the sake of the men who belong in these fields and boats and now find themselves so very far from home. They will dance to remember them, to raise funds and cheer with the price of a ticket and maybe a drink. Performing their own kind of duty.

Because as they creep towards Christmas, their hopes of salvation are falling away.

Men continue to leave, even as news reaches them, of boys who will never return or will return forever changed. Not just in this village but in the one beyond and the one beyond that. A community once connected by its channels, sluices, and dykes, by its flatlands, river and by the overarching sky, now woven together by another hidden network; an ancient place, bound by a new and terrible loss.

John, tied to the smithy by the need for his skills and his care of the few horses who remain, is one of those still left behind

And it was John who had suggested they attend the dance, that afternoon, a week or so after Eleanor had visited Clara, when crossing the river, he found her alone on the road to the marsh.

With her eyes straining against the winter sun and her cold hand in his, Eleanor had briefly forgotten about Lily and the terrible scene in the kitchen; about the letter and the ruin of Clara's face. Lifting her lips to graze John's cheek, she brought her mouth close to his ear and simply whispered her agreement. Accepting the invitation had been a repair of sorts.

But still, Eleanor feels the uncertainty, binding this strange cocoon in which they sit. Where the question of marriage and Lily remain the unseen boundaries that they skirt around, wary and cat-like. Sometimes she catches John's look upon her, intense and quizzical, as though he is trying to break her into tiny pieces and put her back together again. The heat and the anger of that day might have died away, but still everything seems scorched and vaguely brittle. So Eleanor tells herself that attending the dance will be a turning point, a chance to hold their love to the light and let others inspect its colours and patterns. Let others find its flaws.

Now, standing in the garden beneath a navy sky pricked with occasional diamonds, she does her best to ignore the splinters of doubt sticking in her throat and pushes herself forward once again.

With hand and ear pressed against the kitchen door, she waits, shivering in a dress too light for this time of year. In her fingertips, her heartbeat drums, her blood rising and falling as she listens for Lily. Eleanor pictures her, hunkered and tense, mirroring her own posture. Lily on one side and she on this; breathing and seething. Both listening for the other.

She snatches her hand away. Enough. From the drawstring bag at her wrist, she takes the key. Then, for the first time in weeks, she locks the door.

She will not risk Lily following her tonight.

Moving by memory and moonlight, Eleanor hurries through

the darkness and the shadows of the garden, the winter evening like iron against her face. Reaching the road, then the river, she uses the lights of the few remaining fishing boats to steady and guide her on her way. The bridge's silhouette, dominates the night sky, and she imagines John waiting, leaning against the steel and hidden within its shadows. He had wanted to come to the hospital; to escort her, but tonight, it feels safer this way.

She moves on.

From the village drifts the occasional peal of laughter, a strain of a faltering tune. From the marsh, the sudden cry of a bird; sharp and insistent, splits the night and picking up speed, Eleanor concentrates on what's ahead.

John is there. Waiting on her side of the bridge, even though she'd arranged to meet him in the middle.

As she approaches, she watches his outline change, shifting from shadow to contour, to man. She marvels at his stillness, at his ability to hold himself so steady, presenting himself as a moment in time, brought alive by the change of perspective and light. Working slowly around his form, she picks out his edges, tracing the outline of his face and his long work-stained fingers. Making herself as still as he, she indulges herself in this moment, aching for a simpler time. Something lost.

Then he turns. And everything changes. Once more his edges blur and his lines are lost. Straightening and striding forwards John takes her hands in his.

'You came.'

'Of course. Did you think I'd leave you standing here, in the dark?'

'No. But... Lily?'

As he breaks off, the tide of unspoken things rushes in, then out again. Eleanor shrugs, refusing to taint the evening before it has begun. John reaches for her, his hands gentle; his face breaking into a slow, tentative smile.

Tucking her arm in his, Eleanor's chin brushes his coat; the wool, old and worn against her skin, scented by animals and warmth, a spell into which John pulls her. Hope flaring, she breathes him in. Breathing out what she has left behind; a simple exchange. One life for another.

With the power of him wrapped around her, she tugs at his arm. 'Come on.'

They walk on in silence, over the river. The tide is high, close, rushing towards the marsh and sea beyond. Filled with the unstoppable pull and power of its depths, Eleanor imagining herself plummeting, down, into the blackness. She grips John's arm tighter, and he pauses.

'Alright?'

'Too much excitement. Let's get on.'

They quicken their pace, and Eleanor is both terrified and relieved when they reach the other side. She can't remember the last time she was in the village at night. Before them, the flint of the church glistens, frosted against a backdrop of stars; the new moon shines, a bright sickle in the ink of sky.

Down the wide, straight high street, right at the furthest end, is the village hall; the last outpost of the community to which Eleanor has only been a handful of times. Even from here, they can hear the music and laughter that spills from its half-open doors.

As planned, she and John are arriving later, but still a few stragglers linger slowly making their way. Eleanor marvels at the change that has come over the village. Shops, cottage doors, gutters, and kerbstones; all of it muted, gilded mauve and silver. Made unreal, the effect of night and frost is beautiful and unsettling. Everything spoilt, stained, or creased is coated by rime and shadows, hidden away. Leaning into John, she seeks warmth, hoping it will steady her and calm the nerves building within her chest.

Then, just ahead, a soldier and his girl step out from a side street. His left leg is heavily bandaged, and supporting him, the young woman clutches at his sleeve. His crutch catches on the pavement with a slow regularity, the drag of his injured leg filling in the gaps. Moving awkwardly together, the couple's progress is unwieldy and painfully slow. Eleanor wonders how long the journey has taken so far and whose idea it was to go dancing.

Then without warning, the soldier stumbles, falling heavily against his girl. Lunging forward, John catches him by the elbow, only for the girl to push John's hand away.

'We can manage. Thanks all the same.'

Beneath the streetlamp, the girl's skin is taut and yellow, her voice tighter than her smile. Holding up his hands John retreats, and they watch as the girl lifts the lad against her hip, straightening his frame. She whispers to him, her voice determined and harsh. His head stays bowed, and before they move, Eleanor catches a low moan of pain. She looks at John, who looks away.

They follow them along the road, right to the hall. To walk around them seems cruel, even taunting, so they slow, matching their own pace to theirs. Twice more they stop, and each time Eleanor glances at John. And each time his face is unfamiliar and unreadable, his eyes bright but distant. Eleanor shivers. She wants to whisper to him, to bring him back, but she is afraid of the couple hearing her; and besides, she can't think what it is she would say.

Finally, they reach the hall. The girl and her lad peel off, and people move carefully, deliberately out of their way. Keeping her head high, the girl finds a chair and settles her companion; arranging his leg and smoothing back his hair. In the brightness of the hall, she appears even younger, and the boy in even more pain. Busying herself with her coat, Eleanor looks away.

The hall is long; its polished floor glows a warm amber, illuminated by the lamps in each deep recessed window. At tables, each set with a single candle, knots of old men smoke and nurse half-empty glasses. Further back, running the length of the wall, is a row of chairs, upon which young women talk, laughing behind their hands; heads touching as they shoot furtive glances out into the room. The music comes from a gramophone tucked in the corner, next to a piano, poised lid up, ready to be played. Two couples are taking a turn on the dance floor; a jolly farmer and his wife, whom Eleanor recognises from the next village, and beyond them spin a pair of young girls.

The absence of young men is stark and immediate, and the atmosphere, although jovial, lacks the edge that comes with the presence of young, single men. That gentle undercurrent of danger, the impulsive sense of being and sense of fun, where a joke or a fight is just a hair's breadth away. With a jolt, Eleanor realises, that John is one of the youngest men in the room. An observation that she instinctively pushes away.

Without warning, she is thrown back to the days following Alfred's death; when the house was filled with something beyond grief, the feeling that their oxygen, their very being and texture, had been ripped away.

She imagines this happening in homes all around her, this sudden sucking out of life and air, as one by one, hour by hour, the war steals not just the boys but also the life they brought to the places they inhabited. She wonders how the battlefields can stand it; how there can be a place on earth that is vast enough to hold the life, the vitality, the essence of all those vibrant young men.

Her thoughts are interrupted by John, telling her to find a table, while he gets some drinks. Unnerved, unbalanced, she reaches out a hand to stop him, but he is gone in a rush of air and space, leaving her feeling horribly exposed. Picking her way through the drinkers and dancers, she fixes her sights on a small table tucked away at the back, where she reasons no one is likely to join them. Where they can sit in the shadows, together but unseen.

So intent is she on reaching it that, at first, she doesn't feel the tug of fingers at her coat. It is only when she is jerked suddenly backwards does she start. Turning, she finds herself face to face with the soldier's girl who grips her tight about the elbow. The girl's pale face dominated by wide, tired eyes. Eleanor tries to imagine what this girl could possibly want with her. Then it occurs to her that the boy must be in trouble, that perhaps he has fallen again, or his pain has got worse, and the girl needs help to get him upright. Casting about the room, Eleanor searches for John, certain she won't be able to lift him on her own.

'Do you need some help? Has your young man…'

The girl laughs coldly, her huge eyes brimming with disgust.

'My young man is just fine. Or as fine as he is going to be.'

Eleanor's scalp prickles, crawling with confusion and unease.

'Sorry, I don't understand.'

'You don't understand?' The girl's voice is scornful, each word punctuated by the grip of her fingers on Eleanor's arm. 'Well, I understand. That your 'young man' is still here. Still able to walk on his own, still able to work and dance and drink.'

She is breathless now, this strange nameless girl. Breathless with a fury that, try as she might, Eleanor can't understand. Panicking, she tries to prise the girl's curling fingers away. But they only creep tighter.

'Please.' Eleanor looks desperately about the room, still searching for John, for a way out. 'Please let go. I am sorry about your boy, but I don't understand…'

'Don't understand?' The girl's voice rises from its low hiss, and Eleanor feels her cheeks begin to flame. 'Well, understand this. It's time more men were taking their turn, doing their bit. Time men like your fella over there stopped hiding behind their jobs and joined up. Why should you have him here, when my Eddie looks like that and ain't never going to be no good again? You just be grateful that I don't have a feather.'

Her voice, high and uncontrolled, is spiralling now, drawing the attention of others in the room. With one white hand still clutched on Eleanor's coat, the girl points in the direction of the soldier, who, red-faced, sits slumped against the wall. In desperation, Eleanor tries to catch his eye, but quickly he looks away.

The twist of the girl's body is enough to give Eleanor the leverage to break free. She jerks her arm backwards, and the girl falls, clattering into nearby chairs. With the girl's cry ringing in her ears, Eleanor moves blindly through the hall, pushing at people, at tables; trying to find the way out, the way home.

But as she reaches the door, she feels fingers close and clutch yet again, this time gripping at her shoulder, holding her fast. Hurt, furious, Eleanor spins around.

'Let me go!'

But it isn't the girl at her back. It is John.

John, whose hands guide her to the door, leading her out onto the frost-bitten street; where his fingers find their way into her hair, moving in rhythmic, soothing waves. Waves that begin at her crown and end at the nape of her neck, reassuring and firm, as he pulls her face to his chest and mutters comfort into her burning ear.

John who holds her as they stand, locked together, as the music starts up again. Slowly he begins to sway, moving Eleanor's hips, her body, in time with the soft shift of his feet. And somewhere above her tears, he begins to hum, pulling her in, tighter; moving his hands to her waist, resting them there.

In the street, they dance. Away from prying eyes and under the silver slice of moon, they dance for today, forgetting tomorrow; for the days that they've lost and nights they have promised.

Dancing to forget the soldier, to forget Lily and the rest of the world.

CHAPTER TWENTY-THREE

CLARA – JANUARY 1915

Frank has been threatening to do it for months.

Every time he and Clara fight, or he ends up in another fiery exchange of words over a jar of ale, he starts. Jabbering and cursing about how nobody appreciates or wants him, how he is going to show them all. The army is the flag that he pulls out from his pocket, before waving it around.

'You'll be sorry when I'm away, over there.' He shouts, to anyone who'll listen and many who don't.

At first, Clara almost believes him. After years of circular arguments and unfulfilled expectations, the war has given Frank a new angle; one that leaves Clara torn between wanting him gone and wondering how on earth she would feed everyone if he went.

But weeks have turned to months, drifted into a new year and Frank is still here. And Clara has come to see these threats for what they are; hollow, idle. Like her husband. Time and again he has overplayed his hand, hiding behind the words used too often.

So now Clara ignores him.

Because, while the recruiting officer is a train ride away, a ride that will cost beer or baccy money, Frank is no more likely to join up than he is to take holy orders. Effort is what is needed here, and, for Frank, effort is in short supply.

Instead, as the boys of the village continue to leave, trickling out of the wharf and farms, in groups or alone, Frank stays. He stays through the autumn days of stormy skies and bonfires, as the remaining horses, too old to be taken, plough the rich brown earth. Through the sharp frosts and the tears of the mothers who were promised their boys would be back by Christmas, through empty chairs and muted celebrations. Through each of his children's birthdays, through the constant ebb and flow of fights and almost-reconciliations that define their marriage, the river's tides and the ripening wheat. Frank stays through it all.

And while he stays other things return. Postcards, followed by telegrams, black edged letters from Captains and Majors written in copperplate hand, bits of uniform, cap badges. Folded photographs that have been kept close to skin; often torn, broken, or stained. Yet cherished just the same. Pieces of the men who went.

Occasionally, Frank drinks with men on leave, and Clara imagines him slapping their backs, saying he will see them out there, that he is only a week or so behind them. They are to watch out for him, for when Frank Scott arrives, he will give 'em all a run for their money. And sometimes the soldiers, laugh and slap him back, but no one takes him at his word.

Tonight, Clara sits alone, sewing some rag far beyond mending by a guttering light. Her children are sleeping, and she should be too, but instead she lets the quiet of the house settle into her bones.

As so often at times like this, she finds herself thinking of her marriage, of those early days before Alfred died and Frank really began to change. Before every day started with her trying desperately to keep the children out of his way. Just like she knows his Mam used to try and keep Frank out of his Da's.

Not that Frank's father had the excuse of drink to hide behind. By all accounts, Henry Scott was simply a mean bastard drunk or sober; who never needed any excuse to do what he did. It all seemed to come quite naturally.

Her father-in-law has been dead over three years, but it is

several years longer since Frank lived under the same roof and broke bread at the old man's table. Still, Clara knows better than most, that some ghosts go on haunting you just the same.

No one has ever given Clara any reason why Frank always got so far under his father's skin. Eleanor has told her that, even as a child, playing in the dirt of the hospital yard, it was always and inexplicably Frank who was the target of Henry's rage. And if his mother understood, had any inkling of what had cause the familial line to fracture so spitefully and spectacularly, she told no one; just took it upon herself to try and keep the boy safe.

In the early, more tender days of their courtship, Frank would pull Clara close and whisper into the darkness and the roots of her hair the tales of his childhood, all the while biting down on his confusion and pain. And Clara, holding him in her arms, would vow to make it right.

It was Alfred who was the golden child for no more reason than Frank was the outcast. That was just the way Henry had settled on it; that Alfred, following in his father's footsteps, would take on the responsibility of the hospital. Frank, understanding the hopelessness of the situation had left home when he was no more than a boy, drifting about the fen from job to job, from farm to farm, until his dalliance with Clara was cemented by the unexpected urgency and permanence of pregnancy.

They were eighteen when they married, and of course Frank's father stayed away.

Now, with her mending abandoned in her lap, Clara reaches for the simple warmth of their first years, before Henry reappeared in their lives.

Before everything changed.

On that January morning, Clara had woken early, chilled by the frost creeping up the windowpanes. The other side of their bed was empty, and downstairs Frank shivered at the open front door. She had sat on their sagging bed, a child screaming in the next room, as Frank scrambled for trousers, socks, and boots, unable to believe that it really was Henry's voice screeching up their narrow stairs. That Henry, who was down there, crying in the street, had come to Frank.

From the bedroom window, she watched her husband trying to keep pace with his father, ran towards the river; Henry shouting at other men as they went.

Alfred was missing; had been missing on the marsh all night. And Henry had told Frank this was his chance to prove himself. It was up to him to bring Alfred home.

It was three days before they found the body; carrying it, bloated and stinking, back to the hospital, where they rolled it off the makeshift board onto the iron bed.

Hovering in the doorway, holding her children close, Clara had watched her husband lift his gaze from the lump of flesh that had been his brother and look straight at his father. Tears poured down the old man's cheeks, his weathered hands pushing away the men who tried to restrain him. Feeling Frank's eyes upon him, Henry lifted his head and roared.

'You! You useless piece of shit. You should've saved my son.'

His father lurched. But before he could break free from the men that surrounded him, their hands still sticky with marsh mud, their faces frozen by the shock of Henry's words, Frank had spun on his heels and bolted, pushing past her and his children, past his sisters and his mother, who stood weeping on the path.

Thrusting her children towards Eleanor, Clara had started after him; but it was no use. The exhaustion of days spent searching in the cold, of dragging himself through the sea frets, fear and mud fell away as the adrenaline of grief propelled Frank home. Shedding the skin of the past three days, her husband coated himself instead with a cold-hearted rage.

When Clara finally reached him, she had tried to take him in her arms and love him back to life.

And he turned on her. Turned all his anger, pain, and injustice outwards and there, in the narrow hallway of their home, Frank beat her to a pulp.

It was the first time he'd unleashed his fury in this way, but it was the beginning. And the end.

The end of visiting the hospital, the end of any sense of family. Afterwards, only Eleanor ever made the journey to the cottage. Only Eleanor remained.

Now, in the low light of the kitchen, pulling herself from the past, Clara thinks about moving, about heading upstairs, trying to weigh up what would be best. Whether Frank will be less provoked by her sleeping form or by finding her down here and awake.

Tonight, before he left, they had argued, about the children needing new shoes, new clothes. About the fact that she was spending too much and that she never left him alone. His words had been fast and cruel, and now she wonders if the drink will have turned them into blows. And whether it will matter where she is, here by the hearth or upstairs feigning sleep. For, in reality, what happens when Frank comes home is beyond her control. Setting down her mending, she pushes against the arms of the chair. Before the sound of the key in the door makes her freeze.

Clumsy with drink, Frank's footsteps ring out from the hall. Thumping once against the banister, he curses, before appearing in the doorway, leaning heavily against the worn pine frame. As he scans the room and Clara, holding herself taunt, offers up a silent plea that somehow, he won't see her in the shadow of the chair. But even though his eyes are barely focused, Frank grunts in amused recognition.

'Still up, then.'

Unsure whether this pleases him or not, Clara brings her mending back towards her and nods.

Scrabbling hastily at his fly, Frank lurches unsteadily across the kitchen and out into the yard. From the privy, comes a steady rush of piss and its accompanying groans. Clara's stomach turns. Seizing her chance, she has one foot in the hall when the backdoor slams.

'Where the bloody hell are you going?'

She turns, wordless. By the sink, Frank leans uncertainly, his fly half undone, his trousers wet and stained. Despite her revulsion, Clara knows it's best to stay.

'Thought I heard one of the boys.' She turns back to the table, heart thumping.

Snorting, Frank draws out a chair and sits down heavily. Clara, taking the furthest chair, does the same. They regard each other in a silence broken only by the shift of the last embers in the range. Pulling her shawl a little tighter, rubbing one foot against her shin, Clara clasps her trembling hands about her skirt.

'Who was in tonight?' It is she who breaks the silence, unable to bear the weight of it pressing on her chest.

Frank laughs, without a shred of mirth.

'Well, that's a question! Who was in tonight?'

He coughs, spitting onto her clean floor; looking her dead in the eye, he challenges her to comment. Clara looks away.

'Tonight, my dear, we had a soldier in, another one on leave. One of the New Road lads. And what a fucking disappointment he was!'

Shuddering, she thinks of what the lad will have encountered tonight and what else he might have seen far away from here.

'Not even in uniform, for a start. I mean, what th'fuck's that all about?'

She shrugs.

His face twisted Frank lifts his shoulder, parodying her movements; his bulging eyes goad her to comment.

'Not exactly a hero, eh? Same every time. Not one of 'em'll answer a straight question. No, when you get to the nitty gritty, the things that matter, none 'em will hold their heads up and look you in the eye. Not one of 'em will say, 'I've done it. I've killed one of 'em. In fact, I've killed hundreds of the buggers.'

His voice is rising louder, no longer slurred; warming to this well warn subject has sobered him. Again, Clara makes no reply.

'No pride. No guts. Boys doing a man's job. I've said it from the beginning.'

He lifts his hand and then bangs it on the table. Clara starts but somehow keeps the movement in her legs; she won't let him see her fear.

Without taking his eyes from hers, Frank sneers, then fishes in his pocket, pulling out a piece of paper, torn and ragged. With a smirk, and one finger, he slides it across to Clara.

'Read that.' The words are pips, held and then spat between his teeth.

Without a word, Clara takes it, lifting it to the light, tilting it so the shadows fall the right way.

She reads silently, only reaching the end of the first line, before Frank barks.

'Read it out, woman. I want to hear the bloody words.'

Briefly, she thinks of refusing. But she can see the drink is falling away faster than she can run and can see the intention radiating from the depths of his pupils and the muscle at his temple that begins to contract.

So, she swallows. Then reads.

'Lincolnshire Regiment, recruiting marches. Commencing on Wednesday 10th January.'

She looks up. Rolling his shoulders, Frank slides his palms along the table, the tips of his fingers approaching her wrists. Clara tenses and willing herself not to flinch, returns her eyes to the page. She continues to read.

'Recruiting marches will be carried out in the county by detachments of the Lincolnshire Regiment accompanied by Regimental bands.

'3/4th Lincoln Regiment (200 rank and file) – Saturday 23rd January 1915, Train to Sutton Bridge and march to Holbeach.'

Something in Clara rises and then sinks.

The recruiting officer has changed the rules. Tomorrow the recruiting officer is coming to Frank.

CHAPTER TWENTY-FOUR

ELEANOR – MARCH 1915

The weather is turning, the promise of spring curling along the river and snaking around the fen. Last month, Frank left.

Clara, still forbidden from coming over the river, had managed to get a message to John, who in turn told Eleanor.

'Frank? Are you sure?'

John nodded.

'Clara said he joined up after last month's parade. Apparently, he'll be gone in a week.'

Eleanor had found herself assailed by more emotions than she had known it was possible to feel. Relief and joy that Clara would be free to visit her again, undercut by disbelief at Frank's decision. And somewhere, a quiet and inexplicable fear that, for all his faults, the war would swallow up her remaining brother.

Of course, it was up to her to break the news to Lily.

Over the weeks and months since the letter and its fallout, she and Lily have settled into an uneasy existence. Sharing a small house and not speaking being practically impossible and wholly exhausting, their relationship has slipped into a quiet round of civilities and necessities. But every time Lily tries to steer the conversation to Clara, offering excuses and thinly veiled apologies, Eleanor immediately shuts it down.

Telling Lily about Frank was the most intimate conversation they had shared in weeks.

Predictably, Lily wailed, throwing out references to Alfred, how she couldn't bear to lose another brother. Eleanor left the room in wordless disgust, and by the next morning Lily seemed to have dropped the pretence. They haven't spoken of Frank again.

And when Clara arrived with the children, the day after he caught his train, Lily had kept to her room.

Now, weeks later and in the middle of an afternoon streaked with the promise of spring, John is standing at the door; unexpected and clutching a handful of the palest crocus.

At the sight of him, Eleanor is possessed by that silent but familiar need to immerse herself in his appearance, to take in every inch of him, every freckle, the deep lines of grime on his palm, each nick and scar. To memorise the way his hair lifts from the left side of his brow and how, depending on his mood, his eyes drift from brown to hazel.

Shifting, from one foot to the other, John reaches across the stone step, holding out the drooping flowers. Leaning forward, Eleanor kisses his cold, dry cheek.

'Well, this is a lovely surprise.'

He nods, clearing his throat.

She opens the door wider, stepping aside to let him pass. Lily is upstairs, and the kitchen is warm and quiet. But John steps back, exposing something unexpected and unreadable in his face. Looking down at the path, he shakes his head.

'I'd rather go for a walk, if we can?'

A thought, too terrible to contemplate, bites somewhere at the back of Eleanor's brain, then releases with a snap. She fights to keep her reply even, her tone light.

'Lily's upstairs, if that's what's bothering you.'

Smiling weakly, John holds out his hand.

'I'd rather be out in the open, that's all. Been cooped up all morning.'

Eleanor glances behind her; when she turns back, the set of John's jaw and tilt of his head seem harder, more unreadable than they were seconds ago. As if he has slipped a little further away.

Swallowing her dread, she forces a smile.

'A walk then. Piper'll think it's his lucky day.'

John looks startled, then forlorn.

'Let's not take Piper. Not today.'

She looks at the shadows passing over his face.

'Fine, no Piper. But I'll need a coat.'

Despite her best efforts, she can hear the fear in her voice. As she reaches for her coat, hanging heavy on the back of the kitchen door, her hands shake.

John, stepping out into the garden, does not wait; instead he makes his way up the path, past the narrow beds, now alive with fresh green shoots, pushing through the slowly thawing earth, insistent and strong. Eleanor watches him as he stops and gazes out across the river.

Suddenly the warmth of spring slips away.

Pushing her hands deep in her pockets, Eleanor follows, past the new life and the remaining patches of snow. Dirty patches of white dotted here and there, caught against clods of earth and stones, sparking a memory of white paper sprinkled liberally on this very same path almost a year ago. Quickening her pace, she catches up and loops her hand round John's elbow, resting her head against his arm.

They walk along the riverbank, past the fishing boats and shouts echoing from the wharf, the occasional crack of wood and calls of carters. Above them, gulls wheel against a high, white sky, screaming to one another before diving to the boats, hoping for a share of the catch.

Still neither speak.

They walk until the sounds of the village are lost, swallowed up and replaced by the silence of the fen and the flow of the river. Looking up to the lighthouse and the shimmering marsh stretching beyond, Eleanor's uncertainty grows. Unable and unwilling to walk any further, she releases John's arm.

'What's going on?'

John breaks away. Moving to the edge of the path, he leans against a low fence, ancient, warped by the prevailing winds, and stares out across the river. Without looking back, he calls to her.

'Come here, El.' His voice is soft. Soft and impossibly sad, a voice meant for calming animals or placating children. A voice reserved for breaking bad news.

She hangs back, her chest filled with ice and fear. Her feet rooted on the path, and her body refusing to move. She will not step any closer; not to John or whatever it is he has to say. She shakes her head stubbornly.

Twisting from the fence, reaching across the mud and melting ice, John's fingers close about her wrist, pulling her towards him. Firm, decisive. As if something needs to be resolved.

'Eleanor, please.'

He tugs, and she stumbles, landing against his bulk and warmth. Pressed against him, she is overtaken by the sudden and desperate urge to scream, to yell over the brown eddies of water rushing in front of her. To do anything, something to stop what she knows he is about to say.

It is weeks, months, since he came across her and Lily, and in that time, she has almost convinced herself that what she did, what he saw, was forgotten. Consigned to the past and far behind them. But now, standing here, with her mouth filled with mud and salt, and her belly with dread, she knows she was wrong.

John doesn't want her; doesn't want her family. He doesn't love her anymore.

Face burning, she looks up, into the face, she loves that is now so blank and terribly white.

As he takes her hands in his, John's fingers tremble against her palm. He squeezes them lightly, and the tremors travel like shock waves up her arms.

'I've joined up, El.'

The words are chips of ice. That bounce off her shoulders, peppering her face with their needle points, before splintering into the long grass.

In an instant, Eleanor is thrown from one dark place to another. Her thoughts fragment than scatter into an utter, unbearable confusion.

'Why?' It leaches from her, futile and pointless. A single broken word, whining over the river in a voice that isn't her own. Because her own voice, trapped inside her head, is still screaming at the thought that John doesn't love her anymore. Still trying to keep up.

And yet, maybe both things are true. He doesn't love her, *and* he is going. That John would rather go to war than marry her. Would rather be far away. Rather be dead.

In a sickening, dizzying rush, her mind unlocks. Grabbing at his sleeve, she tugs, shaking it from side to side, desperate to wake them both from this nightmare.

'Is this because of Lily? Because of what I did?'

Her disjointed thoughts, now words, are tumbling like rocks, rolling through her brain and out of her mouth before she has a chance to stop them. Small dams breaking one after the other, as all the thoughts she has held in check for so long take on a terrible life and momentum of their own. Tears, hot and angry, pool at the corners of her lips; grabbing at them with her tongue she floods her mouth with salt, fear, and pain. Leaning forward, she retches a rush of bitter liquid into the earth.

John is there. One hand firm on her spine, moves in slow, wide circles, while the other sweeps gently across her forehead. Eleanor lets her head hang, blood pounding in her ears. She longs to turn into him, yet simultaneously, longs to scream in his face and push him from her. To send him spinning out into the fen.

Wrapping his arms around her heaving stomach, John rests his head against her back, nestling his cheekbones between her shoulder blades. His breath is hot and urgent as he whispers in her ear.

'Eleanor. Darling Eleanor. Please…'

She tries to speak, only to be overcome by the need to retch again.

They stand like this. Eleanor gasping and crying; John's head pressed close to her spine, until finally she sags and then stiffens.

Straightening slowly, away from the mess in the grass, she takes John's face in her hands, gripping his jaw, her fingers working with an energy that sits between spite and an embrace.

'I don't understand.'

So, he tells her; how weeks ago, early in the winter, a gentleman farmer by the name of Chapel had brought his horse into the smithy; brought her himself as all his farm hands had joined up.

'She was a grand horse but worn down. Fretful from the minute she set foot in the yard. Exhausted from the work of three horses, the rest of them all in France. Likely dead.'

Eleanor says nothing. John goes on.

'I'm working on the horse when Chapel starts telling me about his son, how he's away, fighting. You can tell by the way he talks, the way he stands, he's proud of him.'

'Then he asked me, whether I've thought about it, joining up. And I laughed, told him the army didn't need the likes of me cluttering up their battlefields.'

'And? What did he say? Obviously, something to change your mind, or we wouldn't be stood here!'

Her anger bites now. Eleanor can't place this man, Chapel. But she knows she hates him, wants to find him, and rip him limb from rotten limb; to stand up square and spit in his smug face.

John flinches at the force of her words, but his voice remains steady.

'He told me they needed men like me. Men skilled with horses. Gave me a paper, a pamphlet and told me to read it when I had the time. That he'd a friend who could answer any questions. But if I wasn't interested, then he'd respect it, would say no more.'

Eleanor laughs bitterly.

'So, one chat with a stranger and your head's turned? One

word from him, and you run off to play soldiers? Just like that?'

His eyes harden, mirroring her hurt and anger with his own.

'No one is playing anything, Eleanor. Surely you don't believe that?'

Ashamed, she bites her lip and looks away.

'And I didn't *run* anywhere. If you must know, I was angry with him at first. This man, walking in, telling me what I should do? I took his paper, but I nearly flung it on the fire.'

'But you didn't.'

He shakes his head.

'No. I stuffed it in my pocket. Forgot all about it, carried it around for days.'

John is speaking quickly now, as if he can't, daren't, stop.

'Every morning, I put off reading it, meant to throw it out. Until one night I couldn't stand it anymore.'

His hands knot and unknot, as he works his way up to the next part. Trying to find the words to explain this decision, whose consequences Eleanor can't let herself imagine.

'The paper explained it… this thing, called the Remount service. A special group, a company, of men who've a way with horses, can calm them and the like. People like me.'

He breaks off, stumbling over his story.

'And then?' Eleanor spits out the words.

'I went to see Chapel, asked some questions. He arranged for me to go and see his man in Lynn. More questions, a medical. And, well… it looks like I'm away.'

'When?'

The question is lead in the air.

'Next week.'

'Next week! John, you can't go to France next week…'

'It won't be France. That's the thing, the Remount Depot, they are based somewhere south, on the coast. Likely I'll never even get to France. We train the horses up, and ship them off, ready for the next batch to come.'

His voice, thick with pleading, is trying to convince them both that this is normal; sane and safe.

Eleanor, refusing to give ground, bats his words away.

'You'll still be gone. Still hundreds of bloody miles from here!'

'Eleanor…' he reaches for her, her forearms shaking in his palms.

'It's done. I've given my word.'

With an edge of steel, Eleanor asks.

'When? When did you do this?'

A pause, just the slightest delay.

'Does it matter?'

Bringing her hands to his chest, Eleanor pushes hard against him.

'Yes, it matters. When?'

She watches his dark eyes cloud, weighing up the cost of truth. Locking her arms against him, she pushes again, until, finally, she feels him give.

'I went to see Chapel at the beginning of February. Just after Frank left.'

Eleanor cries out, before she even feels the pain.

'What in God's name has it got to do with Frank?'

'If a man like Frank goes, what does it say about me if I stay?'

To that, Eleanor has no answer.

'And besides, it's not just Frank. That dance…' John trails off.

Instantly she remembers that evening. The lack of young men, the eyes that fell on them when they walked in. The anger of the soldier's girl and the feel of her fingers on Eleanor's coat. Turning back to the present, she scrabbles desperately; searching for practicalities, for the things she could possibly control.

'What about the smithy? Who's going to look after that while you're away?'

'Rented. Garmouth, Blacksmith in Long Sutton is taking it on. With the number of horses gone, he reckons he can divide his time and make both yards pay. There will be enough rent to keep it going, with that and my army pay.'

'Marry me.' Eleanor seizes him, hands gripping his elbows.

'What?'

'Marry me now. This week. Before you go away.'

'Eleanor, there's no time.'

'There is! Other people have done it. Got a special licence...'

'No, El.'

'Why not?'

She shakes his arms hard. She can't bear it. To be left behind and not his wife, to be no more than a woman he might have loved.

'When we marry, it will be a proper wedding, not rushed. Not just because I am going away.'

'But John, what if...'

He shakes his head, cutting her off. Lowering his face, locking her in his gaze.

'We will marry. I promise. We'll marry when I'm home.'

CHAPTER TWENTY-FIVE

ELEANOR – MARCH 1915

The fine weather has lasted right up to John's last day, but since mid-afternoon there has been hour upon hour of driving rain. They have made no plans, of what to do or where to go; nothing the rain could truly spoil, but as Eleanor watches the fen out back disappear beneath a curtain of water, as she runs from house to hospital and back again, holding her skirts from a sea of mud, she feels a quiet inevitability about the way things have turned out. Almost a pleasure, that her last memory of John will not be bathed in glorious light, too perfect to be real: that perhaps the normality of it all will make it easier to believe in his promise of return.

Finally, in the early evening, John arrives, harried and harassed from his last day; a day spent handing over keys, explaining the quirks of the furnace to Garmouth and hiding away his best tools. Protecting memories, she knows he can barely stand to leave. Seeing him standing there on the doorstep, stooped and sagging under the relentless weight of the rain, Eleanor knows that it is up to her now. To set him right; to hold him up, just long enough to say goodbye and face this last evening.

She reaches out, ready to pull him into the warmth of the kitchen when she feels Lily, lingering behind her. Instantly, her skin and soul turn to ice. This evening won't, can't, be tarnished, touched, or even brushed by Lily. However painful it might be, she will keep tonight for her and John alone.

She owes him that much.

Reaching for her old oilskin, she steps out into the rain, wordlessly steering John away from the house and Lily, looming ghostlike at the kitchen window. Pulling John behind her, she runs to the hospital. Unfastening the door, she pushes him inside, before locking the door.

There is a stillness to this place that never fails to strike her. Tonight it is exaggerated. Perhaps by the relentless rain drumming on the roof, or by the fact she has never been in here alone with John. The hospital is a dead place, and Eleanor has never wanted to bring him here. Until today.

Now as they stand side by side, with the rainwater sliding from their clothes and their footprints slick on the stripped pine boards, it seems that the silence is all that is holding them together.

The rain thrashes unabated against the narrow windows that are set high in the walls. Each week Eleanor cleans these windows, clambering up the old wooden stepladder. The ladder that never leaves this room, never gets used in the yard or the house. Even after all these years, her father's rules still echoing in her ears.

Everything meant for the hospital must stay in this room. They can't risk infection by removing it. Still, Eleanor keeps up the pretence, despite the empty beds and the patients that never came.

The windows — narrow, horizontal panes — are for the purpose of light and ventilation only, opening little more than a crack. But their view across the fen is unique, a perspective that few have ever seen, a frame that captures just the right balance of land and sky. A protected, secret of peace that calms Eleanor, even on the darkest days.

Briefly, she thinks of sharing their secrets, of retrieving the ladder and letting John climb it; of them spending this last piece of stolen time peering out over the low fields, slowly starting to warm with spring's arrival. Taking in the sky that never ceases to amaze and never ever stays the same.

But tonight the view will be rain-smudged and hopeless, not even worth the climb. Not a gift to send John off with; better one saved for later. Something to tuck away and strengthen the belief that he will return.

In the centre of this unfamiliar space, John looks about him, taking in the six beds placed in two neat rows on either side of the room. Each one made up, sheets and wool blankets, tucked in just the way her mother taught her.

Lighting a single lamp, Eleanor sets it down on a small locker; sitting on the nearest bed, she holds out her hand.

John hesitates before walking towards her and folding his hand into hers, the bed dipping as he sits beside her. The smell of fire and ash cling to his hair; she breathes him in,

storing the scent away.

She looks at his hands, soot-stained and calloused, and tries to imagine them in a place far away, leading horses, holding guns. But it does not seem possible that they will do any of these things.

'Smithy all sorted?' It is she who breaks the silence.

'As much as it will be. Reckon he'll do a good enough job to keep things going…'

The sentence remains unfinished, disappearing into the slight shift of air; talking of going is one thing but talk of coming back seems suddenly impossible, tempting fate.

Holding her face in one cupped hand, John kisses her, pressing down with a force she hasn't felt before. She runs her fingers along his skin, absorbing the sudden pressure of his mouth, and the determined set of his jaw.

Pulling away, he rests his forehead against hers.

'Promise me something?'

Tensing, she waits.

'Promise me whatever happens, you'll remember that there

are other places. Places better than this.'

She nods. Then, lying back on the narrow bed, pulls John to her. Resisting, he looks towards the door.

'It's locked. You saw me lock it.'

He nods. Then, breaking into a small smile, he follows her lead, his body falling against hers. Dipping his head, he kisses her once, at the base of her neck, his mouth lingering in the hollow of her throat, his chin nudging at the fabric of her blouse. Pulling him closer, she arches her chest towards his. Lifting his face, John brings his forehead to hers, pressing against damp skin. Eleanor kisses him, her mouth hard and urgent. Moving her hand from his back, she undoes the buttons at the neck of her blouse, not taking her eyes from his, the sound of their breathing drowning out the drumming of the rain.

'Eleanor, we…'

Her fingers fly from her buttons, landing on his lips.

'I want to. Please, leave me this.'

His thigh moves, slowly against hers, and she lifts her leg, until his weight and need settle to meet hers. Pushing his mouth back into her neck, with his fingers tangled in her hair, he lets out a deep sigh. Eleanor responds, surprised by her own body; by her breath, now ragged and short; by the heat she can feel building between her legs.

John breaks away, the lifting of his weight a sudden, unbearable absence.

'Eleanor…'

'Please…' Her voice is high, urgent. Propping herself up, she leans back on her elbows. Her blouse, open nearly to her waist, gapes as she brings her face level with his.

'I want this.' She repeats.

And with one swift movement it is decided as John pushes her back, one hand on his fly, the other scrabbling in her hair. Peppering her neck with kisses, small, fleeting, and sharp, he works at her remaining buttons, pushing his hands beneath the layers. Softly he cups her breast, rough skin lightly brushing her nipple, and Eleanor laughs. Amazed and lost in the feeling, in the relief and the pleasure. She kisses him again, and again; pulling at her skirt, trying to tug beyond her hips. Lifting his body, John takes the weight from her legs, their hands in a tangle, until finally the fabric yields.

They stop. For a second. Both amazed, watching each other; John's hand resting light and almost unbearably still upon the inner softness of her thigh. Then again, his hesitation. Eleanor shifts and fights against it as her need seeks out his.

Eyes tight, she takes in these new sensations; John's fingers, moving slowly at first before growing in confidence, slipping beneath the fabric, and sinking into her softness. Opening her eyes, the beams above her swim, in and out of focus. Her body, both wholly hers and something entirely foreign, seems in danger of drifting, of floating away further and further away.

Then, without warning, the gentle movement stops. Unable to bear it, she cries out, as John eases her knickers down, past her thighs and knees. A fumble, a lifting of hips and then he is there, she can feel him, between her legs, holding the weight of himself slightly above her. She looks up, into his eyes, which even now are questioning. Hooking both arms around his neck, she nods.

They move together.

She feels him push against her, the initial resistance and the first stab of pain from which she turns her head, determined not to let him see. Instead, she presses all the feeling down through her hand and into his back, as he moves against her and into her again and again.

And when they cry out, they cry together, their tears changing into laughter and then back again. Lying together, wrapped in each other's arms, they cling to what they have done. What they have become on this narrow iron bed.

CHAPTER TWENTY-SIX

CLARA - SPRING 1915

The bed might be empty, but suddenly, and for the first time in the recent years of her marriage, Clara finds she has room to breathe.

In the past few weeks, she has woken each day in the early hours, wide eyed and surrounded by the morning chill, as if some unseen hand has ripped away the bedclothes and left her exposed. But Clara knows it isn't cold that is pulling her so abruptly from sleep. It is peace.

Peace that has settled like snow over her small family since Frank left, blowing unseen but deeply felt under the door, lodging itself in every nook and every cranny. Taking hold of her heart.

Drawing the blankets to her chin, listening to her children turning softly in their sleep, Clara thinks about her husband; trying to picture where he is now and where he might have been. Beneath the sheets, one hand creeps tentatively across the bed, fingers drifting, exploring the space, until a mix of guilt and fear brings her up short, and she snatches her hand away.

Frank has been gone for two months now, nearly three, and last week they had received the first news of him. One short note, written in smudged pencil and delivered inside an envelope so creased, and battered at the edges, it looked like Frank had it in his pocket for weeks.

It had taken her days to find the courage to read it.

The note told her no more than the basics; that he was finished with the training camp and due to be shipped out to

France that week. Six scribbled lines in total. Yet still she felt Frank there; hard to pin down, shifty, and vague. Even the thin paper had an inconsequential feel, reeking of reluctance and delay. Only on the third reading did Clara finally take in the words and allow her body to drop with relief. Putting down her head on the kitchen table, she had wept. Not because her husband was safe, but because he hadn't managed to wriggle free of his decision and find his way back home.

Now, in the blackness of the morning, with the lapping of the river creeping through ill-fitting panes, Clara's mind goes over the note again. She pictures it tucked behind the small clock that sits on the mantelpiece, the one her mother gave them when they married and whose tinny chimes now dominate the kitchen. The same clock whose noise always got under Frank's skin, its steady tick causing him to set his jaw and roll his fists. Many was the time Clara had just stopped winding it, yet another way she papered over the cracks that crazed their marriage.

The day Frank left, after she had stood at the station, dry-eyed amongst weeping women, Clara came home and set the clock going, taking time and pleasure in the fitting and winding of the key. It was the beginning. Of the lightening, the reclamation of her days.

And now the note sits there, absorbing every vibration of the clock that Frank hates.

Occasionally the boys ask her to read it, wanting to know yet again where he is, swelling with their newfound pride. And Clara gives them that; happy to play along with the idea that their father is transformed and about to save them all. Out of the corner of her eye, she sees Molly, silently asking Clara how she should behave.

Clara wonders if the note will be the first of many, multiplying into piles of paper, becoming too fat to wedge behind the clock. Or whether Frank is going to leave them in peace.

Because is it easier to be Frank's wife, now he is far away.

Pushing back the covers, Clara swings her legs, searching

the bare boards, first for the rug and then her slippers. With a blanket about her shoulders, she lights a candle and makes her way down the stairs, pausing to listen to the gentle breath of her babes. Just one of the simple things now studding her day with pleasure, things missing for so long that sustain her now.

As she lights the range, the sky is lightening, and Clara turns towards the day. Now, in her solitude, she needs less sleep; inhabiting a body that is free and a mind that's calm makes her able to face whatever life throws her way.

Scraping at the ash, she resets the fire, and thinks about the letter she sent Frank, formal and bland; a reply agonised over for two days and written for duty's sake. She had confessed as much to Eleanor when she called. And Eleanor had simply shrugged.

The truth is, since Frank joined up, everything about Clara's life has changed. No longer the wife of a man who cannot be relied upon, instead she is a soldier's wife. The wife of a man choosing to serve his country, and by association she commands a newfound respect. Women of the village who have previously avoided her, now seek her out; those wives and mothers who move through the streets in knots, talking constantly of pride and fear. Trying to keep their kin close through words, as if words alone will keep them alive. These women smile at her, assuming that she, Clara, feels the same.

She does not.

Clara, happy in her Frank-shaped void, delights in the silence and the rediscovery of the forgotten corners of her life; slowly becoming used to the fact she can clatter unchecked about the house. Grateful that her children can play, cry, and laugh, without fear of what their father might say or do. That she can take the children across the river to the hospital, which they now treat as their playground; rushing around the echoing rooms, trying out each empty bed, as Eleanor, brought temporarily back to life by their relentless and noisy presence, indulges their joy in this strange, unused place.

And for the first time since Alfred's death, Clara's body is her own again. The only marks on her skin are those left from her pregnancies and injuries of old.

Moreover, they have money. Not a lot, but enough. The army pay is regular and to be relied upon; they are no longer beholden to the flow of work and, worse, to those who Frank has chosen to offend. With the occasional bit of mending, and without her husband drinking his wages away, Clara can now look the landlord square in the eye.

The irony is that just as they find themselves with some security, everyone wants to help. By serving King and Country, Frank, it seems, has made them acceptable, and the charity that was always missing now washes over them in waves. Too little, too late.

But Clara forces herself to be gracious, even though she would like to shut the door in their faces or ask them where they were when her children were really hungry and she spent her nights alone and hurting, wishing her life away. Because Clara knows that the future is uncertain and these women, in their neat hats and low honeyed tones, that set her teeth on edge, might be needed later.

If Frank dies.

It is a thought that Clara spends much of her time pushing away. The emotions that Frank's imagined death conjure strangle her mind like river weeds, threatening to drag her under to places she doesn't want to go. Because if Frank dies, this freedom will be permanent. Never again will she have to lie, terrified, her body stiff, as her husband climbs into her bed.

But how would they manage, and what kind of woman wishes the father of her children dead?

She thinks of Eleanor, so paralysed by John's absence that often she can barely make it through the day; waiting for letters and crying with joy when she receives them, only to start worrying all over again the very next day. For Eleanor, the thought of John's death is terrifying and inconceivable, and when she thinks of it, Clara is racked by guilt.

But the truth is, Clara dreams of Frank dying every single day.

CHAPTER TWENTY-SEVEN

LILY – SUMMER 1915

The post is early today.

So when the letter lands in the narrow hallway, Eleanor is in the village and Lily is alone.

Sitting on the stairs, taking a break from dusting, Lily wonders when Eleanor is going to notice the chores she has started doing. For weeks now, Lily has been picking up all the little jobs that once fell to her sister, but, since John's departure, she chooses to ignore.

Lily now completes these tasks, presenting them like gifts and waiting in anticipation of Eleanor's surprise and delight.

Instead, she is greeted with blank looks and often not even that.

Since John left, Eleanor is distracted and cold. The meals she makes are hurried, thrown together from sparse and fragmented things. Lily, ready to grow back into herself and reclaim their old life, watches in frustration and growing anger as Eleanor withdraws.

Stepping down from her perch, Lily lifts the letter from the mat. It is more of a packet than a letter and, pressing down through its layers, she detects something small and hard tucked deep within. The squat, blocky writing, and the strange square stamp confirm that the letter is from John.

Lily had expected John's absence to please her more; being convinced that with him away Eleanor would come back to her. But three months on, Lily is still waiting.

Yet this letter and its possibilities could change it all.

In the kitchen, Piper, having exhausted himself by yapping at the postman, sprawls, exposing his belly to the open door and the warmth of the day. Lily holds up the letter, in the vain hope that the sunlight might yield some hint of its contents.

At first, John's letters had arrived almost weekly, their frequency slowly thinning over time. In the spaces between letters, Eleanor retreats and Lily hears her sleepless, pacing long into the night. The last few weeks has been one such void, and Lily believes that the letter she holds is the first this month; the letter that Eleanor has been desperate for.

She slips the envelope between her palms, and without warning, finds herself back in the night John went away. Standing ghostlike at this very window, watching as he and Eleanor ran along the path, pressed close against the rain. Lily, gripping the smooth stone of the kitchen sink, consumed with a quiet fury, had seen her sister push John into the hospital and close the door.

Lurching across the kitchen, instantly hot and alive with the unfairness of it all, she had grasped the door handle she expected to be locked, meaning only to give it a good shake or bang on the wood, to create some kind of chaos that she hoped would travel through the downpour and push its way under the hospital door.

But to her surprise, the handle had yielded, and as the door sprang open, Lily had fallen headfirst into the yard. Scrambling to right herself, she stood, panting, and exhilarated, first by shock and icy rain. Then by possibility. Overcome and breathless with opportunity, she laughed out loud and wondered if she dared.

What she dared.

Her first thought had been of the river. Of repeating that dark night of months ago and once more wading out from the bank and waiting. But, with all the rain, the river would be running too fast and would be too hungry. And no one would be out and about in this kind of weather, so there would be no one to see.

For Eleanor had other things on her mind.

But if the kitchen door wasn't locked, then maybe Eleanor would have forgotten to lock the hospital door too. Maybe Lily could just walk through the rain and bang hard on the door. Or burst in claiming to be frightened or ill, woken by a terrible nightmare or the storm.

There, in the downpour, Lily constructed scene after scene, each designed to entirely ruin her sister's plans. With her blouse stuck to her skin and hair streaming down her back, exhilarated and oblivious, Lily pressed on, her thoughts racing, pulling her towards the closed door and what she was about to do.

On the hospital step, her hand just above the handle, she had heard it. Beneath the rain, bouncing on the canopy, jarring and out of place.

The sound of laughter. Eleanor's laughter: high and filled with a joy that Lily hadn't heard in so long. Followed immediately by another sound, this one slow and guttural; punctuated with a brief, almost animal cry, repeated and cutting through the storm. Again and again.

Lily's hand had frozen, curled above the handle, the wood rough against her cheek as she leant forward and pressed her ear to the door. The rain suddenly retreating was replaced by the rhythm of those intense and awful sounds. The shock was total and unbearable, turning her blood to ice in her veins. Cramming her rain-soaked hand in her mouth, her knuckles knocked against her teeth as she fought the urge to scream.

Creeping back through the rain and into the house, she'd run upstairs, where she stood cold and alone, her mind filled with her sister's shame. Avoiding the reflection of her own body, white and ghostly in the glass, she had peeled off her sodden clothes, stuffing them hurriedly beneath the bed.

All thoughts of any kind of disturbance or distraction had been forgotten in the face of the realisation that she didn't know her sister at all.

And the terror of the potential consequences.

In the weeks that followed, Lily had been terrified that her sister was carrying John's child and that they would have to marry, despite anything Lily might do. Her relief when Eleanor's monthly rags had appeared soaking as usual in the outhouse was so overwhelming that Lily had doubled over and retched into the rusty water.

What had happened that night didn't matter. It was just a moment in time, changing nothing.

And now, with this letter maybe, finally, Lily has the upper hand.

Walking to the table, turning the letter over, she sinks into the silence, and the knowledge that there is nothing to prevent her opening it. Entirely alone, she could peel back the envelope and satisfy her curiosity right now. And yet she wants to savour it, this feeling of being back in control. It is so long since Lily has experienced the climb onto safe and higher ground that the air feels thin, and she, in turn, feels heady with relief.

She could keep it. Could slip the letter into her pocket and read it later, when she is alone in her room. Commit John's words to memory, before resealing it and pretending to find it on the doormat tomorrow, or even next week. Then hand it over to her sister and bask in her gratitude and relief. And whatever token she can feel inside, well, Lily might just keep that for herself, tucking it away with Alfred's picture, now hidden beneath the mattress. Doubling her own little secret.

Or perhaps she will simply leave it unread and turn its words to ash by throwing it into the fire.

Eleanor need never know it has been delivered at all.

Her nephew's voice ringing out from the garden is an unexpected shock. Without warning Tommy, red faced and panting, appears in the doorway. Billy and Molly loom behind him, as to her horror, Lily hears heavier footsteps out on the path.

Quickly, she moves to cover the letter with her hand, but it is too late.

'She's got it!' Tommy calls back over his shoulder as Clara, and then Eleanor move into view. Children part, spilling into the kitchen as the two women, dishevelled and white-faced push their way through.

'We met the postman, at the top of the road.' Clara is breathless, eyeing Lily coldly. 'He said there was a letter for *Eleanor.*'

Ignoring the emphasis and implication, Lily stares back. She lifts the letter, raising it barely an inch from the table before Eleanor snatches it from her hand. Without looking at Lily, Eleanor checks first the handwriting, then the envelope's seal, before nodding to Clara; a quiet pale confirmation that the letter is intact.

Lily's stomach fills with spite and acid.

Without a backward glance, the letter pressed tight against her chest, Eleanor steps outside. Within seconds, the garden echoes with the bang of the hospital door.

Whispering to her children, Clara turns them towards the garden.

'Out you go. And take Piper with you. I need a word with *Auntie* Lily.'

But whatever it is Clara has to say, Lily doesn't wait to find out. By the time the last child is pushed over the threshold, Lily is already halfway up the stairs.

In her room, face down on the bed, she screams, long and silent. She had been so close. So close to reclaiming some control.

Turning onto her back, she watches freckles of sunlight dancing on the yellowing ceiling and vows that later, when Eleanor is out walking or even asleep, she will try to find that letter.

And while she is at it, she will go back to the hospital. To check that the long box, with the tarnished clasps is still there, nestled snug amongst the linens.

That her unexpected insurance policy is still safely hidden away.

CHAPTER TWENTY-EIGHT

ELEANOR – SUMMER 1915

Standing in the hospital with John's letter clutched in her hand, Eleanor's breath keeps time with her heartbeat, rushing loud and relentless through her ears. Pulling hard at the air that tastes of dust and old soap.

For weeks she has been trapped in a time marked out by the weather, by cleaning the hospital and walks on the marsh. Days counted by the names of boys who won't come home or who come home in pieces that no one is able to claim. Strange in-between hours spent avoiding Lily or sat in Clara's kitchen, just about held together by silence, tea, and the chimes of her sister-in-law's clock.

Eleanor is depleted. Every part of her worn through and hollowed out, all her energy taken up by waking, breathing, and praying for sleep at the end of the day.

She craves movement and longs for exhaustion; to be bone-tired, and able to sink deep into a place where she can't think about things said and things done.

Or ponder what might have been.

In the dead of night, when despite her aching muscles, sleep refuses to come, she returns yet again to the shape of John's body. His lips. His hands. The fit of two of them pressed together on the hospital bed. Trying to summon up something, anything of the woman she was then; through whose sudden boldness she stole the gift of that night, slipping her hands beneath the blankets and down between her thighs. Sometimes she finds release; sometimes she chokes on tears.

Now, in the quiet of the hospital, Eleanor brings the letter to her face; touching its corner lightly to her cheek and convincing both herself and her body that it is real. Disbelief races to urgency, coursing through her like a flame. Collapsing onto their bed, she tears at the envelope, her fingers clumsy with adrenaline.

Inside are several sheets of tightly folded paper. Quickly she leafs through them, her throat constricting, only releasing when she sees that the pages are truly covered by John's strong, blocky hand. She prises them apart as carefully as her shaking hand will allow, anxious to preserve every precious sentence. As she does so, something small, wrapped in the same thin paper, lands lightly in her lap. She glances at it only briefly, her mind refusing to move from the letters and her desperation for John's words.

For one crazy, unreal moment she is filled with the absolute certainty that she is about to read that John has died; only to realise almost immediately that dead men can't write.

But then, just as quickly, she is overcome by the thought that dying men might.

Forcing her tormented mind to slow, Eleanor begins to read.

There are, in fact, several letters, written and dated over the course of three consecutive and recent weeks. The first, as with all John's previous letters, is filled with details of the training camp; descriptions of weather, horses, and the other men, all making her weep with relief. Each word, each crossing out, is a whisper of John, warm on her skin. Desperate to preserve the ink from her tears, Eleanor presses her fingers to the paper, tracing his name.

Setting the first letter aside, she comes to the second, reading now in large, grateful gulps. But soon she is weeping again, this time in fear and despair. Losing sense of the words, she goes over them again and again. Desperate to change what they say.

But nothing works.

The third letter, shorter, only compounds her pain. She reads it twice, before sinking into a stunned silence; her face wet with tears, she fights to take in what she has read.

John is in France.

Despite all his assurances and promises, he is there; stationed barely behind the battlelines, tending frightened horses who, he writes, are out of their depth.

Eleanor feels the same.

She falls back on the bed, and the small parcel, that dropped from the envelope, moves, nudging against her thigh. Through a blur of tears, she retrieves it from the folds of her skirt and, untangling the fragile wrapping, tips the contents into her hand.

In her palm, she holds a crucifix, hung on a thin tarnished chain. The metal is dull, even dirty in places, but its weight suggests it is silver. All four points of the cross are delicately shaped, each end blooming outwards, clover-like and ornate.

Running her fingers over its surface, she holds the crucifix close to her face. Christ hangs before her, stretched out on the cross; His limbs and features finely cast, His head angled upwards, tiny eyes closed, radiating both sadness and an unnerving serenity.

It is unlike the small, simple crosses worn by the women of the village; small smooth crosses, worn even smoother by years of grasping and praying. Picking up the discarded wrapping from the sheets, Eleanor's eye is drawn to something written inside.

Found this in the mud. Too beautiful for here. Rescued. Wear it for me. J x

Dropping the paper amongst the scattered pages of John's letters, Eleanor gets to her feet and, in front of the foxed mirror set above the sink, fastens the chain about her neck. Transfixed by her own mottled reflection, she stares at its outline, nestled in the hollow of her throat; heavy in the shadow of John's kiss. Closing her eyes, she slides her fingers along metal, dip and bone, sinking, leaning into the memory, her body veering between pleasure and pain.

'El?'

Clara.

Her voice jolts Eleanor back to the present. With a whimper, she pushes the crucifix harder, even closer to her throat. Pressing her eyes tighter, she tries desperately to trap that last piece of John against her skin.

'El, can I come in?'

Eleanor opens her eyes, just as the light in the room begins to change. Clara, inching open the door, hovers uncertainly.

'It's just me, El. The boys and Molly are playing with, well terrorising, Piper in the yard.'

Watching her friend in the mirror, Eleanor is unable to reply.

Clara's voice hardens.

'And Lily! She ran off upstairs, tail between her legs, before I could say anything to her, ask her what the hell she was doing with that letter.'

Eleanor turns from the mirror, her hands shielding the cross.

'I thought about following her, giving her a piece of my mind. But I didn't trust myself not to...' Clara trails off, stepping closer. 'Bloody Lily. Thank God we got back when we did. Meeting the postman like that and...'

'He's in France.'

Her own words take her by surprise. Rising from Eleanor's gut, they soar upwards, smashing one after the other into the ceiling, before plummeting to the ground. The floor tips, and Eleanor tips with it. Rushing forwards, Clara snakes a strong arm around her waist.

'What do you mean? France?'

Strengthened by anger and impatience, Eleanor untangles herself from Clara's hands. Making her way back to the bed, she sinks down amongst the mess of blankets and muddled letters. Lifting her hands, she brings them down in a terrible bouncing rhythm, spitting and beating out each word.

'John! I mean John. He's in France. And he promised me he wouldn't.'

Clara winces. Sitting next to her, her fingertips hover tentatively over Eleanor's shaking knees.

'Oh El, it's war. No one can promise anything. John goes where they tell him.'

'But he gave me his word.' Eleanor wails, shrinking away. She can't be touched. The only person she wants to hold her is John.

Raising her hands higher, she slaps the mattress again and again, each stroke harder. Around her, the thin sheets of paper ripple and lift.

Clara grips her wrists. Pressing her forehead against Eleanor's, she holds her in place.

'Eleanor.' Her voice is gentle but determined. 'It wasn't his word to give.'

Eleanor stares into her friends' eyes, trying to tell her that the thought of John dying is sitting right there; a hand around her throat, fear coursing through her body, hardening in her veins and guts.

But she can't find the words. So, she submits. Lets Clara hold her, her eyes and hands fixing her with truth and love.

Eleanor lifts the crucifix from her throat.

'He sent this.'

Clara, reaching for it, twists it towards the light. The chain pulls, and panic bites gently at the back of Eleanor's neck. Immediately she wants Clara to drop it, afraid she is going to rub what remains of John away. She pulls back, and the cross falls again into the hollow of her bones.

'It's beautiful, El.'

Collecting the abandoned pages, Clara deposits them gently in Eleanor's lap. Without a word, Eleanor lays her hands upon them, pressing the paper to her thighs. Minutes pass, silence broken by the sounds of children's laughter and Piper's occasional bark, drifting from the yard.

'Thank you.' Eleanor squeezes Clara's hand.

'For what?' Clara squeezes back.

'For not running a mile.'

Clara says nothing, but pulls Eleanor into a deep embrace, and over her shoulder Eleanor sees Tommy at the door. Forcing a smile, she untangles herself from Clara and beckons him in.

'Is everything...' He stops, glancing back uncertainly at his brother and sister who have appeared on the step. Molly gives one quick nod, and he stutters on.

'We wondered if...'

Molly steps forward.

'We heard... we wondered if... John...'

'Or Da!' Tommy bursts out, then looks down at his shoes.

Going over to her children, Clara pulls them into her arms, calling to Billy, who comes barrelling in from his place at the door.

'Everything is fine. John is safe and...' she shoots Eleanor a look that is impossible to read. '... and I am sure your Da is grand, too.'

Suddenly filled with shame, Eleanor pushes back her hair and, doing up the button of her blouse, tucks John away.

'Your Ma's right. I was just happy to get a letter after a long time. Now, I think there is some of that cake left...'

Shaking his head, Tommy pulls on his mother's arm.

'Ma, you said we could walk up to the marsh. See if they have started on the camp.'

'Camp?'

Eleanor looks at Clara, who throws her son a warning look. 'Tommy...'

But, turning to his aunt, the boy ploughs on.

'Haven't you 'eard? There's a camp coming. For Germans.'

Something within Eleanor clenches then releases. She barks out a laugh.

'Get on with you. There're no Germans coming here.'

She steps forward, smoothing down her nephew's damp and dirty hair; so like Frank, before Da got in his way. Wrinkling his nose, Tommy thrusts forward a face filled with injustice.

'There will be! It's true. Tell her, Ma!'

Stepping out of Eleanor's reach, he plants himself by the door, bullish and defiant. Both he and Eleanor turn towards Clara who, avoiding their gaze, strokes Molly's hair.

'Clara?'

Eleanor waits. Rolling her shoulder, Clara dips her head as if chasing away an irritant no one else can see.

'Tell her, Ma!' Tommy stamps, scattering clods of mud across the floor. His impatience to be off fighting with the desire that his news should be confirmed.

'He's right.' Clara's words are soft, addressed not directly to Eleanor, but her daughter's crown. 'They say there is a camp coming. Prisoners of War.'

CHAPTER TWENTY-NINE

ELEANOR

Clara's words fall into the room like leaden feathers, each dropping too fast, too heavy for Eleanor to grasp. Tommy, whooping in victory, grabs at his brother; the two of them, dashing across the room, where crouching behind the beds, they turn their sticky fingers into makeshift guns.

'Told you. But don't worry 'cause me and Billy…'

Whipping around, Clara swipes her hand in the direction of the door.

'Enough, Tommy. And you Billy. Out, both of you.'

'But…'

She swipes again.

'I said out! You as well, Molly. Take them out into the yard.'

Tommy opens his mouth, but thinking better of it, ducks out the door. Molly and Billy follow, their boots bouncing, indignant.

Eleanor speaks first.

'So, when did you know?'

Clara sighs, brushing hair and sweat from her face with the flat of her hand.

'A week ago, maybe less? I didn't believe it at first. You know what this place's like. One person smells a whiff of smoke, and by dinnertime the whole village is on fire.'

Eleanor's hands scrabble for the cross beneath her blouse, forcing it down against her collarbone. Hurt and irritation flicker behind her eye.

'But you knew?'

'I suppose I did.'

'You knew.' Eleanor says again. 'When were you going to tell me? Or were you going to wait for me to find out some other way? Maybe in the Grocers? Or perhaps you could have told Lily and let her tell me?'

Clara looks away, a flush creeping slowly up her neck.

'Don't be ridiculous, El. Of course I was going to tell you; that's why we were coming here today. But with Lily and the letter, and you so upset. Somehow, it didn't seem important. And I don't really know much, anyway.'

Eleanor's anger builds, fast and hot.

'I'm not a child, Clara. I don't need protecting. I just want to know.'

Sitting on the opposite bed, Clara reaches across the gap, her fingers snaking around Eleanor's shaking hands.

'I know. And I'm sorry, but I was waiting for… for a better day. And yes, I did want to protect you; just once. You've done it for me often enough.'

Softening, just a little, Eleanor places her hand on Clara's. But the peace is short, before her anger morphs into anxiety, rising again.

'When are they coming? And where are they coming to?'

Drawing back, Clara picks at the blankets.

'Sounds like they are going to be up on the West Bank. On the old Port.'

Eleanor's blood cools, pooling in her head, before racing away. 'The Port?'

Clara nods.

'But that means we'll be able to see it, see them. From the riverbank, from the house, even.'

'Well, maybe. But there might not be that much to see.' Clara's tone is even, but there is no conviction in what she says.

Eleanor is already imagining what it will be like, waking up to the reality of these men every day. German soldiers, here; when the man she loves, the man she has made wait, is in danger hundreds of miles away.

Desperately, she tries to think how this can be avoided. She pictures herself hiding away at the back of the house; keeping to the kitchen, tucked out of sight, becoming like Lily, folding up the little freedom she has. Yet again parcelling her life away.

She won't let this happen. Won't let these men — or the people who are bringing them here — keep her inside; away from the places she knows, the places John loved.

Then comes an image, so logical, so terrible, that it overwhelms her entirely. If the authorities have given over the Port, then maybe they have offered up the hospital, too? And she will have prisoners here, in the place where she and John were; where she gave herself to him.

She gasps, suddenly, fighting for breath. Clara starts.

'El. I know it's a shock, but…'

Eleanor shakes her head, fighting to get the words out and make Clara understand.

'What if they want to use the hospital, too? What if they're going to stop paying us to look after it and hand it over? Or put sick or wounded prisoners in here and expect us to look after them? I couldn't stand it. And Lily…'

A look of shock dawns, then just as quickly, Clara pushes it away. 'I haven't heard anything about that. They wouldn't…'

'But how do you know? Surely, it makes sense. This hospital belongs to the Port…'

'Have you had any letters? Anything to say that's what they have planned?'

Shaking her head, Eleanor pictures her father's old desk. She forces herself to think, to back through the small stack of letters she has stashed there over the past few months, searching for something she might have missed. She has been so distracted since John left, maybe there has been something she has overlooked or misplaced.

'Nothing I can think of, but what if they aren't telling us? Planning to do it in secret, in case we tell some one? Or knowing we will say no?'

Pushing herself upright, Eleanor moves past Clara. She needs to check through those papers. Then she will lock the doors; anything to keep this nightmare away.

Molly, playing at the foot of the steps, looks up at the sight of her aunt, but in her panic, Eleanor barges past her.

Hurrying down the steps, Clara reaches for her daughter.

'Eleanor! Eleanor, where are you going? Eleanor… wait.'

At the back door, Eleanor yanks at the catch, clumsy in her haste; without turning she calls back to Clara.

'I have to check, to see what's going on for myself.'

Behind her comes the drumming of feet, followed by Clara's hand, pulling her, turning her round.

'Eleanor, wait. It'll be alright.'

Her sister-in-law is breathless and flushed, Molly close behind.

Leaning forward and lowering her voice, Eleanor hisses. 'You don't know that. It's war, Clara, just like you said. Who knows what might happen? And we?' She waves her hand in the direction of the river, then the hospital beyond. 'We'd be the last ones to know.'

Stepping inside, she shuts the door.

The house is quiet, the kitchen empty. In the garden, Eleanor hears Clara calling the children to her, then the click of the gate. Lily's feet, light on the boards overhead are followed by the dip and squeak of the bed. Crossing the kitchen, pausing at the foot of the stairs, Eleanor rests; one hand on the newel, one eye on the parlour beyond.

She listens for a moment, before stepping into the parlour and carefully closing the door. Into the small room, which even in summer is cold, smelling of damp and the past. The space they never use.

In the open desk lay this month's bundle of letters, sparse and ordered, just as she left them; beneath them are the previous months, read and tied up with string. Hidden in the drawers are years of paper, receipts; broken edges of the past she can't bring herself to throw away.

Thumbing through the pile, quickly at first, Eleanor checks dates, signatures, amounts, and names. Finding nothing out of the ordinary, nothing amiss, she goes through them a second time. Forcing herself to slow, peeling each letter from the pile, she reads as carefully as she can, as slowly as she dares. All the while her heart thuds, one ear and one eye on the parlour door.

Finally, she is satisfied. There is nothing. Nothing about the camp, nothing about using the hospital.

So, just as in the years that have gone before, all they can do is wait.

CHAPTER THIRTY

LILY – SEPTEMBER 1915

Lily waits until she hears the kitchen door close. Then, hurrying to the landing window, watches Eleanor walk along the bank towards the village, basket in her hand.

The morning light, diffused by the mist hanging low over the river beyond is soft; Autumn is settling over the countryside, creeping a little nearer each day.

When Eleanor is no more than a shadow, Lily moves. Dashing across the landing and down into the kitchen below, ignoring the remains of breakfast and the floor she should sweep, she reaches up to the hospital key hanging by the door.

Plunging into the morning chill, Piper charges out behind her, making crazy circles in the dew; grabbing him by the collar she pushes him back inside and shuts the door.

Taking two hurried steps towards the gate, she checks the road. To her relief it is empty. No wagons, no marching prisoners, none of the upheaval of recent weeks. Nothing that might disturb what she needs to do.

There is no denying the presence of the camp and its inhabitants now. Soon after Eleanor had passed on what she had learnt from Clara, the unfamiliar boats had appeared on the river, docking day and night at the wharf, bringing men who began swarming across the opposite bank. Overnight, the late summer air was filled with the sound of crashing wood and metal, the shouts of men and dust. Then, from no nowhere, a line of huts appeared, squat and low to the horizon, intruding on the view that Lily has taken for granted her whole life.

All through September, Eleanor had returned from the village with news of the first prisoners, who arriving by train, were then driven to the camp in a procession of wagons and trucks. Day after day, Eleanor bustled around the kitchen, filled with nervous energy. She told Lily everything she knew, sharing each piece of grim news, in a voice remote and rage filled. And with every word, every small development, Lily had felt Eleanor's desire to unnerve and scare her. Her sister had used the camp to her advantage. Using every unsettling piece of information to punish Lily for Clara, the letters, John leaving, and everything that had gone before.

And Lily had borne it, because at last, after all these months of tension and near silence, something was bringing them closer together. Even though she couldn't bring herself to sit down at the table with her sister, Eleanor was finally speaking to Lily, slowly reopening her world.

And now, to keep it open, Lily has a plan.

But she needs to move quickly, before the prisoners come. The same prisoners who have been marching past the house for almost a fortnight now. A growing line of men, walking less than a hundred yards from where Lily stands on the garden path. Strangers crawling, within touching distance of their life; upright, with barrows and tools. Intact but somehow ragged at the edges, silently walking through the unpredictable fenland weather, heading to the marsh. And in the evening, as Lily watches from the window and Eleanor pretends they don't exist, the prisoners walk back again.

Reassured that for now at least she is alone, Lily runs lightly down the narrow path. Unlocking the door, she steps inside the hospital; all is still, smelling of paraffin and damp. Remembering to slip off her shoes, Lily hurries between the beds, her eyes fixed on the storeroom whose door is slightly ajar. She will not linger.

She knows what she wants and where to find it.

Squatting level with the lowest shelf, hands shaking in anticipation, she slides the linens aside. Her stomach drops, then turns with relief at the sight of the long wooden box, just where she left it all those weeks ago.

Slowly, she pulls at it, angling the edges carefully, tugging the nearest corner, trying not to disturb everything stacked in front. The case, long and awkward, catches on the upright of the shelving; packets and bottles rattle, teetering above. Lily pauses, heart in her mouth, waiting for everything to settle, before continuing to drag the case clumsily free of its nook.

Lightheaded, she sits back against the wall, her hands resting on the dusty wood now in her lap.

For months now, the presence of this long-forgotten box has been her hope. The knowledge that there was something of Alfred left there, preserved and tucked away.

Now, with it there, under her hands, the temptation to look inside is overwhelming. Her fingers stray to the dull brass clasps. But she can't run the risk of opening it now. Later, she promises herself, pushing the case gently to the floor and getting to her feet. Later, when she has it safely hidden in her room, and there is time to deal with whatever memories she releases.

Carefully, Lily restacks the linens, taking the time to check her work. Eleanor can't know the case is missing. Or that Lily has even been there.

Carrying the box flat over her outstretched arms, its joints heavy against the fold of her elbows, she makes her way back to the house. Her mind flitting between jubilation and anxiety, as the box becomes heavier with each hurried step.

Preoccupied, she rounds the corner of the house; not hearing the beat of boots on the road until it is too late. Jolted into reality, Lily loses her grip on the case, letting it slip, graceless from her arms and strike the ground. The crack of wood on stone and Lily's unchecked cry immediately announces her presence to the column of prisoners passing by.

A line of heads turn as one; untold pairs of eyes, all looking in her direction, each searching out the sound.

Frozen Lily stands, one hand flat against the damp brick of the house, the box lying at her feet. Panicking, she imagines the damage the fall has caused, terrified that the ancient catches have sprung open, and the box's precious contents, are exposed or worse spilling across the yard.

But Lily won't move. She has had years of practice at hiding in plain sight, and she isn't about to stop now.

Just one prisoner finds her, there in the shadows. One man at the back of the line, dragging his feet, half a pace behind the rest. Catching sight of Lily, he slows a little more, his eyes flickering with amusement as he steps just slightly out of line. Holding her in his gaze, he raises his hand and smiles.

The interaction lasts less barely seconds. Before a guard at the rear moves the man on with an indistinguishable shout and the flat of his hand. The prisoner, showing no resistance, resumes his sluggish march.

Three beats, three steps, and then all of them are gone. But still, Lily cannot move.

This is the closest she has come to this new reality.

A passing glance, a raised hand; barely anything. But the gesture has passed through Lily like a knife.

That tight smile and quick half-wave, violations of her carefully constructed world; an unwelcome touch from an alien hand reaching out across the void. Standing there, sweat soaking her back, her legs shaking, Lily knows that these men will come again; the next day, and every day beyond that. And she will look upon them and wonder how the fates have twisted to throw these men into her path. How their dark clothes and low, narrow huts have thrown their unfamiliar shadows across her own little piece of earth.

These strange men, setting off each day in the direction of

the marsh.

Just like Alfred.

But unlike Alfred, these strange, unworthy men always come back.

It is thoughts of her brother that bring Lily back to the present, to the case lying abandoned, maybe broken at her feet. Panic blots out her fear and anger and without checking the state of it she drags the case up, into her arms, before struggling along the remainder of the path.

Not until she is in the safety of her room does Lily, set the case down. As gently as her aching arms will let her, she rolls it onto the unmade bed, hardly daring to look at what damage has been caused by the fall.

Amazingly, the case is still fastened, its clasps — stiff with age and neglect — somehow remaining intact. But as she turns it, the crack is immediate and obvious, running almost the length of the brittle and unpolished box. Tracing it with her fingers, she blinks back tears; the web of radiating splinters feels like yet another attack.

She must check the contents. No waiting until she is calm and is sure she won't be disturbed; if anything inside is broken then Lily needs to know.

Clawing the blankets and sheets away, she lays the box flat and with clumsy, practically-useless fingers begins working frantically at the clasps. She tries one, then the other, pushing with impatience, but time and neglect have done their worst. It is clear that the clasps survived the fall due to being all but rusted shut, and the wood, swollen from the damp of the storeroom, means the lid no longer sits true.

Crying out in frustration, Lily sits back on her heels; trying to think, she asks herself, what would Alfred do?

She needs grease, oil; something to work at the layers of tarnish. There must be something in the shed, even in the pantry, something, anything that might do.

Now desperate to hold the contents of the case, Lily propels herself to her feet; only to be halted by a sudden hammering on the back door.

The prisoner.

It can only be him. Somehow, he has managed to slip away, coming back for a closer look. Standing by her bed, Lily is too terrified to move. Glancing at the battered case, she quickly weighs her options.

The hammering comes again. Followed this time by the sound of the back door opening and footsteps crossing the kitchen floor.

Lily tips forward. The room plunges into darkness before spinning back into focus again. She steadies herself against the dresser and curses her stupidity at not locking the door.

Below, the footsteps reach the hall, before halting abruptly at the bottom of the stairs.

'Eleanor?'

Clara's voice: unwanted and familiar but also filled with something Lily can't place.

'Eleanor? You up there?'

Before Lily can decide whether to call out or stay silent, Clara's heavy tread starts up the stairs. Casting one last desperate look at the case lying exposed on the bed, Lily pulls the blankets over it, then rushes from the room.

Clara can't know it's there.

The footsteps quicken, and Lily, stepping out onto the landing, takes control, positioning herself at the head of the stairs.

'Lily!'

Clara is halfway up the staircase, stops, face flushed and breath short.

'Clara.'

Struggling to keep her voice level, Lily straightens, but her mind is still buzzing with the box nestled beneath the blankets and the hope shut behind the bedroom door.

Moving one step up, Clara peers around her. Sensing her sister-in-laws agitation, Lily thinks again of the prisoners on the road.

'Did you see them?'

'What?' Clara snaps her head back to face Lily, so fast she almost stumbles. 'Did I see who?'

'The Germans, the prisoners of war. Marching…'

But Clara isn't listening; once more, she strains past Lily, before glancing back down the stairs.

'For God's sake, Lily, I've no idea what you're talking about. I need to see Eleanor. Is she at home?'

Bristling, Lily retreats into silence. How dare Clara speak to her like that? In her own house. After banging like a mad woman and barging her way in.

Stepping back to the top step, Lily looms over Clara, staring down into the gloom of the stairwell, anger flaring as she realises that her sister-in-law's unexplained agitation has been subsumed by her usual scorn and contempt. She grips the banister.

Then the thought occurs that it would be so easy. To take just one step forward and take Clara completely by surprise. One quick push and all Clara's patronising interference would be lying at the bottom of the stairs. And no one need ever know.

Lily lifts her hand; the stairwell goes soft around the edges and something within her strains, as if it is about to snap.

Then, somehow, Clara is grabbing *her* shoulder, shaking *her*. Everything happening the wrong way round. It is Lily falling backwards, the steps pressing against her calves as Clara's face looms, beads of sweat falling from her hair.

'Lily,' Clara speaks slowly, quietly, but the sense of urgency is red and real. 'Lily, I need Eleanor. Is she up there?'

Without waiting for an answer, Clara attempts to push past her, and Lily, spinning from pain to panic, can only think of the box. Clara can't see it; she can't go in there.

Turning, stumbling, she catches Clara's arm. Yanking her backwards, Lily shouts.

'No Clara. Stop' Clara moves towards her, but Lily stands

firm. 'She's not up here.'

For a second, they stand, Lily's fingers tight about Clara's arm. Eyes locked, neither giving way. It is Clara's desperation that wins out, changing the moments shape.

'Then where is she?'

'In the village.'

'How long? When did she leave?'

'I don't know. An hour? Maybe a bit more.'

'When will she be back?'

'I've no idea, Clara! Eleanor tells me nothing anymore.'

Clara looks like she is about to reply but, thinking better of it, turns, thundering back down the stairs. Lily follows. Curiosity vying with her anger, she calls after Clara as she heads for the door.

'Clara, what's going on?'

'I told you; I need to find Eleanor.' Clara stops by the gate, shoulders sagging, one hand on the latch, her face shadowy and drained. And Lily is filled with an unexpected, creeping dread.

'Tell her Frank's injured. Tell her he's coming home.'

CHAPTER THIRTY-ONE

CLARA -MID OCTOBER 1915

Clara stands on the gravel drive, watching it disappear through banks of hydrangeas and oak. Picking out the shadow of the hall beyond and regretting her choice of shoes. Her feet burn inside her one good pair after walking from the station. Impractical, she sees now, but it had felt necessary to wear her church shoes. Slipping them on, another step towards accepting this role she has been chosen to play.

The respectable wife of an injured soldier, invalided out and on his way home. Waiting for her somewhere beyond these trees.

Pitching on her feet, Clara feels reality jab once again, deep in the pit of her stomach; pinching her guts just as it did when she received that first letter, at the start of September, almost six weeks ago.

The letter, which was the beginning of a series, all written by different people and sent from different places. The first, from his Commanding Officer, told her that Frank had been injured; a serious shrapnel wound to the head. Short, sympathetic, but to the point, written by a man clearly in a hurry. Telling her only the barest of facts. That Frank was being sent to a hospital back in England. He did not know where she should expect to hear more in the following days.

Clara had told no one. Not Eleanor, not her children. Each night as she kissed them, tucking in blankets and turning out lamps, she fought fear and bright flashes of guilt, knowing she was praying for the next letter.

The one that would tell her Frank was dead.

The letter had arrived a week later. This one longer, written in a sprawling and untidy hand; she picked through its slashes and curves, sometimes guessing at words.

A doctor's letter, telling her that Frank was alive and improving. That most of the shrapnel had been removed, but a small piece, lodged too deep, remained. A week or so more and he was hopeful that Frank would be sent to a convalescent home. Hopefully, the doctor had written, somewhere easier for her to visit.

It was then she told Eleanor, who had wrapped her in her arms and whispered, 'My God, Clara, he's alive.'

And Clara, as her head pressed against Eleanor's chest, it was possible to tell if her sister-in-law's voice broke with relief or commiseration.

Then came a third letter, and a fourth. All sent from this place, this imposing, rose-coloured building, whose many blank windows now wink at Clara in the autumn sunlight, golden spots between the copper leaves and evergreens. These letters were written by a nurse, though they claimed to be 'from' Frank; a careful, rounded hand telling her he was 'progressing and looking forward to being well', how the other men 'were decent chaps' and he was enjoying 'the view from the window of the garden and the lawns.' Frank's voice was so absent that Clara wondered if he had been struck mute. There was nothing of her husband on the page.

She imagined this young woman trying to encourage Frank to fill the letter with hope and niceties, to sprinkle it with these strange touches of joy, and, even in her own despair, Clara sent silent sympathy to this faceless being, wondering how many of these letters she was required to conjure up each day.

Between the letters, Clara's panic and uncertainty grew. Every page, every line, talked mildly of progress, but nothing and no one told her what would happen next. Whether Frank would recover enough to return to the front or whether he would, God forbid, be sent back home. Back to her and their old life before the war. Lying awake night after night, she longed to reach out beyond these pages, to grab hold of someone and shake them, screaming in their ear that the home to which they kept referring simply didn't exist here anymore. That she had swept that life into the river and built a new one, in which her husband and his anger no longer had a place.

Then final letter arrived, and she got her answer; the one she had been dreading most of all. This letter was a summons. A kind, carefully worded one, but a summons all the same.

Frank had been deemed unfit to return to active service. His contribution, though much applauded by King and Country, was at an end. Her husband was to be returned, at the earliest possible convenience, to her own loving care.

Taking the letter into the yard, Clara balled the paper into the palm of her shaking hands and wept.

From the shadow of these trees, Clara has watched others — parents, sisters, lovers, and wives — moving through the iron gates. All pinched at the edges, their skin stretched and uniformly grey.

But now she is alone. And she is glad. She couldn't bear sympathy and understanding; a kind stranger walking beside her, making small talk and jollying her along. If she must walk up to that place beyond the trees, she wants to walk alone. To enjoy these last few moments to breathe.

That's why she has walked from the station, even though the letter said that they would send a car. When she wrote back, confirming that she would be coming, she declined the offer. The thought of having to pretend for a minute longer than she needed was too awful to bear. Making out that she was pleased her husband was safe, pleased he was out of it all and finally coming home. It is what most women in England would dream of.

But not her.

Clara moves quickly, her feet on the path before she changes her mind, before she picks up her skirts and runs. With every step she walks a little faster, until, looking up, she realises that the building that was so far in the distance is now looming, towering above her. And there is no turning back.

Yet confronted with the grandeur of its shadow, she can't help but hesitate. Stepping off the path, she reaches out and rests her hand against the trunk of the nearest tree, concentrating on trying to breathe. To her right a great expanse of lawn buffers up to low stone balustrades that run along the front of the house, turning sharply away at right angles.

The house is sheltered from the wind and the world outside by rows of tall pines and wide oaks. Clara hears the occasional bird song and then, unexpectedly a laugh, that tips to a deep, prolonged cough. She looks up. At the corner of the house are a small group of men, arranged in chairs, carefully positioned in the afternoon sun. Amongst them moves a nurse, her white skirts flashing between gaps in the stone. She pauses, leaning over one man, presumably the one who continues to cough.

The sight of them jolts Clara, reminding her why she is here. That she has no business lurking in the shade of this tree, putting off the inevitable.

She wonders if this nurse is the one who wrote Frank's letters. And if she has been watching her, skulking in the bushes, useless and uncaring; not a wife fit to take her husband home.

And a part of Clara zigzags wildly between burning hope and then shame.

She steps back on the path, straightening her hat and lifting the straps of her worn bag, resettling it in the crook of her arm. Taking one final look upwards, she drinks in the front of this impossible house. In normal circumstances, Clara would marvel and build stories in her head about the people who lived here and danced across its floors. But today is not normal in any way.

Instead, Clara climbs the wide stone steps, determined now.

No more stopping.

A heavy oak door stands open, held in place by a large stone, beyond which a second set of doors, glass panelled, are also open. Knowing she is both expected and late, Clara steels herself and steps inside.

Into a room that is oak lined, where shafts of sunlight fall through a skylight reflected in the mirror-like floor. Within their beams, dust glistens and spirals. Clara has never been in a room like this before; one that makes her feel liquid and unsure, as if she should dance and stand incredibly still, simultaneously.

But for all its beauty, the room is strangely empty, every alcove and mantle stripped of their pre-war treasures. At one side stands a desk, topped by piles of paper and a small brass bell. Clara crosses the room, wincing as her heels ring out. They make such a row she is sure someone will appear.

Yet no one does.

On the desk, written in a copperplate hand, is a card, inviting her to ring the bell that sits beside it. She looks about, before tentatively sending one sharp note up to the high ceiling. Instantly her eyes, follow the sound, finding arches of plaster, and ancient faces that stare back, blanked-eyed in silent judgement.

She waits, but still, no one comes. Frustrated, she strikes the bell again, suddenly furious that she has been summoned here only for no one to meet her.

Then, a door at the back of the hall opens, and a young nurse appears, pushing a soldier in a large ungainly chair; one leg is stretched out in front of him, and gauze obscures a good deal of his face.

For one awful moment, Clara thinks this is Frank; that there has been some terrible mistake, and she is going to have to manage him and that chair, back up that drive, through the streets and up onto the train.

Her hand flies to her mouth just as her stomach curls around her mistake. It's not Frank.

The pair pass. The solider looks up briefly; his visible eye, surprisingly blue, stares out at her from a web of cloth and twisted skin. Clara, steps back is overwhelmed by pity. And memories of her own wounded face.

And then he is gone. Spirited away over shining wood, out into the sunshine, the cheery nurse keeping up conversation as they go.

Clara clutches the edge of the desk, horrified. She longs to follow.

'It is very hard the first time you see injuries like that.'

Clara spins around. Standing behind the desk is another nurse. Older, hair grey at the temples. She reaches out, offering her strong, dry hand.

'Sister Anderson. I am sorry for your wait. We seem to be very busy today.'

Clara takes her hand and quickly lets it drop. She gives a small nod of acknowledgement.

The Sister smiles, waiting, and then asks.

'I am so sorry; I didn't catch your name?'

'Sorry… it's Clara… I mean, Mrs Scott, Clara Scott. I've come for my husband… Frank?'

The words come out in a rush, and Clara has the curious sensation of time both speeding up and slowing down.

Sister Anderson nods. 'Of course, we've been expecting you.'

'I know, I'm sorry. I'm late. I walked from the station and…'

The nurse holds up her hand.

'Oh please, don't apologise. We are rather in the middle of nowhere. Most of our visitors are late. I quite understand.'

Still smiling, she steps around the table, and taking Clara by the elbow, guides her out of the hall, into a wide corridor whose floor is striped with the shadow of a carpet, taken up and stowed away.

Opening a door to the left, Sister Anderson steers Clara into a room that is large but, again, sparsely furnished. A deep window bows out, overlooking a small rose garden.

'This, I believe, is what the family call the morning room.

Consequently, at this time of the day, it is a little dark. You wait here, and I'll fetch the doctor. He will go through everything you need to know.'

She indicates a low sofa, upon which Clara sits, setting her bag down on the rug at her feet.

'When can I see Frank?' She blurts it out, hoping to sound eager and concerned. Hoping that dread hasn't poisoned her tone.

The nurse smiles. Every inch of her is so patient and kind that Clara longs to look away.

'Best you see Doctor MacNeal first. Let him explain what's what. I'll bring some tea.'

A final smile and she is gone, closing the door.

I could still leave, Clara thinks. *It's not too late. To just walk out of here and not come back.*

But she won't.

This time she doesn't have long to wait, as the Doctor and the tea arrive together; one more welcome than the other. Clara rises, but the doctor, small, neat, and clearly exhausted, shakes his head, so she sits. Her stomach churns, as the sister joins the doctor, both sitting opposite her in low armchairs.

The doctor peers at her, his tired eyes framed by wire-rimmed spectacles. His voice, rasping and low is heavy with an accent, somewhere from the North.

'Mrs Scott. Your husband has made good physical progress since he has been with us. His injury was indeed a serious one, but he is a fighter. A man, it seems, with a determination to survive.'

Clara fights the urge to vomit.

She tries to concentrate; to arrange her face into a shape that represents understanding and concern. But all she feels is terror pushing, retreating, before pushing back again.

'As I explained in my letter, most of the metal was removed, but a small piece remains, just about here.' The doctor presses on his temple. 'It shouldn't trouble him too much, but...' The nurse hands him a bottle, which he then passes to Clara.

She stares, unable to move, the bottle and his words feeling so far away. Shaking his hand impatiently, the doctor leans further in her direction.

'Mrs Scott?' It is the nurse now. 'Dr MacNeal is suggesting that your husband might require these, just occasionally, for the pain.'

'Pain?'

'Yes.' The softness of the doctor's tone is blunted by irritation. 'As I explained; there may be some headaches, particularly at night. In which case, your husband should take one of these. But sparingly, mind.'

Clara reaches for the bottle, nods once, then drops it into the bag at her feet.

The doctor looks at her, then stands.

'Right, well I am sure you are eager to see your husband. I will get Sister Anderson to bring him to you.'

Wordless, powerless, Clara, nods again.

'Goodbye, Mrs Scott.'

As the door closes, the room fills with a strange, high cry that Clara can't bear, even though it is coming from her. Covering her face, she forces the balls of her hands into her eye sockets. Trying to stem the tears and shut out what is coming next.

Sister Anderson kneels on the rug before her, one hand on her back.

'I know, my love. It has been a terrible, terrible time for you. But it's over. And you are here. And your husband is coming home.'

Thrusting a small white handkerchief into Clara's hands, she gently shakes her shoulders.

'Your life can carry on, just as it did before.'

She stands and then quietly leaves the room. And Clara looks out at the last of the roses and tries not to wail.

When the door opens. Clara barely recognises Frank at all. Never a tall man, now he seems to have shrunk, losing inches from every part. The uniform that he still wears hangs off his stooping frame, its hems dusty and frayed, as if they have spent a lifetime brushing the floor.

His hair, closely cropped, grows in thin patches, and the left side of his skull is marked out by an ugly writhing scar. Clara, imagining it beneath her fingers, gasps, then sucks hard at the air; hot and peppery, it burns her mouth.

The Nurse's smile, broad and pleading, tells Clara this is a test and one she is failing. Bracing her calves against the sofa, she wills her mind to comply and her body to stay upright.

Looking at Frank, she takes him in piece by piece, breaking him down into smaller, more manageable parts. Her eyes fly instinctively to his hands, with which she has been so well acquainted. His wide fingers, protruding knuckles and flat, heavy palms. Hands that have stroked, pinched, and pummelled her skin by turn. In one, he clutches a large, barrel-shaped bag. The other trembles quietly by his thigh.

'Frank?' A question, not a greeting, cast into the air between them. One word pushed through the half smile that her face can't feel.

And this man they claim is her husband stares back, through eyes huge and haunted, from the shadows and contours of a foreign place. He looks from her to Nurse Anderson, who pats his arm and smiles. Clara sees a vein pulse, worm-like and naked at the base of his head.

She shuts her eyes, counts the seconds, before forcing herself to open them again.

'Clara.' Her name is like a cascade of ice water; as if it has been spoken by a stranger.

The fear she has been nursing since she got the letter drops sharply away. Only to be immediately replaced with another kind of terror. One for which she has no name.

CHAPTER THIRTY-TWO

CLARA - WINTER 1915

It is when Reverend Hirst mentions the camp, that Clara sees something of Frank return. That part she had thought lost stirring, then opening one startled and weary eye. Just briefly, it sparks. The lightning flash of anger she has known so intimately, momentarily brought once again to life.

Silently, she curses. The first time a Vicar has ever sat in her parlour, and already she is damning him to hell.

Since Frank's return, visitors have been sparse. At first the local women came knocking, their thirst for gossip barely concealed by the covered plates they clutched. Clara, smiling weakly through a half-open door, had politely but firmly shunned their offers of help. Until the smiles turned to frowns, then whispers and the doorstep was empty again.

Until today, Eleanor is the only one Clara has let across the threshold. And only if she is certain of her ground.

If the nights have been quiet and the sheets of their bed have remained unsoiled.

Only if she hasn't found herself pinned to the mattress in the early hours with Frank screaming at the darkness above, one hand waving at shadows and the other clamped across her throat.

The fear Clara lives with now is new, and unlike any she has known before; manifesting itself in the desperate sounds that issue from her husband without warning, ripping through the cottage and triggered by things Clara can't count, see, or name.

No matter how hard she searches for a pattern to the outbursts and silences, she can't find a way to make them stop.

But now, the Vicar's words hang in the air.

'And of course, I have been asked to visit the German prisoners in the camp.'

Sitting opposite Frank, Clara tries to assess the danger. His left foot remains still, but the right taps. Toe to heel. Tap, tap, rest. Tap, tap, tap, rest. Faster, slower. Then faster again.

She sets her half-empty cup down on the table, safe from the growing tension in her hands.

'Camp?'

Frank breaks the silence, the old menace flaring as his eyes flash back to the Vicar.

'Why, yes. Up at the old port site. Not a large camp, only around 20 or so men.'

The Vicar looks questioningly at Frank, and then with some haste at Clara.

'Did you not know?'

Clara grimaces, then almost turns it to a smile.

'Frank hasn't got out much since he got back. Still finding his feet.'

'Of course. But I am surprised one of your boys didn't mention it. It's the talk of the schoolyard, I believe.'

Forcing the smile harder, brighter, Clara shrugs, her neck growing hot under Frank's glare. Folding her hands in her lap, she searches for words to take the conversation in a safer direction. She opens her mouth, but it is Frank's voice that she hears.

'Why are they here?'

'Sorry?' Reverend Hirst pauses, cup in mid-air.

'The Hun; why are they here?'

The Vicar shifts away from the atmosphere that has lurched suddenly from strained to dangerous. Frank's vowels, tinder-dry, now ready to ignite.

Reverend Hirst coughs.

'They are working on the marsh, I believe. Building new tidal defences. Useful work, at any rate.'

The forced lightness of his tone trails away like vapour. The words of a man beating a hasty retreat. He drains his cup. The tea, barely poured, makes him wince.

'Well, I must be off.'

Clara rises. Frank does not. Instead, his left foot drums faster, his left hand joining in with an opposite and discordant beat. Clara, swallowing hard, crosses the room, rushing to show the Vicar out.

On the step, the Reverend leans close, his voice low. 'Mrs Scott, I feel I must apologise. For mentioning the camp…'

Clara steps forward, holding the door closed and glancing anxiously behind her.

'You weren't to know.'

From the parlour, she sure she hears something smash. And her stomach contracts, acid burning at the back of her throat. Reverend Hirst clutches her elbow, ploughing on.

'But I should have thought. However, it is all new to me; all of this. These brave men coming home, but what to say, what to speak of. It is hard…'

He smiles weakly and shakes his head.

Clara wants him gone.

Another crash, definite and undeniable. Clara shifts against the doorframe, trying to block out the sound and stay upright.

The Vicar unaware, leans forward, his hands on her wrist.

'I will pray for you, Mrs Scott. You and your husband. And seeing you in church on Sunday, seeing all of you, it would be such a joy.'

She nods, watching as he makes his way to the end of the street. When he stops to talk to a woman on the corner, Clara turns, throwing herself inside. In the shadows of the hallway, she summons the strength to re-enter the parlour and face what she might find.

She walks slowly, opening the door with care; three cups lie in pieces about the hearth, the rug a mess of china and tea.

The drumming of feet and fingers has stopped, replaced by a silence so heavy, so close, that it seems to push up against her body, making it hard to move.

Frank is pulled up, curled child-like, in the crook of the chair; smaller than Clara has ever seen him. Feet on the cushions, his arms wrapped tight around his shins, Frank's hands grip alternate wrists; his fingers squeezing, then releasing, his knuckles turning from white to red, to white again. Yet another pattern Clara can't read, another warning she doesn't know how to heed.

She edges further into the room and the sobbing starts; so gentle, yet so insistent that it causes Clara unbearable pain. China crunching beneath her slippers, she backs away.

Stepping out into the yard, she looks up to clouds so complete and lowering, she finds it hard to breathe. Dragging cold, metallic air across her teeth and tongue, she forces it into her

The yard walls, remaining in shadow, are still white with morning frost. Pressing her fingertips to the brick, Clara feels the ice burn. She remembers last winter, when Frank left, and she was settling in to being. She shrugs off her shawl; torturing herself with the cold and what she has lost.

All the peace she gained usurped by this stranger, who cries out in the night, kicking and punching his way out of his dreams. The same man who will sit, day after day in silence, flinching no matter how gently she sets the kettle down on the plate. Who will suddenly fall on the stairs clutching his head, only able to move when the pills she crams into his mouth start to take effect. Pills that are already dwindling; pills Clara has no idea how to replace. Stiff with fear and exhaustion, she wonders how much longer she can bear this.

The scuffle, scrabbling and scratching, appears from nowhere and comes from high up on the wall. Clara turns her head to see a flash of brown. On top of the brickwork sits a rat, lifting its pointed nose to the chill. Fear grips her, and she raises both hands, desperate to send the creature away.

The rat moves; streaking along the wall, before leaping onto the roof of the neighbouring privy roof. Feet threatening to slide from beneath her, Clara heads back to the kitchen and slams the door.

She can't stand a repeat of last week. Not after today.

It had begun with a muffled thudding, that escalated into swearing and sudden insistent cries. Clara, scrubbing the previous night from the bedroom floor, had flown down the stairs, only to be greeted by an open door, an icy wind and Frank standing on the back step, barely balanced, his left shoe high in his shaking hand.

'Bastard.' His words echoed around the narrow yard. 'Get away, you bastard! You hear me?'

As Clara watched, bemused, Frank launched his shoe. Sailing high through the air, it hit the back wall.

'What in God's name…'

Continuing to scream obscenities at the bricks, Frank removed his other shoe; howling, and possessed by an anger that even Clara couldn't recognise as his own.

Closing her fingers about his elbow, Clara had interrupted the throw, the shoe dropping at his feet.

'Rat. Look over there, huge fucking rat!'

Clara stared. Into a yard, empty of rats, but littered instead with all manner of other familiar objects, all thrown by Frank.

'I can't see any rat.'

It was the wrong thing to say. She enraged him. Almost toppling from the step, Frank grabbed at the shoe, spitting venom into the freezing air.

'I'll bloody kill the fucker…'

On either side of the yard, doors began to open, accompanied by whispers and the sound of clogs on stone. As the presence of curious women swelled around them, the first voice was anticipated before it was heard.

'Everything all right, duck?'

Without looking up, Clara called back.

'All fine. Thank you.'

Stepping in front of Frank, she gripped his shoulders and guided him back inside. Her touch, at first tentative, had grown stronger as she felt the fight slip from his frame. Then, leaving him hunched at the table, staring at his sweat soaked palms as if they belonged to another man, she stepped back into the yard and, under the eyes of her neighbours, piled into her apron each thing her husband had thrown. A brush and pan, his shoe, a wooden ball, a tin of polish, a broken plate. And, only when she crossed the kitchen step, did she hear the women's doors close?

It is the thought of those women that drives her inside now.

Even though she would rather die than hear those sobs that are coming from the parlour once again.

CHAPTER THIRTY-THREE

ELEANOR - FEB 1916

Before Christmas there had been talk of leave, and the thought of John had burnt through the frosty nights until the anticipation had become more than Eleanor could bear.

But it hadn't happened. And, with Clara trapped on the other side of the river and the presence of Lily still unbearable, Eleanor spent Christmas Day alone.

Locking herself in the hospital, she lay on their bed, between the unchanged sheets. Turning her face to the thin pillow and convincing herself she could catch John's scent, could inhale the very last of him; trying to will into being the tips of his fingers, brushing against hers. Remembering how her skin had puckered and pulled under the pressure of his mouth, she lifted her hips and let her own hands replicate his touch.

Then, prising up the loose board and lifting the packet of letters from their hiding place, she curled in on herself and read each letter once again. Finally, she wrote him one more, pouring into it all the crippling longing of her days.

Now it's January; three weeks since she last received a letter, and John has never seemed so far away. Since being in France, his letters have been maddeningly brief, lacking details other than he is well, that he misses home, that the other lads are generally to be relied upon. Signed *unfailingly with love*, they always leave Eleanor wanting more.

Even though, deep down, she knows she won't find John on those thin sheets of paper; amongst script so faint that often she must hold it up to the light to read it. For these letters are merely markers, precious evidence of John's continued presence on this earth.

It is too much, she knows, to ask for this man of few words to pin himself to paper, to preserve himself for her in carefully chosen words. So, unable to step into his world, she works harder to pull him back into hers, clinging to the belief that, when all this is over, John can and will tell her everything. That, on his return, they will lie together, whispering their secrets, both filling in the blanks of time.

But until then, she searches for him in the places they have always been. In the wide-open landscape where she has known and loved him, finding pieces of him on the riverbank and the marshes, in the taste of samphire, where the salt of him dances on her tongue. In occasional warm breezes that blow down the river, heavy with the promise of sea air.

And always in the tangled linen of the barely made hospital bed.

Today, standing on the riverbank, she searches the sky. Looking for a trace of him in the dark, forbidding clouds. Clouds, which have been pushing down on the open fields all week, bursting, clearing, before rolling in again. Resolute, immovable, rolling banks of granite, touching the earth with steel fingers; teamed with a sharp wind, gusting since the early hours. The river, a swirling mass of mud and water, rushes beside her as she turns Piper towards the marsh.

And somewhere in the distance she hears the call of the prisoners and their guards.

It amazes Eleanor how quickly these men have become part of this landscape; their camp and their presence, at first so resented and feared by the village, now settling into the everyday. Just another of the changes and challenges the war has thrown their way.

She is neither drawn to these men nor repelled by them. Her thoughts, like most of the villagers, are too taken up with their own thoughts to give space to these strangers either way. After a letter arrived from the Port Authorities ensuring her, there were no plans to use the hospital as part of the camp, the men had fallen from her mind, quickly becoming an irrelevance. Something else lingering on the fringes of her days.

While Lily continues to make a show of cowering as the prisoners pass the house, Eleanor barely looks their way. Their silhouettes, now familiar and distant against the marsh skyline, fail to raise her curiosity in any way.

She continues, the rain-sodden ground oozing underfoot and Piper, belly deep in mud and delighted, pulling on his rope. Eleanor tugs back, cursing him, despite knowing she only has herself to blame. The foul weather and her own mood have kept them both indoors for days. The short forays into the garden or along the river path have done little to curb the dog's energy levels, and his constant barking and whining are the only reason Eleanor is out here today, with her head down against the wind and her thoughts in disarray.

She remains unaware of the prisoners until they are right in front of her, the sounds of their work having been snatched up and thrown back to The Wash by the wind. Only when the rope goes taunt, and Piper is up on his hind legs barking, does Eleanor realise the men and their guards are merely a few feet away.

She stops, frozen by the unexpected. Beyond the fence, between her and the river, the men, alerted by Piper's yapping, look up as one, their curious eyes all looking her way. Eleanor's cheeks burn. This is the last thing she needs today.

Yanking hard on the rope, she begins to retract her steps, but Piper has other ideas. Filled with joy at the sight of so many new people, the dog lunges, catching Eleanor off guard and off balance. Through her frozen fingers, the rope flies and Piper is away.

'Piper! No!'

Making one desperate grab at the rope, she loses her footing, landing heavily on all fours.

For a moment she can't move, glued to the earth by cold, mud and humiliation; not to mention the pain in her joints. Piper, having ducked beneath the fence, is jubilant in his escape, his barks now met by the calls of men and deep throated foreign laughs.

Reaching for the nearest post, hauling herself to her feet, Eleanor finds herself face to face with a man. Standing on the other side of the fence, his face, pale and slender, hovers somewhere between amusement and concern. His long woollen scarf and heavy coat are both streaked with filth. There is even mud in his fine, sandy hair.

'You are hurt?' His voice, light in tone, is heavily accented, its delivery stilted, immediately marking him out as a prisoners of war.

Unsure what to say or feel, Eleanor's hand tightens on the post top. Out on the marsh, Piper continues to bark.

'Are you? Hurt?' The man asks again, his brow heavy with concern. Rousing herself, Eleanor gives one quick shake of her head.

'No. I don't think so. Just…' She looks down 'Muddy.'

Light laughter drifts between them, as if they were casually passing the time together in the street or on a train. The prisoner waves a single dirty hand at his own body.

'I think I am the same.'

Despite the mud, humiliation and herself, Eleanor smiles; the prisoner smiles back, but his reply is cut off by a shout.

'Schafer! Back to work. Leave the lady alone.'

A guard, barrel chested, strides towards them, ankle deep in mud and fury. He carries both Piper and an immediate air of unpleasantness. The dog's tongue lolls in excitement, his scrabbling paws marking the man's khaki tunic with wide, earthy tracks.

The prisoner nods once at Eleanor before retreating.

'Wait.' She calls after him softly, not wanting to get him into more trouble but somehow not wanting him to slip away.

He pauses, holding her gaze with a quizzical smile.

'Thank you; for checking, I mean…'

His smile widens, just slightly. Then, with a brief glance at the approaching guard, he walks quickly away.

'One dog.'

Piper is dropped into Eleanor's unsuspecting arms, ensuring that any clean inch of her coat no longer stays that way. Humiliated, Eleanor looks up to the guard's disgruntled face.

'Thank you. I...'

'You need to keep better control of that dog, Miss. I am sure you are aware that we have prisoners of war working here and...'

'I know. I'm very sorry. With the weather, Piper hasn't had much of a walk these past few days. He got over excited and...'

'Miss, your domestic dramas are of no interest to me.' The guard is already turning away. 'Just keep control of your dog. We've enough to contend with. If you hadn't noticed, there is a war on.'

Breathless, Eleanor glares at the man. Setting Piper back into the mud, she turns to home, just as the threatened rain begins in earnest. Vertical ice, that slips past her ruined collar, to trickle down her back. Head down, she marches forward, tugging and cursing Piper who, temporarily subdued by adventure and weather, now trails in her wake.

Her anger at the dog, now inflated by the words of the guard, becomes tears of rage and indignation that mingle with the rain. How dare he dismiss her as some silly woman knowing nothing of the war? An irrelevance, unaffected. Yet again, the absence of John strikes her. This time as a physical pain.

She thinks of the prisoner's words, the stark contrast to those of the guard only adding to her discomfort. With Frank's return keeping Clara at home, the man's concern is the first genuine kindness she has experienced in weeks; the only flicker of warmth. And it has come from a German, whose countrymen John is fighting, hundreds of miles away.

Misery, cold and confusion propel her onwards. Pushing the afternoon's encounters to the back of her mind, she concentrates on the ground in front of her and the number of steps she takes. But landscape around her — road, verge, sky — all merge into a hopeless sea of filth and water; everything brown or grey.

Until peering through the rain, she is arrested in her bleakness by something that jars. Stopping her in her tracks.

There, outside the house, leant against the fence, is a bicycle. A bicycle with mud coated wheels, leather panniers and worn saddle. Startling, unexpected. Out of place.

But somehow not.

She walks towards it, blood rushing in her ears. Her stomach tips, her body immediately unbalanced and liquid. Her vision narrows, either side falling away into blackness. Her eyes can only see the bicycle. Piper's lead goes slack in her hands, and he makes a dash for the open gate.

She reaches forward. Her shaking hands lingering over the cracked leather of the seat, before running along the length of the frame; caressing the cold metal, studded with a thousand raindrops. Brushing all of it, every inch, with the lightest touch, Eleanor wills it to be an illusion. A product of her own feeble and inconsistent emotions. A result of her encounter with the prisoner and the guard, this relentless wind and rain.

Standing there in the road, her hands barely resting on the metal, she is transfixed. Frozen. Until a cough, soft and nervous, brings her to her senses. Snatching her hand away, she snaps her eyes up.

A boy, peak capped, stands beyond the gate. Unable to meet her eye.

At his feet, Piper barks once, before spinning off into the garden again, oblivious to his significance. Eleanor shakes her head.

The boy looks down. Fumbling, he reaches beneath his dripping cape, then with cheeks rain soaked and flaming, he takes one step towards her and presses the envelope into her hand.

'Sorry, missus …'

Instantly Eleanor's fingers curl around the paper, the edges, already soft and soaked, moulding to the shape of her palm.

The boy inches forward, and Eleanor moves, just slightly. A

quiet dance of sorrow before the boy is passed and gone.

The air about her fills. With rain, the scent of earth, ash, marsh and sea. A gull cries as, behind her, the river rushes on its way. Darting about the garden, Piper barks furiously at the sky.

And suddenly John, so hard to find, is everywhere. All around her.

Eleanor opens the envelope.

CHAPTER THIRTY-FOUR

ELEANOR

She reads it once. Then, with the paper wet and tight in her fist, she closes the gate and turns once more to the wind and rain.

There is no bursting and clearing of clouds now, just this relentless downpour, rivalling the evening John went away.

Her heart pounding, driving through her body and infecting her limbs, Eleanor runs, head long, face thrust up high, as if to meet the storm, arriving soaked and choking at the bridge.

The footpath is slippery, alive with water, and below the river thunders unchecked. Thrusting the sodden mess of the telegram deep into her pocket, Eleanor moves, along the semi-open sides of the bridge; right to the centre, where, with the marsh in front of her, she finally stops.

Where she screams once; long and loud. Then begins to climb.

Gripping the iron with frozen hands, thrusting her face through the bridge's careful geometry, she lets the frigid air bite her already raw cheeks. And there, half hanging over the bridge, in the cold, familiar companionship of rain, finally her tears begin to flow.

The river, wide and ochre, swirls beneath her, its muddy eddies circling and breaking repeatedly against the pillars. The tide, high and swollen by days of rain, moves below in a terrifying formation.

Eleanor leans further forward, then climbs higher. Blinded by tears, she feels her foot slip from the girders then catch, before slipping again. She clings, suspended; both terrified and thrilled by the pull of the wind. Gasping, then screaming, she pushes her grief out, throwing it to the gathering darkness, fighting against the overwhelming urge to lean further. The urge to release her frozen fingers from the steel and let herself plummet into the bursting river below. Letting the seething water claim her, provide the answer.

The way to obliterate it all.

The hospital and her sister. The bicycle, the boy, the telegram. The promise she never kept.

Let the water take it. Like it took Alfred, almost took Lily. Let it take it all away.

She stays there, undecided, weeping. Clinging to the ironwork, her body thrown sideways, buffeted by the wind tearing along the river and across the fen.

Stays there for as long as it takes for the weather to deaden and claim her feelings. And only when she is completely numb, does she climb down and turn to home.

When she arrives, Lily, predictably hysterical, grabs at her arms, moaning in pathetic relief before she is even through the door.

'Oh Eleanor, oh thank goodness. Where have you been?'

Unable to speak, Eleanor shakes her off and closes her eyes against Lily's questions. Her muscles ache, and water, streaming from her sodden clothes, pools on the floor.

Undeterred, Lily reaches out again, her panic now frosted with rage.

'Look at the state of you!'

Drawing out the nearest chair, Eleanor falls into it. The heat from the range, despite burning her calves, does little to ease the violent shivering that courses through her body.

Relentless, Lily pushes on, throwing out words like arrows.

'You've been so long, out in this terrible wind and rain. And Piper, left alone in the garden? I found him, whining at the door, soaked, with his rope still on. I was so worried. Eleanor, are you listening?'

Hand shaking, Eleanor tears at her collar, frantically but silently pressing her ring against the cross at her throat.

She must say something. Anything to stop Lily's pathetic tirade. But the words, she can't let them come.

'I thought something had happened... Eleanor, how could you? It was... it was like that awful night all over again.'

Eleanor looks up, and Lily stops. Finally shocked into silence by whatever it is she sees in her sister's face.

Unable to keep her head up, Eleanor presses her face deep into her hands, her fingers forming an icy cage around her skull. She speaks just one forced, muffled word.

'Dead...'

Her nails curl inwards, repulsed by her own voice.

Feeling Lily's hand closing on her elbow, Eleanor shrinks away. She grips tighter at her face, her skin burning from wind, tears and rain.

'Who's dead?' Lily is kneeling at her sister's side. Too close. Her hands, insistent and desperate, worm their way up onto Eleanor's sodden lap. She flinches as if her flesh is held against the heat of a flame. Every fibre, every muscle stretches to its limit. Every nerve disjointed, yet strangely alive.

Anything could happen.

Lowering her own hands, she pushes Lily's away. Forcing herself to meet her gaze, Eleanor watches realisation, too bright, too yellow, creep into her sister's eyes.

Eleanor stares, holding Lily in furious challenge. Finally, she spits out the words. She will leave no doubt.

'John. John is dead. John is never coming home.'

She watches; tracking Lily's features as one after the other they rearrange themselves. Hastily ordering their response into the expected and acceptable, settling into a mask of shock and disbelief.

But in the dim light, with the sound of wind and rain at the panes, Eleanor sees then snatches it up. Lily's first reaction. That bright spark of triumph that first flared, flashing like a diamond in the depths of her sister's eyes.

Eleanor leans forward and slaps her.

Leaving her Lily cradling her face, she walks out the room.

CHAPTER THIRTY-FIVE

ELEANOR- FEB 1916.

Since the arrival of the telegram, each day has been knitted to the next by splintered sleep and darkness. Eleanor's head aches, permanently. Her only respite, a silent numbness, through which the occasional and crippling terror of realisation rises unseen.

She is determined not to let the pain catch her. Even though she feels its pungent breath stalking her; teeth snapping at her heels, but it can only pounce if she allows herself to be still.

So from first light until dusk, Eleanor drives herself, moving from house to hospital and back again. Cleaning, folding, sweeping, drowning herself not in the river but in a tide of practical and mechanical things. From sunrise to sundown, she wraps herself in the rough blanket of work and routine.

It is night-time that haunts her, when grief pins her to the rumpled sheets, and nothing can keep at bay what she has. No matter how much her body aches, screaming for rest, the darkness always pulls her back to the truth.

When in the moonlit mirror, she glares, marble eyed with rage, at the woman she finds there. Whose past mistakes, delays and unkept promises shine from her pale face and lay tangled in the strands of her unwashed hair. Lifting her nightdress, Eleanor examines, through half-closed eyes, the places John touched, places she can no longer bear to let her own fingers stray. Into the hollows of her belly, flat and taunting, she balls her fists, screaming silently about what should have been.

And not once has she allowed Lily to comfort her. Not once has her sister even spoken John's name.

It is the middle of the second week when Clara arrives.

Clara, whose grip is immediate and firm, her voice thick with apologies and tears. Eleanor feels her body stiffen.

'I came as soon as I could. Frank...'

Eleanor shrugs.

'Makes no difference when you came. Or if you came at all. There's nothing you can do or change.'

Clara smiles weakly.

'Doesn't mean I shouldn't try.'

Eleanor arranges cups on the table, no saucers, her eyes fixed on the task.

Clara watches her silently, taking the offered cup.

'El. I don't know what to say. When I got your note...'

'As I said there is nothing to say.'

Eleanor is haunted by the truth of her words. There has been no one to talk to, and she is glad of it; worried now that if she starts, she won't know when to stop.

'How'd you get away?'

Clara looks at her.

'What d'you mean?'

'From Frank; how did you get away?' She needs to change the subject.

'Oh,' Clara shifts uneasily, trapped by Eleanor's furious gaze, but she goes on. 'Grocers. He thinks I am at the Grocer's. Where's..?'

'Lily? Upstairs. Keeping out of my way.'

Eleanor pushes her ragged fingernails into the tabletop. She has nothing else to say.

Clara's hand creeps across the table.

'I lit a candle. Yesterday, in the church; for John.'

'He doesn't need a candle.' Her fury comes from nowhere. 'No candles. You call in on the way back and blow the bloody thing out.'

Clara recoils slightly but shakes her head.

'I mean it, Clara! I won't become one of those women. Lighting candles and sitting around, weeping uselessly in churches.'

Clara's voice is gentle. 'Fine. But Eleanor, candle, or no candle. John's not coming back.'

Eleanor looks at her in disgust.

'Is that what you think? That I'm sitting here waiting, hoping he will walk through the door? Or for a letter, telling me they got it wrong?'

Again Clara reaches for her, but Eleanor pushes her chair further away.

'I know he's dead.'

Stalking from the room, she returns with a brown paper bundle that she drops into Clara's lap.

'What's this?'

'John's uniform.'

Clara's hands fly from the parcel, and Eleanor laughs cruelly at her shock.

'Yes. His uniform. It arrived on Monday. With a letter. His Commanding Officer said that he hoped it would be a comfort.'

Lifting the parcel to the table, Clara asks, 'And is it?'

Eleanor snorts.

'No. It feels like what it is. Something abandoned. Dead and cast off. He probably never wore it. Was probably never even his.'

Pacing now, she falls back on the thin comfort of ceaseless movement. She longs to be out in the hospital, working hard and mindlessly.

'Eleanor. Stop.'

Getting up from the chair, Clara grabs at her.

'Look at me.'

Her face is white but determined.

'I'm here.'

Eleanor pushes back, her own palms hot against Clara's hands.

'But he's not. He's not here, and I can't feel him anymore. Can't remember his voice, his smile. Not the colour of his hair.'

Clara strokes her wrist, her thumb dry and cracked, catching on the protruding bones.

'It's shock.' She whispers. 'It'll come back. All of it; I promise. It's all still there, just the shock's hidden it away.'

Wrapping her arms about her body, Eleanor retreats, violently shaking her head.

'It won't. I know it won't. And it's my own fault. All I've got left is a ring, a cross, scraps of paper and cloth. If I'd married him, instead of getting trapped here, then maybe I would deserve to find him again.'

Her face stricken and wet with tears, Clara retreats to her seat, pulling her hands into her lap.

'El, I don't know what to say.'

'Then say nothing. I don't expect you to. But no candles. I don't want people talking, whispering. I won't have John reduced to just another thing this family have lost or broken...'

Clara frowns. 'What do you mean?'

'The Port, Alfred, Lily. Everything.'

'No one thinks...'

'Of course they do.' Eleanor laughs. Turning from Clara, she jabs at the river and the village beyond. 'And you, you of all people, know they do. But not John. I won't have them thinking of him like that.'

Silence, broken by the creak of a floorboard from above. Clara tries not to glance up as Eleanor speaks again.

'What I need is answers, Clara. Maybe I can't see him because a piece of him is missing. All these months, this time he's been away; it's sitting there, this great gaping blank in my mind and I need to fill it. I need to find out what he saw, what he did.'

Clara's eyes instantly harden as her familiar, steady challenge rises through her pity.

'How can you possibly do that?'

Eleanor's cheeks colour, but her voice is steady.

'I don't know. But I know I'll go mad if I can't find a way to get close to him again.'

Biting her lip, Clara nods.

'What about the letter? The telegram and the one that came with that.' She waves at the uniform. 'When Frank was injured, some Major or something wrote to me. Told me a bit, anyway.'

'They told me nothing; just that he had died of wounds behind the battlelines, that he 'knew no pain'. No word about who was with him, what he said.'

She pauses.

'I've been thinking. Maybe Frank…'

Clara picks up her now-cold cup, then immediately sets it down hard against the table. Her reply is razor sharp.

'Frank?'

'Maybe… I could talk to him. About things over there, in France. He could tell me things, about places, things John would have seen.'

Clara's answer is slow, weighed down with the effort of control.

'But they weren't near each other; John and Frank. They were in different places, different regiments. Doing different things. Nothing about it was the same.'

Resting her hands on the table, Eleanor leans forward, her face taut and urgent.

'But surely he could tell me something at least. Anything would be a start.'

Clara shakes her head.

'He wouldn't be much use. You know what he is like.'

Her voice, flat, fights for neutrality, as if she is willing the whole conversation away.

Eleanor pauses; her eyes fixed.

'Maybe I'll pop in. See for myself.'

'No!'

Clara pushes herself away from the table, startling them

both with the strength of her response. Quickly, she continues in a low, softer tone.

'I mean, he isn't up to talking about things just now. In a few weeks maybe, but please not yet.'

Eleanor eyes her curiously, before nodding and dropping the subject.

CHAPTER THIRTY-SIX

CLARA – APRIL 1916

Pegging out last night's sheets, Clara pushes her face into the spring breeze. After wrangling Frank through another fear filled night, she has left him sitting in the parlour, staring at the empty hearth, a mug of tea rapidly cooling by his hand.

And Clara sets about her day; another in the endless string. Each made up of strange, irregular shapes, whose edges cut her peace and sanity clean away. Hours, minutes, seconds; angry shards of uncharted time, into which Frank wakes either silent or incoherent, and Clara retreats, keeping the children out of his way.

Since Reverend Hirst's visit, the camp that has become the focus of his rage.

Whenever Clara sees the prisoners, marching through the village in their ragged lines, their clothes dusty and rough-hewn, she finds herself studying their faces. Each time looking a little harder and wondering if they have the same nightmares, too. If, nestled in the hollow of the abandoned port, the night air rings out with the screams of men; men who continue to fight the enemies they believe are still breathing down their sweating, sleeping necks. If these strangers sleep like Frank, with their fingers curled around eachothers' throats; or if they take it in turns to hold the next man's head as he cries out, thrashing in the darkness.

Each time they pass, Clara fights the urge to reach out and lay her hands on their swinging arms. To still their tramping feet and ask them if they know how to make the screaming stop.

And she wonders who it was. The one who maimed her husband. And why he hadn't finished the job.

Clara is heaving the last sheet onto the line when she hears the front door close with a snap. Pushing the peg onto the fabric, she hurries inside, calling out, trying to keep her voice calm and low, 'Hello?'

If one of the children has been sent home from school, whatever happens, they can't be allowed to burst in on Frank. Not after last night.

But the kitchen is empty. Clara moves into the hall, where her stomach plummets at the sight of the parlour door standing ajar. She darts forward, ready to retrieve whichever child has ventured in there, praying that Frank, after his night of sleepless terror, has finally fallen asleep.

But there is no child. And worse, no Frank.

His armchair sits empty.

Blind with terror, Clara runs the length of the hall, throwing herself into the street, she looks wildly up and down. In an open doorway, a woman scrubs furiously at her stone step, but the road is empty. Stepping out onto the cobbles, Clara cranes her neck, desperate to see past the corner, willing Frank to be lingering in some alley or doorway.

There is no sign.

'Looking for that husband of yours, love?'

The woman sets down her brush, leaning back against the door. The street spins as Clara fights to keep her reply light.

'You seen him?'

'A minute or so since, went down that way.'

Lifting a thick, wet arm, her neighbour points in the direction of the wharf and Clara swears quietly under her breath.

'Everything all right, duck? I did call out, said hello, but he didn't seem to hear.'

'What?... Oh, yes. Everything's fine... just he has forgotten...'

Clara trails off; her mind racing with desperate thoughts of the previous hours and Frank's terrifying unpredictability.

Heaving herself upright, the woman makes her way across the street, her eyes alive with unspoken questions and mock concern.

'I expect he fancied some fresh air, a lovely day like today. After all, we've not seen him out much since he got home.'

Clara says nothing. Stepping around the woman, she scans the street again.

'Nice to have him back, though? After all that time away?' The woman's face twitches with a smile that makes Clara's blood run cold. She wants to scream, to ask her what she means. Even though she knows.

Because everyone knows about Frank and the state he is in. It is reflected in every murmured hello and barely met eye. The echoes of his shouts that bounce like fleas through the night and off the terrace walls; sounds relived at first light, in conversations held on street-corners and in backyards.

So instead, she nods.

'Yes. It's good to have him home.'

When she heads back inside, she's careful not to slam the door.

In the hallway, Clara finds herself trapped by agonising indecision, between terror and rage. Should she go out searching? Or stay here, ready to catch him when he arrives back in a state? Whatever state that might be.

Briefly, she thinks of asking Eleanor for help, then remembering her request to speak to Frank all those weeks ago, changes her mind. Eleanor's grief remains raw and explosive; Clara can't take the chance.

Since getting home, Frank has been no further than the back alley, occasionally slipping out of the gate, where he leans against the wall and smokes; while Clara stands silently in the yard, making sure he doesn't stray.

What can have possessed him to leave the house now? And where has he gone? The woman had mentioned the wharf, but what could he possibly want down there?

Then, as she paces the hall, a vision lapping at the edges of Clara's mind sets her skin off, prickling with realisation and fear.

Frank is headed for the river.

And then, after the initial heart stopping terror, comes the relief; a wave of warmth, so intense, so complete that Clara can't help sinking into it. Quietly, decisively, she steps back towards the kitchen.

Standing by the range, Clara winds her clock. Resting one hand on its wooden case and laying the other lightly against her chest. Closing her eyes, slipping into the ever-thickening silence, she wills her body to find the rhythm she lost months ago.

And when she finds it, Clara simply carries on with her day. With movements, deliberate and practiced, she constructs a show of normality. Cleaning, washing breakfast plates, adding coke to the range; all the time aware of a growing sense of anticipation that settles in the pit of her stomach, only to fly upwards and dance wildly at the base of her throat. Again, and again.

As she waits for the knock that she knows is coming.

She wonders who will deliver the news to her. Who will try and comfort her, and how she will react. In the smoky glass of the kitchen window, she practises rearranging her eyes into some semblance of shock. Pulses of self-loathing course through her, only to be overtaken by a greater force; the rush of desperate and crushing salvation. More than once she almost crumbles, and lurches for the door, only for those selfish, hopeful thoughts to keep her where she is.

If she can wait this out, can hold her nerve until Frank reaches the river, then, maybe, she will finally be released.

The knock comes just before two. Ringing out with an authority that shakes the passage walls. Clara glances at the clock; time enough to receive the news before the children come home. Trembling at her callousness, she waits.

The rapping comes again. This time louder, more insistent

and accompanied by a muffled shout.

The afternoon light cutting across the kitchen falls in bright shafts, through which Clara stares down the passage, towards the front door.

Again, the banging.

Clara is sure that she will never move. Her mouth is dry, and the urge to laugh comes from nowhere. Again, it comes; that rapid, unrelenting tattoo. This time with a finality; the sound of desperation. The sound of someone bringing news.

She draws herself up. From being paralysed by reluctance, Clara, possessed by urgency, runs the length of the hall.

'I'm coming.'

Hand on the catch, gulping at hot air, she counts silently, slowly, before finally opening the door.

On the step stand two men. A policeman and a farmhand she recognises from the other side of the village, someone Frank worked with, off and on, before the war.

Behind them, three women hang back, their faces a blur of intrigue. Clara looks down.

And there is Frank, shrunken, and tear-stained. But very much alive. Inside her head, Clara hears someone scream.

The men are holding her husband upright, but still his legs, bending out at odd angles, sag about the knees. He wears no coat, and his trousers are caked to the thigh with cloying mud.

Slowly, he lifts his head.

'Mrs Scott?'

Clara stares.

'Mrs Clara Scott?'

The policeman tries again, his impatience obvious. Behind him, the women lean closer.

'Yes…' Clara whispers, trying to catch hold of it all, the men, Frank, the women; everything before her that is refusing to come into focus, that insists on staying unreal and remote.

The policeman steps forward, his companion following suit;

Frank jerks towards her. A ragdoll, lolling, his head now down, his eyes roaming the ground.

'Believe this gentleman might belong to you.'

Even now Clara thinks of denying it. Him. Of closing the door and pretending that Frank is no one she knows. But then she sees, over her husband's bowed head, the row of curious and accusing eyes, each fixed upon her.

'He… he's my husband.'

All those faces, staring; blank and hard.

Clara stammers.

'I … I've been so worried… I thought he had… gone for a walk.'

The huddle of women and their whispers are growing steadily in number. Glaring at them the policeman gestures towards the open door.

'Maybe, Mrs Scott, we should get our man here inside.'

'Oh!' Even now, despite her fluster and shame, Clara longs to keep Frank out. To keep the reality away.

But her feet, betraying her, step aside.

'Of course…'

A strained smile from the farm hand and Frank is propelled into the hall. His feet, catching on the edge of the step, drag and bump along the boards. Clara, her back flat against the hall wall, almost shouts. 'You see? He doesn't want to be here. Neither of us want this.'

But instead she says nothing. Just absorbs the impatient sigh of the policeman as she steps around him to close the door; shutting out the women still standing in the street, bathed in their gossip and glee.

'Where to, Missus?' The farmhand grunts, as Frank sags ever lower at his side.

Hurrying forward, temporarily brought to her senses, Clara pushes at the parlour door.

'Sorry, in here. Bring him in here.'

Half carried, half dragged, the men set Frank down heavily by the window, dropping him into his abandoned nest of unread newspapers and blankets. And proving she is a wife who cares, Clara removes his wet shoes; lifts a blanket from the pile and drapes it around his thin, trembling shoulders. As her hand brushes his arm, Frank flinches. The policeman clears his throat.

'Perhaps a word, Mrs Scott?'

Blushing, she nods, following the men into the hall.

'I'll be off.' The farmhand is already at the door.

'Thank you…' Clara begins, but the latch clicks, and the man is gone.

'Your husband is, I believe, not long back from the war.' The sunlight has vanished now, leaving the policeman's face little more than a shadow. Shivering, Clara leans against the wall.

'That's right. He's been back a few months now.'

She glances at the parlour door, lowering her voice to a whisper.

'He was injured… it's taking some time for him to recover. To become himself.'

The policeman nods, his face stern.

'And does he do this often?'

'Do what?'

'Wander, Mrs Scott. Get lost. Become so disorientated and distressed that he is unable to find his way home.'

She shakes her head, both angry and ashamed.

'No. He hasn't left the house for months. Not until today.'

'I see.'

Then, almost unable to bear the answer, Clara asks, 'Where was he? Found, I mean?'

'A young lad found him wandering across the fields. Making no sense; kept shouting out something about looking for the camp. The lad followed him and sent his friend off for me. By the time I arrived, your husband was quite distressed.'

Bowing her head, Clara forces out the next question.

'He wasn't by the river?'

'The river? No, thank goodness. If I were you, Mrs Scott,

I'd be keeping a closer eye on your husband. A man who has fought for his country deserves some care. Some attention. And maybe keep your door locked?'

His face is stony, cold with accusation, and Clara's heart sinks as she leads him to the door; beyond which, the voices of those women continue to rise and fall.

After he leaves, Clara heads to the kitchen, where, sinking into a chair, she weeps.

Frank has no intention of ending his life. Clara sees that now. He is set on a course she can't understand; driven by experiences she will never know. But once again, Frank's behaviour is dragging her family back to their lowest point.

No longer is she the wife of a soldier, seen through respectful, grateful eyes. She is the wife of a lunatic. And a poor wife, at that.

One who can't keep her husband secure and his reality out of the village's way.

CHAPTER THIRTY-SEVEN

ELEANOR- JUNE 1916

'Eleanor, please!'

Clara holds tight to the door as one startled, bloodshot eye peers out from the hall.

Eleanor stares back, confused. She has already been to the back door and found it locked.

'Clara? What's going on? Let me in.' Eleanor pushes against the door; it heaves back in response.

Clara's voice is low and desperate. 'Today is not a good day. Please, Eleanor, just go.'

'Are you ill? Let me in. I can help.'

The eye shakes as Clara pushes harder against the door.

Eleanor's concern turns to anger. That Clara should shut her out like this when she, Eleanor, needs her help. When she needs to see her brother.

In this anger, she finds realisation.

'It's Frank, isn't it? Has he hurt you? Or the children? Clara, just let me in.'

Stealing a quick look behind her, she sees the twitch of skirts, and a curtain fall.

Again, the door nudges back against her foot.

'Clara!' she hisses. 'What's he done?'

'Nothing! He's sleeping. Eleanor, I'll come tomorrow to the hospital. But please not now.'

Dropping her eyes, Eleanor inches away from the door,

immediately feeling Clara's weight ease. Seizing her chance, she charges, shouldering the door with a final, desperate push; Clara staggers back as Eleanor falls ungainly into the hall. Grabbing at each other, they stay upright. Rocking, breathless. Staring.

'What's going on?' Eleanor speaks first. Clara waves her hands, her eyes gleaming.

'Shh. Frank is asleep.' Shaking her hands free from Eleanor's, she turns for the kitchen. Eleanor follows, past the parlour door that is shut and silent.

Already at the table, Clara holds her head in shaking hands. Eleanor sits, dizzy with confusion and a growing sense of shame. Never before has she forced her way into this house, into anyone's house.

'Clara?'

Clara, her face still covered, sighs.

'Keep your voice down. Don't wake him up.'

'Has he been wandering again?'

Clara's hands fall, revealing eyes, sharp and wide. 'What do you know about that?'

'Not much since I haven't seen you in weeks. But I've heard things, in the village. Where's he been going?'

Clara sags.

'He's trying to get to the camp. He's got close a couple of times but then he seems to…' she trails off.

'Seems to what?'

'Forget where he is or start screaming, crying. Then, usually someone comes along, scoops him up, brings him home.'

Clara runs her hands through her hair, her wedding ring rolling on her finger.

'They bring him back, and he goes quiet. Or gets angry. Or, if I'm lucky, he sleeps for days.'

'Have you told anyone?'

Clara laughs; hollow and harsh. 'Eleanor, the whole bloody village knows.'

'I mean a doctor. Have you written to that place, the hospital he was in? Maybe they could help?'

'And who'll pay for that? No. We're on our own.'

'You've got me. Or I thought you had.'

Clara looks at her, exhausted.

'Eleanor, I've barely been able to leave the house. And when he sleeps, if he sleeps, there are errands to be done. Will you have a cup of tea now you're here?'

Eleanor watches Clara as she moves around the kitchen, each movement meek and measured. Filled with guilt at the real reason she is here, the questions that, despite what Clara has told her, still dance in her mind, unanswered.

She tries to push the thoughts away, but her mind refuses to follow.

'How are the children?'

'Scared. And Molly's angry, but she hides it well. The other kids are giving them a hard time. Saying that Frank,' Clara inclines her head to the wall, 'is mad.'

'Speak to the schoolmaster!'

With a hollow laugh, Clara whispers.

'What use would that do? He probably agrees. And besides, it's hard to prove them wrong.'

They drink their tea, Eleanor searching for a safer place from which to restart this conversation, but between her grief and Clara's despair, she is trapped. So, despite resolution, made and repeated quietly to herself as she stood in her own kitchen, she steps into the place she knows she shouldn't go.

'Have you asked him, why he wants to go to the camp? Is it to do with the things he saw? In France?'

'No! I haven't asked. And don't you ask either.'

Clara's face, flaming now, is split by the tight, white line of her lips.

'I mean it, Eleanor. You've no idea what it's like living in this house, with him. Trying to read his moods. The endless crying… the shouting, the stench. I can't, won't stir it all up.'

Eleanor listens. But still, she refuses to drop her gaze. Her grief is sitting there, a rod running the length of her spine. A rock in her chest, pressing at the edges of her reason, blunting the force of Clara's pleading.

'But if you haven't tried, how do you know…'

'Know what?'

'Know that it won't help. Telling you might help him somehow.'

'For God's sake, Eleanor. No! I can't take much more.'

Clara's face is wet with tears, an odd clicking sounds coming from the back of her throat.

'Please…'

In the yard something bangs, and both women start. Immediately on her feet, Clara casts an anxious look into the hall, but the parlour stays quiet. Hurrying to the back door, she slides the bolt and peers out.

'The gate, blown open.' With another glance behind her, Clara dashes out and across the cobbles.

Eleanor seizes her chance.

Closing the kitchen door behind her, she moves into the hall, towards the parlour door. Her mind is racing, but there is no time to pause, no time to think; turning the handle, she steps inside.

The room is dim, its curtains drawn against the June sun, casting a thick green light across the mismatched furniture. The air, stale and close, throws her back to Lily's room, two years of despair. The absence of hope.

In a chair by the window sits Frank. Huddled, shapeless. Despite the heat, he is covered in blankets; he seems somehow shrunken, little more than a body beneath a pile of rags. Eleanor fights the shock of his appearance. She knows her time is short.

Listening for Clara, she hurries towards him, her feet

catching on the rug as she goes. Stumbling, she lurches, one hand landing heavy on her brother's arm. With a cry, he jolts awake, eyes immediate and terrible against the darkness, panic etched in every line of his face.

Terrified and desperate, Eleanor holds her hands up, pressing her finger first to his lips and then her own.

'Shh, Frank, it is me... Eleanor. I've... I've come to see you.'

Shrinking from her touch, drawing his knees up, Frank pushes himself back, into the crook of the chair.

'What... what'd you want?'

His voice is high and uncontrolled, his eyes rolling. Ducking down beside him, she tries desperately to calm his agitation.

'Just to see you. That's all. See how you are...'

'Clara!' Frank shouts, his neck stretched tight, reaching high over her head. 'Clara!'

Then, pulling at the blankets, tugging them up to his face, Frank turns his head, first this way and then that. Sweat beads across his forehead, filling the room with a sour, animal smell.

'Frank... please...' She has never seen her brother like this, seen anyone like this, and she knows that she should move away. But her questions are still there, unanswered. And this might be her only chance. She pushes on.

'Frank...' She whispers, urgent and rapid. 'Frank, I need you to tell me. About the war. About what happened over there.'

Clara is behind her now. Her feet stamping out Eleanor's betrayal on the boards. Even without turning she can feel her fury.

But she doesn't care.

For her, grief is everything now. Pushing up and consuming her, impossible to check. Propelling her through the streets, it has brought her here. She can't stop now.

'Eleanor...' Clara speaks and the room tips, but Eleanor fights; against every nerve that jangles and the sweat now pooled at the base of her spine. Against the pain, so raw, clawing in her chest. Writhing and alive, reawakened by her sudden, furious resolve.

Frank is shaking, pulling away from her hands, and with every twitch of his limbs, every jerk of his head, Eleanor's anger grows; spiralling, out of control, snapping the final threads of her patience.

With furious tears coursing down her cheeks, she lunges forward. Grabbing at his face, pulling his head towards her, she snarls, 'Tell me. What did you see in France?'

Her face close now, pressed against his. Pushing her fingers deep into the hollows of his cheeks, she forces his terrified eyes to meet hers.

Clara yanks on her shoulder.

'Eleanor! Stop!'

But there, in that second, beneath her fingers Eleanor feels something change. In the tension of her brother's jaw, the set of his teeth, the years fly away, and suddenly they are children again, fighting in the yard.

Frank wants to hurt her. She knows it. She can *feel* it. Just like he did back then. To win the fight and silence her. Eleanor holds on tight.

Struggling against her, Frank jerks his head, left, right, then back again. But Eleanor holds firm, lifting her fingertips and pressing her nails deep into the stretched and waxy flesh of his cheeks.

She spits her words, carefully, deliberately into his face.

'I need to know… what was it like… why… how…'

It is too much.

Frank roars. Twisting from her grasp, he flings his head away, kicking out and sending Eleanor to the floor. Her arm, outstretched, knocks the poker from its stand; it skids across the hearth, the sound of iron on stone ringing across the floor.

Now it is Frank who looms over her, his face crimson and contorted.

'Hell!' He screams. 'Nothing but bloody hell. And that's the truth.' The words are hissed into her face, his spittle sour at her mouth.

Clara sobs, frantic, pulling at them both.

But still, this is not enough.

Scrambling, both hands on his chest, Eleanor rises, forcing her brother back. She is not done yet and within her she feels a fractured triumph. For herself, for Clara and her children. That she alone has broken his silence.

But she needs more.

'Why hell? Define hell.' She pushes him hard. Caught off balance, he strikes the wall. Grief making her determined, anger making her strong. She has broken him; she can see it.

But still she pushes on.

'Don't be a coward all your life, Frank. Tell me!'

She has him in a corner now. Back against the wall, frozen, he stares. Not at Eleanor but beyond, eyes fixed over her shoulder. Then, his face drains, and without warning, he falls.

Descending into a sound that is like nothing she has ever heard before.

Animal screams, bursting forth, echo around the small room. Turning from her, Frank begins scraping at the plaster, pulling at the walls. Beneath a sheen of sweat glisten the scratches she has inflicted, a mark of the chaos she has left.

Eleanor recoils. Peeling herself from the dusty floor, all her triumphant anger retreating. To be replaced by overwhelming shame.

She did this.

Sweeping Eleanor aside, Clara descends, wrapping her arms around her curled and sobbing husband, whispering gentle words that Eleanor cannot hear. Should not hear.

Slowly, she reaches out, but reaching behind her, Clara slaps her hand away; she half turns, her eyes hard and bright with disbelief. Her face hot with betrayal.

'Go. Now!'

Eleanor flees. With Frank's screams ringing in her ears, she wrenches open the door, expecting she will find the whole village there, lined up in the street, waiting to judge her family yet again.

But the road is silent; only sunshine and shadow stand on the cobbles; there is no one to see the horror on her face. Head down, she hurries, desperate to distance herself from what she came for and what she has done. She is less than ten feet away when she hears the door slam.

'Eleanor.'

She stops but does not turn.

'Eleanor!'

Suddenly, Clara is alongside, in front of her, her face white; the front of her dress stained with something yellow and vile. Recoiling, Eleanor tries to step away, but Clara's hands close about her arms, like irons. She pushes closer.

'Don't you dare! You can bloody well stand there and smell what you have done.'

Eleanor pales, but she holds Clara's eye.

'I had to know.'

'You! You had to know? I warned you. I begged you. Not for his sake, but for mine.'

'I'm sorry...'

'Sorry? For what? The fact you made him lose control of his guts? Or that he hasn't told you some lovely tale to take away your pain?'

Eleanor says nothing. Clara grips her arms tighter, before pushing her away. Her face is twisted, eyes shadowed and blank.

'John's dead. And I'm sorry, more than you can ever know. But this,' She waves her hands over her soiled, wretched clothes, 'This won't bring him back.'

Clara turns on her heel. And without looking behind her calls out.

'Until you can accept that, don't come here again.'

CHAPTER THIRTY-EIGHT

LILY - LATE JUNE 1916

Walking back to the house, Lily wades waist deep in half-ripened wheat, skimming the bobbing heads; letting them drift beneath her palms. On the horizon, the marsh shimmers beneath a June haze. Swallows swoop and wheel amongst the first lasting heat of the year, through air soft with summer's sudden tranquillity.

Unlike the atmosphere at home.

In another month, if the weather holds, they will begin the harvest, men and their horses coming right up to the hospital land. In the past, Lily has made a show of hating it; the days of shouting and calling, all those people so close.

But there is no one to pretend to anymore.

Eleanor, lost in grief, is impossible to reach; each week slipping further and further away. The early fury and nights of weeping, now replaced with silent indifference, through which Lily moves unnoticed and unacknowledged. Every morning, she lies in bed, wondering if Eleanor will speak to her today.

But even though it cuts Lily to find herself such an irrelevance, she has found, buried in the silence and unseeing, a new freedom, which she takes advantage of most days.

Each day she walks. And each day the distance grows slightly longer; at first by a few yards or steps, heading in a different direction or setting out at different times of the day. At first, she had walked only across the fields, keeping to the land tucked behind the house, but recently she has ventured along the river, half hidden by the lea and curve of the bank. And yesterday, for the first time in months, she found herself standing in the shadow of the bridge.

Each day, she returns and waits for Eleanor to confront her about where she's been.

It hasn't happened yet.

Reaching the edge of the garden, Lily pauses in the long grass. Beyond the lupins and hollyhocks, Eleanor kneels, poking half-heartedly at the sun-baked ground, working at the same few inches of soil, automated and aimless.

Standing there in the shadow of the hospital, Lily decides that things can't continue this way.

She makes her way along the side of the house, slipping unseen into the kitchen, where she fills a mug with tepid water. After quenching her own thirst, she refills the mug and heads outdoors.

As she approaches, she sees Eleanor tense, only to focus with even more intensity on the dirt.

'Eleanor?'

Lily holds out the mug, but still Eleanor keeps worrying at the ground. Biting back anger, Lily pushes the mug closer.

'Eleanor, you need to drink. It's too hot.'

Eleanor drops the trowel. Without looking up, she reaches for the water, her throat rippling as she drinks. She sets the empty cup down on the ground between them, as if handing it back is too intimate. Lily fights to keep her voice level and light.

'Do you want more?'

'No. Thank you.'

The thanks are an afterthought, but inside Lily smirks.

'I don't mind.'

'I said no.'

Eleanor resumes her digging, working with the same unreachable aimlessness. Lily wants to scream. Instead, she moves closer. Her shadow, falling across the grass, touches her sister's face; Eleanor flinches and shifts back into the sun.

'I understand, you know. About John. About how you feel.'

Silence, heat, sudden stillness. Lily tries again.

'Eleanor, I said, I know how you feel.'

One laugh, short, mirthless, but Eleanor's eyes stay fixed on the ground.

'How can *you* possibly know how *I* feel?'

Lily flushes in anger and in triumph. This question, for all its scorn and indignation, is the most Eleanor has said to her in weeks.

'Alfred, of course. You know, Eleanor, how much I miss him, every single day.'

The trowel lands with a dull thud on the baked ground. Eleanor turns to her sister, finally meeting her eye. Her face, etched with disgust, is painted with disdain.

'Don't, Lily.' Eleanor holds up her hands.

'But I loved him.' Lily whines. 'I know what it's like to feel this…'

In an instant, Eleanor is up, drawn into an immediate tower of looming rage.

'He was your *brother* Lily. Our brother. John was…' Eleanor stops, pressing her hand against her throat. 'It's not, it will never be, the same.'

Pushing past her, Eleanor heads towards the gate; Lily, shaking with indignation, is hard on her heels. Determined that Eleanor will no longer dismiss her, furious that she has claimed such a monopoly on grief.

'No! You're wrong, Eleanor. Alfred's death…'

Eleanor, spinning around, cuts her off.

'You know what happened to Alfred. We, you, saw his body.'

Lily flinches as the June heat drains away. Instantly she is back, trapped in the cold of the hospital, faced with silent, exhausted men. Her brother, discoloured and swollen, lies half covered on the bed. Surrounded by cries of her mother, the terrible curses of her father. Recoiling from the pinch of Eleanor's fingers, as they press deep into her arms.

Fighting the memory, she stares at her sister.

'At least you've been spared all of that.'

'You see!' Eleanor sprawls across the path, her arms wide and fists clenched. 'That's just it. You don't understand at all.'

Lifting her head, gulping at the air, Eleanor cries out. 'That's the thing that no one understands. I don't want to be spared. I want to know. I want to see a body, to see and taste what he suffered. I want it all.'

'Eleanor…' Lily recoils, horrified. The days of silence, the indifference. Everything of the past weeks. All of it is preferable to this.

'Don't you see? I *want* the truth, to know his story. I want, need, what you have and take for granted every day.'

They stand, neither moving, as all the weeks of silence lie shattered, splintered at their feet. Until, finally, Eleanor turns, dropping to her knees, ready to attack another patch of earth, before her attention is caught by something on the road.

And even though she is still reeling from Eleanor's outburst, Lily hears it too. The familiar echo of boots on the road. Prisoners, back from the marsh; back from walking the same paths as Alfred, jumping the same creeks in places they've no right to be. Her recent walks have never taken her to the marsh, and they are the reason why. Lily might be hoarding courage, but these men represent the last genuine shreds of her fear.

Eleanor stands, pushing herself forward, into the sounds that are growing louder, each footstep more clearly defined than the last. Calls, shouts, a whistle, a laugh, all ringed with rising dust. The music of camaraderie that, coupled with the heat and the fallout of Eleanor's words, steals Lily's breath and fills her with the urge to run.

In all the months the prisoners have been here, since the first time she was taken unawares, Lily has been careful to keep herself hidden whenever they pass.

But Eleanor has never hidden. Now, walking along the fence, she presses ever closer to their approach, stepping into their shadows, which are touching the garden; long and lean. Lily moans and, without turning, Eleanor spits, 'Lily, go inside.'

But she can't. She is caught, the moment and the heat refusing to let her move.

Out on the road, the shadows are becoming men, their dirty feet drumming on the road. Closing her eyes, Lily counts the beats, and her mind, tethered to the rhythm, tries to push the prisoners on their way.

Suddenly, the sound changes, descending into a shuffle of stones and irregular beats, accompanied by urgent shouts. Confused, Lily opens her eyes.

The lines of men are split, disordered, and at the rear a prisoner lies, motionless on the road. Through a tangle of bodies, Lily can see his sprawling legs, his head crooked in the dust. Other prisoners gather around him, their voices panicked, alien and low. Out front, one guard shouts, as another picks his way through the crowd.

Then, from the corner of her eye, Lily sees something, someone, move. A flash of blue and white as Eleanor darts through the gate, out onto the road.

CHAPTER THIRTY-NINE

ELEANOR – JUNE 1916

As yet unseen, Eleanor waits, her body taut with the consequences of her inexplicable actions; filled with both an electric energy and a curious immobility. Standing in the road, she can no longer hear Lily's cries.

Minutes pass and still the men remain unaware of her presence, all their attention entirely on the prisoner. On the man whom she now recognises as the one who spoke so kindly to her the day the telegram arrived. She watches as his limbs twitch and then still, his pale hair, dark with sweat, flat against his livid skin. Briefly, his eyes open, before rolling back into his skull.

Eleanor knows the signs of heatstroke, the scourge of a summer spent in the open fen. Under unforgiving skies and unrelenting sun, the locals have learnt the hard way that sparse shade and deceptive sea breezes make the marsh a dangerous place to spend the length of a burning day.

The prisoner remains propped against the knees of a companion, while others pull frantically on his arms.

'Anton? Hörst du uns? Anton?'

'Schafer! Can you hear us? Schafer, stop buggering about; come on, open your eyes.'

'Wasser. Gib' ihm Wasser.'

'Water, he needs water.'

Eleanor watches as a canteen is passed from hand to hand, and with it, growing panic. Snatching it from the last outstretched fist, a guard lifts the bottle to the prisoner's gaping mouth, where it tips with a dreadful ease. The merest trickle wets his lips before dripping, useless, to the parched earth.

'Damn! More water, we need more water.'

This is her chance. Hoping her voice won't let her down, Eleanor calls out.

'I have water.'

As what feels like a thousand tired eyes turn as one, a thrill passes through her body. Finally, she is seen.

'Water.' Eleanor repeats. 'I have water. And a hospital.'

The words, ridiculous and huge, hang in the stifling air. Immediately self-conscious, Eleanor points towards the house.

'There.'

A voice booms from the left. Even before she turns towards it, Eleanor recognises the inflection and sneer. It is the guard who chided her for Piper's escape; his stiff, greying moustache, now beaded with sweat, bristles with the effort of being polite.

'Water would be most appreciated, Miss. And if there is a hospital that we haven't been told of, then maybe a doctor could help.'

Ignoring his barely concealed scepticism, Eleanor replies.

'There's no doctor, but we have beds.'

'No Doctor? So, what kind of hospital is this?' Grimacing with disbelief, the guard steps closer. Eleanor's fists curl, her nails sharp against her soaking palms. Lifting her head, she looks straight ahead. 'The kind that is here. The kind you need.'

He raises an eyebrow. Behind him comes a shout. The first guard, cradling the prisoners head, leans closer.

'Sir, I don't like the look of him.'

The officer swears, and the swell of power knocks against Eleanor's rib. She has what they need. For the first time in forever, she is in control.

'He,' She points. 'Has heatstroke.'

She aims for confidence.

'Too much sun, not enough water. Or shade. Because you've had him working out there in this heat all day.'

The guard chokes. Shaking but emboldened, Eleanor continues. 'Heatstroke is serious. He could die.'

She sees it. The fear, flashing beneath the anger.

Without taking his eyes from Eleanor's, the guard shouts, 'Private Wilson, let's take this *lady* up on her kind offer. Get hold of Schafer. Private Brody? Keep the rest of them out here.'

Eleanor's heart constricts, then lifts. Fighting to keep her face steady, she nods, as a knot of men haul Schafer to his feet.

'Follow me.'

The garden is empty; Lily is nowhere to be seen. With cruel delight, Eleanor muses that maybe, finally, she is giving her sister something to worry about. Hopes she is watching from the house, frightened and unseen. From behind her comes a groan, barely masked by unintelligible whispers of encouragement and the sound of heavy feet moving over stones. Two languages lap her ankles, wrapped about themselves.

She moves quickly, not looking back, worried she will lose her nerve. With sounds of illness and exertion trailing her, she moves through the gate, past the house, where Lily's white face flashes briefly at the window. Triumphant, Eleanor smiles.

They reach the hospital; unlocking the door, she steps aside. 'In here.'

The room is dark and cool. Blowing with effort, the men move to set Schafer down on the bed.

Their bed; her's and John's. With its memories and unchanged sheets.

'Not that one.' Her tone, sharp and breathless, is enough to make them freeze.

Private Wilson blows out audibly, casting her a weary look.

'Sorry.' Eleanor stumbles for an explanation.

'That one's broken, one of the legs. The next one,' she indicates along the row, 'is fine.'

Wincing, they manoeuvre Schafer, setting him down none too gently on the mattress. He lands with a moan.

The Officer, steps forward. 'Since there is no Doctor, perhaps you could attend to him in your capacity as a Nurse?'

Eleanor laughs, shaking her head.

'No doctor. No nurse, either. Just a hospital.'

The Officer frowns. Ignoring him, Eleanor walks to the small sink. She fills an enamel jug and three mugs almost to the brim, before taking them to the bed where the other prisoner and the Private stand panting.

'Water.' She announces, handing both a mug. With muttered thanks, they drink greedily; the accent of the prisoner reminding her again of the risk she is taking.

Handing Wilson the final mug, she nods towards Schafer.

'For him. But just sips; don't let him gulp.'

The officer looms, still frowning, at this situation he doesn't understand and can't control. Eleanor feels the surge of power once again.

'This man needs a doctor.'

She nods. 'I agree. But as I said, there's no Doctor here. Head into the village, ask for Dr Cook.'

Flinching at orders given by a woman, the officer clears his throat and looks to the group gathered around the iron bed. Efforts to give Schafer water are having little success, and his face remains pale and clammy. Lifting his concerned gaze to that of his superior, Wilson slowly shakes his head.

A look of irritation passes over the Officer's face.

'You!' He points at the second prisoner. 'Come with me. Wilson, keep an eye on him. I will be back with the doctor as soon as I can.'

Making for the door, he looks at Eleanor. 'All this is most irregular. I would suggest that you head back into the house, let Wilson deal with it now.'

Eleanor's rage ignites and flares.

'I will stay where I see fit, in my house, my hospital. Especially when he,' She points towards Schafer, 'Is lying in one of my beds.'

Shaking, she braces herself for his response, but unbelievably, the Officer turns, pushing the prisoner out before him. For a moment there is silence, before it is broken by a laugh. Eleanor spins. Wilson grins.

'Not sure old Stewart has been spoken to like that before. Let alone by a woman.'

Ignoring the comment, Eleanor approaches the prisoner's bed. 'How is he?'

'You tell me; you're the nurse.'

'I told you, I am not a nurse!'

'Oh ay? But you've a hospital in your backyard? Seems a rum do to me.' The guard's eyes, bright and full of mischief, provoke in Eleanor a lightness she had thought lost. Despite herself, she smiles back.

'It's a long story, one we don't have time for.' She gestures at Schafer's pale form. 'He needs cooling down. Can you take off his shirt?'

Back at the sink she fills a bowl and looks for cloths.

'Thought you weren't a nurse?' Wilson fumbles with Schafer's shirt buttons, pulling the rough cotton aside.

'This isn't nursing. It's common sense.'

Wilson sits Schafer up, and together they peel back his shirt, exposing a shoulder, knotted, and scarred; puckered and livid, a red ribbon of skin running hard against the white. Eleanor wonders if John's body was buried with such marks.

She feels Wilson's eyes on her.

'Alright?'

She nods. Pulling the shirt from Schafer's back, she fights the temptation to run her fingers along the twisted ridge, wondering if the feel of it will tell her what she longs to know. If the answer to John's missing months rests in this ruined flesh.

Instead, she thrusts her hands into the tepid water, soaking, squeezing the cloths. She hands the first to Wilson.

'Sponge him down.'

Taking one herself, she lays it gently across Schafer's neck. Then steps away.

She could soak another cloth and help Wilson, but she doesn't; unable to trust her hands to stay away from that scar. Looking at it, the way it snakes over Schafer's shoulder, grazing his collarbone, Eleanor feels so close to the truth that it hurts her heart.

'Ugly bugger, ain't it?' Wilson cuts through her thoughts. He lifts the cloth, gesturing towards the scar.

'That, there. Not a pretty sight.'

He looks at her face. 'We can put his shirt back on, if it's upsetting you like?'

'No. I told you. We need to cool him down.'

'Sure?'

She nods.

He carries on, working in silence. When the cloth is warm, she hands him another, cold and soaking from the bowl. One more cloth, a change of water and Wilson speaks again.

'Lots of the prisoners have 'em. Scars. Worse than his.' His face is tight with something Eleanor can't read, something so intimate she looks away.

'Sorry, I shouldn't have said that. Don't know why I did.'

'I don't mind, really.' Eleanor's tone is light, even though she is finding it hard to breathe; as if she is balanced, teetering on the edge of an abyss, reaching down towards the knowledge she craves. Willing both her heart and thoughts to slow, she feels her way, working out how to proceed.

'Do they talk about it? About how they got the scars?'

Wilson shrugs. 'Not to me, not to any of us. But maybe to each other, in their own language and late at night.'

Wilson's eyes darken, and she wonders what he's seen. Thinking of Frank, and his terror, she pulls back, trying a different path.

'I suppose them speaking a different language… well, that can't help.'

'Most of 'em have a bit of English. Enough to get by. Schafer here, he's nearly fluent.'

Wilson laughs.

'Speaks the King's English better than me, does old Anton.'

Plucking the information from the still air, Eleanor stores it away. She looks at the prisoner's pale form.

Anton.

His name feels like a gift; his presence, a defining moment. This man from far away has changed this place forever. Their first true patient. The realisation makes her brave.

Dipping another cloth, fearless now, she hands the rag to Wilson.

'What about you? Have you got any scars?'

Wilson stares at her in disbelief; is silent so long that her heart drops, certain she has gone too far. And then he laughs.

'You say what you think, don't you? No, Miss, I've no scars to speak of.'

'Eleanor, please.'

'Eleanor.' He repeats it softly. 'George.'

The bed behind her suddenly seems both closer and further away. She steps back, the mattress pushing into her calves, filling the moment with silent memories and the taste of John in her mouth. That need, that desperate urgency rising again.

She pauses, gathering her thoughts.

'Have you been over there? To France?'

George dabs at Anton's skin until it glistens.

'No… Eleanor.' Soft, hesitant, he tries out her name. 'No France for me. Just here.'

His tone is quiet but final, shutting down her questions and closing the path.

She turns to Anton. He appears more relaxed; the low moaning having all but stopped, he is slipping towards sleep. She lays her hand lightly on his forehead, moving briefly to his chest, her fingers itching as they brush across his scar.

'He's cooler.'

Lifting his feet, Eleanor untangles the sheet, gently drawing it up and over his legs.

'Let him sleep.'

The two of them, Eleanor and George, stand either side of the bed. Without the cloths in their hands, they are suddenly awkward.

'You go on, now.' George breaks the silence. 'I'll wait with 'im. That doctor, he's bound to be on his way.'

Eyes still on Anton, Eleanor shakes her head. Leaving means facing Lily, whose reaction she wants to keep at bay. And besides, she isn't done here.

'I'll wait.'

She brings two chairs to the side of the bed. But George hovers, shifting from foot to foot.

'Do you have a privy I could use? All that water, you see.' He nods to the empty mugs.

Leading the way to the door, Eleanor leans out into the yard; flinching in the sudden afternoon light, she shows George where he needs to go.

'You'll be alright? In 'ere with 'im?'

He nods at Anton whose eyes remain closed, his breath regular and deep.

'Think I'll be safe, don't you?'

Still, he looks unsure. Eleanor nudges him forward. Suddenly she wants him gone. 'Go. I'll be fine.'

He holds up his fingers. 'Two minutes.'

Only when he is out of sight does Eleanor close, then bolt the door.

Standing, trembling by Anton's bed, she takes his features in. His hair, now beginning to dry, is a fine strawberry blonde; his cheekbones are high, almost sculpted, and beneath the raw red of sunburn, a fine cascade of freckles bridges his nose. His sleep is contented, his breath regular. The water, the bathing, have worked their magic; the doctor isn't needed; perhaps he never was. No matter, it has bought Eleanor some time.

With shaking hands, she lifts the damp sheets, inching them from his body while watching his face. Just slightly his eyelids flicker, his head shifting against the pillow; Eleanor freezes, but immediately he settles again. How young he looks, how vulnerable and alone in this narrow bed.

She peels the sheet away, draping it lightly over his ankles. His hands lie palms down, his fingers, long and still; the dirt of the marsh is creased about his nails. They are unlike John's hands, unlike the hands of any man she has ever known. They are, she thinks, the hands of an artist. Of someone earning his living amongst paper and ink.

Her eyes travel the length of his body, along his navel where fine, downy hair grows. His chest is smooth and, like the rest of him, pale and slight. The comparison to John's body, with its breadth and dark, abundant hair, is immediate and stark.

Her gaze comes back to the scar. Beginning at the collarbone, where, jagged and raw, the skin is twisted and unnaturally stretched. Against the rest of his body, so fine and unblemished, the scar belongs to another landscape, leaping out like the border to an alien terrain.

Eleanor reaches forward; her fingers, held in mid-air, begin to shake. She braces her elbow, gripping it with her other hand, but it makes little difference. Straining, she listens for the sounds of George on the path, but the thudding of her heart, coupled with the ragged rush of her breath, make it impossible to hear.

She needs to act now.

With a gasp, Eleanor lowers her hand, letting her fingers settle, ghostlike, on the rim of Anton's puckered skin. Immediately she recoils, snatching them away, before forcing her hand down again. Tentatively, along the seam of flesh, over each ridge and bump, her fingers creep. Her skin prickles with sweat, excitement and fear, waiting for something, anything to fill her. Waiting to find the truth that she is so sure is there.

Up and down her fingers move, drifting over ruined flesh; she wills the magic of realisation to begin.

Then from the garden come men's voices, muffled but getting closer. Eleanor freezes, her hand still in place. She has run out of time. Desperation biting, she presses her fingertips hard into Anton's raised skin.

Without warning, his eyes fly open; his pupils, wide with panic, gape against the grey of his eyes. Eleanor yelps and snatches her hand away, but Anton is too quick. One grab and his long, white fingers hold her wrist fast.

Their eyes lock as Anton presses her fingers back to his ruined skin.

The voices are outside the door, the boots on the step.

His face open and steady, Anton pushes Eleanor's hands in harder, so hard that she feels the sharp edges of his collarbone beneath his ruined skin. Something rises within her, rises and then stills.

The handle turns, as hands push against the locked door.

"'ello. 'ello? What's 'appened? You alright in there?' George's voice is high and alarmed.

Eleanor tries to pull her hand away, but still Anton holds it close. She can feel the scar burning, writhing beneath the flat of her hand.

Slowly, Anton lifts his head, pushing his mouth to her ear. Eleanor's body tenses with fear, longing, and anticipation. She is ready for the truth, whatever it might be.

Above the insistent banging at the door, Anton whispers. 'Thank you.'

CHAPTER FORTY

CLARA - JULY 1916

Clara hasn't seen Eleanor for weeks. Not since that awful day when Frank and Eleanor had locked themselves together on the parlour floor; spite, rage and grief etched on their faces. Both reduced to something so base, it was, and remains, beyond Clara's comprehension, still filling her with the same revulsion and fear that made her cast Eleanor out into the street. The fear of being tainted by their wildness, that sudden, inconceivable lack of control.

But still, the absence of Eleanor is a sore that festers, spreading into weeks of loneliness, compounded by Clara's own confusion. There are days when every part of her longs for Eleanor and their friendship, for her old life, and the return of everything they have lost in this war.

So it is to Eleanor that her thoughts and hope spring when the knock comes at the door.

With one quick glance, she confirms that Frank is still in the yard, sitting hunched on a kitchen chair. His gaunt face, half in shadow, his hands, working their way around each other; fingers flicking and grasping at things that aren't there.

Clara steps out of the kitchen, collects herself, then opens the door.

Dr Cook stands there.

Within seconds, Clara's mind flies, from blank to every terrible possibility.

'I haven't called for you.' She blurts it out, too unnerved to care how rude she sounds.

Smiling, the doctor tips his hat and Clara's thoughts turn immediately to Frank. Pulling the door to behind her, she whispers, 'There is no one ailing here; you've the wrong house.'

Again, Dr Cook inclines his head, giving Clara a slight, strangled smile. The man — young and relatively new to the village — seems as uncomfortable as she. Maybe more.

'You are right, Mrs Scott, I haven't been called. But...' He looks behind him. 'But there is something I would like to discuss with you. Maybe inside?' Removing his hat, he indicates the closed door.

Clara hesitates. She can't have him in the house, but neither can she have him standing out here. There is enough for the neighbours to feast on already, what with Frank's vanishing acts and the noises that crash through the night. Against her better judgement, Clara steps aside.

She leads him to the parlour door, then, changing her mind, directs the doctor to the kitchen; away from the place where the echoes of Eleanor's visit still linger. Silently, she checks the window, making sure Frank is still safely in the yard. In this run of warm weather, he has taken to sitting outside. While the nights are just as bad as ever, the recent days have been quieter, more predictable, and Clara takes her relief where she can.

Without speaking, she draws out a chair from the table and indicates to the doctor he should sit. She fills the kettle and tries to quash the thousand crawling thoughts that are scurrying through her mind. She is sure he is here for Frank. Maybe someone on the street, a neighbour sick of the late-night screaming, has been to see him. Or has the hospital sent him, deciding after all these months, for some unfathomable but wonderful reason that Frank should go back? Clara's heart lifts at the thought. Glancing at Frank sitting beneath the sill, she reaches forwards, gently pulling the window shut.

'Mrs Scott?' Dr Cook's voice is soft. 'Mrs Scott, won't you sit down?'

Clara keeps her back to him, her reply unsteady.

'When I've made the tea.'

'Please…' He speaks slowly, feeling his way. 'I don't… I am afraid I don't have time for tea. But I do very much want to talk to you.'

Putting down the pot, she turns reluctantly to the table, where the doctor, half standing, points to the opposite chair with his open hand. Clara flushes with indignation; how dare this man tell her to sit in her own damn house?

But she sits because she wants this over. No matter what he has to say, after everything she has been through, it can't be any worse.

Clara decides to get in first.

'If this is about Frank, I don't know what you've heard, but he's much better now. This sunshine, it's done him a power of good. He's out there now, in the yard, sitting out there, meek as a lamb…'

The words tumble, one into the other, each coated with a brightness she doesn't feel, her obvious desperation undermining everything she says.

Dr Cook smiles weakly.

'That's good to hear, Mrs Scott. But I am not here about your husband.'

He draws in a short, barely audible breath, and Clara waits.

'I've come about your sister-in-law.'

'Lily?' Lily is the last person she expected him to bring up. 'What's she done now?'

'No, although this does affect her. No, my concern, if that's what it is…' He trails off. 'My concern is about the other sister. Eleanor?'

At the sound of her friend's name, Clara experiences a simultaneous softening and hardening of her heart.

'Eleanor's ill?'

'Not ill, as such. Perhaps troubled?'

Clara can't make head nor tail of the things he is saying. She wishes that, whatever it is he wants, he would just come out with it and stop this talking in riddles.

'Troubled? Is this about John?'

'John is the young man she recently lost? Her fiancé?'

Clara nods. Her mouth is dry; beneath the table her fingers pluck at her skirts.

'Then, yes, in a way. Mrs Scott, forgive me; it is hard to know where to start.'

'Maybe the beginning?' Clara wishes he would get to the point. She is no nearer knowing what he wants, and Frank won't stay put forever. She looks towards the yard. 'My husband, he will need me...'

'Sorry, I see how...'

'Please, just say what you need to.'

'Last week.' He stops. 'Last week I was called away from my rounds to attend to a prisoner who had taken ill, a man from the camp. The guard who summoned me was convinced that man was dying. They called me as the army doctor was away.'

At the mention of the camp, Clara's body clenches; straining, she searches for any sound that will confirm Frank is still in the yard. The doctor continues; Clara forces herself to attend to his words.

'The man, the prisoner, had been taken into the hospital, where I was told Eleanor was attending to him.'

The doctor pauses, letting what he has told her sink in.

Clara stares, trying to imagine Eleanor willingly letting a prisoner in. Yet maybe she was only doing the decent thing, the thing any reasonable person would do? Love and loss surge into powerful protection, and Clara refuses to let her shock show.

'Helping out, then; offering charity where it was needed.' Clara juts out her chin, defiant. 'Sounds like Eleanor.'

Fiddling with his cuffs, the doctor blushes.

'Of course, no doubt that is true... I am sorry, I am not explaining the situation well.' His colour deepens. Lowering his eyes, he speaks again. 'It is more the fact that when I arrived Eleanor... Miss Scott seemed to be alone with the prisoner, for how long we are not sure. And, well, it appears that she had deliberately locked the hospital door.'

Clara absorbs the information. It makes no sense; why would Eleanor have done such a thing? And what does this doctor want from her? Again, she glances to the yard, her head beginning to throb.

Oblivious, the doctor ploughs on.

'And the other sister...'

Clara looks at him intently.

'You mean Lily?'

'Yes, Lily... Lily was, well, most distressed by the incident. Terrified, in fact; it was incredibly difficult to calm her. She kept repeating how concerned she was, is, for her sister.'

Clara bites back the urge to laugh. That Lily should be talking to a doctor about Eleanor's state of mind is too much.

'Lily claims to be terrified of most things. I wouldn't put too much weight on that.' She rises from the table, desperate now for this man, who knows nothing, to be gone. Whatever it is he wants or intends, Clara knows that his presence can only mean trouble.

'Mrs Scott,' The doctor's tone is pleading. 'Obviously you know more, about the family circumstances and, of course, you may be right about Lily...'

'Oh, I am.' Clara interrupts him. 'I'm most certainly right about Lily.'

He nods quickly.

'Of course, but I do feel that, perhaps, this time she may have cause to be worried.'

Clara sits down again.

'Lily told me about losing her brother, then her parents. All after losing the port; so much grief in one family, your family.'

The Doctor's voice is heavy with empathy, willing a tragic but loving family into existence.

Clara almost laughs.

'And those young women are still stuck out there, all alone in a place that feels... well, remote; lost to time.' Shaking his head, the doctor continues. 'Put simply, Mrs Scott, I am worried about Eleanor, worried about the balance of her mind.'

Clara reply is sharp. 'You think Eleanor is going mad? Is that what you mean?'

Dr Cook's eyes soften. 'I think she is grieving and lonely and would welcome the support of a friend. Maybe, if things are, as you suggest, better here with your husband, then you could find time to pay her a visit?'

'No one is setting foot over there.'

Frank's voice — raw, unexpected — slices through the kitchen. Leaping up, Clara turns to see her husband looming in the doorway. Her heart goes cold. For the first time in a long time, she is face to face with the man she knew before the war.

'Mr Scott.' The doctor, now on his feet, extends his hand. 'How nice to meet you.'

Although his face suggests it is anything but. Blood crashes through Clara's ears.

'I was just talking to your wife...'

'I know. I heard.'

The doctor's weak smile disappears as Frank, stepping forward, slams his hand onto the tabletop. Cups rattle, and for a second, Clara's heart stops.

'Heard all of it. Eleanor...' Frank barks out the name. 'Eleanor is *my* sister, is she not?' His face is tight with anger, a vein throbbing at his throat. There is no trace of the past month's weakness, no sense of fear, as if what he has overheard has transformed him into something of the man he was before. 'Those things you say she's done. You should have told me, not her.'

Frank throws his arm in Clara's direction, and she wills herself not to duck. The doctor flinches, as Frank leans further, deeper into his space.

'My apologies, Mr Scott. Your sister is clearly grieving, and I thought that maybe what she needed was a friend. I heard in the village that while you were away, your wife and she had been close and…'

Clara wants to punch them, punch them both. This stupid doctor for coming here and interfering, and Frank for what she knows he is about to do.

Stepping forward, now with both hands on the table, Frank twists his mouth up to the doctors retreating face. 'There are no friends for that bitch in this house. And if anyone's going to visit her, it'll be me. I'll make sure she never lets a German bastard in again.'

'You need to leave.'

Clara speaks softly. The doctor nods and, to her relief, Frank doesn't stop her ushering him out.

As she shepherds him down the passage, she thinks of apologising, but she can't find the words. And besides, she is sick of it, of making excuses for Frank; his words, his moods, for everything that isn't her fault.

And besides, she isn't sorry. Angry, that's what she is. That this doctor would come here, with his half-baked thoughts and intentions, and leave with no idea of what he has done. Of what she will be left to face. Alone.

Stepping down into the street, the doctor reaches out, putting his hand on her forearm; his face is ashen, any fragile bravery swallowed by Frank and his rage.

'I fear, Mrs Scott, I may have made things worse.'

Clara nods.

'No doubt you have.'

She is filled to spilling with anger, for the doctor, for Frank and this nameless, faceless prisoner. For every man in the whole damn world.

Dr Cook turns away, then turns back, fumbling in the black bag he carries; his eyes darting up and down the street. Balancing the case on his crooked knee, he uncorks a small glass bottle.

Grabbing at Clara's hand, he prises open her fists and shakes something hard and round into her palm. Leaning close, he whispers. 'Sleeping pills. Just two. They should give you enough time to get across the river and back again. Time to visit your sister-in-law, to warn her.'

Then he is gone. And Clara drenched in a shocked silence, feels her fingernails digging neatly around the two tablets, right into the centre of her palm.

CHAPTER FORTY-ONE

CLARA – LATE JULY 1916

There is a storm coming. Clara can feel the change even before she opens her eyes. Without leaving her bed, she senses that the heat of the previous days has shifted; settling into a new and strange heaviness, a tightening of the air.

The temperature can only rise so far before something explodes.

It's been three days since the doctor's visit. Days filled with quiet terror, time filled by checking windows and locking doors. Days Clara has spent sweltering in the heat of the shuttered house, fretting about what would happen if Frank managed to leave.

Hours made all the more unnerving by the fact Frank hasn't mentioned the doctor's visit, not even once. Instead, he has wrapped himself in a silence so complete and brittle that Clara knows it cannot possibly last.

This morning, the heat is already unbearable. Pushing, relentless into their small room; its intensity almost a match for the atmosphere within.

Careful not to wake Frank, Clara shifts her face against the pillow, searching for just an inch of cool. Briefly, she closes her eyes, only to be confronted yet again by those small white tablets, now wrapped up in a handkerchief and stuffed at the back of the dresser drawer. In the past few days, she has taken them out more times than she can count, each time wondering if and what she dares. And the longer she waits, the more she feels the danger grow.

Today.

It has to be today.

After breakfast, Clara sets about it. Frank is sleeping late, but every so often she hears the creak of the bed, sometimes a groan, and her stomach fills with hatred; the children flinch. Looking up at the ceiling, she prays silently that Frank will stay where he is. It will be easier that way. Pulling Molly to one side, trying to keep her voice steady, Clara hands her a paper bag filled with apples and bread.

'Keep the boys outside today, love. Your Dad's had a bad night; he needs to sleep.'

Molly shoots her look and, worried she will betray herself before she even starts, Clara quickly moves her daughter towards the open door.

'Just today, please. With it being so hot and all…' She trails off. 'There's plenty in the bag for lunch. Eat it in the churchyard, under the trees where it's cool.'

As an afterthought, Clara lifts her purse from her apron pocket, pushes two ha'pennies into her daughter's hand. 'Get some sweets for afters.'

It is enough. Molly leaves, calling their good fortune to her brothers already playing in the street and, before she can change her mind, Clara shuts the door. And slides the bolt.

Now alone in the hall, she springs into action, moving before she has time to think. Retrieving the tablets from the dresser, she carries them through to the kitchen, dropping them into a shallow pie dish with hot, trembling hands. Here she grinds them, reducing them to a fine powder with the end of her rolling pin, working with one ear trained on the room above.

Next, she sets the kettle on the range and, waiting for it to boil, moves around the kitchen gathering everything she needs. She makes the tea, strong and dark, lacing it with more sugar than Frank usually takes. Finally, from the pie dish, she spoons the powder, keeping her hand low and steady, wary of spilling a single grain.

Two tablets are what she has. Two tablets alone. This is her only chance.

Lifting the spoon, Clara holds it in the curling steam; power followed by fear scratching at her throat.

Closing her eyes, she plunges the spoon in, just as Frank's feet thump upon the floor.

'Clara? Clara!'

His voice, although loud, is still unsteady with sleep. If she moves quickly, she can keep him upstairs.

Clara snatches at the mug, sending tea slopping across her wrist. She bites her lip and fights the urge to scream. A minor spill, no more than a few drops, but still, she needs to take better care. Cradling the mug, both hands tight about it, she moves out into the hall, ignoring the heat against her palms; upstairs the sounds of movement are becoming louder, more insistent. Voice shaking, she calls out.

'Stay there, Frank. I'm on my way. I've made your tea.'

Carefully, her hands trembling, her eyes trained on the liquid lapping at the rim of the cup. Frank, now out of bed, stands at the bedroom door, his feet and chest bare, the scar on his head livid and proud through the stubble of his hair.

'Thought you might want a cuppa.' She smiles. Frank stares. Heart pounding, she lifts the cup, nodding towards the unmade bed.

Frank grunts, lips curling. 'I need a piss.'

Swallowing her disgust, Clara tries again. She can't afford to be provoked.

'Get back into bed. I'll bring the pot.'

Another grunt, but this time with a nod. He turns, and she follows, plunging back into the heat and stink of the room. Setting the cup on the dresser, Clara reaches beneath the bed. Black spots dance before her eyes, and her temple throbs. She hands the pot to Frank, who fixes her with a sneer. Fumbling at the fly of his pyjamas, he leans forward, releasing a stream of pee, filling the room with the stench. Looking away, Clara reaches for the bedpost, afraid she might faint, but then Frank finishes. And the room settles. He thrusts the pot in her direction. Wordlessly, Clara takes it, sets it down by the door.

Sitting back on the bed, Frank swings his feet up and leans back on the pillow. Willing her hands steady, Clara hands him the tea.

Unable to watch him drink, she leaves the room, taking the pot with her. As she walks down the stairs, the dark morning urine shifts and slops, just as the tea had moments before. Her mind and muscles are screaming, but Clara forces herself to remain calm.

In the privy, surrounded by humidity and fear, she flushes away her husband's waste. Bracing herself, one hand on the wall, she retches once. Head hanging over the pan, she wonders how long the pills will take to work. Or if they will work at all.

It is twenty minutes before she dares go back to check. But from the moment she sets foot on the first step of the stairs, she is enveloped by a silence so complete that Clara knows the pills have taken effect; that her plan has worked.

In their bed, Frank sleeps deeply. Unnaturally so. His face, turned towards her, is pushed deep into the pillow. His slightly-swollen lips hang open, every second breath a rasping snore; saliva trails from the corner of his mouth. Clara shudders.

The room, hot and airless, is sour with sweat, but Clara won't open a window. She plans on being back before the pills wear off, but she can't risk Frank waking, in one of his fits, alone and unchecked. As she lifts the mug, a floorboard groans beneath her feet and, dogged by the feeling that she is running out of luck, Clara hurries from the room.

In the kitchen, she washes away any trace of what she has done, before leaving by the back door. Locking it firmly in her wake, she checks it twice before she believes it secure.

The yards on either side of hers stand empty; offering up

silent thanks for one less thing to negotiate, Clara hurries on.

By the time she reaches Eleanor's gate, she is panting, her breath stolen by the heat, anticipation, and fear. Resting her hand on the latch, Clara gazes up at the house. Images of Eleanor and their argument knot themselves within her chest. But she must do this. There is no choice.

Catching sight of the hospital, Clara thinks of the prisoner and reminds herself why she is here. With one final steadying breath, she opens the gate and heads towards the house. The kitchen door is closed, the back window open only the merest of cracks. Peering inside, she sees the table littered with breakfast things. Butter left out in the heat, melted into a pool of yellow. The room is empty, neglected. Clara lifts her fingertips, tapping gently against the glass; a timid ring, the sound of someone who doesn't want to be heard.

From the direction of the hospital comes the clink of metal on stone. Looking around, she sees Eleanor in the doorway. At the sight of her and without thinking, Clara steps out of the shadow of the house, immediately putting herself in view.

Eleanor freezes. Hands shielding her eyes against the sun, she says softly, 'Clara?'

Clara takes another step forward, Eleanor too. And then in the next moment, they fly to each other, each wrapping the other in their arms. Standing together, between hospital and house, drenched by the sun. And drowned by love.

It is Eleanor who pulls away first. Holding her friend by the elbows, Clara notices how, above deep shadows, her eyes dance with an unnatural shine.

'Clara, I'm so sorry for Frank… the things I did and said. For upsetting you.'

Clara shakes her head. 'It's alright; please, Eleanor. Really, it's alright.'

And standing in the garden, Clara realises that she means it. Pulling Eleanor back towards her, she whispers, 'Eleanor,

I don't have much time. There's something I need to tell you.'

Eleanor draws back. Her face is pale in the sunlight as she tugs Clara towards the hospital.

Clara resists, looking towards the house. Eleanor shakes her head. 'No, Lily's in there.'

So Clara follows, into the hospital, where her feet echo on the wooden boards. The first bed — the one nearest to the door — is unmade; pillows and sheets crumpled and awry.

Clara turns to Eleanor. 'Are you sleeping in here?'

She shrugs.

'Sometimes. And besides, it's cooler in here.'

Fetching two metal framed chairs, Eleanor sets them down in a skinny patch of sun.

'I know.' Clara says. 'About the prisoner, about you and him being holed up together in here.'

Eleanor's head flies up. Her eyes are startled but defiant.

'I should've expected I'd be the talk of the village.' Clara can feel her anger, goading her to a response.

'I wouldn't know about the village. Frank's seen to that.'

Reaching for Clara's hand, Eleanor squeezes it in apology. The ground they're on is not yet solid; Clara knows it, can feel it. But there is no time for small talk and niceties, no time to find a gentler way in. With visions of Frank and those ground up pills crowding into Clara's head, she pushes on.

'It was the doctor who told me. Turned up on the doorstep out of the blue. Telling me how worried he was about you.'

Spots of colour flare on Eleanor's cheeks. 'I might've guessed. Yes, the good doctor was scandalised. Lectured me in my own kitchen about who I should and shouldn't be bringing in here.'

'He told me you were trapped over here, lonely. He thought you needed a friend.'

Eleanor's laugh is bitter and biting as it bounces off the floor. Too loud, and Clara fights the urge to shake her into silence. 'Hasn't anyone told him? That I have lived like that for years?'

'But a prisoner, Eleanor? Bringing a prisoner, a German prisoner, in here? Of all things.'

'Clara, he was ill. It looked like he was dying out there in the road. What was I supposed to do?' Eleanor's face is full of indignation. But beneath it, Clara hears a quiet plea for understanding.

'The doctor said you were alone with him. What were you thinking? Anything could have happened.'

Eleanor looks her directly in the eye.

'He could barely move. He wasn't in a fit state to do anything. And besides, it was the guard who left me, left us, alone. Went out to use the privy.'

Eleanor's voice hardens with each word, and Clara knows she should tread carefully, but time is evaporating; every minute, every second slipping by faster than the last.

'And according to the doctor, you locked the door?'

Silence. Eleanor refuses to reply.

'Eleanor. Why would you do that? What's going on over here? In your head?'

'Nothing's going on, Clara.'

Desperate now, Clara tries a different tack.

'I know it's been hard for you since John.' Visibly, Eleanor stiffens, but Clara carries on. 'But this kind of thing, it won't help.'

'Why?'

Clara looks down, longing to lose herself in the shadows playing at her feet; anything to avoid the real reason she is here.

'Eleanor. If I know, other people will. And they'll have plenty to say.'

'Let them say it. What do I care? The man was ill, I helped him. That's all there is to tell.'

'Trying telling Frank that.'

Eleanor's face freezes, her eyes widening.

'Frank knows?'

Clara nods, the thought of the pills and what she has done, hot and scolding at the front of her brain. Overwhelmed by panic, she grabs at Eleanor's hand, her words a tangled, urgent rush.

'Yes, he knows. He overheard when the Doctor came. Eleanor, you know how he is about the camp. Even the thought of the prisoners... you saw what he was like, how unpredictable; angry. That's why I came, to warn you. He was so furious with the doctor that...' she trails off.

'That what?' Eleanor speaks slowly; fear now undeniably etched on her chalky face.

Clara fights to get out the words.

'That the doctor slipped me two pills. Right there on the doorstep, told me they were pills to make Frank sleep. To give me time to warn you.'

Hands shaking, she reaches for Eleanor, desperate to convey the gravity of what she has to say.

'Eleanor, Frank knows. He has barely spoken since the doctor came, but I'm sure he's planning something. And Eleanor...'

Her voice catches, tears coursing down her cheeks.

'I don't know how to keep you safe.'

CHAPTER FORTY-TWO

ELEANOR – LATE JULY 1916

Eleanor makes promises to Clara.

In the face of her sister-in-law's fear, and the risks she has taken to warn her, Eleanor wraps Clara in her arms and swears she will put Anton out of her mind, telling her that helping him had been a one off, never to be repeated.

She is careful to refer to Anton only as 'The prisoner', knowing that admitting to knowing his name will only increase Clara's alarm.

But even as her sister-in-law sobs against her shoulder, Eleanor silently pushes her fear away. She knows what Frank is capable of, but the connection she felt with Anton, that single powerful moment, is enough to override it all. With her hand on his scar, Eleanor had finally felt it, that surge of strange, wonderful hope. The quiet certainty that the answers she wants are out there, within her grasp; and not even Clara's desperate warnings are enough to make it die.

It is to that hope that she secretly clings as she walks Clara, their hands clasped, to the top of the riverbank. She is both reluctant and eager for her sister-in-law to be away.

'You'll be alright? Do you want me to come with you?' Eleanor asks, ashamed by her quiet expectation that Clara will refuse.

Clara shakes her head. Out of guilt, Eleanor persists.

'What if he is awake or wakes up in a terrible mood?'

Clara smiles weakly. 'Pills or no pills, Frank always wakes up in a

305

terrible mood. And if Frank sees you, who knows what he will do?'

Eleanor tightens her grip on Clara as habit draws her eyes out across the river, towards the camp. Watching intently, Clara tugs hard on her hand.

'Please, Eleanor.' She pleads. 'Put that place, those prisoners, out of your mind. Nothing good can come of this.'

Eleanor nods. Trying to burn the site of the camp onto her brain, she drags her gaze back to Clara, her heart lurching at the panic smouldering in her friend's eyes.

'I promise.'

As they part, Eleanor offers up a silent prayer, against the shame that pricks as she thinks of the danger Clara has put herself in by coming here; and what she is likely to face when she arrives home. All to warn her, to keep Eleanor safe.

And yet, despite all of it, Eleanor knows she can't keep her promise.

For the rest of the day, she works, aimless and hard, in the hospital, then the garden, making sure to stay out of the house. With every fleeting glance of Lily, she wonders if her sister knows that Clara's been here today; all the time knowing that neither will speak of it.

Just as they haven't spoken of the prisoner. Even though he is with them every day. He is the reason Lily keeps to the house and Eleanor the places outside, the hospital, the garden, the marsh.

Just as he is the reason that in the early evening, exhausted and hopeless, Eleanor makes her way back to the riverbank, her eyes drawn once again on the camp.

Two hours ago, when the prisoners and their guards passed the house, Anton was there, right at the centre. And Eleanor had convinced herself that the group had slowed a little as they reached the house; that their tired faces had been alive with new connection. Something that might, if it were allowed, begin to grow.

It is undeniable that the red-faced officer still stares straight ahead, his mouth a tight, dark line. But it isn't the officer Eleanor cares about. It is Anton who she is interested in; Anton's gaze and fleeting smile that she seeks. Since that day, when her fingers ran the length of his scar and his hands curled about her wrist, Eleanor has become utterly convinced that Anton is the key to understanding the truth, the answer to finding all John's missing pieces and bringing him back to her. For Anton has been where John has been, and Anton can bring back everything that is lost and far away.

In the evening, when the air is still or the wind blows in the right direction, Eleanor listens, picking out the sounds of the prisoners as they return to the camp; calling to each other over the crash of tools being stored away. And she watches the soft swells of yellow, blooming through the dark as lamps are lit.

But now, there is nothing, just a strange and growing sense of calm.

Eleanor shifts, stretching her legs over ground baked hard with weeks of heat, grass burned yellow, leaving just the occasional patch of clover, wilting through the deadness with a defiant twist of green. Turning from the river, she looks east, where purple shadows are beginning to collect, moth-like; hovering and swelling on the horizon of the marsh, bruising the sky at the edges. Air that has been so lazy and languid for days, is now stirring with a strengthening breeze. The river, no longer golden, is a swirling sheet of indigo, carving up the land.

The last few fishing boats are heading for the bank, where fisherman work quickly, unfurling sails and taking down masts; confirmation, if Eleanor needed it, that the evening will bring a storm. Timber piled on the wharf sits covered with tarpaulin that flaps and slaps.

Reluctantly, she turns, heading back towards the house. The evening feels separated, cleaved in two by some unseen and undefined magic. The openness of this land, the way it can change so completely in the blink of an eye, looking so different depending on where you stand; that is what Eleanor loves about this place. What John loved, too.

Now, with storm shadows crowding about her, the familiar tide of grief breaks, washing over her once again. Slipping her hands beneath her collar, she touches the cross. As her fingers graze her collarbone, she thinks once again of Anton. And her promise to Clara recedes.

The small kitchen window is a warm frame of light, within which Lily moves. Eleanor picks her way through wilting flowers, their colours muted by the storm clouds and twilight; drawing in one final lungful of petrichor, she heads inside.

At the sound of her entrance, Lily looks up. Just as the first crash of thunder sounds.

'It's starting.' She says, more to the room that to Eleanor.

Eleanor nods once. Then leaves.

Late into the evening, she watches the storm, tracking its progress as it rolls around them; moving out onto the marsh before coming back to engulf the fen and the small house once more.

Midnight finds her, eiderdown wrapped, her back wedged against the window frame. She sits with her hands against the glass, mesmerised, before a sky bursting from edge to edge with dancing light, each raindrop bursting anew as lightening splits the clouds and the lighthouse beam moves mechanically through the dark.

And still the rain comes. Pounding, heavy curtains of water that part, only to close again, blown sideways by the gusting wind. Below, the lawn is a sea of petals, as the roses, one by one, fall victim to the storm. Eleanor stares at their teardrops, each white against the earth and dark, snaking stones. Each one a ghostly echo of the past.

Then she sees it. Unexpected, unlooked for, out in the wild blackness of the night.

Just a single light, bobbing along the outline of the wharf; a lone night watchman checking all is safe.

Despite her cramped and chilled body, Eleanor does not

move from the window.

Then come the other lights.

Not the watchman this time. Or the beam of the lighthouse. Or lightening refracted through the rain. These lights are coming from the direction of the camp.

Intermittent at first, the merest pinpricks of gold. Dipping, flaring, barely visible, erratic in their dance along the horizon. Within minutes, they are joined by others, the pinpricks growing as the distance between them shrinks, only to suddenly move further apart. Lights that separate, huddle, then separate again, each time the distance a little wider than before. As if they are searching for something.

For someone.

Exhilarated, fascinated, Eleanor swipes at the window, wiping away the clouds of her breath with excited hands. Pressing her face close to the glass, she peers uselessly through the raindrops that continue to chase each other, stubbornly obscuring her view. She fumbles in the semidarkness, groping for the window catch, her knuckles knocking on the edge of the wood. Kneeling up on the sill, she thrusts her face into the rain. Immediately the wind answers, making a grab for the frame, trying to tug it from her hand. Eleanor pulls back, planting her feet square on the floor, bracing her hips against the window recess. Tentatively, she tries again, leaning forward, straining to hear over the roar of the storm. Within seconds, her face and her nightdress are soaked. But still, she waits; hanging there frozen, ignoring the water that runs like a river, down her back.

A cry, a shout. Something. Somewhere out there, in the dark. Eleanor leans towards it. Further than she should. Further than she dares. But it is impossible to pick out anything more amidst the rushing of the river and the thrashing of the rain.

Finally defeated and dripping, she closes the window and pulls her head back in.

But she watches. And misses nothing.

She bears witness as the rain begins to soften and one by one the lights go out. As the wind drops, rises, and then drops again. She is present, waiting, when the heavy purple clouds slip away to reveal bright flashes of a half-formed moon.

And she sees the shadow.

The one that might have been a man. Follows its shape as it slips down the banking and lets itself in at the garden gate. Its slight, long limbs moving swiftly over the bruised petals.

CHAPTER FORTY-FOUR

ELEANOR

The next morning, long before Lily is awake, Eleanor slips out.

Past Piper, who still slumbers by the unlit range; out into a world that is studded with raindrops and coated with the scent of the storm. Making her way across the lawn, her footprints dark in the newly soften earth, she is both terrified and excited by whatever, whoever, she might find.

The door of the hospital is closed, but its lock, twisted, hangs down.

With her heart hammering, Eleanor climbs the two narrow steps, and lightheaded with anticipation, steps inside. Pulling the door closed behind her she waits, allowing her eyes to adjust slowly to the lack of light. Breathing softly, she can feel her blood hot, pounding at her neck. Pulsing at her wrists. Disappointment threatens as she scans the narrow room.

But then she sees it. Someone is there, lying motionless on the bed.

Anton. It must be. She can barely breathe.

Suddenly her mind is full with all she wants to know, questions that have been forming and bursting then forming again, ever since John died. Born of her grief, bubbles of longing and pain that continuing to press and jostle.

Slipping off her sodden shoes, Eleanor makes her way to the figure. It remains curled, fox-like, on the bed, her feet almost soundless on the floor. With each step her vision flares, until the room is alive with colours and dancing shapes, a strange shifting perspective that makes the walls on either side move in towards her, only to pull immediately, sharply away. The building rocks on unseen, watery foundations and her limbs feel like they belong to someone else.

Stopping short of the bed, she pauses, forcing herself to still her mind and quieten her thoughts. Desperate as she is, she must take her time. The potential for danger, of every kind, is real, and she can't risk announcing her presence yet.

After waiting so long, she won't waste this opportunity.

Then, without warning, the thought occurs that it is not Anton lying there, but some unknown prisoner with whom she has no connection. Someone whose scars she hasn't seen or felt.

Or not a prisoner at all. From nowhere comes the conviction that the sleeping soul is Frank; followed by an image of Clara's terrified face yesterday.

With fear and desperation taking control, she leans closer. Her relief is instant.

Even in the dim light and her agitation she can see the figure is not Frank. The limbs, tucked up and inwards, are slender and slight; nothing like her brother's cruel, knotted arms.

And besides, Frank wouldn't have been sneaking around in the storm like a thief. Frank would have come straight to the house and banged on the door, shouting, hammering, letting her know he was here. Even now, after everything he has been through, Eleanor is convinced that Frank would want his presence felt.

And after Alfred, Frank would never lay down and sleep on these hospital beds.

Across the floor runs a line of muddied tracks, a path of debris pulled in from the storm that ends at a pair of worn boots, set neatly at the side of the bed; paired as if by an obedient child, one careful not to spoil the sheets. It seems such a strange, oddly tender thing that, even through her fear and excitement, Eleanor smiles.

It is the sort of thing John would have done.

With one hand holding tight to the cross at her neck, she moves to the far side of the bed. Still, the body does not stir. There is no movement beyond the gentle rise and fall of his chest; whoever it is remaining sunk within in a sleep that is deep and absolute.

Lowering one hand, light and tentative, Eleanor brings it down to the crumpled sheets. She leans over and looks directly into the sleeping face.

Anton.

She chokes back a sob of relief, a stilted echo that rises and breaks the silence of the room. Anton stirs, briefly, then pushes his head deeper into the pillow.

Despite the care taken over his boots, the sheets are streaked with mud. His clothes too are caked, coat and trousers, all dark with water.

Eleanor thinks of the clothes that, in the early hours of the morning, she had pulled from the trunk beneath her bed. Alfred's clothes and her father's. Folded and tucked away, until grief subsided, or a use could be found.

No one ever imagining a use such as this.

As she assembled them, running her fingers over their seams and patches, seeking out her mother's needlework and some of her own, she had thought of the men who had worn them; what they would have said about her plan. The plan formed the moment she saw the shadow she hoped was Anton's flit through the gate.

Now Eleanor takes in the length of him, this man, reeking of wet animal and the river. Clearly, he has made his way along the banks, balancing right on the edge of the rising tide.

She lifts her eyes from his muddied hems to his shoulders; one pushed into the mattress and the other raised, twisted away from her in sleep. Recalling the scar buried beneath his sodden, stinking layers, she feels the need to find their previous connection; almost without thinking, she reaches out her hand.

Instantly, Anton's eyes snap open. His face, now frozen, is white, luminous with sleep and shock. Snatching her hand away, Eleanor stumbles backwards, her feet clattering clumsily on the uneven boards.

As if it is she who shouldn't be there, she who is in the wrong.

'Sorry...' she cries out, then immediately stuttering to a whisper, 'I... I didn't mean to wake you...'

Pushing his heels against the mattress, Anton retreats to the top of the bed. For a second, he stares in silence, then holding up his hands, vigorously shakes his head.

'Please... please....'

Reaching down, his eyes still on hers and pupils wide with panic, he gropes blindly for his boots.

'I am sorry... me, I... I only meant to rest awhile... not to fall asleep...'

Desperation comes off him in waves. Slipping from the bed, he grabs the nearest boot and fumbles with laces made stiff and uncooperative by layers of drying mud. Fear leaping within her, Eleanor reaches out again. She wants to steady him, to slow him, and most of all to convey, somehow, that he must not go. But Anton shrinks away, flattening himself against the bed, terrified.

She retreats, holding her hands up, spreading her fingers to their limits. Lowering her voice, she speaks softly, as if to a wounded child, all the while her mind flitting wildly between here and the house, offering up fragmented, silent prayers that Lily remains asleep.

She cannot lose this chance.

'Please...'

Anton, focused entirely on the boot in his hand, tugs at the knot, wiping mud from his palm and then staring in horror at the ruined sheets.

'So sorry, so sorry. Oh God, I... fallen asleep. I plan to be gone before... I only mean to rest. Please...' The force of his foot into his boot releases a fresh stench of the river, and

Eleanor knows she is right about where he has been.

Boots on, Anton tries to dodge around her, eyes fixed on the door.

'I go, I go. This was a bad mistake.'

'No!' Fighting against the lurch of her heart, she steps directly into Anton's path.

'Please... I mean no harm... I go...'

And Eleanor realises with a jolt that he is scared, terrified, that he believes she wants to keep him here, ready to hand him over and send him back to life in the camp.

Forcing herself to calm, she reaches out, laying her hand on Anton's shoulder. Deliberately, she presses the place where she knows his scar begins. Or perhaps ends. Through the filthy layers of cloth, she feels for the ridge of his collarbone, pushing down, until it bites, deep into her palm. Locking her eyes to his, she wills their previous connection back to life.

Silently, she pleads, begging him to trust her. Beneath her hands she detects a stillness, remote but growing. She whispers.

'I want to help. Please, tell me how.'

Anton's eyes are wary; the iris so grey it is almost indistinguishable from the whites. At the centre, around his pupils, glows a steel ring of blue. Eyes that should be cold but somehow are filled with warmth.

With her hand still on his shoulder, Eleanor watches as hope and confusion move in rapid succession across his face. Seconds turn to minutes, until finally, shaking his head, Anton's eyes scan the room.

'No, it is kind, but no... it is no good for you me being here. I bring trouble... please, I must go.'

She steps closer, pressing harder, her fingers sinking into folds of wet wool. Knowing and not caring that her desperation is on show.

She has to keep him here.

Battling to keep her voice low, she scrabbles for an explanation, searching for the right things to say.

'I can take care of myself. And besides, it is morning now.' She waves to the high windows and the fens beyond. 'All these open fields? I don't fancy your chances of finding somewhere else to hide.'

Anton shifts uncomfortably and Eleanor wonders how much he understands. Private Wilson told her Anton's English was good, but she can't be sure. One more risk she is adding to the many.

'There are many channels, ditches. I will use these.' His voice is uncertain. But it is clear he understands.

Eleanor's heart lifts. Catching on to hope, she tries again.

'The dykes? Plenty of those. All filled with water, especially after last night's rain. And all of them run along fields that will be full of men looking for you.

His face falls. She knows she is winning. Trying to conceal her excitement, Eleanor speaks again.

'Wait here. Until dark, until the fields are empty. Hide here. I can bring you food and clean clothes. Keep an eye out while you rest.'

Anton sinks to the bed, his shoulders sagging. She removes her hand, and the connection snaps; but no matter. She has won.

'One day only.' He holds up one hand. 'Less than one day. I stay only until dark. Maybe not that long.'

Eleanor nods, hoping her face does not betray the excitement surging in her chest.

'Until dark, then.' She steps back. 'Wait there.'

Hurrying to the door, propelled now by possibility, she plunges her feet back into her rubber boots. She must act quickly; bring the promised food and clothing before Anton changes his mind. Looking out, she checks the garden, glancing up to the road before she leaves. The broken lock means she can only trust that Anton will remain.

The house, when she enters, is quiet. As soon as the door is opened, Piper bolts, running into the garden, nose down. Terrified that he will alert Lily to Anton's presence, she follows him and slips on his rope, waiting with one eye on the hospital until he relieves himself before returning him to the kitchen.

Wasting no time, she retrieves the clothes from where she has hidden them, flat beneath her eiderdown, the ghosts of long dead men.

Then she checks on Lily, peering around her slightly open door. Despite last night's storm, Lily sleeps deeply. Her sister's peaceful form jars, unsettling Eleanor in a way she can't explain. But the feeling is fleeting, instantly overtaken by the relief that she has more time to put her plan into action. At the landing window she catches sight of her reflection, barely recognising the woman she sees. Her pinched skin is marked by an unnatural flush, sitting high on her cheeks. Unnerved, she turns quickly away and heads downstairs.

In the kitchen she gathers as much food as she dares. Taking down jars, cheese, bread, before losing her nerve and putting more than half of it back. With just her and Lily living here, their stores, never abundant, are now scant, and each time she places something in the basket she is certain that Lily will notice its absence; that it will be a lack of bread and jam that betrays her.

For far too long she collects far too little, until a sudden terror that Anton will have left forces her back to the hospital through the growing morning light. Holding the bundle of clothes and supplies close, Eleanor keeps her head down, for once grateful for their isolation. And for the fact it is Sunday, so the other prisoners won't be walking this way today. One less pretence to keep up.

As she approaches the hospital, the broken padlock catches her eye; an eye that is now alert to anything that might betray her. Betray them. Glancing quickly towards the house, she unhooks the padlock, hiding it in her dress pocket where, sagging through the fabric, it lies cold against her thigh. She straightens her back; a broken lock won't undo her now.

Inside, with the door pulled tight, the hospital seems different. The air feels almost rarefied, reminding her of a church. The silence so intense and thick that Eleanor is sure the room is empty, that Anton has changed his mind; deciding, despite her gentle pleading, it is better to be on his way.

But then she sees it, the movement of a thin shadow rising against the rough walls, behind an unused screen. Anton is still here.

She steps forward, her legs elastic with relief. Softly, she calls his name. 'Anton, it's me.'

Slowly, he emerges, moving awkwardly, with the posture of a man who has run hard and then held his body still for too long. She passes him the bundle of clothes, catching a flash of gratitude before his face fills again with concern.

'You are sure… the risk…'

She nods. 'I know the risk. And besides, we agreed. It's just for today.'

'I hope they will not come here… the guards… not first, at least…'

'Why?' Eleanor is puzzled and suddenly filled with the dread of conviction that the hospital will be exactly where the men might look.

'I did not escape alone… two of us left…'

Truly terrified now, Eleanor spins, as if expecting to see another prisoner lying curled on another bed.

'No, no!' Anton raises his hands. 'Two of us left. But my friend… he was caught… that was the plan. He was caught and he will send them the other way.'

She stares. 'A trick?'

'Maybe a trick…' He smiles softly. 'But now, maybe, we have some time.'

Grasping at thin threads of relief, Eleanor nods towards the clothes. 'Put those on and then you can eat. I'll wait outside.'

She reaches the door as Anton calls out, shrugging off the woollen coat. 'Hey, I realise, please… I don't even know your name. Will you tell me, maybe?'

She smiles. 'Eleanor.'

'Eleanor,' his accent adds the dips and inflections to her name in just the wrong places. Yet it fills her with warmth and, despite the danger, she feels happier than she has in months.

'I am Anton.'

She laughs softly.

'I know.'

Waiting outside, she listens to him moving, his feet shuffling on the creaking boards. A sudden groan that makes her wonder if his scar aches or hides a deeper pain. She adds it to her list of questions and hopes a day will be enough to ask them all.

Because now he has taken the clothes and her name, there is much he owes her. Stepping back inside, she finds him dressed in a jumble of faded memories. Anton points to his wet clothes, neatly folded and piled on the floor. Even as a fugitive, it seems that Anton is particular in his habits.

'You must hide, burn them. I bring no trouble to you.'

Scooping up the clothes, Eleanor stuffs them under the opposite bed and then hands him a heel of bread. From the tap, she draws a mug of water.

'Sorry, it's not much, but I was worried about Lily. I'll try and bring more later. Maybe tea, something warm to eat.'

Anton stops tearing at the bread and looks up, his eyes wide with fresh alarm. 'Lily? Who is Lily?'

'My sister.' Seeing his panic, Eleanor adds. 'Don't worry, she sticks to the house. Lily is…' She pauses, searching and failing for the words to describe Lily. 'We aren't getting along. She never comes in here.'

But Anton is not convinced.

'I did not know. But now I think, maybe…' he shakes his head. 'Some of the other men, they say that they see two women here. One in the garden,' He points at Eleanor. 'And one sometimes at the window. I never see her but…'

He breaks off.

'But what?'

'But I think maybe this is your Lily. The other men, they call her *Geistermädchen;* the ghost girl.'

Eleanor shivers.

Anton returns to the bread, but his eyes, flitting back to her, are full of his own questions. Eleanor, determined not to say more, turns away. She won't waste precious time on Lily.

'You are married?' Anton's mouth is full; his manners temporarily forgotten by his obvious hunger.

Eleanor stiffens. Raising his eyebrows, he points to her ring.

The bluntness of his observation is unnerving her, but at the same time, it gives her hope. She rubs softly at the gold. Anton waits.

'That was the plan.'

He looks at her questioningly. His eyes, intense and unblinking.

'I was going to be. Married.'

Realisation dawns. Slowly, Anton shakes his head. 'I am sorry.' Then, with a directness Eleanor already expects, 'What happen? No, wait. Let me guess. The war. All the time this war. *Verdammt!* I am right?'

That familiar, choking grief. She can't let it overwhelm her. With an effort, she presses it down.

'He was killed, in the spring.'

'His name?' Anton holds her eye, daring her to look away. Again she feels that knot of fear tangled up with hope.

'His name was John.' And just like that, she has handed him to a stranger. Delivered in the words of the past.

'You loved him?'

Blinking back tears, she looks at her hands. 'Very much.'

Anton sighs. 'I am sorry. None of this is any good.'

It is her turn. One question. The first in payment for his.

'Are you married?'

Behind the mug at his lips, she sees Anton smile. His drawn features, briefly transform, filling with life.

'Yes. I marry Sophia just before the war. But I know her a long, long time.' He speaks, as if summoning his words. 'And…' he holds up one finger. 'And I have a son... Franz... you would say Frank.'

She smiles at his sudden lightness but does not speak, silently willing him to go on.

'I have seen him only once...' Anton's face twists, his grey eyes becoming dark. 'But now, a letter... and the boy is sick.' He gestures, vaguely, in the direction of the camp. His face does not leave hers.

'A letter from Sophia came telling me this. It was written last month... so this is why I must go.'

Talking of his family has made him restless, tearful and Eleanor worries that again he will try to leave.

'Best we keep you safe then, so you can get away tonight.'

Anton nods stiffly, bringing the water up to his mouth, the mug's rim knocking against his teeth. Preparing another question, Eleanor attempts to steer the conversation closer to where she needs it to be. To what she needs to know.

'When you get back to Sophia, what will you tell her?'

He laughs. 'So many things. And I will tell her how you help.'

Frustrated, Eleanor tries again. 'About the things you have seen, the things you have done?'

'I will tell that the camp, really, was not so bad. The food was terrible, but,' He shrugs. 'Not so bad.'

Eleanor stares in disbelief.

'Even though they worked you half to death? On the marsh, with no water?

Anton shakes his head.

'We had water. That day was my fault. Trying to prove I was strong man.' He lifts his arm, flexing it, and despite herself, Eleanor laughs. Anton smiles.

'So, no. The camp is not so bad. But I need to see my son. You understand?' She nods, and feeling even more questions gather, she tries again. Instinct tells her to keep her tread light.

'But what'll you tell her about before?'

Anton frowns, head on one side. Very still.

'Before?'

Mouth dry with anticipation, she edges forwards, finding her way to a place closed to her. Yet still she asks.

'Before the camp. What will you tell her about that?'

Silence unspools unseen and unchecked into the room as Anton's face switches from open to unreadable, becoming a patchwork of shadows. His reply is cloaked in an emotion that Eleanor can't begin to describe.

'No. I will tell her nothing. There is nothing of that time she needs to know.'

Something sparks within Eleanor. Whether it is shame or anger, she can't decide. Suddenly the room feels both too big and small for the two of them. But this is not over.

Anton needs rest. More food, more sleep, then she knows he will talk.

She gets to her feet.

'I will leave you. And Lily will be wondering where I am.'

His expression softening, Anton reaches for her hand.

'Again, thank you, for doing this.'

His grip tightens. His eyes, although bright, appear empty at the centre. As if a part of him has been lost. In that same choked voice, he whispers, 'Your questions, I... I hope you understand.'

Before Eleanor can reply, from the direction of the house, comes the sound of a door slamming. Both start and then freeze, paralysed in fear. The first to move, Eleanor, waves Anton behind the screen before edging towards the door. She opens it just a crack. The garden remains quiet, the lawn still covered in the remnants of the storm-damaged roses, amongst which a thrush tugs a worm from the wet grass. Eleanor waits, her heart slowing as she tries to convince herself that the noise was nothing. Just Lily, back from a trip to the privy, and going inside.

Telling Anton to bolt the door, she heads back to the house. To her relief, the kitchen is as she left it. Nothing amiss or out of place.

Eleanor works, distracted and aimless, keeping one eye on the hospital, letting the other drift continually towards the clock; planning how, in the dwindling hours left to her, she is going to get to the answers that she seeks. She knows time is short, leeching away, and talking about John has reignited the urgency of her grief. She is terrified, yet strangely alive.

She is so distracted by the things she plans to ask, that it is over an hour before she heads upstairs and finds Lily gone.

CHAPTER FORTY-THREE

LILY

As the storm began, Lily listened to Eleanor, pacing in agitation, while she, Lily, sat calmly on her bed. Watching the lightning flash white against the ceiling, possessed by a strange, creeping stillness. As the rain and wind wrapped themselves about the house, their music drowning out the familiar throb of the river, Lily embracing the moment, had found herself silently and undeniably brave.

It was a courage rooted in anger, which had grown unchecked since Eleanor had let the prisoner into their world. Nurtured and fed by her sister's refusal to apologise or even acknowledge what it was she had done. As fast as Eleanor retreated beyond compassion and reason, Lily's anger had crystallised, cocooning her within its shell. When Lily realised that Eleanor was sleeping in the hospital, her overwhelming emotion had been relief. And her bravery had begun to swell.

But still she chose to hide herself from the prisoners, watching their daily passage from the upper floor. Pouring silent scorn and hatred onto their heads, as they violated and corrupted the place Alfred loved; and the life Lily has carved for herself.

Over the past week, she has found it surprisingly easy to conjure Alfred, the brother from whom she previously took her cunning and strength. Each morning, sliding the box from beneath her bed, Lily has allowed herself to imagine his laughing eyes and easy nature; whispering to him as she polishes and cleans its contents.

It has helped beyond words to have Alfred's gun.

Found on the marsh before her brother's body, the gun had been her father's one solace. Taking it apart, piece by piece, he had checked, cleaned and oiled each and every part, polishing its wood and metal over and over again. As if tending his gun, he could bring Alfred home again.

Until finally, in his grief it had been abandoned. Hidden away in the hospital, untouched for years. Until Lily discovered it, that day in the storeroom, and claimed it for her own.

At first, she had been sure that Eleanor would know it was missing. But as the distance between her and Eleanor continued to widen, barely bridged by a few passing, almost indistinguishable words, the gun's absence had remained unremarked upon, unnoticed.

With the storm raging, Lily cradled the gun close, bending her body around its shape and the memories of her brother. She remembered him showing her how to open the chamber, loading and unloading the cartridges. How occasionally out on the marsh he would let her fire it, straight into the wind. Standing tall, with Alfred behind her, her shoulder recoiling from the force of the shot, her cries of wild joy and terror had mingled with Alfred's deep approving laugh. The images had filled her with a fire of lost courage and possibility; things she could barely remember how to feel.

Bringing the gun back to life has been like finally bringing Alfred home.

Now, waking into the cool relief of morning, it is the first thing that Lily checks first, before dressing and heading downstairs.

From the hallway, she can hear Eleanor, busy in the kitchen; opening cupboards, then quickly closing them again. Her scuffed and muffled movements are the sounds of a search.

Immediately, Lily thinks of the gun.

Slowly, she advances, her feet soft on each step. Looking towards the kitchen, she stands, half shadowed and unnoticed in the doorway, watching. Eleanor's actions are fleeting and strangely hesitant; her thoughts clearly far away. Leaning a little further, Lily grips the wood of the frame, ready to swing herself out of sight should Eleanor turn.

On the kitchen table stands a basket, surrounded by small parcels, some loosely tied, others spilling open, revealing hastily assembled food. Piper sniffs around the table, searching out the spoils. Her back to Lily, Eleanor drifts in and out of the shadows, reaching for one thing and then another, picking things up before setting them down. Her hair is shaken loose from its pins, her blouse untucked; everything about her appears careless and half-formed.

Then suddenly Eleanor stills completely, as if listening to something outside. Pulling herself out of the doorway, Lily tucks herself into the wall.

Breathing slowly, she turns back to the kitchen, in time to see Eleanor sweep the last of the small parcels into her arms and head towards the larder. She returns minutes later, with the end of yesterday's loaf, which she adds, along with two remaining parcels to the basket. Then hurries out the door.

Only when she is sure that Eleanor is not coming back does Lily dash across the kitchen, to the small window behind the sink. There, in a garden reinvigorated by the storm, Lily watches Eleanor duck, quick and silent, inside the hospital, pulling the door tight behind her. Lily follows. Slipping out into the morning, closing the kitchen door to prevent Piper following her. Keeping to the path, she moves quickly, desperate for the safety of the hospital's shadow. Instinct pulls her to the darkest place, overgrown and neglected. The spot where no one ever goes.

Except today she is wrong. Because before her lies a path newly beaten through the grass, the undergrowth flattened.

Amongst the weeds and the nettles, Lily drops down to her haunches and waits; still, listening.

And through the walls the sounds come. Drifting out, shaping themselves into jagged, splinters of memories; each shard-like, stabbing and impossible to arrange in any kind of order. Memories of those men, prisoner and guards; their shadows moving through the garden, long and dark on the kitchen wall. Their voices, gravelly and grave. And the silence, after Eleanor ushered them into the hospital, so long, so intense that Lily had vomited into the mixing bowl.

Crouched there in the grass, she recalls Eleanor, white faced and silent, as the guards had carried the prisoner away; avoiding the eye of Dr Cook who had demanded that the man be returned to the camp.

Now, unable to believe what she is hearing, Lily pushes her hands down hard over her ears, blocking out the voices that are coming once again.

Getting to her feet, she turns and runs.

Back in her room, Lily howls. On her knees, sunlight pooling weakly about her, she struggles to breathe, struggles to think.

That voice. The one she heard through the walls, both familiar and foreign. Getting stronger, louder, refusing to be kept at bay.

She longs for Alfred, yearning until every part of her aches. She screws her eyes tight, but still he floats stubbornly, tantalisingly just out of reach. Crawling across the floor, she scrabbles under the bed, pulling the box towards her, into her lap. She sits as if in prayer, the gun in her hands, its metal cold beneath her palms as she tries harder. Pushing at the present and pulling at the past. She can feel it, hear it. Alfred's voice; right there, becoming clearer, telling her exactly what it is she must do.

Then finally, gradually, her brother's face, his features, drift into view.

But it is not Alfred who stares back at her. It is Frank.

And the answer is clear.

Rushing to her feet, wrapping the gun in a blanket, Lily heads for the stairs. She moves quickly, before she can become overwhelmed by the certainty of what it is she must do.

The kitchen is quiet, empty of anything other than the chaos of crumbs left by Eleanor and the dog's gentle snores. Beyond it, the garden is cool, emptier still; across the river the bells of the church peal, rolling across the water one by one.

Lily lifts the gun higher. Bulky beneath its woollen shroud, she holds it close to her chest, and steps out, her feet heavy on the still-damp path. She remembers Alfred, how he would march out, gun in his hand, gleaming and always on show. Closing her eyes against the terrible reality of the present, she sets about convincing herself he is still there, still directing her movements, still shaping her thoughts. That his longed for voice still whispers deep in her head.

She continues along the path, out of the shadow of the house, edging closer to the embankment and river beyond. She longs to turn, to steal one final glance at the hospital, but she won't. Forcing herself to keep her eyes straight ahead, concentrating on the distant clamour of bells, she presses on, out onto the road. Turning from the marsh, she heads towards the village.

With each step, Lily fights the urge to go back; only to remember what going back would mean. Recalling what she heard, squatting in the weeds behind the hospital, she begins to shake. Doubled over in the empty road, trapped between sky and fen, she is paralysed by the weight of change. Eleanor's betrayal has put them both in danger, and their only chance of safety now waits on the other side of the river.

In her room, within those familiar walls, Lily had been so sure she could hear it; Alfred's long silent voice, reawakened and telling her exactly what she must do. But now, out here on the road, exposed, fields all around, all she hears is fear; drilling at her temple, rattling through her bones. With each step, Alfred's voice has become smaller, quieter; finally drifting entirely away. To be replaced by those voices of betrayal and danger coming from within the hospital walls.

The gun is tucked by her side now. Alfred told her to carry it, all the way. Then hand it to Frank, presenting him with the answer. And she had meant to.

But now, without Alfred's quiet urging, the gun is too heavy, and as the folds of the blanket that conceal it slip, every step is harder to take.

Terrified and frustrated, Lily turns from the road. Half-climbing, half-sliding into a narrow dyke, she struggles to keep her footing. Gathering an armful of straw from the edge of the newly harvested field, she makes a nest and, careful to keep it above the waterline, slips the gun into its depths. In trepidation, she lifts her head from the muddy channel and checks the road. All is empty, all is still.

The church bells are silent now, and the final whisps of cloud have cleared, leaving the sky a pale, tentative blue. Overhead, a heron, emerging from the weeds of the river — arrow straight and dark against the horizon — flies in the direction of the marsh.

Leaving the gun means Lily is no longer dragged down by its weight. But she can't shake the fear, pinching and pulling at every part of her, refusing to drop away.

But she must keep moving, must get to Frank. Her last remaining hope.

Clambering up from the dyke, she steps on, towards the bridge, towards the village into which she hasn't set foot for months, for years. But all the fear she had believed she felt in the past is nothing, not compared with today.

The village, like the river road, is silent. In front of her looms the church, its doors open against the heat which, despite the storm, is already starting to build again. Within its depths, Lily can make out the shadowy shapes of the villagers standing shoulder to shoulder. She imagines them heads close, hands clutching gloves, caps and prayer books. And she wonders what they know.

Are they whispering about the man hiding beyond the river, cowering and sheltered in their hospital? Or are they entirely ignorant of the fact that anything is amiss? That anyone has got away?

Steadying herself against the low wall, Lily pulls in the air around her. The churchyard, just a handspan away, is filled with the scent of earth and dying flowers. Thick and cloying, it snakes beneath her tongue, coating her teeth; filling her mouth with the taste of decay.

Without permission or warning her eyes flick to the right. Seeking out the dark corner where Alfred lies.

She allows herself just the briefest of glances before spitting, quick and hard over the wall, down into the long tangle of grass.

And pushing herself straighter, Lily moves. In search of Frank.

CHAPTER FORTY-FIVE

CLARA

Pulling herself into the shadows of the yard, her hips against the wall that is still wet with rain, Clara listens to the excited whispers drifting from the neighbouring yards. Her blood runs fast and cold.

'Two of 'em tried apparently. A hut was damaged, you see, in the storm. Guards were moving 'em, and they made a run for it. Caught the first one straightaway, he didn't get far.'

'But the other one, he's still missing?'

'Out looking for him now, they are.'

The unseen woman's voice drops, and Clara, straining to hear, pushes her face closer to the soaking brickwork. Its surface is rough against her burning cheek.

'… one of the guards reckons they know where he's gone…'

Terror, black and beetling, crawls through Clara's stomach. Suppressing the urge to cry out, she grinds her heels against the yard. Her thoughts fly to Eleanor as she crouches nearer to the wall.

But whatever is said next is lost in a string of quick, yapping barks. Clara curses, and by the time the dog is sworn at and silenced, the women are turning to their doors.

'See you in church.'

Church. Clara hasn't been to church for years. She had never been that regular about attending, but before she married Frank, she went often enough to stay respectable. But church would be the place to be today; packed, and bustling with gossips hiding beneath stained glass and hymns. All of them shuffling, eyeing each other in the lull between blessings and prayers; waiting impatiently for the release of the churchyard where news of the prisoner's escape can be freely shared.

For the briefest moment, Clara considers slipping into the pews, holding herself still as she seeks the information she craves. The idea vanishes before it even truly begins.

Yesterday's visit to Eleanor, all that business with Frank and the pills, has left Clara exhausted and on edge. Every shadow snatches her breath, and every sound is enough to cut her through. She daren't stray from the house, not today. After what she's got away with, the things she's done; it could so easily be her they are whispering about in church this morning.

For the thousandth time, she thanks her lucky stars that Frank was still sleeping when she got back from the hospital, even though he had woken in a temper, ranting, and with a raging thirst. That had been the least of her worries.

Still huddled by the wall, she tries to catch hold of what she's just heard, grabbing desperately at the words that float like cobwebs, ghostly and just out of her reach. She needs to know more about this prisoner and his escape, so she can assess the danger for herself.

Maybe she could send Molly to church instead; get her to creep in after the service starts or hang around the graveyard just as it ends. Let her daughter's sharp eyes and ears find out what there is to know.

But what if the things Clara suspects are true? And Molly hears Eleanor's name mentioned? No, Clara needs to keep her children away from this; they are best at home with her. The boys, too; they will have to be kept inside. She can't have them bursting in, filled with tales of manhunts and the like. Not today.

Turning back to the house, she sees Frank, framed by the kitchen window, sitting rigidly at the table. Yesterday's unnatural slumber had been followed by a restless night, in which neither of them got more than thin fistfuls of sleep. Both trying to keep to the edges of the sagging mattress; Frank on his back, eyes wide, staring up into the blackness, and Clara curled, tucked up like a comma, sinking into the sound of the wind and rain. As the house shook with the force of thunder, Frank had flinched, but neither of them had spoken a word, unable to break a silence so hard, so complete.

Then, in the early hours, as the wind dropped, and the lightning ceased, Clara had felt it. A creeping change, the energy within the room noticeably shifting, as if reset by the storm. Frank's strange lethargy that had characterised the last few days is cracking, and a new restlessness is moving into its place.

Still, Frank hasn't mentioned the doctor. Or what he heard. Not one word has passed his lips about Eleanor or the prisoner she had taken into the hospital. But watching the way his lips curl and his fingers twist continually in his lap, Clara knows it is all he thinks about.

The news of this escape must be kept from him, no matter what it takes.

She should go in; make him some breakfast; try and settle him with a cup of tea, somewhere she can keep an eye on him. But despite all these things she should do, Clara can't make her feet move, can't step back inside the kitchen, back into the fog of panic that refuses to lift. It is impossible to think inside the house.

And Clara needs to think. Of a way to reach Eleanor, to make sure her sister-in-law is safe, and to find a way to put her own reeling mind at rest. She needs to know that Eleanor has kept those promises Clara dragged from her, that she has stayed away from the camp and its inhabitants.

But Clara had one chance; those two tablets were her one golden opportunity. And she has used it.

Pacing, walking the same patch of cracked and damp ground, it occurs to her that perhaps she could go to the doctor and ask for more; could go now, before any of her family even have time to notice she is missing. Maybe she could find the man and explain. But what if she is right? What if that prisoner *is* the same one, and he's hiding over there? Clara remembers how shocked the doctor was about Eleanor's behaviour before; surely, if she is right, this time things will only be worse. He is bound to report Eleanor, and then who knows what would happen?

No, all Clara can do is keep the rumours from Frank and keep him inside. Every second she stays out here worrying is a second that someone could be knocking on her door, searching for the prisoner or just wanting to pour poison in Frank's ear.

Heart plummeting, forcing herself to accept that the best hope she has is to stay close to home, she heads towards the house. Behind the glass, Frank shifts, half stands. Panicking, Clara bolts for the back door.

CHAPTER FORTY-SIX

ELEANOR

The first thing Eleanor does when she realises Lily is missing is waste time. Precious time that she loses to the paralysis of disbelief; time spent willing her eyes to fill the space in Lily's tangled bed.

Seconds slip by, becoming minutes, until finally, faced with the undeniable truth, Eleanor finds the strength to move. In desperation, she opens cupboards, looks under beds and behind doors, moving all over the house, searching spaces too small to contain anything but dust. All logic abandoned, it is as if she is playing a parlour game, looking for an errant child on a rainy day, not a grown woman. A woman who never leaves the house.

A woman who has only disappeared once before.

The thought of the river rises from nowhere, consuming Eleanor with dread. Her veins filling with its muddy waters, her mind catching and spiralling, mirroring its current.

And with it comes a terrible hope, followed hard and fast by red bursts of spitting shame.

Running from the kitchen to her own room, Eleanor throws open the window, letting it hang carelessly and wide. The catch slips, bangs, then slips again as she leans out, the ledge dagger-like, pressing against the bones of her hips. Beneath a watery sky, life continues. It is a Sunday river that faces her; just a few boats on the water and the wharf empty, its timber still covered, saved from the worst of the storm.

No errant women, no obvious emergency. At first glance, all is serene. Thrusting her face further out, Eleanor starts to call Lily's name.

And then she sees them.

The soldiers, like ants. Starting at the camp and fanning out, moving in lines along the opposite bank. A silent formation, slowly heading her way.

There is no sign of Lily, no matter how much or in which direction Eleanor twists her body, trying to see. Just these men. Zigzagging, splitting the bank, from top to bottom, then back again, their black shadows marching beside them. Heads down, she watches them search methodically. Not in the crazy, haphazard way she had searched for Lily only moments ago, but with a purpose and deliberation, that takes them further from the camp and ever nearer to the bridge.

Her thoughts of Lily drop away, only to reappear, tangled up with the images of these men and what it all means. Possibilities, scenes — imagined and real — crowd her mind, jostling, tumbling. The skyline shifts, jolting in time with her now wild, thudding heart. Disorientated and dizzy, Eleanor pulls back into the room, slamming the window shut; her eyes fighting to adjust to the sudden change of light. Sinking to the floor, she balls her fists, pushing them hard against her eyes, grinding her knuckles into her sockets, bone on bone. She must think.

She can't stay here, trapped in the house, idle and waiting for what might come. She thinks of Anton, hiding in the hospital, of how she stopped him leaving, stopped him from making his escape. Whatever happens next will be her responsibility, a direct result of the decisions she has made.

Climbing up from the floor, she looks again.

The men are still there, still moving, but their progress appears slower than before. The storm has made the riverbank perilous and hard to negotiate, and some men are floundering at the water's edge. She watches as they board the fishing boats moored there, lifting the folded sails, and ducking beneath.

Maybe she has time.

The minute Anton looks up at her from his ball of sheets and blankets, Eleanor knows he understands.

'I am found?'

Shaking her head, she attempts to reassure him, quickly holding up her hand. But seeing how it trembles there in front of her, she pulls it away. She can't fail now.

'Not yet, but…'

She pauses, wondering how to frame what it is she needs to say. How to warn him but at the same time achieve the impossible and make him want to stay.

'The men, the soldiers, are out there. I saw them, over on the other side of the river.'

She sees his immediate panic recede, only to be replaced by resolve as he begins pulling at the tangle of sheets, searching for his boots and tugging on her father's coat.

'So, I have time?'

Anton is looking for her agreement, reassurance and, knowing she hasn't told him the whole of it, Eleanor starts to turn away. He tugs her back gently, his hand about her wrist tightens in panic as his expression darkens. His face is alive with concern, but his eyes, grey and wide, still regard her with trust.

'It is not just the men?'

She shakes her head. 'Lily's gone.'

At first there is silence, before Anton surprises her with a laugh, low and steady. 'The ghost girl has left? I think we did not expect that!'

Sitting down on the nearest bed, he lowers his head into his hands. His neck, pale and vulnerable against the collar of Alfred's old shirt, stirs a memory; a moment tied to something familiar that Eleanor can't place. John's face, shadowy and fragmented, flashes up behind her eyes and then just as quickly slips away.

Legs like lead, she drops onto the mattress, just inches from Anton. Suddenly overtaken with danger and impossibility, she whispers, 'I'm sorry, I never thought...'

He silences her, placing his hand gently on her knee. Through the thin cotton of her dress, she feels it, the warmth of another. One whose hand is steady despite it all.

'Please, no. I should not have come here. And no matter what you said, I should have gone.'

Lifting his hand from her leg, he takes her fingers in his. Resting one finger on her ring, he asks, 'I wonder what he would think? John, if he was here?'

Eleanor looks at him. Her mind brims with panic, yet still the old sense of desperation rises. She knows that her chance for any kind of answer is slipping away. Hearing John's name nearly undoes her, but at the same time it brings her purpose, her need, back into focus. Pulling her hands from Anton's, she brushes at the scalding tears waiting behind her lashes, determined to keep them at bay.

'I don't know what John would say. What he would think. Sometimes it feels like I barely remember him at all.'

Anton smiles sadly. 'I think he would say I should not be here. I need to go.'

Her heart cracks. It is like giving John up all over again. Her one and only chance to find those answers, to understand what he went through is being taken away.

And it is Lily's doing yet again.

On his feet, Anton looks up and around, his eyes urgent and intense.

'The door is bolted, yes? Now tell me; is there another way out?'

Eleanor stares at him, her grief sinking below a wave of disbelief. 'You can't mean to go out there, not with all of them looking for you. Surely?'

'You have a different plan, perhaps? Better to move, to keep going than sit here and wait.'

She shakes her head, desperation and fear switching to anger, her mind swimming and unable to keep up. 'But there's nowhere to hide. The fields, the marsh, it's all too open. You'll be seen from miles away.'

But it is as if she hasn't spoken. Anton, pacing the length of the room, runs his hands up and down the walls, muttering words she can't understand.

'Anton, listen, please; you won't stand a chance.'

He turns, the calmness in his eyes undercut with a steely determination. She can sense everything changing, shifting before her. His feelings, his intentions, everything in the room is suddenly too hard for her to place.

'I say before, the ditches and dykes. In these I will hide.'

Again, she opens her mouth to protest, but Anton stops her.

'Maybe I return just briefly to the trenches. But this time they will get me home. Back to Sophia. And my boy.'

It is just a passing reference to a war she doesn't understand. But it is enough to remind her why she kept him here. Her hand touching the cross at her throat, she nods, just slightly. And, as if sensing a shift, Anton smiles.

'Now tell me.' He points upwards. 'These windows? Do they open?'

CHAPTER FORTY-SEVEN

CLARA

Behind her, the gate opens.

And for one ridiculous moment, Clara, flooded with the warmth of relief, convinces herself that all her fears are unfounded. Eleanor is here.

Somehow, she will have to keep her out of Frank's sight. But if she's here, then it means she isn't holed up with the prisoner on the other side of the bridge. Weak with hope and gratitude, Clara steals one look at Frank, who is once again hunched in his chair. She turns, plans already forming, towards the open gate and the figure standing there.

But it is not Eleanor.

It is Lily.

From the step, twisted half to the gate and half to the house, Clara stares.

Horrified, she almost topples down into the yard. Fighting to regain her balance, she cries out as her wedding ring knocks smartly against the glass. Just briefly, Frank looks up, his eyes sharp but also unseeing. Then he looks away.

Clara's relief is hot but fleeting, swallowed up and overtaken by shock.

Stepping down to the yard, she heads towards Lily, trying to fathom what her presence could possibly mean. And how quickly she can send her on her way.

'Lily? Why are you here? Is it Eleanor?'

Lily doesn't answer. Instead, she looks around the yard, her eyes ranging, wild; like an animal in a trap. Her left foot drums constantly, each heaving breath giving the impression that any second she will bolt. Clara reaches out, but Lily steps away. Whatever the reason for Lily's appearance and whatever it costs, Clara needs her gone.

'Lily!' Checking quickly on Frank, desperate he shouldn't see, Clara grabs her by the shoulders, pushing her up against the yard wall. Lily's dress is pale against the wet brick, but her face is paler, and being out in the world seems to have stolen her voice. Clara watches her sister-in-law's thin, white throat rippling with the effort of angry gulps. Her hair hangs about her face in sweaty clumps, and her sleeves and hem are stained with mud. Aware that Frank is far too close, Clara's heart thuds.

'Is Eleanor with you?'

'Eleanor?' Lily's eyes lock with Clara's, her voice rasping through bared teeth. 'Eleanor is busy. With company at home.'

Clara knows why Lily is here. Now she understands.

Bringing her body closer to Lily's, Clara tightens her grip, her fingers clutching at soiled fabric and protruding bones, trying to find enough purchase to turn her sister-in-law towards the still-open gate. But with a strength that comes from nowhere, Lily pushes back, her body falling suddenly and hard against Clara's.

The force, immediate and unexpected, sends Clara staggering, her foot catching on an abandoned pail. The crash of tin on stone reverberates like thunder around the yard.

And, from the corner of her eye, Clara sees it.

Frank's shadow. Rising from his chair, coming to loom at the window before crossing to the door.

And Lily sees it, too. With eyes fever-bright, she calls out in the direction of the house.

'Frank? Frank! You need to come.'

Struggling to her feet, Clara lunges; summoning and focusing every ounce of strength. She propels Lily towards the deserted alley.

'No, Clara. I need Frank. There's a man…'

Clara pushes again, this time harder. Sending Lily spinning backwards. She is so nearly gone, so nearly out of the yard.

Lily yells. Turning her body inside out, she twists her frame, becoming all angles and elbows. She lashes out, cracking Clara, hard, on her jaw.

'Frank!' She rears up, wild and louder over Clara's shoulder. 'Frank, there's a man in the hospital.'

Clara's arms are around her waist now. Doubling Lily over, folding her almost in half. But still Lily's words keep coming, getting higher, becoming clearer, bouncing off the walls.

'A prisoner, a German hiding…'

'Stop!' Clara screams. Bucking against Lily, she slams her hips into her body in desperation.

'Let her go.'

The voice comes from behind them, cutting through their frenzy. Both women freeze, then, releasing her hold on Clara, Lily turns her head towards the house. But Clara only holds tighter, pulling Lily against her own churning belly, swallowing the bile that is bitter in her mouth.

No matter what happens, she won't let Lily go.

'Frank?' Lily's voice climbs, soaring up and far beyond Clara; out of her arms and her control. Gripping tighter, Clara feels the pinch of muscle and Lily's breath, fast and close, hot on her neck and arms. She longs to drag her closer, then push her far away. But before she can do either, a hand on her shoulder wrenches Lily from her grasp.

'I said, let her go.'

Frank, looming above Clara, pulls Lily out from her now shaking hands. His sister shivers under his touch.

His other hand, lifting from Clara's shoulder, draws back, before landing closed and hard against Clara's cheek.

And the world descends, from sunshine to instant midnight;

the inky black she has fallen into so many times before. And the last thing Clara feels is a boot lifting her, high from the floor.

CHAPTER FORTY-EIGHT

LILY

At the sound of bone on flesh, Alfred's voice is silenced; and the last of the vision that has sustained Lily through the empty streets shatters and drops away.

And there is only Frank in the yard.

The brother she has barely seen these past two years, and whose face is twisted, his eyes darting every which way.

Beyond his legs, Clara lies motionless and bleeding, sprawled out upon the stone. Frozen in horror, Lily waits for Frank to realise, to acknowledge what he has done.

Instead, grabbing her wrist and pulling her to him, Frank lowers his face to hers. 'Where? Where is he, the bastard?'

Lily recoils, suddenly weak with exertion and shock. Barely hearing the question, she is aware only of Frank's breath, a near sensation of heat and noise. That and the rag of Clara's body.

Frank moves closer; his fleshy lips tight and wet with spittle, the grind of teeth livid against her ear. His voice, quieter now, is soft with menace. Each vowel, pebble-smooth with threat. Within his face, so sallow, his eyes are fixed, dead and wide.

How could she have believed that Frank was the answer, the way to reclaim what was lost? Her mind races, engulfed by the black certainty that by coming here, she has simply walked into another kind of danger. Looking up into the distorted face of her brother, all her anger with Eleanor falls sharply away.

'Say it again, Lily.'

With both hands tight around her upper arms, Frank shakes her. Her neck snaps back, and every joint jars.

'The Hun. Tell me again where he is.'

He is roaring now, lent over her, pushing at her terrified silence. At his feet, Clara moans and a child's muffled weeping seeps out from beyond the kitchen door.

There is nothing left but fear.

So, she tells him.

With a scream of triumph, Frank thrusts her out through the gate, leaving Clara silent and alone on the yard floor.

Together they move, Frank's fingers still tight on her wrist, his gaze set in the direction of the river, turning onto the high street where they are greeted by the dull discord of untrained voices floating from the open church door. With the service still in progress, the streets remain as quiet as before. Glancing sideways at her brother, Lily searches for a hint of recognition, any kind of remorse for what she has witnessed, what he has just done. But there is nothing, only the grim, white lines of fury and determination ringing his lips. Tentatively, Lily attempts to tug her arm away, only for Frank to pull her closer.

'Keep up.' He spits the words out, high above her. 'We don't want that bastard getting away.'

Along the high street, past the station and the village green, they move. Still, they meet no one.

Only as they approach the bridge does Lily feel Frank's pace begin to slow and his grip begin to loosen, until, at the edge of the bank, he abruptly stops. Tight at his side, Lily waits, not daring to hope he has come to his senses. Or that perhaps he has remembered Clara and is ready to turn for home.

'Frank?' Her voice falters, barely more than a whisper.

There is no response, only that faraway gaze and the steady, painful pressure of his fingers in the flesh of her forearm. Then in an instant, his hand moves from her wrist to the small of her back, before twisting itself in the nape of her hair.

'You go.' He pulls at the roots, Lily gasping as her scalp burns. Propelling her forward, Frank releases her, sending her staggering onto the bridge, where she falls against the steel.

'Go on. In front, where I can see you.'

Legs trembling, Lily steps out. On one side of the bridge is Frank. On the other, Eleanor. And the prisoner. She wants to stay here, on the bridge, forever, because disaster awaits her no matter which way she turns.

It is then she sees them. The soldiers, down below, moving in groups and heading towards the bridge. Some beating at the long grass, with sticks and high rhythmic strokes; some by the water's edge, where they poke amongst the mud and reeds. A wolf of a dog pulls on a rope at the centre of the bank. The sight of them, the sound of them, brings Lily to a stand-still, there above the thundering river. She could weep with sweet relief.

They are the end to this, the answer; there below her. These men, appearing so suddenly and from nowhere, whose presence she has shunned and railed against all these months. Lily takes it as a sign.

Jubilant, she calls to Frank, her fear almost forgotten now he is no longer her only hope.

'Frank! Frank!'

Her brother walks towards her, his gait beating its strange and uneven time, his expression impassive, even in the face of Lily's wild cries.

Again, Lily looks down. The men below pause; calling out to one another. Pulling herself to the edge of the bridge, Lily leans further, fighting the heady rush of relief and fear, both magnified by the song of the water beneath.

They have heard her.

But then, shaking their heads, the men turn to stare in the opposite direction. Lily's heart lurches. Convinced they are heading away; she shouts again to her brother, running towards him, her aching body screaming in protest.

'Frank!' Her voice is high with excitement, thin with relief. 'Look. Down there. Soldiers!'

Frank stops. His eyes are glazed, his lips slack. Acknowledgement, when it comes, is slow and strangely distant. Unnerved, Lily grips his arm, gesturing below.

'There, on the bank. They're looking for him.'

Something flickers; she catches it. Something hot and white, dancing around her brother's pupil; a flare of understanding, spiralling outwards, then settling into a sneer. Shaking her off, he lurches unsteadily across the path, peering through the steel. Lily follows his gaze, watching it roam the riverbank and drift out towards the marsh before retreating to blankness. Frank shrugs, turning back to the path.

Confusion muddying her joy, Lily pursues him. She tries again.

'Don't you see? We can tell them. They must be looking for the prisoner, and we know —I know— where he is. You could shout, down there; tell them. I am sure they heard me before.'

But still Frank ignores her, setting his shoulder, and rolling his body, his eyes fixed and unseeing.

Below, the men stand, their backs to the bridge as they gaze hopelessly towards the marsh.

'Frank. We need to tell them. Tell them they're looking in the wrong place.'

Walking on, Frank glances briefly, coldly over his shoulder.

'Let them be. This is for me to sort. Come away.'

Lily stares, refusing to understand.

'But we could tell them. Let them come and take him away. Then there would be no need for any of this, nothing, and Alfred's gun, I could just put it back...'

The words are out before Lily has time to understand what it is she has said. Yet their effect is immediate and arresting.

Frank stops. Spinning round, his face split by a slow, crooked smile. Lily's stomach drops. Reaching behind her she clutches at the cold steel of the bridge.

The scar that Lily has been trying to ignore glints in the strengthening sunlight, standing proud against her brother's sallow skin. He laughs, a strangled bark, that simultaneously freezes Lily and makes her want to run.

'Alfred's gun. Alfred's bloody gun.' Frank shakes his head. 'I underestimated you, Lily.'

Stepping closer, peeling her from the side of the bridge, Frank draws her back to him, pulling her into his side, jamming her hip hard against his.

And once again Lily is forced to move in time with her brother's clumsy gait; left hip rising, stiff and jarring, right leg swinging out far too wide. She is exhausted; from emotion and walking farther than she has in years.

Once over the bridge, they turn awkwardly, onto the road that runs down to the hospital. There are no soldiers here, no one at all; the whole of the village, the whole of the world, continues to look the other way. Frank's hand remains tight at her elbow; his scent — musty and sour — is overwhelming, and Lily fights the urge to retch or scream.

Onwards they roll, driven by the unnatural rhythm of her brother's stride, thigh to thigh, weaving unsteadily across the road. At times the river comes close, too close, the sound of water rising to pound unrelentingly in Lily's ear; Frank's wild and jerking body threatening to tip them both headlong down the sodden bank. Then, without warning, she finds herself pulled in the opposite direction, twisted towards an entirely different path, spiralling towards the fen, her feet dragged through dust and stones.

And all the while Frank says nothing, lapsing back into silence, broken only by occasional snorting breaths that end in unreadable moans. As if there is a pain building somewhere deep inside of him; an agony he is determined to suppress.

Finally, they pass the toll house, the last house of the village, beyond which only the hospital, lighthouse and marsh lie. As they step into its violet shadow, Frank lowers his head, his voice hot and sudden in the tangles of Lily's hair.

'Nearly there, Lily. Nearly there.'

Every bone, every muscle, every sinew of Lily's body is desperate to pull away. But she is trapped, a wren beneath the wing of a crow.

'So where is it? The gun. Where did you hide it, eh? Clever girl.'

Frank's excitement drips oily and foul, and Lily's breath falls to the earth. Briefly, she thinks of denying him, of ignoring the question. As his ribs push closer, biting into her shoulder, his arm against her cheek, again she searches desperately for Alfred. Longing for his voice to rise up, just as it did in the house, to tell her again what it is she should do.

But Alfred is gone.

There is only Frank now; his face up close and curling round to glare at her. Only Frank's hands; pinching the bones of her wrist so hard she's afraid they will snap.

'The dyke.' The words slide out, stinging her lips with betrayal.

Frank smiles, and his rank breath shifts across her face. Pushing her in front of him, hand tight on her elbow, he whispers, 'Show me where.'

CHAPTER FORTY-NINE

ELEANOR

It is Eleanor who climbs the ladder first, pushing hard at the window, determined to show Anton how it opens no more than the merest crack.

Eleanor who, despite her panic, can't help but stare out at the fields beyond, that run away from her, one acre at a time. She remembers the night that John left, her intention of showing him this view and what she had given him instead. And then immediately wonders how she can think of such things at a moment like this, with another man's life and freedom, at stake.

The land before her opens ever wider, the horizon expanding by the second as she stands, vulnerable and exposed; balanced on the narrow step of this ladder, standing trapped and powerless with Anton waiting anxiously at her feet.

And yet there is no one to see her. And nothing to see, except the bright flash of sun on the stubble of newly harvested wheat; nothing to hear beyond the call of a lark, rising into the sky. Bringing her hands to the open window, Eleanor lets her fingers run through the breeze. Forgetting her fear, just for a second.

'Eleanor?' Anton's earlier calm is now rapidly slipping away. His pale eyes blaze up at her, shot through with panic, his jaw tight with anticipation and resolve.

'Please, let me see.' Forcing herself back to the present, she climbs down, her sweat-slick hands slipping on the ladder.

Reaching the floor, Eleanor steps aside, allowing Anton

to spring up, moving two rungs at a time; the exhaustion of this morning forgotten, swept away by circumstance. Eleanor glances towards the door. Anton is now intent on the window and its frame.

'It's no good.' Her voice trembles. 'You see, it's too small.'

Making no reply, Anton pushes against the hinges; delivering his full weight in short, desperate bounces against the glass, pausing only to wrench at the window frame. His face is alive with concentration as his slender shoulders move in frantic waves. For a moment there is silence, a drawing back of his body that Eleanor reads as defeat, before Anton throws himself completely at the window. A snap, like gunfire, cracks through the hospital as the window flies up, way beyond where it should be. Knocked off balance, Anton leaps to the floor, the boards trembling beneath his weight.

Eleanor steps away, her heart hammering.

Above them gapes a void, newly created and entirely open to the fen; the window hangs haphazardly on what remains of its hinge.

One final push and the inner frame gives way completely, falling into the undergrowth below. The outer frame clings, cracked and dangling. Eleanor is sure that the sound of its descent will bring damnation upon them; that the soldiers will spring into action from nowhere, brought by the call of splintering wood and breaking glass. But from where she stands, gazing up at this bright spot of sky and whisps of trees, the only movement is the ebony whirl of disturbed crows, their cries ringing out across the fen.

'Please,' she calls up to Anton. 'Please let me check.'

Reluctantly, Anton descends.

Eleanor climbs again, balancing herself in that familiar spot, the view yawning even wider. Again she scans the landscape, fast, feverish. But there is not a soul to be seen. By some miracle, the fields remain empty.

'You see?' Anton calls up from the floor. 'Nobody, nothing is there. It is the best time for me to go.'

She looks down, into the strain and impatience lining his face. This, she knows, is the time to climb down and let him make his escape. But still, she can't let him go.

She grips tight at the remainder of the sill, the splintered wood stabbing at her palm. The outer frame hangs above her head, precarious and rotten. Her voice wavers as once again she clutches at broken straws. 'It's further than you think down there, and all that glass; what if you cut yourself? What then?'

'Eleanor, please.' The edge of his words is unmistakable now. A warning that time, — *her* time — is running out.

Still, she ignores him, stubbornly staring at the vast land and distant trees, watching the remaining wheat ripple, golden wave after wave, bowing in the breeze. Trying desperately to think of some way to make him tell her what she needs to know. Closing her eyes, John's face swims into view. Barely half formed before it fades, just as it has so many times before; each time his features softer than the last. And no matter how hard she pushes her lids together, she can't hear his voice.

Bringing her hands down hard on the fractured wood, she cries out in frustration and pain.

'Why? Why will no one tell me?'

Beneath her feet the ladder rocks violently, as uncontrollable anger pushes out, spilling from the very centre of her grief. Anton's expression flicks between desperation, bewilderment and concern.

'Eleanor, please! I do not understand. I am sorry, but... I must leave. Whatever my friend has told them will only buy me very little time.'

She shakes her head, and again the ladder sways. Her need to keep Anton here is now complete and all consuming.

'No.' Her voice rises to a screech. 'You can't leave. Not until you tell me! Tell me what it was like over there.'

Letting go of the window, she waves wildly to the east, hands pointing in the direction of the marsh, trying for the hundredth time to imagine the place John went to and what lies beyond.

'Over where?' Anton's foot rests on the ladder. His brow is creased and his words, stilted and clipped, are the words of a man fighting to keep control.

'Eleanor, you make no sense. I need to go.'

He gestures at the door and hisses. 'Men, the guards, they are out there. You know this. You have seen them. Time, it is running out. Tell me, over where?'

Furious, weak with rage at his stupidity and wilful misunderstanding, she hisses.

'The bloody war! Over there in France. Tell me, what did John see? What did he touch, smell, taste? That's what I want to know.'

Anton's hands fall from the ladder. His face, recently so animated, is now blank, slipping into a land of shadows. Stepping away, his reply is no more than a whisper.

'Why? Why do you want to know this? What do you hope for?'

Eleanor's legs ache: the balls of her feet throb from standing balanced on the ladder. Trembling, she lowers herself, fingers inching from the ruined window, creeping down the wall. Seating herself on the top rung, she breathes out her reply, sending it over Anton and his distress, fixing her eyes on the tangled bed; the first in the row. Her mind slipping back between the sheets, reaching for a man she can no longer feel, tracing the outline of a face that insists on inching away. Wretched tears blur her surroundings, washing everything with a sweep of grey and pain.

'I want...' She stops and then begins again. 'I want — need — to bring him home.'

CHAPTER FIFTY

LILY

It is Lily who retrieves the gun, clambering into the dyke where her earlier footfalls remain pressed into the wet earth. Lily, who makes her way into the deep rain-soaked gully.

Despite her showing Frank exactly where the gun is hidden, pointing out the mound of hay, undisturbed and still above the waterline, no amount of persuading will make him move.

Even as they approach the dyke, Lily senses it. The change in her brother, in his manner; in the roll of his walk and his breath, that takes on a rasping, awkward rhythm, as if he is fighting for control.

At the edge of the dyke, he steps back, recoiling, whilst at the same time pushing Lily forwards, so hard she has to fight to keep her footing on the muddy bank.

Away from her brother, so unexpectedly released, Lily's body is filled with an immediate, dangerous lightness. For that moment at least, she is free.

Briefly, she thinks of running, but one look at her brother stops her in her tracks.

Standing alone in the middle of the road, Frank's arms are wrapped, tight around his body, his hands jammed into his armpits. His back is rigid, his eyes flitting between Lily and the dyke beyond.

Unnerved, Lily freezes.

'Just get the gun. Go…' Unhooking one hand, Frank waves

at the ditch. 'Get it now, before that bastard gets away.'

Lily flinches. Then moves.

Easing herself down and along the soft, tilting ground, yet again she pictures the soldiers, wondering if they are moving towards them or heading away in the opposite direction.

Desperately, she tries to think of a way to end this. Make it all go away.

Then, without warning, she begins to slip, her feet sliding along the same tracks she left earlier. Her thoughts now consumed only by the need to stay upright, she leans into the bank, grabbing at reeds and tufts of yellowing grass, slippery from last night's rain. Feet planted wide, she halts her slide. Limbs shaking, she reaches down; with her free hand, she moves first the straw and then, gingerly, the blanket.

The gun is there. Undisturbed, untouched by hand or water.

And from here, Lily can't see Frank.

Yet she can feel him. Hear his laboured breathing and the anxious shuffle of his feet. She waits, catching her breath. Her body aches, each joint and muscle pulling against her in protest.

Leaning into the bank, she gazes up to the sky, where whisps of clouds drift lazily towards the marsh. Wishing herself up amongst them, light, floating; free. Far away from her brother and everything she has set in motion. Far from Eleanor and her selfish stupidity. Far from what handing over the gun will mean.

'What you doing?' Frank's voice ripples with anger. Or possibly fear.

Snapped back to the present, and with trembling hands, Lily presses on. Edging lower, tightening her grip on the rough grass, she pushes her weight into her right foot and leans. Her fingers brush against the wood of the gun's butt, just as her left foot slips, and she slides down, heading rapidly to the water beneath.

'Oh!' Grabbing at the weeds again, she scrabbles for firmer ground.

'What?' Frank's voice is loud yet seems somehow even further away. 'Is it there? Fuck's sake Lily, what's going on?'

Pulling herself in tight to the bank, she hangs there, panting. Seconds pass, and she breathes hard and fast into the long grass, unable to speak.

'I… slipped. It's… It's still here.'

'Then hurry up.'

Lily nods in response, even though Frank can't see her. As if they are making everyday conversation, and this is a normal place to be. Her foot hangs there just above the gun, still half covered. She could kick out. Just hook it with her foot and send it spinning down into the peaty water beneath.

Then she remembers Clara, left lying on the cobbles in the yard. And it is terror that pushes her on and makes her reach out. Moving inch by inch, until finally, her fingers close on the once-polished wood. One final pause and she pulls. The blanket, falling away, lands in the water beneath and Lily exclaims under her breath, not wanting to alert Frank again. Carefully, she drags the gun up, hauling it through the wet grass, trailing it behind her, as she begins to climb.

Emerging from the dyke, she rests, exhausted, on hands and knees. Immediately Frank is upon her; his face white, his body pitching back and forth.

'Give it to me.'

There is no other way now. And besides, she is desperate to get the gun out of her hands, to have the decision made and done. She reaches out, towards her brother, towards those eyes, unreadable and unblinking.

Then it comes. A sound cutting through the air, something close by fracturing, splintering; the crack of wood and the ring of shattered glass. Lily's eyes fly towards the hospital.

Frank flinches, his hands flying up, over his head, before the strange rhythmic rocking of his body returns, intense and more pronounced. Then, for a second, the world is still. Frank stares blankly into the void created by the sound, his feet planted in the road, his torso bobbing. His eyes lost.

Gingerly, Lily reaches out, touching his sleeve, her fingers ghostlike on the fraying edges of his jacket.

'Frank?'

Instantly, he snaps back.

Recoiling, he snatches the gun from her hands and pulls it close to him. Breaking it open, he grunts at the loaded chamber, before snapping it closed. Reaching out, he hauls Lily back to him. And gun on one side, Lily on the other, held together by disjointed motion and a terrible sense of dread, they continue on their way.

The trembling starts as they move off the road and down the bank, increasing when the hospital in finally is view. With their bodies pressed so tight together, at first Lily is unable to pinpoint in which of them the sensation begins, and where it ends. Whether the palsy that is vibrating through her hands is Frank's gift to her or the other way around, she can't tell.

Inching away from his clamminess, she fights a growing nausea. Longing to be free of the constant movement and insistent rocking. Desperate to escape the stink of him; his sour, unwashed smell, that clings harder with each uneven step.

But still Frank pulls her back. The nearer the hospital gets, the tighter his hold. The more their bodies pitch and shake, the more deafening his silence becomes.

They move on, awkward, close. Not quite as one.

They are at the gate now. Beyond which, Frank hasn't stepped in years. Stealing a look, Lily searches for recognition, any trace of memories that might check his purpose or slow his stride. But Frank continues; staring straight ahead, pulling them both ever closer to the hospital door. His skin, grey, shines with sweat and sunlight, his scar snaking white and knotted through the thinning patch of dark hair. His face appears completely familiar and yet, at the same time, so out of place. As if someone has taken him apart and then put him back together in entirely the wrong way.

Finally, they are here, on the path just yards from the hospital, where its bolted door, the garden and the house all jump out at Lily in sharp relief. Every brick, leaf and line made more vivid and yet more unreal by her brother's presence. She stands, stunned by the enormity of what she has done. Bringing Frank to the hospital. In the state he is in, a gun under his arm and Eleanor and the prisoner on the other side of this door.

Frank pauses, and hope jumps up from the depths of her belly, burning at the back of her throat, only to be quelled by the cold terror of her brother's voice, sudden and close to her ear.

'When I say so, you need to knock, Lily. Knock hard on the door.'

Despite her fear, Lily shakes her head.

'I can't... I... think we should go.'

Frank laughs, and Lily freezes.

'Go? Oh no, Lily. No, you knock. Knock loud, let 'em know we're here.'

Despite his commands, Frank's body continues to tremble and twitch. Shuffling, hampered, he pulls her forwards, bringing them, inch by inch, ever closer to the shuttered door. With one awkward movement, he lifts Lily away from him, hoisting her up onto the narrow steps. Again she feels it; that same dizzying lightness, the same freedom, the relief of being away from her brother. But all too quickly it is replaced by the dawning realisation that, suddenly unsupported, she is about to fall. Toppling forward, palms outstretched and desperate, Lily clutches at the air. Righting herself just in time, she yanks her hands away from the wood of the door.

'No!' Panic bleeding into her whisper, she turns to find Frank backing away. Confused, she watches as he makes his way along the front of the hospital, rounding the corner half hidden in the scrub of weeds and windblown stunted trees. Here he stops, his silhouette dark against the fields and now cloudless sky.

The gun is set high against his shoulder. And it takes a

moment for Lily to realise that it is pointing directly at her.

Hand hard against her mouth, she suppresses a moan and her bladder releases; hot urine and shame spilling, splashing down her thigh. Grimacing, Frank turns the gun towards the hospital.

Slowly, he mouths 'Knock.'

Again, Lily shakes her head, openly weeping now. Her heart jumps, biting at each and every one of her joints, and her blood runs fast and hard, rushing in her ears. Leaning away from the building behind her, Lily falls against the wooden pillar that supports the hospital roof. Summoning what little courage she has left, she searches her brother's twisted face; desperate to find some connection and willing him to see sense.

But Frank only raises the gun higher, swiping at the sunshine in a wild, terrifying arc. He takes one step towards her, and in terror, Lily whimpers, then knocks on the door.

CHAPTER FIFTY-ONE

ELEANOR

Reaching upwards, Anton's slender fingers seek hers. Gripping her hands, he guides Eleanor down, rung by rung. Sobbing, blind and clumsy in her grief, she relies entirely on him — this man she barely knows — to bring her safely down. His arms reach out to comfort her, his face a mask of concern.

With her feet on the ground, Eleanor's anger returns. Slapping her hands flat against Anton's chest, she pushes him away. Stunned, he holds his hands up in the air.

'I am sorry, I never meant...' his voice trails off, swallowed by a frigid silence, broken only by the sounds of the fen drifting through the shattered window above.

Immediately, pity tempers her rage.

'I know you meant well. Everyone means well, but the letters, the uniform. All the things they sent back. John isn't there, in any of it. Nothing of him is in any of those things. And without him, I am lost.'

Anton reaches out again. This time she submits, allowing him to guide her, wordless, to the nearest bed. Falling onto its thin mattress, she clutches at the metal frame, fighting the urge to lay down, to press her swollen eyes into the cool, clean sheets. Instead, she focuses on Anton, watching his expression shift from sympathy to blankness and then back again.

She waits, eyes on his torment, until finally he speaks.

'It is a terrible thing you have lost. These things you have to bear. But Eleanor, I cannot help.'

'Why?' She wails. 'You've been there. Seen the things he saw. Walked where he walked. Tell me! Tell me how he felt.'

Shaking his head, Anton's eyes move from hers, coming to rest on the open window; reminding her yet again of the danger he, they, are in. It is ridiculous to delay him in this way. But the grief of the past months, the pain, the longing that burns within her chest, refuses to release her. She can't let him go.

Twisting her body, closing the narrow gap that Anton has placed between them, Eleanor takes his face in her hands, pulling his gaze back to hers.

'Tell me.'

For a moment he does not speak. Then, bringing his hands to hers, he holds them in place. His eyes burn with something she can't identify, something that makes her fingers press hard and insistently on his cheeks. When finally he answers, his words are hoarse, torn from his throat, his breath gentle on the bridge of her nose.

'What you ask is not possible. I cannot tell the story of another man. A man I have never met.'

She begins to protest. 'But you know…'

Lifting his fingers from hers, he presses them firmly against her lips.

'I know the war *I* fought. Only this. Where *my* feet stood, the things *my* eyes saw, the food *I* eat. I know a war filled with both life and death. But it is my war. And my war alone. Not John's. Not yours. I can tell you a story, but it will not be what you want.'

Eleanor's tears slide unchecked down her cheeks. She grips harder, the ridges of his cheekbones sharp beneath her hands, her fingers trying to match the tightness in her chest.

'So how do I find him?'

Anton smiles, though his own eyes are wet. Again his fingers curl about hers, now returning the pressure of her own.

'Listen; that is how. In places he knew, listen only to the beating of your heart. John is not on some battlefield far away. He is here, inside of you.'

Moving her hand, peeling it carefully from his face, he presses it close to her chest, before laying his own hand on top. 'You see? Wait, rest awhile. Your heart is talking to you.'

Bringing her other hand to rest on his, Eleanor allows herself to sink, deep, deeper into the beats within her. Closing her eyes, she senses the darkness of the proceeding weeks begin to separate and watches as, slowly, John moves into view. Against her ribs she pushes, pressing harder, steadying her breath, lost in the rhythm of her body.

'You see?' Anton whispers.

And she does. But when she opens her mouth to tell him, it is Lily's voice that replies.

Followed by a different rhythm. This one hammered on the bolted door.

'Eleanor?'

Anton and Eleanor stare at each other, their hands still pressed together, resting on her chest.

Neither speak. Neither move. Eleanor's heart races beneath their fingers.

The calling and the knocking are followed by a rattling of the door handle, turning hopelessly in the dim light. The bolt gives, shifting slightly as Lily leans against the door.

'Eleanor! Please, Eleanor. I know you're in there.'

It is Anton who moves first, pulling his hands from Eleanor's and pushing himself up and across the floor.

Above the sound of his feet, clumsy and chaotic upon the bare planks, the knocking comes again. Lily's pleas bleed into the hospital, swelling, feeding the terror Eleanor feels.

'Eleanor, please. You must open the door.'

Standing, fingers at her lips, Eleanor signals silence to Anton, who has one hand on the ladder. She makes for the cupboard, disappearing, then emerging with a bucket, which she slams down into the depths of the sink. The sudden clang of metal against ceramic rings out, hard and bright, piercing the tension.

'Eleanor?' Lily calls again, questioning. Now desperate.

Turning to Anton, Eleanor lifts her hands from the bucket. Slowly, deliberately, she brings them back to her heart.

Through her tears, she calls out.

'Just a second, Lily, I'm about to mop the floor.'

Then, with one last look, she waves Anton upwards, to the terrible, gaping scar of the window, tears streaming down her cheeks. He nods, just once.

Resting her right hand on the tap, Eleanor lifts the other high into the air; three fingers extended.

Three, two, one…

She opens the tap, as wide and as far as it will go. The sudden rush of water against the pail is deafening. And beyond its thunder, Anton moves.

The water crashes, overflowing. And again, through its roar, Lily calls.

But Eleanor's eyes, her attention, are entirely on Anton.

Watching as catlike, nimble, he clambers up the ladder. Flinging one leg over the sill, then the other, he pushes himself through the window, a gleeful child down a helter-skelter; body half in, half out, head suspended in mid-air.

He smiles, and despite her terror, her grief and sadness, Eleanor smiles, too. Removing her hand from the taps, she returns it to her heart.

One last look, one last push.

And he is gone.

Sagging and lightheaded with grief and relief, Eleanor turns off the tap. Water pooled at her feet, glints in the abundance of sunlight that streams through the ruined window; its shattered frame and hanging splinters casting new and unfamiliar shadows over the glistening floor.

Again, it comes; Lily's voice rising over the hammering of her fist on the wood.

Stepping through the water and the drifting light, with one last glance at the space that gapes jagged above her, Eleanor makes her way towards the sound of her sister and whatever it is she faces.

Pulling back the bolt, finally she opens up the door.

Before her, trapped in a gaze that struggles to adjust, is Lily. Her face is tear streaked and alive with terror; her hand still raised, as if surprised by the space that suddenly gapes in front of her. Her body is surrounded by brightness and the unmistakable stench of urine.

'Eleanor...' Her voice is low, thick with warning.

Starting to step forward, out onto the narrow stone step, Eleanor steadies herself, one hand still on the door, ready to close the remnants of the previous hours from view. But as she moves closer, Lily's eyes widen, stalling her with one short but desperate shake of her head; her hand no longer raised now grips the pillar at her side.

And beyond her, the unmistakable and yet unthinkable shape of her brother, stepping slowly into view. Eleanor's gut freezes.

'Frank?'

At the sound of his name, Lily whimpers, falling completely and heavily against the veranda's wooden frame; closing in on herself, as if she is making space for Frank, as the shadow of her sister shifts and falls away, Eleanor sees it. There, undeniable, set hard against Frank's shoulder is the long-forgotten profile of Alfred's gun. The past. Held high and waving wildly right there in front of her.

Leaning out of the doorway, into the acrid stench of her sister's fear and the warm air, her confusion and disbelief make her ridiculous and bold. But how, how is Alfred's gun out there, out in the garden wrapped in Frank's wavering hands? When she knows that Alfred's gun is in the hospital, safe and hidden away. Instinctively, she turns, glancing over her shoulder, towards the store; its door still stands open, affording her a glimpse of its carefully ordered and ancient shelves and stores. Trying to convince herself that she is right and what is before her can be explained away.

Can be unseen.

Then, from somewhere inside, amidst the chaos of tangled sheets and water, comes the sound of splintering, falling wood; the final fragments of the shattered frame shifting, before giving way. A final, brazen crash of destruction splitting the air.

Instantly, seamlessly, Lily's whimpers transform, rising into screams. She lunges, throwing herself towards her Eleanor, just as Frank twists his face and roars; his words, unheard and indistinguishable. The final duet of siblings; sounds that are too close, too terrible to separate.

Frank flies backwards, and the earth, the walls and Eleanor's bones vibrate with one final, terrible sound.

Reaching out, Eleanor grabs Lily, pulling her towards the hospital. Face to face, for the first time in months, she holds her sisters gaze, watching as her eyes widen.

Before she slips through Eleanor's hands, crumpling to the hospital floor.

EPILOGUE

MAY 1917

They winter in Clara's cottage, each curled around the other's grief, hidden away from the rest of the village. Eleanor nursing and Clara healing, safe in the knowledge that Frank is and will remain far away. The doctor has seen to that.

For it was the doctor who found them. Having been summoned by Molly and arriving to discover the tattered remnants of the family they had once been.

Coming first upon Frank, his body hooked and cowering. Alfred's gun, still beside him, accusing in its heat.

Then Eleanor. Bathed in weak sunshine and a pool of spreading red, holding Lily at its centre. Eleanor who had, from those first spinning moments, known that her sister was gone. With no parting words, not of fear, nor venom, nor regret. Just blank, startled eyes and rapidly cooling hands.

And Anton was nowhere to be seen. The search for him almost entirely forgotten in the face of what Frank had done. What Lily had unwittingly unleashed.

Through the coldest of months, and under the cover of darkness, Eleanor visits the churchyard, standing in silence, her feet sinking into the wet earth beneath which her sister lays. Finally reunited with Alfred.

In the chill of those evenings, with her eyes closed against the stars, ice, sleet, or rain, she searches the rhythm of her heart. Body still and barely breathing. Not until she finds them; not until she catches the scent of iron and horses or feels the familiar ridge of a twisted scar.

Today, the train is on time.

The children chatter at the window, Piper winding himself around their legs, watching as the village, wreathed in steam, slips slowly from view. Silently Eleanor inclines her head; to the river, the camp and what is left of the port. And finally, to the hospital, now abandoned and empty, paying her respects one final time.

Then, winding her hand around Clara's, Eleanor lets her mind drift, slowly and completely, out and towards the sea.

AUTHOR'S NOTE

In the Spring of 1881 the new port in the village of Sutton Bridge, Lincolnshire was finally completed. Sitting on the banks of the River Nene the port had been billed as the answer to all the village's hopes and dreams, and on 14th May 1881 the first boat, the SS Garland, entered the dock.

Less than four weeks later, on 9th June, the port began to collapse, falling piece by piece into the river. It was not rebuilt in any form for over a hundred years.

Yet on the opposite bank the small isolation hospital built to serve the port remained. Stocked and waiting for the sailors that never came. My great-great-great-grandfather Edward Burton, having been appointed the hospital caretaker, lived there with his family in the attached house. On the event of Edward's death the mantle passed to his son, Henry who then passed it to his daughters Mary Allett, known to all as Alice, and Rose. Henry died in 1906, just months after his 18 year old son Alfred Herbert drowned on the marsh.

Alice was engaged, to a solider whose name is lost to time and who never came home from World War 1. He sent home a crucifix, given to him by a French soldier who was later killed. I treasure it now as I do Alice's engagement ring.

Following the death of her brother Alben and his wife Sarah Jane (my great-grandparents), Alice brought up one of their six children Ivy. Ivy was my grandmother and my mother, Sadie was born in the hospital house.

The hospital was not official closed until 1950 when it was

sold by the Port authorities. In the almost 70 years my family looked after it, the hospital was stocked and held in readiness.

In all that time it never cared for single a patient.

All the characters in this story are fictional. Eleanor is not Alice. Lily is not Rose. Their father Henry was no monster.
There was no Frank, no Clara or their children. All their tormented relationships and hardships are entirely imagined.

But the landscape, the fallen port, and most importantly the hospital are beautifully, hauntingly real.

ACKNOWLEDGEMENTS

The writing of a novel is a long and often solitary process, particularly when this is your first rodeo and the landscape changes daily from open vista, to impenetrable forest or sheer rock face.

So many people have sustained this journey to publication, by believing in me, offering support and guidance, love and food.

To Isabel Costello I offer thanks for her unwavering belief, constructive criticism and the ongoing ability to push me beyond where I thought I could go. This book would not exist without you; thank you!

To Sidra Ansari and Laura Besley who showed me it was never too late to write and gave me the courage to share my work.

To Emma and Rebecca, my podcast buddies, friends and so much more.

Thank you for always being there.

And to Jenny for everything.

To Northodox for taking a chance on this book; I am still pinching myself now! You guys are amazing.

And to my agent Jemma McDonagh who always has my back; thank you Jemma.

To my family, there are too many thanks to give for all the love, support and encouragement. But a special mention to Stella for her numerous proof reads.

To Matthew and my children, I love you.

NORTHODOX PRESS

FIND US ON SOCIAL MEDIA

www.northodox.co.uk

@northodoxpress

@northodoxpressofficial

@northodoxpress

@northodoxpress

@northodoxpress.bsky.social

www.northodox.co.uk